The Witches' Tree

Jacqui Campbell-Elliott

For Ian

Without whose love, patience and unwavering support I
would never have completed this book.

And in memory of my beloved sister Rose.

Acknowledgements.

Thanks to Soraya for making me finally put pen to paper after talking about writing this novel for so long, and for her help and advice about all things supernatural, as well as being a source of constant encouragement.

Heartfelt thanks to Mary for her friendship, unending support and invaluable proof reading skills

A very grateful thank you to many friends for the time they spent reading my manuscript and offering their invaluable advice.

Finally, thanks also to Marie O'Regan for all her helpful suggestions and encouragement.

The Witches' Tree

'Life must be lived forwards but it can only be understood backwards.'

Sören Kierkgaard.

PROLOGUE

December 1851:

The day began like any other in the small Highland township of Corriglen. When she awoke that morning, she lay savouring the feeling of contentment that wrapped around her like a cloak. She caressed her distended belly and smiled. Her baby, due in a little under three months, had given her barely a day's discomfort during this her first pregnancy for which she was thankful; she hoped the child's delivery would be as straightforward.

She rolled out of the bed, drawing in a sharp breath as her feet touched the cold, packed-earth floor and then, dressing hurriedly, tended the peat fire which Douglas had lit before he left. As she straightened up, rubbing her back to ease the ache, she glanced through the croft's tiny window.

Although December, the weather was fine if cold. In the distance, a weak sun glinted on granite mountain peaks softened under their first frosting of snow. Nearer to hand she glimpsed the weather-stained stone of a neighbouring croft almost hidden by a stand of native oak and rowan trees, their skeletal branches profiled against a pebble grey sky.

Then she saw the crow.

It strutted around a patch of bare ground and she shuddered; she knew that crows were birds of ill-omen. She held her breath. Fly away! Please fly away. At last it shook its feathers and, with a hoarse 'kraak', rose into the air. She could hear its strident calls echoing for some time through the morning air long after it had disappeared from view.

Her legs felt weak and she sank down onto a stool by the fire. As its warmth enveloped her, she breathed in deeply and scolded herself for being so foolish; getting upset like this couldn't be good for the baby. After all it was only a bird, one of God's creatures and she should rid her head of such superstitions.

She touched the cradle beside her, stroking the smooth oak and running her fingers over the outline of rowan leaves and berries Douglas had carved into the wood to protect his firstborn. She pictured her husband as he had been the night before, straining his eyes in the candlelight, as he worked to get it finished in time for the birth.

He had been gone only a few hours and she missed him already. He was away fishing with some of the other men from the township. Life on the croft was not easy and food was scarce, so she hoped the day's catch would be a good one. Her mouth watered at the thought of the sweet-tasting mackerel Douglas would bring back; with precious little meat to be had it was a welcome supplement to their otherwise meagre diet.

She put up a hand to her cheek and her mouth curved into a smile as she imagined she felt again the brush of her husband's lips as he had crept out at first light. This is no good, she thought, I can't sit here day-dreaming. The morning was drawing on and Douglas would return before nightfall. She stood up feeling much calmer and pushed all thoughts of the crow to the back of her mind. Busy with daily chores, she hummed softly as she carried water from the nearby burn, swept the floor and baked a batch of floury bannocks.

Later, as she stirred a pot of nettle soup suspended from a hook above the fire, she gasped as the child inside her gave a hefty kick. He was a lively one for sure. She knew her baby to be a boy. She could still hear the words of the wise woman from Invershee who had arrived at the township a few months ago to visit a neighbour with a persistent fever. On passing her, the old crone had put a hand on her barely rounded belly and pronounced, 'You'll be delivered of a fine son.'

She felt a stirring of unease at the recollection. For a moment it had seemed the old woman was about to say more but had thought better of it, merely frowning before going on her way. She wondered now, as she had then, what the crone had been about to tell her.

Thrusting aside the memory, she left the soup to simmer and set the bannocks to cool on the windowsill, glancing again out the window as she did so. Dark purple clouds were massing above the far mountains. It looked set for a storm and she hoped Douglas would be back soon. Her husband was an excellent sailor and had made many similar trips without mishap.

She pictured him striding towards her, his arms held out as she ran to greet him - though perhaps running was a bit ambitious in her condition. 'Hello there, lass,' he would call and, despite her heaviness with child, he would swing her round as if she weighed little more than a wee girl, before kissing her until she had no breath left to speak.

Still, she was aware of a growing disquiet, like a worm wriggling into a good apple, undermining her sense of well-being. She gazed out through the gathering gloom, hoping to see the welcome figure of her beloved husband appear. There was no sign of him.

But the crow was back.

This time it lit on the dry stone wall outside the croft. She wrapped her arms protectively around her belly and willed the bird to be gone, but it only settled obstinately on its perch, its black feathers and heavy black bill glossy in the half-light.

It turned its head towards her. She stared at it and the crow stared right back, its beady eyes full of malevolence. She forgot her earlier vow to ignore such foolishness and a wintry hand gripped her heart.

The Witches' Tree

* * * * *

CHAPTER 1

Maggie MacQueen stared at the man standing in front of her. *I don't know you,* she thought. But of course she did. This stranger was her fiancé; he looked like Ben, sounded like Ben though the words he spoke were not Ben's....they couldn't be. She frowned, trying to concentrate on what he was saying.

'I'm in love with someone else.'

She noticed he hadn't shaved and his shirt was creased; he was usually so neat, and particular about his appearance. The sound of her heartbeat thudded in her ears. *This isn't happening. He can't mean it.*

'I don't understand.' She struggled to get the words out, and swallowed hard.

'We have to call off the wedding.'

She heard what he said but it didn't make any sense. Everything was arranged. As was her way, nothing had been left to chance. Ben began pacing around the room, trying to justify his behaviour with some meaningless explanation.

'But......' was all she could manage. She couldn't frame a single coherent sentence, never mind utter one. He continued stumbling on. She saw a slight sheen of sweat glistening on his forehead and his eyes strayed around the room, studiously avoiding hers. The import of what he was saying finally drilled itself into her brain. *He does mean it. He's really leaving me for someone else;* for his sweet-faced secretary of all people. *What a cliché,* Maggie thought, stung by the bluntness of his confession.

Nothing in his voice when he had phoned earlier had prepared her for this. Now here he was, a week before the wedding, telling her it was all over; their relationship was finished, dead, discarded like yesterday's empty pizza box. She felt the old panic rise. She couldn't lose him. What about the life together they had planned? If he went she would be on her own again. *I can't bear it*, she thought, biting down hard on her bottom lip.

She shook her head and dragged herself back into the moment.

She saw him eye her uneasily. *What does he think I'm going to do?* She had an overwhelming urge to scream and shout and smash something but she fought against it; she had learned early in life that being in control was what mattered. So she stiffened her back and fisted her hands tightly by her side as he ripped apart their future.

'I'm so, so sorry, Maggie.' Ben made a move towards her, as if about to offer some banal words of comfort. She shrank back.

He was sorry? How dare he pity her? She felt consumed by a mixture of rage at him and sorrow for herself yet she was damned if she would go to pieces. Her head pounded and her legs trembled as if they were about to dump her unceremoniously onto the floor. A sense of despair at her own impotence seized her but she willed herself to be strong and raised her chin, staring back at him with eyes like flint.

'I see. I'd better start cancelling all the arrangements then,' she said, her voice as brittle as winter.

He stood there, his brow furrowed and his arms hanging loosely by his side. 'I...' he began.

Maggie cut him short. 'Just go, Ben' she said, her words clipped and precise. 'For God's sake just get out.'

She folded her arms tightly across her chest and closed her eyes; she couldn't bear to look at him anymore. She heard the door click shut and stood for several moments, her nails biting into the soft flesh of her palms as she clenched and unclenched her hands. She felt as if the blood in her veins had turned to ice and the very marrow in her bones was frozen solid. *This cannot be happening.* Over and over the phrase repeated itself in her head, lodged there like a tape track on continuous play.

Gradually, however, she became aware of another more insistent voice. *Ben's gone. He's really gone.* Why she had not seen this coming? How could she have been so blind, so stupid?

She began to pace up and down the room, touching things as she went: magazines placed just-so on the glass-topped coffee table, a neat arrangement of her favourite white carnations and lilies in a crystal vase on the mahogany bookcase, and the cushions, in warm browns and russet, plump and inviting on the expensive, tan leather sofa. She paused before the well-polished, silver frame of the only photograph on display. It showed a smiling, dark haired man holding a young child on his shoulders, the child laughing in sheer joy, head thrown back, her hair windblown.

Everything was just as it had been before Ben arrived. *But nothing's the same and never will be again.* The future she had so carefully planned was not the future now before her. She flung herself down on the sofa, for once not caring she was crushing the cushions so carefully arranged, and lay there dry-eyed as she went over and over everything Ben had said until her brain ached.

Later, as she packed away the oyster-cream wedding dress, folding the delicate, silken fabric in layers of tissue before returning it to its box one last time and consigning it out of sight to the back of the wardrobe, Ben's words again rang in her ears.

'I'm in love with someone else.'

She sank down onto the bed and took the air tickets out of their folder. Staring at them, she wondered if she would ever get to see Kenya now. She had a sudden urge to rip them up and scatter the pieces like confetti over the floor – *not a good image*, she thought, stifling a sob. It was tempting but she wasn't going to fall apart, she told herself. She had to stay in control. It was an accusation Ben had flung at her as he tried to justify his betrayal.

'You're always so sure of yourself, so organised. Sarah is such a light-hearted, spontaneous sort of person.'

Well, bully for Sarah, Maggie thought and threw the tickets into a drawer. She didn't care if she never saw Kenya. It would always be associated in her mind now with crushed dreams and a broken heart. She slammed the drawer shut and then buried her face in her hands.

To hell with control. There was no-one here to see her and it was a relief to let the tears come. She slid to the floor and wept without restraint. It was as if she had been punched in the very centre of her being, and the ache of it filled her. The same feelings of despair and abandonment she'd had as a child, when her father had left her and her mother without a word, overwhelmed her. When that happened she had vowed she would never again experience the sense of helplessness, the awareness of having no control over her own destiny, she had felt then. So, as she grew up, she had planned her life and future with great care; because if you did that, you stayed in control and bad things didn't happen. Yet, here she was once more, suffering the pain of her father's loss in Ben's betrayal.

How she got through the next few days, she didn't know, but get through them she did. Presenting a stony face to the world, she parcelled up her hopes and cancelled all her dreams, only dissolving into misery as she got through her own front door. If it had not been for Rachel she would probably still be wallowing in salty self-pity.

Rachel had called round and found her in tears of regret and recrimination. As all good friends should do in such circumstances, Rachel listened and soothed and made countless cups of coffee. But when Maggie began to sob yet again, 'How could he do it?' she had heard enough.

'You need to get away. Take yourself off and have some time alone to make sense of what's happened.' She paused to sip her umpteenth coffee before continuing. 'I know you're hurting, Maggie, but it's not all your fault. Ben has to take some responsibility for letting things go so far without speaking out. You can't control other people's feelings or actions you can only take care of your own.' Suddenly her eyes lit up. 'I have an absolutely brilliant idea.

You should go to Tigh-na-Bruach! It'd be perfect.'

So, the next day, Maggie found herself driving a hire car from Glasgow airport towards the northwest coast of Scotland, and something in her responded to the wild grandeur of the scenery: the vast emptiness of the moor lands of Rannoch, the towering splendour and haunting sense of history besieging Glencoe, and the serene beauty of the lochs. She was returning to her ancestral roots and the notion somehow soothed her.

When she arrived she was too tired to do more than take a cursory note of her surroundings. The place seemed clean and tidy and she was glad to simply tumble into bed at the end of a tiring day. For once she slept deeply, bone weary and emotionally spent.

Now here she was sitting in the garden of Rachel's cottage in a remote Highland glen. She had better make the best of it and find some way to restore her self-esteem, prepare to face the world again. What a good friend Rachel was, Maggie mused, yet they were so dissimilar. Rachel, gregarious and fun-loving, never took anything too seriously, least of all relationships. She, on the other hand, was searching for stability, a sense of belonging, a future mapped out in front of her; casual romance wasn't part of her long-term plan. In fact, she decided, romance of any sort had no part in her future; she was done with love for good.

As she sat on the grass, leaning back against the warm, greyish-brown bark of a rowan tree, for a moment she was strangely comforted. She gazed up through its fernlike leaves and slender branches reaching towards a sky of cerulean blue. It was as if time had stopped and she wished this peaceful afternoon could go on forever so she would never have to think about her life and what had happened ever again.

She sighed and looked down at the book she had picked it up at the airport bookstore, "A History of Celtic Scotland." It had seemed a good idea to find out about the country, its ways and culture if she were going to be spending some time here. Her father's Scottish blood might course through her veins but it was a place she had never visited.

Not in the mood for reading, she put the book aside and contemplated the whitewashed stone building in front of her, with its small, deeply-set windows and sturdy, wooden door. It was a bit battered and in need of a lick of paint but, even after nearly two centuries, still resisting the ravages of time. *No doubt it's seen its share of laughter and tears over the years*, she thought. She recalled Rachel's description of it.

'My God-mother left it to me. It's a bit basic but it's got all the necessary. You know, electricity and water. I've even had an internet connection and a shower put in. There's no central heating but there's a fireplace to burn wood and peat.' She had paused. 'However, it *is* a bit remote.'

Maggie smiled now at the memory. She couldn't imagine Rachel enjoying being away from the bright lights for very long. Rachel loved city life, the noise, the people, the sense of urgency accompanying you wherever you went. But to Maggie it had sounded the ideal place for her to hide away and recover some semblance of dignity and self-respect.

As she lazed in the garden, the sun was warm on her face, the air soft on her skin. She could feel the rough bark of the rowan tree through the thin jumper she wore; it felt like the one enduring, reliable thing in a shifting world. Her eyes closed and she relaxed as the stillness around her calmed her jaded spirit. Before long she had drifted into that elusive world somewhere between sleep and wakefulness.

She was walking on the hillside behind the cottage. She looked down in delight. The turf was springy beneath her bare feet. It felt good and she wriggled her toes in the cool grass. A light breeze ruffled her hair and she pushed a stray curl behind her ear. Lifting her face to the sun, she savoured the solitude and tranquillity of the moment and the place.

She turned and looked back. The stone cottage settled staunchly below her at the bottom of the hill, windows sparkling in the bright sunlight. It had an air of sturdiness, resolutely defying the rigours of the Scottish climate and the assault of time, solid as the hills surrounding it.

The picture-book image shimmered like a mirage. She rubbed her hands over her eyes.

That's odd.

The cottage still sat there snugly under its roof of weathered thatch …though she could have sworn the roof was grey slate.

She stared.

It no longer looked like Rachel's cottage at all.

This was a single-storey building, the walls of rough, grey stone - and where had the back door gone? And the rowan tree…? A cat stretched its black body sinuously on the broad, stone windowsill as it soaked up the sun's rays. There had been no sign of a cat when she had arrived last night and she was damn sure Rachel didn't have one. She stood nonplussed for a moment longer, wondering what was going on. *It must be some kind of optical illusion,* she thought, probably due to the stress she was under. Hesitantly, she began to retrace her steps.

All at once the air around her took on a decided chill. The breeze had dropped and there was absolute silence; even the birds had stopped singing.

Maggie paused, and half-turning, glanced back. A figure stood further up the hill behind her.

It was a young woman in a long, grey gown, her fair hair flowing over her shoulders.

'Hello,' Maggie said. 'I didn't see you there.' Her voice had an unnatural quality to it in the eerie calm.

The woman did not answer but took a pace forward. Maggie resisted a sudden urge to step back.

Then she saw the woman's eyes. They were a translucent grey and full of the most unspeakable anguish.

Maggie forgot her fear.

'Whatever is it?' she cried, 'What's happened?'

The woman still made no reply but took another step forward, reaching out towards her. Tears glistened on her gaunt, pale face and she opened her mouth as if to speak.

Maggie's eyes flew open and she peered around. She was not on the hillside at all, but in the garden. She could feel the solid presence of the rowan tree once more at her back and there was no sign of any woman in a grey dress. The cottage looked exactly as it had before with its whitewashed walls and slate roof; the cat was nowhere to be seen. She frowned. She must have fallen asleep.

She shuddered and struggled to shake off the vestiges of the vision that still lingered at the edge of her consciousness, trying to dispel the sense of foreboding which gripped her.

It was no longer warm. The sun had dipped behind a cloud and the breeze had sharpened. Maggie shivered again, and not only from the drop in temperature. The dream had seemed so very real. She picked up her book and walked slowly and thoughtfully along the stone path to the back door. As she lifted the latch she stole a quick look over her shoulder. The hillside was deserted. A few delicate fingers of mist crept across its contours. Maggie shivered and hurried inside.

She busied herself in the kitchen; she had not eaten since the plastic meal on the plane. The cupboards were stocked with basic necessities and she sent a silent *thank you* to Rachel for arranging everything with a woman who lived along the glen. She had been only too willing to make up the bed and to get in some provisions for the visitor.

Maggie put a light to the fire laid in the hearth and soon the tiny living room was warm and cosy. The earthy scent of smouldering peat filled the air and the reflected flames danced over the polished, old, oak furniture which stood against the walls. She felt calmer now and dismissed all thoughts of the afternoon's experience as the work of her emotional state and an over-active imagination. She tidied away the dishes and, leaving the fire burning low, went upstairs to bed, hopeful of a good night's rest.

Her sleep, however, was restless, punctuated with more dreams, this time of Ben and the figure on the hillside; Ben on a white horse galloped towards the woman in the grey dress who stood in his path, her mouth open in a silent scream. Maggie watching, shouted, 'No!' as it seemed he was about to ride straight over her. At the last moment Ben swerved and swept the woman off her feet, gathering her up into his arms as he rode off into the mist which rose to swirl around them.

Maggie awoke from the dream soaked in sweat. She could still hear the horse's hoof beats and it took her a heart-stopping moment to realise what she was hearing was the sound of rain driving against her bedroom window. Her heart still pounding, she pulled the bedcovers over her head and tried to compose herself for sleep once more.

Outside, under a starless sky, the rowan tree stood alone in the corner of the old, walled garden as it had done for well over a century. Now, its leaves shivered at the rain's onslaught. Its branches dipped and swayed as the wind grew in strength. Deep down its roots reached into the dark, peaty soil anchoring the tree firm and strong. Maybe its longevity did not make it unusual in the natural world, but this rowan tree had, for over one hundred and fifty years, stood sentinel, protecting a dark secret. And, despite the violence of the growing storm, that secret remained.

CHAPTER 2

The next morning Maggie woke feeling tired. She had spent the rest of the night curled under the covers, sleeping fitfully. But now the sun's rays were edging through her bedroom window and she determined to make the most of the day. Perhaps a walk down to the village and a pub lunch would cheer her up. She dressed quickly and was finishing her breakfast toast when she heard a soft knock at the back door. She opened it to a smiling face and a 'Good morning, lass. I hope you're settling in fine? I'm Jessie Ferguson.'

'Hello', replied Maggie, for a moment at a loss as to who the woman was and what she wanted. Then she realised this must be the person Rachel had called to prepare the cottage for her visit, 'Hello', she repeated more warmly, 'I'm Margaret MacQueen, though I'm usually called Maggie'. She smiled in return. 'Do come in,' she added, opening the door wider.

'Well, I'll not be stopping, but I'll step in for a wee minute if that's alright.' Jessie Ferguson followed Maggie into the kitchen.

'Can I get you a cup of tea?' Maggie offered. 'It's just made.'

'Thank-you but no, dearie. I've only called round to make sure you're alright and you'll not be needing anything.'

She was a small, neat woman with small neat features, probably in her fifties Maggie judged and, according to Rachel, happy to keep a neighbourly eye on the cottage when Rachel wasn't there. Maggie reassured her on both points.

'I thought the rain and wind last night might have disturbed you.' Jessie Ferguson's soft brown eyes reflected a motherly concern. 'It was quite a storm and I always think these things sound so much fiercer in the country than in the town. Not that I get up to town very much myself,' she added with a cheery smile, 'but I've heard it said that's the way of it.' She patted Maggie's arm. 'And you do look a little washed out, dearie.'

'I'm fine, thank you,' Maggie declared, as she picked up her cup and plate and deposited them in the sink. 'Though it's very kind of you to call,' she added, smiling brightly.

After Jessie Ferguson had left, having first extracted Maggie's promise to visit her later in the week 'for a cup of tea and a wee blether,' Maggie walked out into the garden. The berries on the rowan tree glistened redly in the morning light and she could smell the rich, leafy scent of the earth. Her spirits lifted a little as the sun's rays fell upon her face. Everything looked so fresh and newly washed, she reflected. How wonderful it would be if a little rain could wash away the hurt and humiliation she was feeling.

Maggie looked around. There was no sign of the cat anywhere this morning and she glanced warily up at the hillside behind the cottage. Nothing stirred. No ghostly figure stood there with arms outstretched, reaching out to her. There was merely the grass and a few straggling gorse bushes, still displaying a few bright yellow flowers like tiny, golden cushions amid their dense spiny growth...

Then all at once she sucked in her breath. A chill ran up her spine. Carried faintly on the breeze came a whispered *'Help me.'* She stared up at the hill but all was as it should be. She strained her ears and again she heard it like a sigh, an exhalation. *'Help me.'* The plaintive voice drifted towards her and then came utter silence. She stood there for several more minutes, clasping her arms around her, as the panic which had squeezed her belly gradually subsided.

She breathed deeply, mentally chiding herself. Not only had she thought she might see the phantom from her dreams standing there in broad daylight but now she was hearing things; the sound had surely been nothing more than the gentle soughing of air moving among the tall grasses. It was so unlike her to indulge in such imaginings. Her stressed state, the nature of the place and the air of timelessness which seemed to possess the landscape, were leading her astray into such fancies.

She turned and went back into the cottage. She needed a good long walk to banish such foolish notions and steady her nerves. Quickly washing up her breakfast dishes, she then found a warm sweater to ward off the September chill, and strode off down the single track towards the village.

'There are several houses and cottages not too far away on the loch side with a shop for groceries.' Rachel had told her. 'A little post-office too, and a pub if you're desperate for company... mind you I think everyone in there, except the barman, was over seventy when I called in,' she had added, grinning.

Maggie enjoyed the walk. It was good to be out in the fresh, clean air and she would miss her daily jog around the park near her London flat while she was away; walking was a good substitute and there was plenty to see.

The track was edged on both sides by deep ditches and she could hear the gurgling of water as the run-off from last night's downpour flowed down from the hills to the loch below. Low, stone walls followed the ditches and she admired how skilfully they were built, standing as they did against all weathers without benefit of bonding material. She wondered about the people who had constructed them, imagining their lives were hard and, at times, desperate as they laboured on the crofts struggling to provide for their families as best they could.

She was pondering this when she rounded the corner and saw the village of Invershee spread out before her. She had driven through it when she had arrived the evening before but, concentrating so much on trying to follow Rachel's tortuous directions, she had barely noticed it. Now, seeing it from this vantage point, she thought how picture post-card perfect it looked.

It was exactly as she imagined an old crofting community would be with its scattering of traditional, stone-built, white-washed cottages interspersed with a number of other single storey dwellings of more modern construction. Some of the buildings crowded around a central green space and Maggie noticed children playing there, no doubt making the most of the fine weather and the fact it was the week-end. The sound of their voices and occasional laughter carried clearly on the still air.

Sunlight played upon numerous, rocky islets which seemed to float here and there on the surface of a loch and, on the far side of the water, craggy mountains etched their outlines against a sky of sapphire blue. Maggie could see a narrow road winding its way uneasily between their lower slopes and the shore.

She stood for a minute or two longer enjoying the scene, absent-mindedly picking one or two lusciously plump blackberries from the bramble bushes at the roadside, and appreciating their musty richness as she popped them into her mouth.

She carried on down the track and made her way into the village, stopping momentarily to watch a heron on the rocky shore. It stood motionless, its head hunched between its shoulders, gazing into the shallow water. Then, in a sudden flash of movement, it stabbed downwards with its beak. The next moment it was up and away with a swift spread of wings, its raucous cry echoing loudly in the stillness. *Oh dear, failed to get your lunch*, Maggie thought and, now feeling hungry too, went off in search of the pub Rachel had mentioned.

She found it set back from the road and paused to admire the building and its setting. It stood overlooking the loch, surrounded on three sides by a fringe of well-established trees of oak, ash and alder with a scattering of rowan. Three-storeys high, it was built of large blocks of dark grey granite. The window frames and sills were painted a brilliant white and there were tubs overflowing with scarlet geraniums around the entrance, a little past their best now but still providing a glorious splash of colour. "The Loch Shee Inn" she read, and above the doorway, the inscribed legend, "Angus Cameron, licensed to sell wines and spirits."

At that moment the door sprang open and a young couple came out, holding hands, laughing, carefree. An image of herself and Ben last Easter flashed into Maggie's mind.

They had been spending a long week-end in Brighton when he had proposed. She remembered it as if it were yesterday. As they were walking along the street, he had suddenly stopped.

'What do you think about getting married?' he said. No romantic build up, no sense of occasion or going down on one knee. He had simply come out with it and Maggie accepted readily.

And why not? She knew he cared for her; he often brought her flowers and other small gifts: a pair of pretty jade earrings, a book she had once mentioned she would like to read, a box of her favourite sweets. She admired too his air of quiet composure. Not a passionate man, he was, nevertheless, a warm and considerate lover, and Maggie believed a relationship based on mutual respect and a deep affection was a far better foundation for a happy marriage than one where instant attraction and sexual fireworks were the deciding factors. She had seen too many of the latter fail – not least, that of her own parents. Everything seemed to be going the way she had planned for since she was a little girl - home, a career, maybe children, but above all a settled existence.

Well, she had certainly got that wrong, hadn't she!
She chewed her lip as the words Ben had uttered so curtly echoed and re-echoed in her mind.
'I don't love you anymore.'
Thinking about it now, Maggie recalled he had seemed rather distracted, distant even, as the wedding approached.

She had put it down to pre-wedding nerves but now she reflected he had probably been trying to pluck up the courage to tell her how he felt. She would never have believed he could be so deceitful, never would have imagined he could be diverted from his life's plan by emotional considerations. It only proved she had not really known him at all.

She hugged her arms around her, trying to ignore the feelings of sadness and raw anger churning away as she gazed out over the loch lying peacefully under the shadow of the distant mountains. Taking a deep breath, she pushed the bitter memory aside and, turning quickly on her heels, went into the Inn.

A dark haired, dark-eyed man was polishing glasses when Maggie entered. 'Good day to you, lass, what can I get you?' he called out cheerfully from behind the bar.

She looked up at the sound of his voice and saw him studying her as she approached. His was the practised appraisal of a man who enjoyed women, she thought, as his eyes swept over her figure. She stood quite still and watched him until their eyes met. *He could at least appear a little embarrassed at being caught out – eyeing her up and down as if she were goods on display in a market.* She gave him a frosty look. He seemed unconcerned and repeated his question.

As Maggie read the menu, she was aware of his continued observation. What did he see, she wondered; pretty ordinary looking, even features but with little make-up on and thick brown hair scraped back in a ponytail, *Not his type at all,* she imagined. She looked up and, in a tone barely this side of arctic, ordered lunch.

'I'll bring it over to you as soon as it's ready,' he offered.

Still feeling piqued at the way the barman had looked her over, Maggie wandered to a table by a window overlooking the loch. *Typical macho male,* she thought; she would ignore him when he brought her food. Settling into her seat, she gazed around. The bar was starting to fill up as people began drifting in, ready for a good pub lunch to set them up for their afternoon activities.

Several family groups clutched information leaflets of "Things to see and do in and around Invershee," excitedly planning the rest of their day. Others, with heavy boots and binoculars, studied maps and debated the next stage of their trek through the glens and across the hills. The rest, mostly local Maggie surmised, were snatching a quick sandwich or ploughman's lunch, although she also heard a couple of American voices raised above the general hubbub laying claim to their Scottish ancestry. She noticed several old men at the bar and smiled to herself. They fitted Rachel's description of 'everyone being over seventy'; Maggie imagined they came every day more for the company than for a drink, a sort of daily social club.

The atmosphere was warm and welcoming, and she began to relax, enjoying the fragrant scent from a peat and wood fire burning in an old, stone fireplace mingled with the smell of freshly-cooked food.

The inn was evidently old, about three hundred years she guessed. The thick oak beams of the ceiling had darkened through centuries of exposure to peat and wood smoke and there were curiously-shaped tools nailed to them at intervals. They looked like relics from the once-active, crofting community and she stood up to take a closer look at one curiously-shaped implement fixed to the beam above her head.

She stumbled when a man's voice close to her ear said, 'Here's your lunch, lass.' Maggie felt someone grip her arm, steadying her. She let out a strangled gasp and abruptly turned around, trying to brush away the hand as she did so. His grip remained firm.

'I'm fine. You startled me that's all. You can let go of my arm, now,' she said, her voice icy. 'You can let go,' she repeated, glowering at the barman when his hand remained where it was.

'Sorry, I didn't mean to make you jump.' He grinned and

moved away. Maggie fell back into her seat.

'I didn't hear you coming.' She felt the heat rise in her face at her awkwardness and looked quickly down at the food and drink he placed in front of her. The soup smelt appetising and she was certainly hungry now.

'It's a croman,'

'What?' Maggie looked up, wishing he would leave her alone so she could start eating.

His smile was friendly and open but Maggie merely stared back at him, a slight frown creasing her brow. She could feel herself becoming irritated. Why didn't he let her get on with her meal?

'What is?'

'The tool you were examining so intently a moment ago. It's called a croman. It was used for lifting potatoes in the old days.' He didn't appear at all put out by her offhand manner.

'Really? Thank you for telling me,' she said her tone clipped and precise.

'Well, I'll leave you in peace to enjoy your meal' and he turned and made his way back to the bar.

Maggie watched as he paused here and there to exchange a few words with several visitors or give a casual nod of acknowledgement to people he knew. He seemed very much at ease with the customers and they with him. *Fancies himself as a bit of a charmer*, she thought. She knew she had been short with him when he was only being friendly but she really was not in the mood for conversation. Probably in his early thirties, she judged, but not at all the kind of man she was attracted to; dark, gypsy-like looks and deep set brown eyes didn't appeal to her. She went for the Nordic type, tall and lean with fair hair and blue eyes like Ben.

All at once, she realised how much she missed him. Ben was always good company and a longing for him swept over her. She stared down at her plate and wondered what he was doing and, more to the point, who with...*good old Miss Spontaneity, Sarah,* she supposed.

She remembered the way her heart had leapt into her throat when she had opened the door to him the day after his bombshell announcement. *He's come to tell me it's all a mistake and he does want to get married after all,* was her first thought. His words soon dispelled that notion.

'It seems such a shame to waste the tickets. One of us might as well use them,' he said, his hands shoved deep into the pockets of his tailored, grey slacks, his eyes everywhere but looking into hers.

She clenched her hands; they itched to reach out and slap his handsome face. How could she have been so foolish as to imagine he had changed his mind? Not able to trust herself to speak, Maggie marched into the bedroom and retrieved the tickets from the drawer where she had flung them. *How could he be so insensitive?* She returned to confront him in the doorway and, with great deliberation, tore the tickets in half then thrust them at him without a word. Not even waiting for him to turn and leave, she slammed the door in his face; mean-minded and petty, yes, but for a moment so satisfying.

Whatever was she thinking? She didn't care what he was doing. In fact, she hoped he was full of regrets and even more miserable than she was. Unwelcome tears gathered in her eyes and furiously she dashed them away. She was not going to cry again and certainly not here in public. She sat for a moment trying to gain control of her jumbled emotions.

Taking a deep breath, she thrust aside all thoughts of Ben and attacked her meal with relish. The soup was delicious and the roll freshly baked.

As she sat finishing her glass of wine, she pondered what to do next. A stroll around the village might be nice, and then a visit to the church perhaps. She had glimpsed it hidden away among a grove of trees on her way to the Inn. She loved old buildings and an afternoon wandering around it and the graveyard appealed to her present mood.

She carried her dirty plates and glass over to the bar and, as she did so, the barman came to take them from her.

'That was very good, thank you.'

'I'm glad you enjoyed it. You certainly looked in need of something when you came in. You had a face on you that'd turn milk sour. In fact I sent Caitlin there to check that the milk in the fridge hadn't curdled, didn't I Cait?' he called to a raven-haired girl serving customers further down the bar. Caitlin looked up, grinned and, shaking her head as if used to such banter, carried on pulling pints.

'I've a lot on my mind at the moment.' Maggie managed a pinched smile. *The genial, mine host at work,* she thought sourly.

'By the way, I'm Angus Cameron.' He put out his hand to take hers, apparently not at all fazed by her cool tone. After a moment's hesitation, Maggie shook his hand briefly. Before she could introduce herself, he went on, 'I'm thinking you must be the lass staying at Tigh-na-Bruach. He leaned his arms on the bar. 'Mollie, is it? Or Meg?' He regarded her solemnly but his eyes were twinkling.

'Actually, it's Maggie, Maggie MacQueen', she said in a prim voice; she had a feeling he already knew her name. 'How did you know, anyway? Where I'm staying, I mean.' She looked up at him and then wished she hadn't when she saw the humour in those warm, whisky-coloured eyes. She quickly looked down again and began twisting the stem of her empty wine glass.

'You only have to sneeze here in Invershee and they know about it in the next village before you've had time to take out your hankie.' He chuckled. 'Besides, Jessie Ferguson is my aunt. I bumped into her this morning and she mentioned you were at the cottage'.

'Oh, I see. Well, I'm off to look around the village now.' Bidding him a brisk farewell, Maggie made for the door as he began to wipe down the bar.

She was tempted to glance over her shoulder to see if he was watching her but forced herself to walk through it without looking back.

Angus leant his elbows on the bar and stared after her. There was something about her ….maybe it was the air of vulnerability; she had a bruised look, as if someone had dealt her a hefty blow. She might appear composed and distant but he sensed a whirlpool of emotion contained beneath the calm exterior. 'I've a feeling I'll be seeing a lot more of you Miss Maggie Macqueen,' he murmured.

CHAPTER 3

Maggie wandered off towards the village, lingering briefly to watch the children still playing on the green. How lucky they were, she thought, to have no idea of the troubles and heartaches waiting for them in the adult world. They were right to enjoy their time of happiness and irresponsibility now while they were young. She sighed and moved on, finding the village shop close by.

It was the Aladdin's Cave of all village shops, full of everything from shoe polish to Satsumas, from charcoal to Chardonnay. Maggie made her way through stacks of peat and bundles of kindlers jostling for space by the entrance and then wandered passed shelves crammed with tinned goods and fresh vegetables, flour and biscuits, paperback books and aspirin, and freezers stocked with ready meals and ice-cream. She picked up a carton of milk, some Cheddar cheese and a loaf of crusty bread, enjoying the mixture of smells pervading the air; the exotic scent of oranges and bananas melding with the fragrance of soap powder and the sharp, lemony tang of midge repellent. She debated whether to buy a bottle of wine and then decided she would. It would be pleasant to enjoy a glass or two at night in front of the fire before she went to bed.

She stood for a while reading the notices fastened to a board on the wall at the side of the counter. There was to be a night of fiddle playing in the village hall, Mrs. Muir had a pair of laying hens for sale, while Donnie Macgregor would do odd jobs for a very reasonable price. Adverts for window cleaning, cakes for special occasions and puppies free to good homes were pinned next to ones offering lessons in Scottish country dancing or a course in quilt-making.

Someone had lost a cat and she studied this notice carefully, wondering if it might be the black cat she had seen lying in the sun on the windowsill of the cottage. But no, this one was a tabby answering to the name of Charlie,

31

"last seen the day before yesterday in the area of the church". She would keep an eye open for it when she went round there.

She approached the counter and for an instant was struck by something familiar about the motherly-looking woman who came to serve her. Maggie shook her head; she was imagining things again. She paid for her shopping and exchanged a few pleasantries about the weather.

Once outside, she strolled slowly towards the rear of the long, low, brick and wood construction which housed the shop, intending to have a look at the rest of the village before visiting the church. At the end of the building she noticed a small extension had been added and that the door to it stood open. On the wall beside the entrance was a sign which read 'Herbal Solutions.' Interested, she decided to pop in and have a look around.

The moment she walked through the door such a medley of sights and scents swamped her senses she felt overwhelmed. The sweet, flowery smell of jasmine, aromatic rosemary and thyme, the spicy fragrance of basil and the warm, aniseed scent of fennel, feathery-leaved dill and chervil assailed her nostrils mingling with many other wonderful smells she couldn't identify. Great bunches of dried herbs and flowers hung from the ceiling and terracotta pots full of leafy vegetation spilled across the floor, making manoeuvring through them a somewhat tricky operation.

The walls were lined with shelves crammed with all manner of bottles and jars containing a myriad of colourful mixtures and blends. Scented candles burned in odd corners, their flames fluttering in the gentle draught which sneaked in through the open doorway. Chime bells tinkled melodically set in motion by the same quiet movement of air. Scattered sticks of incense added their exotic fragrance to the already heady atmosphere. There was no-one to be seen anywhere.

Maggie began wandering around picking up various items, reading labels, sniffing contents, admiring the huge assortment of lotions and potions on display. So entranced was she, she nearly jumped out of her skin when someone tapped her gently on the shoulder.

'I'm sorry, have you been waiting long?'

Maggie whirled round. She had not been aware that anyone had come in and it was a moment before she could gather her thoughts to summon up the words to reply.

'No, no', she stuttered, 'I was having a look around. I hope that's alright?'

'It's perfectly fine, you carry on.'

The woman standing before her smiled. She was probably about her own age, Maggie guessed, and had the most glorious auburn hair she had ever seen. The rich red of autumn leaves, it fell in waves, curling around her face and tumbling over her shoulders, its coppery tones enriched by the dancing candlelight. Her cat-green eyes were regarding Maggie thoughtfully.

'Are you alright? I seem to have given you a bit of a fright coming in unexpectedly like that. I only popped out for a wee minute to see a friend and I didn't realise anyone had come into the shop. Would you like to sit down for a moment? You look a bit shaken.'

Maggie nodded, her heart hammering against her ribs. The woman disappeared behind a curtain patterned with sunflowers at the back of the shop and reappeared almost immediately with a chair and a glass of water. Maggie felt rather silly. After all it was the second time today that she had reacted like this when someone had taken her by surprise.

'I'm really sorry to put you to such trouble. I don't know what's the matter with me lately. I seem to be jumping at the slightest thing.' Maggie took a couple of sips of water and then, to her absolute chagrin, her eyes began to fill with tears. She blinked rapidly.

'You're probably a bit run down I expect. You *are* rather pale.'

The woman's voice was soothing as she moved over to retrieve a small, blue bottle from a shelf behind her.

'Here, you should use this,' and she handed the bottle

to Maggie. 'It's a special tonic,' she added seeing Maggie's look of alarm. 'It's Marigold Syrup from a very old recipe handed down in my family from mother to daughter. It's made from the ordinary marigold flower, you know the one? The kind you might find growing in your granny's garden - thick green stems and bright sunshine yellow petals.' Her smile was engaging as she went on. 'Anyway, this is a great tonic and certainly won't do you any harm. In fact it wouldn't hurt for you to take a little now,' and, still talking, she reached over behind the tiny, wooden counter and fetched out a tea-spoon. 'I often take it myself when I'm feeling a bit under the weather.'

Taking the bottle from Maggie's non-too-steady hands, she poured out a small dose and offered it to her. Maggie, like a child, obediently opened her mouth and swallowed it down. It was not at all unpleasant, sweet and sticky, a bit like honey.

The woman smoothed down the long, multi-coloured skirt of her dress, and then looked directly at her visitor. 'I've a feeling you've had a big shock lately, and I don't mean now, today. But something's happened recently that's really shaken you up.'

Maggie gazed at her. 'How could you know that?'

'I can tell things about people.' The woman's eyes were still fixed steadily on Maggie's face, her expression concerned.

'I don't want to talk about it.' Maggie jumped up, almost knocking over the chair. 'Thank-you for your trouble but I have to go now.'

'I didn't mean to upset you. I'm so sorry if I have.' She patted Maggie's hand. 'It was lovely to meet you and we'll meet again I know.' She smiled. 'I'm Bridie MacInnes, by the way, well Bridget really. I was named for the Goddess, but since I was a wee girl I've always been known as Bridie.' When Maggie looked uncertain she added, 'Brighid was the Pagan Celtic Goddess of fire, fertility, and healing.' She laughed, and whirled around, her arms outstretched to encompass all that made up her little kingdom. 'Rather appropriate don't you think?'

She was so full of passion that Maggie, unable to resist her enthusiasm, smiled back. Bridie continued, 'You can usually find me here most days if ever you do want to talk, or maybe if you'd simply like a friend.'

Maggie relaxed. Bridie had been welcoming and sympathetic and she, herself, had been less than gracious in face of the other woman's kindness.

'Thanks, Bridie, I appreciate that, and maybe I'll take you up on your offer.' She could certainly do with a friend at the moment. 'My name's Maggie. I'm staying down the glen at Tigh-na-Bruach, for a week or so.'

'I know,' Bridie replied smiling. 'I'll look forward to seeing you while you're here.'

Maggie took her leave with a promise to return soon but, instead of making her way along to the church as she had planned, decided she would go back to the cottage. Her emotions were all over the place and she was tired.

By the time she got there, the sky had clouded over and there was a chill in the air. She shivered and raised her hand to lift the latch. As she did so she felt the shape of a warm animal body wind itself through her legs. A little startled, she looked down expecting to see the black cat from yesterday. There was no cat. There was no sign of a cat or any other creature.

She caught her breath and shivered. Stealing a glance at the hillside she imagined for a moment she could see a shadowy figure standing there, silent, motionless. She stared harder but there was nothing. *My nerves really are shot to pieces*, she thought as she opened the door and hurried inside.

A little later, with a fire burning in the grate and a large glass of wine in her hand, she concluded her imagination had got the better of her yet again. Feeling a little less on edge she settled down into a chair and opened her book. She turned to a chapter on Scottish folklore and began to read.

"The Bodach is a creature of Celtic myth found in both

Irish and Scottish folklore. In Ireland it is a shadow-like spirit, black as ink, slinking and sly, capable of changing its shape at will. Children are warned that if they are naughty, the Bodach, or Bogey-man, will come down the chimney at night and carry them away."

The room was cosy, the pretty, floral curtains closed against the falling darkness. Flickering flames in the hearth were reflected on the highly-polished surfaces of the old oak furniture around the room. Curled up in the ancient leather armchair, Maggie struggled to concentrate on what she was reading

"In Scotland 'Bodach' (or Bothach) is a Gaelic term for an old man;, in bygone days, it was used as a derogatory term by Scottish fighting men when referring to the peasantry though in more modern times it is often used as a term of affectionate teasing for an older adult such as father or grandfather. However, it is also used, as in Irish myth, to describe a mischievous, shape-shifting imp or faery often appearing in the guise of an old man. Unlike his Irish counterpart, however, the Bodach is not a creature of nightmares but has the gift of 'second-sight' and so is respected for his wisdom…… ..."

The words started to blur as her eyes grew heavy. The day out in the fresh air coupled with the wine, the disturbed sleep of the night before and the warmth of the room began to have their effect. Soon she was asleep, no longer reading about the Bodach but dreaming of him.

She was in the same room, the fire was still burning, but in the chair opposite to her sat a very old man. His silvery white hair hung down to his shoulders and his beard was long and silky. Although his figure seemed lean, his features were big and strong, his face weather-beaten as if he had spent much time out of doors. Faded blue eyes gazed at her now, unwavering. *He looks kind,* she thought.

The strange thing was that she felt no surprise, no fear or shock at his sudden appearance. She simply accepted he was there. He made no movement but remained seated by the fire, one hand firmly gripping a tall, dark wooden staff carved with many curious designs and symbols. He wore a black suit, shiny with age and the boots on his feet were dusty as if he had travelled many miles. He spoke not a word.

Maggie gazed at him, a little uncertain. *He looks real enough*, she decided, and raised a hand as if to reach out to him. As if he had read her mind, he gave a slight shake of his head and she paused. Still, he did not speak. With his eyes fixed upon her, he slowly withdrew his free hand from a pocket and held it out to her. In his palm lay a small, flat pebble with a symbol like an angular letter B inscribed upon its surface, and she could make out the initials C. R scratched below it. She leaned forward to take a closer look but, as she did so, his figure began to waver, his outline becoming hazy and smudged until all that was left was a vague impression of his presence. Then that too disappeared and he was gone.

The phone was ringing. Gradually the sound penetrated her consciousness and she awoke with a jerk, disorientated, half asleep. She staggered up from the chair and reached for the receiver. It was Rachel.

'How are you? How are things going? Have you been out yet or are you still hiding yourself away and moping?'

'Hold on, one question at a time.' Maggie laughed.

She pictured her friend at the other end of the phone probably pacing around her stylish flat anxious to know how Maggie was surviving out in the back of beyond. It was really good to hear her voice.

'I'm fine,' she went on. 'The cottage is lovely and

I'm really enjoying the peace and quiet,' which, she realised, was true. Despite the feeling of wretchedness which hovered in the background of her waking moments and the weird dreams troubling her sleep, she was relishing the change and the chance to recharge her mind and spirit. She told Rachel about Jessie Ferguson's visit that morning and then of her walk down to the village.

'And did you go to the pub and get an eyeful of the hunky barman yet?'

'As it happens I did, though he isn't only the barman, he's the landlord. Angus Cameron. He seems very full of himself and not my type at all,' Maggie was quick to add.

Before Rachel could press her further, she went on to describe her meeting with Bridie... 'She seems really nice and friendly.'

They chatted on for a while longer, in particular about the state of Rachel's love-life, currently non-existent, although she had high hopes of the guy who had recently moved into the flat opposite.

When she finally put down the phone, having managed to reassure her friend that she wasn't moping, that yes she was sad and felt betrayed by Ben's behaviour but she was trying to get over it, Maggie felt more cheerful than she had for a while.

For a few minutes she reflected on the dream she had had before Rachel's call and, in her mind's eye, could see the stone the old man had held out to her. The angular letter B cut into it looked like a runic symbol, but she wasn't sure. And the initials so carefully scratched on it, what did they signify?

Maggie wondered why the image remained so clearly etched in her mind. Usually, once she woke, her dreams faded so quickly she had difficulty remembering them. She shrugged her shoulders, deciding to forget about it and try to get a good night's sleep for a change. To her surprise, she did. For the first time in weeks her sleep was dreamless and undisturbed.

CHAPTER 4

She woke early the next morning to the sound of rain pattering against the bedroom window. She didn't need to get up yet, she could have a little longer snuggled under the covers, secure and warm whilst the weather did its worst outside. The rhythmic tapping of the rain, the gentle scent of lavender from the bedclothes soothed her as she drifted between waking and sleeping.

She thought back to her first meeting with Ben.

It had been in the street. She was rushing to catch a tube train her arms full of books and files she was taking home to prepare for a display being mounted at the museum where she worked. He was striding along engaged in conversation on his mobile phone and not looking where he was going. The streets were crowded, people everywhere intent on getting to wherever they wanted or needed to be.

Ben had accidentally knocked her arm as he walked passed her and she dropped everything. Books and papers scattered and she fell to her knees, trying to retrieve them before they were kicked away or trodden on by other hurrying feet. At her cry of alarm Ben had stopped full of apologies.

'I'm so sorry,' he said. 'I didn't see you,' and he had bent down to help her. She looked up, a disparaging remark on the tip of her tongue, and had found herself staring into eyes of the most brilliant blue. He gave a broad grin and added, 'I'm really not safe to be let out on my own.' She couldn't help herself. She grinned back. They ended up going for coffee; she missed her train and he never got wherever it was he was rushing to.

They continued to see each other, their relationship gradually developing into something more significant. After his proposal she began looking forward to marriage. It would give her the sense of order and constancy she craved. Her father's desertion of her as a child had left her bereft and confused. She was determined life would never again take her unawares.

Well that was not to be the way of things now, she reflected still half-asleep. Her safe, predictable future had disappeared in a flash like fairy dust with Ben's perfidy. Without warning, a feeling of such bleak emptiness swept over her that she buried her head in the pillow and wept. Finally, as the tears dried up, she grew calmer and felt marginally better.

A curtain of rain still shrouded the hills when she went downstairs. It looked set to continue for the rest of the day but she didn't fancy being confined indoors. She needed milk so a quick foray to the village was in order. Foolishly, she had not packed any clothes for wet weather and she could hear the rain now assaulting the kitchen window. Not relishing getting soaked to the skin, she had a quick look around for the waterproofs she was sure Rachel had mentioned.

Unable to locate them, she found Jessie Ferguson's phone number on a list by the telephone and rang to explain her predicament.

'I think Rachel said there are waterproofs and boots somewhere, but I can't find them. Do you happen to know where they might be?'

'Och, aye dearie, they'll be in the press.'

Maggie frowned. She had a sudden vision of trawling through the 'For Sale' ads in the local newspaper in search of wet weather clothing.

She was contemplating this when Jessie went on, 'You'll have seen it, dearie, a small cupboard in the front porch. Behind the door?' she added as Maggie remained silent; she didn't remember seeing such a thing.

She found her voice. 'Oh, right! Thanks,' and

readily accepted Jessie's invitation to call in on her on her way back from the village.

There wasn't a soul to be seen when she drove into Invershee; no chattering tourists or walkers or even local people for that matter. The shop was empty too, apart from the woman who had served her yesterday. Again Maggie experienced a fleeting stab of recognition ... something about the woman's eyes was familiar...but she shrugged the feeling off; she was being foolish. Having bought what she needed, Maggie drove back up the glen.

She passed the turn off to Rachel's cottage and, following Jessie's directions, carried on along the track, which became narrower and more rutted the further on she went. She slowed down and, as she carefully rounded a bend, saw Jessie Ferguson's cottage sitting squarely at the roadside. The track stopped here. In true Highland fashion the rain was relentless and beyond the croft Maggie could barely make out the faint outline of hills and then mountains, climbing into the distance.

How must it have been long ago when fierce clansmen strode those hills and swooped, like vengeful demons out of the concealing mists to fall upon their enemies? She imagined their restless spirits haunting the Highlands, their ghostly battle cries echoing across the rough desolate heath lands. Gazing out over the grey landscape, Maggie sensed the distant memories and long-held secrets enshrouded in its peat-sodden, timeless terrain; past and present irrevocably entwined. She shuddered. All this thought of ghosts brought back her dream of the woman in grey and she wondered again if that was what it had been, simply her mind playing tricks on her.

Shaking herself back to the present, she saw the name, Myrtle Croft, painted in large letters on the gate which stood open for her. The cottage was white-washed like Rachel's and, even through the rain, Maggie could see tubs of multi-coloured flowers crowding around the front door which, like the window frames, was painted a glossy black. She parked the car and sat quietly for a moment contemplating the cottage and its surroundings.

It was clearly a working croft for there were sheep dotted about on the near hillside, shorn of their fleece and seeking whatever shelter they could find. Further off, she could see some cattle lying placidly in a field. The pervading silence was interrupted by the loud barking of a couple of dogs, which Maggie hoped were secured in the large shed she could see alongside the cottage. The hen run was empty of occupants but she expected the hens were cosily encooped, sheltering from the inclement weather, and there was a well-used saw-horse standing by the front wall beside which a great stack of logs was heaped; no doubt in anticipation of a harsh winter.

Taking a deep breath, she hurried along the flagstone path to the door. It opened as she reached it and Jessie ushered her in to stand dripping in the tiny entrance hall.

'Come in, come in. What a dreich day it is!'

Having divested Maggie of her waterproofs, Jessie bustled her into the sitting room and into a large, well-worn but comfortable arm-chair beside a glowing wood fire. The sweet smell of baking hung in the air and Maggie sniffed in appreciation, her mouth watering at the thought of floury scones straight from the oven. Jessie produced a towel and then busied herself in the kitchen making tea as Maggie began to dry her hair which was hanging round her face as if she had recently stepped out of the shower.

All at once, she sensed she was no longer alone and with a quick start she turned and jumped up, her hand flying up to cover her mouth as she let out a small 'Oh!' of fright. Angus was leaning casually against the door frame, his arms folded, watching her.

'You obviously make a habit of creeping up on people, scaring them half to death!' she snapped, sinking back into the chair

Angus grinned. 'I wasn't creeping and I did knock before I came in. However,' he said, giving a little bow, 'I do apologise Miss MacQueen if I "scared you half to death"....yet again!' he added as an afterthought. 'I really don't mean to make a habit of it.'

Maggie scowled at him. However, a sense of fairness made her realise she was partly at fault for daydreaming, so in more moderate tones she said, 'I'm sorry for biting your head off. I was miles away and I didn't hear you come in.' She raked her hand through her hair and then flashed him an apologetic smile.

'You should do that more often,' he said.

'What?'

'Smile.' Angus continued to regard her steadily.

'I haven't had much reason to, lately.' She sighed and her face became serious again as she gazed into the flames, biting her lower lip.

As the air between them began to grow heavy with unspoken words and thoughts, Jessie came hurrying in with a tray of tea and the hoped-for scones. Angus leapt from his relaxed position, and taking the tray from his aunt placed it carefully on a small, side table next to Maggie.

'I thought I heard you come in, Angus. I hope you two have been getting acquainted? Now help yourself to a nice warm scone, dearie,' Jessie said, turning to Maggie. 'They're fresh out of the oven.'

The conversation ebbed and flowed around her as Angus and his aunt discussed the weather, trade at the Inn and snippets of village gossip. Maggie, able to contribute little – apart from saying she had met and liked Bridie - knowing nothing of the people and places they mentioned, sipped her tea and, whilst Angus and his aunt exchanged chit-chat, she sneaked quick glances at him through her eyelashes.

Her impressions of him yesterday had not been wrong, she decided. He had an easy charm and a rather wry sense of humour. His affection for his aunt was obvious in the way he spoke to her and Maggie supposed some women might find his rough-hewn looks attractive; there was certainly nothing fine or delicate in his build or features. *He's so unlike Ben,* she reflected, who had a slim, almost athletic, physique. She bit down hard on her lip to suppress a quick pang of longing.

She turned back to her scrutiny of Angus. His was a strong face and no doubt, once he had set his mind to something, he would not give up until he had achieved whatever it was he wanted. He reminded her a little of her father. Maggie had loved her father to distraction but it had not been enough to make him stay. One day he had been there, the centre of her existence, the next he was gone.

Remembering him now, she felt the all-too-familiar, deep-rooted ache of loss spread through her. She blamed his departure on her mother; some people should just never marry, Maggie reflected. Her mother had not looked after him properly, she was always off doing other things, meals were disorganised and never at set times, the house was a shambles. Amidst it all her mother had flitted from one interest to another, beautiful but selfish, with little room in her busy life for a husband, much less a child. Maggie did not think her mother had even really noticed he was gone, but *she* had. Seven-year old Maggie had felt his absence like a physical pain. She didn't know why he'd left and she never found out. Her mother would never discuss it.

'Leave it, Maggie,' she would say, 'it's over and done with.'

But Maggie had missed his solid, dependable presence as if an arm had been amputated. Though rarely expressed in words, she was aware of the warmth of his love for her every day in a dozen different ways; he would listen attentively to her stories about school, make her favourite dinner when her mother was absent, stroke her hair as he said goodnight. She recalled the touch of his fingers on her face and way his voice softened as he murmured,

'Night, Night, my lovely lass. Sleep tight.'

After he went she had prayed every night for him to

come back to them until her knees were sore and her throat ached. She had promised to be so good that he would never go away again but it was too late. He was killed a month later in a car crash on his way to work. She never forgave her mother.

Maggie sucked in a deep breath and, rousing herself from her reverie, turned her attention back to Angus. His hair, a rich, dense brown, was a little too long for her taste. It grew thick and unruly and gave him a rather untamed air, as if he cared little for convention. She could picture him as a pirate swashbuckling his way across the high seas or perhaps leading a gang of ruffians on raiding parties across the Highlands or, maybe even, commanding a band of rebellious Jacobites against the Redcoats during the '45 uprising. She wondered idly what he looked like in a kilt. Rather impressive she thought, and felt the warmth flood her face at the image she had conjured up.

A little later Angus left, having delivered the newspaper he had brought for his aunt. He had been surprised to find Maggie there when he stepped familiarly into the room after a perfunctory knock at the front door. He had been thinking about her all that morning and then there she was, perched on the edge of a chair, her feet bare and her hair hanging round her face in damp, dark curls. A towel lay discarded on the floor. She was clearly unaware of his presence and he had watched her silently for a few moments.

She looked more rested than when he had seen her yesterday. Her cheeks, kissed by the firelight, had a rosy glow, and coppery highlights glimmered in her chestnut-coloured hair. He'd felt a sudden urge to touch it and let its long, fine-spun softness run through his fingers. Maybe he made an involuntary movement as if to do exactly that, or maybe some sixth sense told Maggie she was no longer alone because, all of a sudden, she had abruptly leapt up from the chair like a startled deer catching wind of a stalker.

He had found the conversation over the tea and home-baking interesting, not for its content but for the opportunity it afforded him to study Maggie a little more. Something about her commanded his interest but he was damned if he could work out what it was. After all, she was nothing like the type of woman he was normally attracted to with her pinched, pale face and haunted eyes. He had again detected the undercurrent of strong feelings kept rigidly in check as he had on their first meeting. And yet she had a very expressive face; every emotion displayed for all to see.

He recalled how her eyes had flashed when she scolded him for startling her, the quick smile of apology, and then the signs of strain when she sat lost in her own thoughts. She appeared relaxed sitting in her chair but he saw how her hands frequently fiddled with the braid on the chair arm or touched her hair, and now and again he caught her biting her bottom lip. Once, a look of such desolation shadowed her face that he almost leapt up to go and comfort her. It took some effort for him to remain seated; somehow he didn't think she would appreciate his rushing over and putting his arm around her.

Later, as his aunt regaled him with stories of the pine marten she had seen sneaking around the chicken coop, he glanced over at Maggie and saw a quick blush stain her cheeks. He wondered what she was thinking. She was certainly a woman of contradictions; maybe that was what intrigued him?

He might have a word with Bridie and see what she made of Maggie MacQueen, he mused as he drove away; she was always good at working people out. He and Bridie had a close relationship. There had been a little dalliance some years back when they were both full of the energy and curiosity of youth but their brief affair had ended amicably, and, in the way of people who understood each other, once the brief flare of passion was spent they

had discovered the bonds of a deep and abiding friendship.
Yes, he would speak to Bridie.

CHAPTER 5

After seeing Angus away, Jessie settled back into her chair. 'He's such a considerate lad,' she said, smiling. Maggie thought he could hardly be described as a lad but murmured agreement with the older woman's sentiment.

'He knows my John's away at the Farmer's Market in Dingwall,' Jessie said, glancing at a wedding photograph on the mantelshelf above the fire. 'Angus likes to make sure I'm alright.' Absentmindedly, she rubbed her leg. 'I've a touch of rheumatism at the moment or I'd have gone too but I can't be managing all the walking and standing about you do at those places. I'm better off here resting as the doctor said.'

Maggie, half listening, was still thinking about Angus as Jessie chattered on.

'He seems to know what he's about though he's new here. Took over the practice from old Dr. Gordon six months ago. Mind you his family's from these parts so he's a local man more or less and he's a very pleasant manner on him.'

She paused and Maggie, aware of a sudden silence, reproached herself for not paying proper attention. She smiled at Jessie and nodded.

'Now, what was I saying before?' Jessie continued. 'Oh, yes, I was telling you about Angus. He's my brother Alisdair's boy. He died when Angus was a wee boy of nine. Such a lovely man he was, Alisdair, and a good brother to me.' Her voice shook a little and she took a deep breath as she went on. 'But the trouble was he was a drinker, you know. Well, of course you don't know, dearie', she said, leaning forward to pat Maggie's hand and smiled. 'But such a good, caring man when he was sober, and such a sense of fun he had. He'd a fine voice on him too,' she added, a faraway look in her eyes. 'People were always asking him to sing and oblige them he would without any bother, never refused anyone. Angus absolutely adored him. Aye,' she went on sadly, 'it was the drink was his downfall. He couldn't refuse that either. Fell into a ditch one night, he did, after too many drams.' She didn't elaborate further.

Maggie felt a tug of sympathy for Angus. She knew as well as anyone what it was like to lose a beloved parent at such a young age.

'What about Angus's mother? Is she still alive?'

Jessie looked up from her memories, 'No, she died last year, Cancer. Took her in a matter of weeks. No, it's only Angus and the three girls now."

'The three girls?'

'Aye, his sisters. There's Fiona, the eldest. Lives in Edinburgh. She married a teacher and teaches school herself. Then there's Ailsa. She's a fiddler with a Celtic music group. They travel all over playing at Ceilidhs and festivals and such like. She's a lovely voice too.' Jessie smiled proudly. 'She takes after Alisdair for that. And then there's wee Caitlin, the youngest. But of course you'll have met her if you've been to the Inn. She sees to the food and helps behind the bar,' she added seeing Maggie's puzzled expression.

Maggie nodded, recalling the pretty, dark-haired girl pulling pints when she had gone there for lunch.

She became aware Jessie was looking at her with a concerned expression on her face.

'Well, that's enough of the family history for today,' the older woman said, briskly. 'Now, how are you doing, dearie? You're still looking a wee bitty pale.'

'Oh, I'm getting on alright. I really love it here. It's so peaceful and pretty.' Maggie glanced across the room. Through the window she could see a fine rain was still falling steadily, obscuring the surrounding hills. 'Even on a day like today,' she said smiling. She took her courage in both hands. 'Actually, there was something I wanted to ask you. I hope you won't think it's too silly'. Maggie hesitated, wondering how to bring up what was on her mind.

'Well, ask away dearie and I'll do my best to answer you.'

Maggie decided it was probably best to come straight out with it. 'Do you believe in ghosts? Or spirits? Or that kind of thing?' she finished lamely, leaning forward in her chair

'Well, that's a question for a body to answer!' A slight frown creased Jessie's brow and she went on, 'I suppose I do, in a way. I mean I don't believe in the kind of ghosts you see depicted on the telly. You know all white sheets and clanking chains. That sort of rubbish,' she said, dismissing such media portrayals with a wave of her hand. 'But I do believe in an afterlife so I expect there are such things as spirits. I've never actually seen any myself, but I know people who have, or at least claim to have seen one. And sometimes you can sense a kind of presence, as if there is someone there but when you look closer there's nothing. It gives you a kind of spooky feeling.' She shivered involuntarily, and then looked curiously at Maggie. 'Why, dearie, do you think you've seen a ghost?'

'Well, No….that is I don't know. I thought it was a dream but now, well I'm not so sure.' Maggie paused for a moment and then plunged on. She described first of all seeing the cottage looking so very different to the way it looked now. 'There was a cat on the windowsill too and the rowan tree wasn't in the garden. It was really weird. But it must have been a dream or perhaps some kind of hallucination,' she added. 'I have been a bit stressed lately.'

'Well, the rowan's been there for as long as I can remember and I don't know of any cat.' Jessie frowned again. 'But the strange thing is you've described the cottage exactly as it used to be.'

Maggie stared at her, round eyed. Her heart beat quickened and she leaned further forward, intent on what Jessie was saying.

'It used to be a black house at one time, a fair few years ago now.'

'What on earth's that?'

'Och, they used to be common here in the Highlands.

They had dry stone walls and a turf or heather roof. People lived at one end and the animals lived at the other with a partition between.'

Jessie chuckled at the expression on Maggie's face. 'At least they were warm in the winter. Anyway,' she continued, 'someone bought it and converted it. Built an upstairs and slated the roof. And of course they put in a back door and built a proper chimney. In the old days the hearth was in the middle of the floor with a hole in the roof for the smoke to escape.' She gazed at her young visitor.

'What a very strange experience you've had, dearie. It must have been quite un-nerving.' She looked at Maggie. 'Is that what you meant about seeing ghosts?'

'In a way,' Maggie replied, 'but it was much more than that,' and she went on to relate her strange encounter with the woman in grey. 'She seemed so real and then she simply disappeared as if she'd never been there,' she finished. 'She seemed so real,' she repeated, 'and filled with so much suffering.' She twisted her hands in her lap wondering if the other woman would perhaps think she was slightly crazy. 'And then, yesterday when I got back from the village, I thought I saw her again on the hillside.' A shudder ran down her back at the memory.

Jessie's expression was unruffled as she leaned forward and clasped Maggie's restless hands between her own. They were warm and firm, thought Maggie irrelevantly, sturdy, working hands calloused in places and beginning to show signs of age, but the action calmed her and she returned Jessie's gaze.

'It's possible you may indeed have seen the woman you describe, dearie,' the older woman said gently. 'It's strange, because, when you first asked me if I believed in ghosts, I said though I'd never seen one myself I knew someone who had. In fact I was thinking of Morag MacIver who used to live in the cottage where you're staying.' Maggie gave a little exclamation of surprise, as the older woman went on. 'I remember her telling me about it.'

She released Maggie's hands and settled back in her

chair. 'It was shortly after she lost her husband, Donald. Very sad, it was. Killed in an accident with a tractor, and she was, well, completely distraught as you'd expect. He was all she had. They were never able to have children of their own you see, which, I suppose,' she added thoughtfully, 'is why she was so fond of her god-daughter and left her the cottage when she died. That's your friend isn't it?' Maggie nodded.

'Anyway, Morag told me she was out on the hill one day and this woman in a long, grey dress appeared, wringing her hands and weeping. Morag, of course, was grieving for Donald but she said, as she made to go towards her and offer some comfort, the woman simply vanished. Morag said it really unnerved her. She didn't go out onto the hill again for some time after that.'

Maggie stared at the older woman. Maybe she really had not been dreaming after all. 'Did Morag ever see her again?'

'Yes, two or three times more, I think, and the same thing happened. As soon as Morag made to move towards her she was gone. But I remember her saying the woman's sadness was so great it seemed to fill all the air around her until she, Morag I mean, could hardly breathe. Everywhere became icy cold she said.'

Maggie nodded. 'Yes, that's exactly what it was like for me too. It was as if the woman was surrounded by a cloud of grief.' She frowned, chewing her bottom lip. 'I wonder who she is. Maybe there's some way we can find out if she actually existed. If she was a local woman there must be records somewhere.' She looked hopefully at Jessie who gave a slight shake of her head.

'I wouldn't know about that, dearie.'

Maggie remembered reading somewhere that ghosts often appear to people who are particularly susceptible to the atmosphere of a place; usually somewhere that something truly tragic or evil has occurred.

'Maybe Morag saw the ghost because they had both lost someone close to them,' she suggested tentatively.

'You know a kind of shared sorrow or something like that.' She sat quietly for a moment, speculating, not sure where this line of thought was taking her.

Jessie interrupted her thoughts. 'You could perhaps speak to the Minister, dearie. He might know of some tragedy in the past. Or maybe Bridie could help. She's into that sort of thing. You know spirits and such like, being psychic as she is.' Her voice softened. 'I've a lot of time for Bridie. It's a shame things didn't work out between her and Angus.' Maggie's eyes opened wide. 'Oh, yes, they were...what is it they call it nowadays? That's it, an item. Yes, at one time I had high hopes for the pair of them. But it wasn't to be.' She sighed. 'But there we are, that's the way of the world. People have to make their own choices in matters of the heart.'

Maggie wondered why she was disconcerted at the thought of Angus and Bridie together. *It's nothing to me who he sees*, she thought, and stood to help as Jessie rose from her chair to carry the tea things through into the kitchen.

As Maggie was leaving, having thanked the other woman for her hospitality, Jessie put a hand on her arm. 'You know dearie, we've another local mystery you might be interested in. You'll probably hear about it if you're here for any length of time. That one might be easier to solve than trying to find out about your woman on the hill. Mind you, no-one over the past one hundred and fifty years has been able to discover who she was.'

'Who's that?'

'The Unknown Maid.'

Maggie stared at her. 'The Unknown Maid?' she echoed.

'Och, it's an old tale from hereabouts. My Gran told me she heard the story from her great-grandmother. Apparently some young woman was found wandering on the hillside by where you're staying. Well over a hundred years ago it was, and I believe she died very soon after she was discovered.' Jessie frowned and then continued. 'A young man found her I think, if memory serves me right. Out poaching I expect. Anyway, they never found out who she was or where she'd come from. She wasn't from this village evidently. She's buried in the churchyard with the simple inscription 'Maighdeann.' Locally she's known as The Unknown Maid.'

Maggie gazed at the older woman. 'Has anyone done any investigating recently?'

'Not that I know of, dearie.' Jessie shook her head. 'But I should think it would be difficult after all this time to find out who she was.'

'Maybe, but I could ask the Minister about that too. He might have some ideas.'

Maggie turned and hugged Jessie, and thanked her once again, saying she would do a little digging and see what she could find out. She promised to let the other woman know if she discovered anything.

The rain was still falling as she made a dash for the car. *Not a day to go exploring a church* she decided and drove home, her head buzzing with ideas and possible ways of discovering the identities of the two mystery women. She felt a tingle of excitement at the thought of the challenge ahead. At least it would provide a diversion from constantly thinking about her own troubles and misery.

Because she now knew Morag McIver had claimed to have seen her too, Maggie was convinced she had not dreamt or imagined the woman in grey; what she had seen had not been a living, breathing person but some manifestation from the past.

She shook her head. Was she, a sensible, well-adjusted young woman of the modern world now accepting without question that she had seen a ghost? She needed to sit and think the whole thing through calmly and was thankful when she arrived back at the cottage.

Later, with a fire burning in the grate, and a little more in control of her emotions, she resolved to go about this puzzle in the same way she would tackle any other, in a logical, methodical way. She was, after all, well used to examining and researching fragments and snippets of information to discover how they fitted together to reveal the bigger picture. She would start with what she had observed...

She closed her eyes and conjured up an image of the figure she had seen, focusing as hard as she could on the clothes the woman was wearing. The dress had definitely been grey and of some serviceable material, *probably drugget*, she thought. There were no frills or flounces, simply a small, plain collar, long sleeves and a skirt falling straight to the ankles; the sort of dress a woman of a fairly low station in life might wear to church during the 1840s or 1850s perhaps, though, Maggie recalled, the dress had looked stained and dirty.

Was the woman wearing a wedding ring? She hadn't noticed but then she had not been looking for one and it was not something easily seen from a distance. Maggie frowned and concentrated. She was sure the woman wore no head covering...her hair fell loose about her face... and she had no shawl of any kind.

Satisfied she had remembered all she could Maggie sipped her glass of wine, planning what to do next. She should confirm she was right about the clothing being mid-Victorian or thereabouts. Suddenly she jumped up. *Of course!* She had her laptop with her. Bringing it had not been a conscious decision, merely an automatic reflex as she was rarely without it at home. She ran upstairs to fetch it down.

She spent the next few hours on the internet and confirmed she was right about the style of clothing. She also unearthed a mountain of information about life in the Highlands during that period which might prove useful. Pleased with what she had achieved, Maggie began to put everything away, glancing, as she did so, at the old carriage clock on the mantelpiece. It showed three minutes to eight. She had been so absorbed in the research time had simply flown by. As she turned to go into the kitchen to make a cup of tea, she heard a loud rap on the back door.

Maggie froze. She held her breath as her mind raced. Who on earth could that be at this hour? She glanced again at the clock. It was quite late for someone to be calling unannounced. Jessie would be at home and surely would have phoned first if she intended to visit. She didn't know anyone else in the village well enough to think they might drop in without warning. Maggie stood absolutely still listening, her hands clenched by her sides. All she could hear was the regular, monotonous ticking of the clock and the gentle tapping of rain against the window pane.

The sound wasn't repeated and Maggie began to relax. *Stupid woman*! All this reading about mythical creatures and delving into the past was making her paranoid. It was probably simply a branch from a tree falling against the door; the fact that the only tree near the cottage was the rowan at the end of the garden did not occur to her.

She debated whether to go outside and check but decided if there had been anyone there they would have knocked again. So she went into the kitchen and, finding little to eat other than some pasta and a tin of tuna, busied herself making a quick meal. She would need to go into the village in the morning to get some more supplies. *Porridge!* She would get some porridge oats. She hadn't had porridge since she was a child.

She remembered how her father would stand in the kitchen at home stirring the pot on the stove and listen to her chattering away about girlish things. The appetising smell of porridge cooking, the rich aroma of freshly made coffee and the occasional musky whiff of her father's after-shave were inextricably linked in her mind with this scene. It had always made her feel warm and cared for. He would smile in that indulgent way he had which made her feel as if she were the most important person in his life, that she mattered.

She bit her bottom lip. Then why had he left? It was the question which continued to torment her. It was one to which she had never found a satisfactory answer and it hovered there at the back of her mind, taunting her; *maybe it was you he left, maybe you weren't loveable enough.*

Now Ben had left her too! She must be at fault in some way. There had to be something wrong with her. Tears of self-pity stung her eyes and she was tempted to give in to them. But no, she shook her head and sipped her tea. She would simply not let herself get involved with anyone again. She was clearly no good at relationships so she would avoid them in future, not allowing anyone close to her emotionally. She was not foolish enough to expose herself to such heartbreak a third time.

All at once she felt tired. A headache threatened and an early night seemed sensible. A couple of aspirin and a good night's sleep was what she needed and then she would be ready for whatever tomorrow might bring. As she went to lock the back door, she resolved to have a quick look around outside to make sure all was as it should be. The unexplained noise earlier had unsettled her and it would put her mind at rest to discover the cause of it; whether it had indeed been a tree branch as she supposed.

Taking a deep breath, she edged the door open a few inches and sneaked a quick peek outside. There was nothing out of the ordinary to be seen. It was still fairly light. She had forgotten that, whilst down in London it would be dark by now, up here in the Highlands she was much further north and so daylight lingered longer. Without realising it she had been holding her breath and now she let it out in a long sigh of relief.

She opened the door wider, glancing around as she stepped outside. She could see no sign of anything which might have caused the sound she had heard. Everywhere was calm and quiet. The rain was easing off and there was a slight breeze rustling the leaves of the rowan tree. The hillside was empty; *no ghostly figure tonight*, she thought.

As she went to shut the door, her foot knocked against something on the step. Looking down, she saw it was a small stone or pebble and her heart skipped a beat. Surely it couldn't be...? She bent down and picked it up. It was warm to the touch. Slowly she turned it over in her hand and saw a strange symbol and some scratched initials. It was the same pebble she had seen in her dream of the Bodach. She jumped back into the kitchen and, slamming the door shut, quickly shot home the bolt. Her legs were shaky, her head spinning, and she collapsed onto a nearby chair feeling as if at any moment she might faint.

CHAPTER 6

After a few minutes, when her heartbeat had returned more or less to normal and she felt her legs were capable of carrying her, Maggie walked into the sitting room. Still clutching the pebble, she went over to a lamp. Uncurling her fingers, she studied it under the light. Yes, it looked identical to the one in her dream. There was the angular letter B carved into the stone and the initials C.R. scratched onto the surface beneath the symbol.

She didn't understand it. How could she be holding in her hand something she had dreamt about the night before? *Unless I'm dreaming now*? She did what she always did as a child if she wasn't sure that something was real, she pinched herself; she had pinched herself so hard and so often when told of her father's death she had livid bruises on her arms for weeks. Now, as then, she felt the sharp nip of fingers squeezing her flesh; she wasn't dreaming, this was real.

But if that was so, *what does it mean*? That the Bodach had really had been in the cottage sitting in a chair by her fireside? How could it be? Her head started to ache again with the wild thoughts chasing around her brain. She placed the stone on the small oak table by the window. She needed a good night's sleep and then she would be able to think it all through in the morning with a clear head.

Sleep, however, was the last thing that came. She tossed and turned, nightmares troubling her throughout the long hours of darkness; dreams in which she opened the back door and saw the Bodach standing silent and unmoving, the woman in the grey dress leaned over her bed and wept tears of such anguish that Maggie woke with tears filling her own eyes, Ben lead the white horse over the hillside and then became Angus with Bridie walking ahead strewing sweet-smelling herbs in their path - she could smell their scent even in her sleep - and, throughout it all,

Jessie Ferguson handed out tea in cups bearing the strange symbol, the angular letter B.

That's ridiculous was Maggie's waking thought. She stretched and yawned. Despite her disturbed night, she was ready to face the day and put it to good use. She would go down to the village shop as she had planned and then visit the churchyard. Perhaps she would also try and speak to the Minister if she could locate him.

With her morning's activities planned, she dressed hurriedly and, seeing the rain had relented, went over to open the bedroom window. The sun was struggling to break through the clouds and she leaned on the sill, taking a deep breath of morning air. As she did so, her hand nudge against something small and hard and she looked down. Her eyes widened when she saw the Bodach's strange pebble lying there.

She was sure she had left it downstairs last night. She must have picked it up again without thinking and brought it upstairs with her. She held it again now. It was odd, but once more it was warm, as if someone had held it recently. She dismissed the thought. Obviously the sun, weak though it was, had warmed it as it lay on the sill. Absent-mindedly she slipped it into the pocket of her jeans.

After a quick breakfast of toast and coffee, she set off at a gentle jog towards the village. The sun had won its battle and now shone brightly although it was still chilly. As before, she could hear the rippling of the water, tripping over stones in the ditches running alongside the track, and birds sang in the trees and hedgerows as if elated at the freshness of the day. She slowed for a moment, charmed by a robin perched on the wall, its bright red breast puffed out as if delighted by the melodic yet plaintive song it warbled, before flying off.

As she picked up her pace again she noticed some of the leaves on the trees she passed already beginning to display hints of the golden bronzes, the sharp, vivid reds and showy yellows to come. With so many trees, autumn in this part of the world must be a riot of vibrant colour. *I'd love to be here to see it.* The thought came unbidden to her mind. Her feet faltered, their regular, rhythmic thudding on the road interrupted momentarily, as she examined the idea.

There was nothing urgent to draw her back to London, except her job of course; maybe she could arrange a sabbatical from the museum and use it to do some research into the old crofting communities she had thought about the other day. She recovered her former steady pace and carried on, the idea of staying on at the cottage at the back of her mind, inviting, appealing, tantalising.

In a few more minutes she was in the village and, deciding to call at the shop afterwards so as not be encumbered with shopping bags, she made directly for the church.

It was an impressive building she thought, not because of its size... it was not large... but because of its air of solid impregnability. It had stood here for over two hundred years and would stand for hundreds more she had no doubt. Like the Inn, it was built of huge granite blocks, solid, well-jointed stones, weathered and dimpled with lichen and moss, its roof a sombre grey slate. The entrance door of heavy, blackened oak opened easily at her touch, the hinges well-oiled from constant use. As she entered the body of the church she could smell candle-grease and beeswax mingled with the exotic fragrance of lilies lingering in the air.

Light spilled through the stained glass window behind the altar illuminating the gloomy interior and creating patterns of glowing colour on the well-worn flagstone floor. Maggie ran her hand over the back of a pew, its wood gleaming in evidence of hours of dedicated polishing. She slipped into a seat at the back of the church and sat for several moments letting the atmosphere of mellow peace soak into her.

Later, as she wandered among the gravestones, some ancient and leaning at strange, gravity-defying angles, others newer and defiantly upright, she paused now and again to read the inscriptions wondering about other people's lives, other people's sorrows. Then, she noticed a man making his way towards her. He was dressed all in black and for an instant she thought it was the Bodach. Her heart leapt into her mouth and she stood as transfixed as a moth on a collector's pin.

As he drew closer, however, she saw his cheerful countenance and twinkling eyes and, breathing a sigh of relief, offered a tremulous smile.

'Hello there,' he said as he approached, 'I saw you looking round the church earlier. I'm the Minister here, Euan Cameron,' and he put out a plump hand to shake hers. 'Can I be of any assistance to you, young lady?' His hand-shake was warm and firm and she silently chided herself for letting her imagination play tricks on her once again.

He looked like the traditional image of Father Christmas minus the red robes and beard, she thought, round and jolly with a beaming smile. White hair stuck out in tufts above his ears whilst the rest of his head was hairless and shiny. He seemed so friendly and approachable that, after the initial pleasantries, she began to tell him about the phantom she'd seen on the hillside and that she was looking for the burial plot of "The Unknown Maid."

He listened in silence, his eyes never leaving her face. 'Well,' he said thoughtfully, 'that's quite an experience you've had, my dear. Being a Minister of the church I would never disavow the existence of spirits of course, although I think of them more in terms of the soul.' He hesitated a moment as if pondering how to proceed. 'And, perhaps,' he continued, 'there *are* those few tortured souls who find it hard to surrender their previous earthly connection for one reason or another. There are plenty around here who certainly believe it. I, however, must have faith in a compassionate God and I cannot think that He would deny such tormented beings His mercy and forgiveness.' He must have caught a flicker of disappointment on her face because he patted her arm and continued. 'I don't doubt for one second, my dear, that you did indeed see something, sense something unusual and strange. But what it was..." he paused and shrugged his shoulders, "who knows? Maybe Hamlet was right and there are indeed "more things in Heaven and earth ..." than we ever dream of.'

He broke off and then, nodding his head, smiled, 'However, there is something I *can* do to help and that's show you where The Maid is buried. Come along with me now,' and, taking the lead, he trotted off down a path towards the rear of the churchyard.

Maggie followed a little more slowly, thinking about what he had said. After a moment, he stopped. 'There she is,' he announced, somewhat dramatically, she thought, as he flung out an arm and pointed towards a large slab of granite embedded in the ground. It was positioned close to the boundary wall and partly obscured by clumps of long, feathery grass. 'The man who takes care of the churchyard can't get his grass-cutting machine up here,' he said, as if apologising for its neglected appearance. Maggie approached the place and gazed down.

The word "Maighdeann" was carved in large letters at the top of the stone. She could see an inscription of some sort below it and knelt for a closer look. The stone was well-weathered, with lichens clinging to parts of it but she could make out some words, though she did not know what they said. They were in a language other than English and she guessed it was probably Gaelic. She looked up at the Minister.

'Do you know what the inscription says?'

'I do indeed,' he nodded and, leaning over, read out the words, before offering their translation.

"Herein lies a maid unknown,
Who is known to God alone."

Maggie felt tears prick the back of her eyes and she rapidly blinked them away. How sad that this young woman had had no-one to identify her when she died alone on the hillside and then was buried here un-mourned. She looked more closely and was able to distinguish a date.

"1852".

Euan Cameron hovered beside her as if hopeful of providing further assistance if needed.

'Is there a written record of her being found or something like that somewhere?' Maggie wondered aloud. There was a moment's silence and she looked around.

'Of course! There are the Parish Records. I'm sure I remember reading about it when I first became Minister here. It's a few years ago now but if my memory serves correctly...' His voice trailed away as he turned and began to scurry back along the gravel path towards the church.

Maggie watched him go and then rose to her feet ready to follow. As she stood, she caught a faint movement to the left out of the corner of her eye. She turned and gazed towards a small group of indigenous trees further along the wall where she thought someone or something had stirred.

There was a slight breeze and she could see the branches gently swaying. She put up her hand to shield her eyes and focused hard. For a moment she imagined she detected a black-suited figure standing silent and still in a darker patch of shadow between the trees. She narrowed her eyes and peered harder but there was nothing. She really did need a break. Time off from work and from her hectic life in London would not be such a bad thing she reflected. She turned away and hurried along the path taken by the Minister.

When she found him in the vestry, his clothes were a little dusty and his face was creased in puzzlement. 'I can't put my hands on the records at this minute. They're not where I thought they were.' Maggie must have looked crestfallen, and he went on, 'But as soon as I locate them I'll let you have a look through them,' and with that she had to be satisfied. She took her leave after thanking him for his help and promised to call back in a day or two to see if he had traced the misplaced registers.

She strolled along the pathway towards the gate lost in thought. *How awful it must be been to die alone and so young.* She wondered why the woman had been on the hillside and what had caused her death. It was strange no-one in Invershee had known who she was; the village must have been a lot smaller then with fewer people. So, Maggie reasoned, she must have come from somewhere else, further away along the loch-side. But why? What or who had she been seeking?

As she reached the gate and went to lift the heavy iron latch she saw Angus approaching the church.

'I thought it was you I saw wandering about amongst all these dead folk,' he said by way of greeting.

She gave a brief smile. 'Churches and churchyards happen to be a particular interest of mine. You can learn a lot about a community from such places. And I've always been especially interested in history. I like to know about the past and how people lived their lives.' She thought the last bit sounded slightly pompous so she added, 'Anyway, shouldn't you be pulling pints or something instead of accosting women in the street?'

He grinned. He had a slightly crooked grin, she noticed, which was rather appealing. 'First of all, we're not in the street,' he countered, 'and secondly, I'm not, as far as I am aware, accosting you, although,' he said thoughtfully, 'I probably could if you'd like me too?' He raised a quizzical eyebrow and leaned against the gate, effectively trapping her on the other side of it.

It was hard to resist his lazy charm. 'I don't know about that. Can I think about it and let you know later?' She smiled back. A little innocent flirtation, she thought, couldn't do any harm and she was sick of feeling miserable all the time.

Angus was pleasantly surprised to discover that she had a quick sense of humour. It was true he had seen her in the churchyard earlier but he had not meant to speak to her until he saw her coming towards the gate. He had been speaking to Bridie about her and she was less than encouraging.

'My impression of Maggie,' she said, 'is that she's been deeply hurt recently by something or someone and I think you ought to be very careful if you're intending to get involved with her.'

When he denied any thoughts of a serious relationship, she looked at him knowingly. 'Even a short-lived little affair such as we had…delightful as it was,' and here she dimpled at him sweetly, 'may be more than she can cope with right now. My feeling is that she's quite fragile. If you take my advice you'll be friendly but that's all.'

Seeing Maggie now he realised he did not intend to follow Bridie's advice. He had an idea. 'Do you ride?' he asked without preamble.

'Ride?'

'Yes, ride. You know horses.'

Taken aback by the unexpectedness of the question, Maggie stuttered 'Well, not for ages. I mean…that is… I haven't been on a horse since I was a girl. My father…' she drew a deep breath and wrinkled her brow. 'My father used to take me to the local Pony Club. He took me,' she repeated. 'I used to go every week… but then I stopped going.' She looked down at the ground as if studying patterns in the gravel. 'Why?' she asked in a small voice.

Angus pressed on. 'I thought you might like to go riding with me tomorrow. I keep a couple of horses in the field behind the Inn. Riding is one of the things I do to relax. If you've done it before you might enjoy it while you're here.'

Maggie lifted her face and looked at him. His eyes, which she had seen glinting with humour a moment earlier, were regarding her seriously. She considered his invitation.

It might be fun to get up on a horse again; she had loved riding when she was a child. She returned his gaze and smiled shyly. 'I think I might at that.'

They arranged she would come to the Inn the next day about ten-thirty, and Maggie watched him as he sauntered away with a casual wave wondering whether she had been wise to accept his invitation.

CHAPTER 7

Once Angus had disappeared from view, Maggie's doubts grew. Maybe going horse-riding with him was not such a good idea. After all, she didn't know him or anything about him. *For Heaven's sake*, she chided herself, what on earth did she imagine was going to happen. She was a grown woman fully in control of her own life and her own actions. A morning spent horse-riding was an innocent enough activity and he was probably only being kind.

Nevertheless, she decided it wouldn't hurt to call on Bridie…she had intended to anyway …and quiz her very discreetly about Angus. According to Jessie Ferguson they had a past so Bridie obviously knew him very well and the other woman's opinion may help her to understand what kind of man he was.

She wandered towards the village shop taking her time and looking around appreciatively. Invershee really was a very pretty place, so tranquil and undisturbed. It was as far removed from the clamorous crowds and noisy, frantic life of the city as she could have found. The trees and foliage everywhere were flourishing and verdant, and the surrounding hills and mountains made it seem safe and protected.

The village green was deserted today apart from a couple of dogs wandering around busily engaged in sniffing every blade of grass they encountered. She supposed the children were in school and looked around to see if she could pick out the building which housed it. She guessed the long, low building at the back of the green must be it. It had a large fenced off area around it which was probably the playground, and stickers on all the windows; in all likelihood, displays of the children's work.

After picking up what little she needed from the village store, she walked along to Bridie's shop. As before, the light was dim with flickering candles illuminating the darkest corners, the air perfumed and seasoned with all manner of fragrant, spicy scents. This time when Maggie entered, the smell of beeswax also hung in the air and she could see the other woman engaged in packaging what looked to be bundles of candles at the back of the shop.

Bridie looked up as the shop bell tinkled and at once hurried forward, surprising Maggie with a warm hug. 'I was thinking about you only a minute ago and here you are. Come along to the back and we can sit and have a chat.' She turned and made her way nimbly through all the pots and plants and boxes littering the floor. 'Would you like a coffee?' she called over her shoulder to Maggie as she tried to negotiate her own way through the same pots and plants and boxes without knocking anything over.

'That would be lovely,' Maggie said as she wondered how best to broach the subject of Angus.

Bridie set about making them both a drink whilst Maggie glanced around. The room was clearly used as some sort of office as well as a work area. There were papers and files heaped everywhere. Masses of books crowded the shelves of a tall, rather ramshackle bookcase in the corner; books on herbs and flowers as well as a wide assortment on crystals, exotic oils, horoscopes and one rather intriguingly entitled "Book of Spells". Pushed against one wall was a small work-table on which fresh herbs, bottles of perfume, tiny little glass jars of brightly coloured liquids and, what to Maggie looked like, long pieces of string were assembled. The smell of beeswax was even stronger in here. Bridie noticed the focus of her attention.

'I've been dipping candles all this morning. I always use beeswax. It holds the scent so much better than tallow and it's easier to work with.'

When they were finally sitting with a cup of steaming coffee each, it was Bridie herself who brought up the subject at the forefront of Maggie's mind. 'I saw you talking to the landlord of the Inn earlier didn't I?'

She sounds concerned Maggie thought and

wondered why. Unexpectedly, a small pang of jealousy shot through her; perhaps the other woman still cared for him. Bridie looked at her curiously and then went on, 'You were both standing by the church gate and seemed to be having quite a heart-to-heart.'

'Not really. He asked me if I'd done any riding and whether I'd like to take one of his horses and go out for a ride with him tomorrow.'

'And are you?' Bridie glanced over at her as Maggie tasted her coffee.

'Well, I said I would. I'm supposed to meet him in the morning.' Bridie remained silent. 'I thought it might be rather fun,' Maggie continued. 'Why? Don't you think it's a good idea?'

Bridie nodded her head. 'I'm sure it *will* be fun. Angus is very good at fun.' She paused for a moment. 'I don't mean that quite the way it sounded.'

Maggie stared at her. 'What do you mean?'

'I mean Angus is good fun to be around and he'll make sure you enjoy yourself. It's simply he doesn't take anything very seriously. Except, perhaps the Inn, he *is* serious about that.' She eyed Maggie pensively. 'Look, Maggie, I know I don't know you at all really but, as I said the other day when we met, I do know things about people.' She put out a hand as Maggie opened her mouth to interrupt. 'No, let me finish. I'll tell you what I told Angus.' Maggie's jaw dropped even further and her eyes grew round. 'I said I thought you'd had a bad experience recently and you were feeling pretty raw about it still. I suggested he should be friendly but nothing more. He's an attractive man and most of the young women in the village are half in love with him. I know for a fact Isobel Duncan, the schoolteacher, is sweet on him. But he's not interested. He's not into commitment or any kind of permanent relationship.' Seeing Maggie's shocked face, she added, 'I thought you should know that's all.'

Maggie could hardly believe her ears. 'Are you telling me you and Angus have been discussing me?'

'He came to see me and asked me what I thought about you. I think he's attracted to you and isn't quite sure how to deal with it. I don't want you to get hurt again.'

Maggie's cheeks were burning. 'How dare he!' She could hardly get the words out. 'And how dare *you* presume to know what is or isn't good for me!' She jumped up from her chair. 'If I decide I'm attracted to someone, I'll choose what I do about it, not you or Angus. And if, in the process, I get hurt then that's my business not yours or his. I'll cope with it.' She took a step towards the door. 'I'm a grown woman Bridie. I don't need you or anyone else to look out for me.' She spun round and dashed out of the room, sending a couple of earthenware pots crashing to the ground as she ran through the shop.

Bridie was up on her feet in an instant. She had made a mistake. She should have kept her mouth shut and let events take their course. Maggie was right, she had no business interfering. These thoughts flashed through her mind as she dashed after her. Maggie was about to fling open the shop door, and Bridie could see, from her pale face with its two bright spots of red staining her cheeks, she was furious.

Maggie heard Bridie shouting. 'Maggie! Maggie! I'm sorry, I'm so sorry. Please don't go.' She stopped and stood stone still with her hand on the door knob. She turned to face the other woman as Bridie came up to her and put out a conciliatory hand.

'Maggie, please, please let me apologise. You're quite right it's absolutely nothing to do with me whether or not you and Angus get together.' She took Maggie's hand in hers and gave it a gentle squeeze; it was ice-cold. 'It's only that I've never known him come to me before to ask my opinion of someone he's met,' she continued, 'and it surprised and then worried me.' Maggie remained silent as she met Bridie's eyes. She could see that the other woman regretted what she had said, and slowly relaxed her grip on the door handle. Reluctantly, she allowed Bridie to lead her back to the office.

Clasping her hands tightly together and taking deep, calming breaths, Maggie watched as Bridie make fresh coffee. She couldn't recall a time when she had been so angry and upset…apart from when Ben had told her he was leaving her for someone else, she thought bitterly. Then an image from her childhood flashed into her mind.

She was sitting hunched up with misery in a corner of a hotel lounge watching her mother who was dressed in black silk with a creation of feathers and veiling set at a jaunty angle on her head. She was flitting and fluttering from one man to another, smiling and flirting without any sense of propriety. Maggie was sickened by her behaviour. Her father, not long buried, was lying alone in the cold earth and her mother was acting as if she were at a party. Seven-year old Maggie felt the slow burn of anger grow and grow until she had flung herself from the room unable to bear it any longer.

She had run out into the gardens and kicked at a wooden bench until her new patent leather shoes were scuffed and scratched beyond salvation. The reality of her father's death descended over her like a suffocating blanket and she struggled for breath as tears of rage and loss coursed down her cheeks. Her mother didn't even notice she was gone. The shoes were ruined and later assigned to the rubbish bin; the question of how they had got into such a state was never raised.

Bridie thrust a cup of hot coffee into her hands and Maggie looked up. 'Thanks,' she managed tight-lipped, as she curled her frozen fingers around the welcome warmth.

Bridie sat down opposite her as before. She spoke quietly. 'Look, Maggie, I really didn't mean to upset you. Please believe me and please, please forgive me. Everything you said is true and I'm a nosey, interfering old besom.' This last she offered with such a disarming smile Maggie couldn't help but respond to her obvious sincerity.

She nodded. 'It's okay, I believe you. You thought you were acting in my own best interest. I understand that. But you know, Bridie, I'm nearly twenty-seven and I can look out for myself. You're right about my having had a really upsetting experience lately, which I *will* tell you about some day, soon.' she added as she saw Bridie's raised eyebrows, 'when I'm ready. But the thing is I'll get over it, I am getting over it. So you see there's no need to worry about me.' She sat staring at her coffee for a moment and then looked directly at the other woman. 'Can I ask you something?'

'Of course.'

'Are you in love with him?'

Bridie laughed. 'Who? Angus? Whatever makes you think that?'

'It was something Jessie Ferguson said. She told me you and Angus had had a...' Maggie struggled to find the right word... relationship.

'Well, I'd hardly call it that. It was only a brief fling. Anyway, it was years ago and I was never in love with him, nor he with me. We were both very young and it was a bit of fun that's all. We're simply good friends now.' She smiled broadly when Maggie winced at the phrase. 'Yes, I know it's a cliché but it happens to be true. He really is my best friend. If ever I need help or advice I go to Angus. He's very generous and good-hearted beneath that rather cavalier attitude of his.' She leaned forward, her elbows resting on her knees and looked directly into the other woman's eyes. 'You've every right to be angry and I don't blame you, but please Maggie can we be friends now?'

Maggie managed a smile of sorts, relenting a little in the face of Bridie's openness. Her eyes lost their look of hostility and she said, 'I suppose so, since you've grovelled so nicely.' Her voice took on a more serious note, 'But you should know I'm not looking for any meaningful relationship as far as Angus, or anyone else for that matter, is concerned. I've had my fill of those recently and if all he wants is for us to enjoy a morning's horse-riding it's fine by me. That's all I want too.

'You're right, of course you're right. I'm being a mother-hen. Make sure you let me know how you get on though. I shall want to hear all the details,' Bridie said laughing. Maggie smiled and nodded and the women parted on a promise that Maggie would call in the next day after her outing with Angus.

She was halfway home before she realised she had meant to ask Bridie about the pebble with the strange symbol on it but, with everything else that had happened, it had gone right out of her head. She fingered it in her pocket. It didn't matter; she would ask her tomorrow and also tell her about the woman in grey.

The rest of the day and the evening passed uneventfully. There were no mysterious visitors, no-one came to call and she saw and heard nothing strange or otherworldly. She spent most of the time researching life in the 19th century on her laptop or reading. For the first time since arriving at the cottage she felt a sense of peace and something approaching contentment. She drew the curtains against the gathering dusk and sat for a while sipping a glass of wine, watching the flames of the fire burning brightly in the grate. Despite her earlier misgivings, she had to admit she was looking forward to the morning.

She had adored riding lessons when she was younger and was heart-broken when she had to stop going after her father's death. Her mother flatly refused to take her. She always had some excuse.

'I'm much too busy,' she'd say. 'I've far more important things to do than ferry you here, there and everywhere.' Or she'd wrinkle her nose in distaste and say dismissively, 'I don't know what you like about horses,

Maggie. They're nasty, big, un-predictable animals, smelly too. Go and read a book or something.'

Funnily enough the smell was one of the things Maggie remembered most and liked best. She loved helping with the mucking out …it was something all those learning to ride, however young, had had to do. She closed her eyes recalling the warm, musky smell of the horses, the pungent aroma of the stables and the clean, fresh smell when the new straw was put down.

She gave a wry smile. She was certainly looking forward to being up on a horse again, to feeling the power of the animal moving beneath her as she rode along, but if she were honest she was also looking forward to spending an hour or two in Angus's company. She was still aggrieved he had talked about her to Bridie and she would have words with him but, nevertheless, it would give her a chance to get to know him a little better. After all he couldn't be all bad if Bridie liked him.

She decided to go to bed and try and get a good night's sleep. Once upstairs she took the pebble out of her trouser pocket and laid it carefully on the bedside table. She must remember to take it tomorrow and show it to Bridie.

Sleep came quickly and she dreamed, not of a woman in grey nor even of Ben, though she did dream of a horse. This time she was riding the white stallion, racing across grassy plains hoof beats thudding on the green earth, splashing through the surf at the edge of a vast, turquoise-coloured ocean and then trotting gently as the horse's hooves kicked up heaps of bright, autumn leaves carpeting a forest trail. And all the time, though she couldn't see him, she sensed someone was there, behind her, in front of her, watching her.

She woke briefly only once in the night, certain she could hear a baby crying. She strained her ears. No, the sound was gone. *Must be a cat*, she thought sleepily before tumbling back into her dreams

CHAPTER 8

In the morning Maggie woke to the sun painting the wall by her bed with a golden glow. She stretched and yawned and then, recalling the dreams, felt herself blush. *For Heaven's sake, what romantic nonsense*, she thought. She threw back the covers. Her jeans and a warm sweater would have to do for her morning's ride, she had nothing else suitable.

As she climbed out of bed her glance fell on the bedside table. Surely she had put the pebble there last night? It was not there now. Frowning in an effort to remember, she ran down the creaking, wooden staircase and looked around. The pebble lay on the small table under the window. She looked at it for a long moment trying to decide whether she had been mistaken about where she had left it the previous night. No, she distinctly remembered placing it down beside her as she got into bed.

As she went to pick it up, she somehow knew it would be warm. It was. She rubbed her fingers over its surface, tracing where its polished smoothness became uneven with the letter carved into it. A trickle of uneasiness slid down her back. This was getting decidedly unnerving. She would definitely have to talk to Bridie about it, though what she would make of it all Maggie couldn't begin to imagine.

She hurried to get dressed and, after a quick cup of coffee, jogged down to the village. The remnants of a morning mist were floating like wisps of white veiling over the glassy surface of the loch as the sun began to warm the day and she took deep breaths of the sweet Highland air. It was a good day to be alive.

When she reached the Inn, Angus was waiting. 'Good, you're here. I've borrowed Caitlin's riding hat for you, I think it should fit.' His tone was brisk as he handed her the hat and then strode off around the back of the building to a large field beyond. Maggie looked after him in surprise and then followed slowly; if cool and distant was the way he wanted to play it that was fine by her.

When she reached the field she saw the two horses were already saddled, gently nuzzling Angus as he held their reins. He spoke softly to them in Gaelic.

'What are you saying to them?'

'Och only that they're beautiful creatures.' He smiled briefly. 'I was also warning Freya here,' he said as he indicated the pretty, chestnut-coloured mare on his left, 'she's about to have a novice on her back.' The look he gave Maggie was serious. 'Generally, she's the quieter one but she can be a bit skittish if she's a mind to. Merlin is always a handful so I usually ride him' and he turned patting the neck of the big bay stallion standing snorting noisily beside him.

To Maggie he looked a magnificent animal, almost seventeen hands high she judged, his reddish coat gleaming and his black mane and tail long and silky. The horse shook his head as if eager to be off now Angus was here.

'I thought we'd take a gentle amble along the forest track until you feel comfortable about being on a horse again. Then, if you're okay, we'll have a short canter over the hill.'

Maggie's hands gripped the riding hat tightly and she bit her lower lip.

'If you'd rather leave it for another day…?'

She shook her head. 'No, I'm ready,' she said firmly, and approached Freya with a confidence she was far from feeling. She let the horse nuzzle her for a moment and then allowed Angus to give her a leg up onto Freya's back. Settling into the saddle, she relaxed a little. It felt good to be astride a horse again and she began to look forward to the ride. With accustomed ease Angus mounted Merlin and, signalling her to follow him, headed off towards a distant line of weather-beaten oaks and lofty pines.

They rode in silence, Maggie enjoying the gentle motion of the horse beneath her and welcoming the sense of freedom from all that had been engaging her mind for the past few weeks

Angus slowed until she rode up alongside him, undaunted by the silence between them, occupied in trying to sort out his own tangled thoughts. He was very aware of her closeness. Every now and again he caught a hint of the delicate flowery perfume she wore and it sent his nerve endings dancing.

After leaving her at the church gate yesterday, he had questioned the wisdom of his impulsive invitation, going over in his mind all Bridie had said. If Maggie was as deeply hurt by some previous relationship as Bridie suggested, how could he pursue a casual affair with her which might cause more hurt? His face set in stern lines. It went against his nature, used as he was to going after what he wanted with a single-mindedness of purpose, but he had decided he would wait for her make the first move.

Maggie, noticing the seriousness of his expression, was about to make some light-hearted, comment when Angus moved ahead of her into the trees.

Immediately they were enclosed in soft shadows, shafts of sunlight penetrating the canopy of trees, illuminating small spaces here and there in the wooded gloom. Maggie thought she understood what people meant when they likened being inside a wood or forest to being in a church. A sense of sanctified stillness and calm hovered in the cool air and yet the wood itself was neither silent nor still.

The leaves of the trees rustled and stirred as they rode by, fern fronds waved gently in the slight movement of air and she was aware of the muffled thud of the horses' hooves as they trotted along the dark, hard-packed earth of the woodland path. Birds twittered and fluttered from branch to branch high above her head, disturbed by the intrusion, whilst all around her Maggie sensed the swift movement and stealthy sounds of small animals scuttling and scampering through the undergrowth. Permeating all was the earthy smell of leaf mould and damp bark intermingled with the resinous scent of pine needles. She felt a sense of peace and well-being steal over her and allowed herself to relax fully and enjoy the moment.

Before long, however, they were through the wood and emerging onto the open hillside beyond. Looking around Maggie realised they were quite close to Rachel's cottage and was just about to remark on this when Angus turned in his saddle towards her. The challenge in his voice was unmistakeable.

'Are you ready for a little more action now?'

Without waiting for her reply, he gently nudged his horse's flanks and Merlin took off at a swift gallop. Maggie had no time to decide whether or not to follow. Freya, seeing her stable mate disappearing over a rise in the ground, lengthened her stride and set off after him. Taken by surprise Maggie could do little but cling on to the reins and try to dig her knees into the mare's flanks so she wouldn't lose her balance and fall off. She muttered all kinds of imprecations against Angus under her breath and, as she crested the hill, she saw him pulled up way below her. He was laughing and she felt her face redden as she managed finally to slow the mare's pace to a steady trot.

'You idiot,' she snapped as she approached him, 'I could have been thrown.'

He merely shrugged and gave an amused smile. 'Well, you weren't. Anyway at least you've shown me you know how to handle a horse so I won't have any worries about letting you ride Freya in the future.' Maggie ignored the tone of admiration in his voice and just sat there glaring at him until he turned his horse's head away and cantered off nonchalantly towards the bottom of the hill.

She was speechless. *What an arrogant so-and-so.* If he thought there was any way she was going out riding with him again he was sadly mistaken and she'd tell him so in no uncertain terms as soon as she caught up with him. She followed slowly, still seething, holding the reins firmly to prevent Freya racing off again.

The sun disappeared behind a cloud and all at once the air took on a familiar chill. Over to her right Maggie caught a glimpse of Rachel's cottage and she encouraged her horse to pick up its pace, wanting to get off the hillside as quickly as possible. The atmosphere had become thick and dense and she shivered, glancing around her. Soft tendrils of mist were drifting across the grass. Then, without warning, the mare reared, throwing her to the ground.

Maggie landed with a sickening thud which knocked the breath out of her body. She could feel the hard earth beneath her and, overhead, the sky had taken on a dismal greyness. For a moment she simply lay there and closed her eyes, wondering what had happened and trying to assess whether she was hurting anywhere. She didn't think she'd broken any bones which was good. She still held the reins with one hand and sensed the horse trembling and shaking beside her. Something had definitely spooked the horse and she was just thinking she should try to get up and calm the frightened animal when Freya reared again, the movement wrenching Maggie's shoulder almost from its socket. The reins were torn from her grasp and she let out a short cry of pain as the mare plunged away down the hill.

She must have fainted momentarily because, when she came to, Angus was kneeling over her his voice full of concern.

'Maggie! Maggie, are you all right? Are you hurt?' She saw the relief rush over his face as she blinked and tried to move. 'Come on, let me help you up' he said and slipped his arm under her shoulders.

The pain see-sawed through her, every muscle screamed with it and she felt pinpricks of sweat sting her forehead as she sobbed, 'It's my shoulder. I think I've done something to my shoulder.'

Angus helped her to her feet and she stood swaying against him. A searing pain shot down her arm and she felt sick. She hoped she wasn't going to faint again and tried taking in deep gulps of air but that made her more light-headed. His arm was around her and, though she wanted to pull away and tell him to go to hell, for the moment she was simply thankful for the support.

She wondered how she was going to get back to the village. Even if she succeeded in remounting Freya, she didn't think she would be able to hold onto the reins. She could see the horse now standing close to Merlin, the occasional tremor still rippling along her flanks. *Poor thing*, she thought, something had really panicked her, and Maggie had a good idea what that was. The thought had barely registered, when she felt Angus stir. Before she realised what was happening, he swung her up into his arms and strode off in the direction of Rachel's cottage. The rapid movement jolted her shoulder and she closed her eyes against the sharp, daggers of pain which sliced through her.

All the way to Tigh-na-Bruach Angus silently berated himself for the stupid, reckless fool that he was. She had called him an idiot and she was absolutely right. He had been showing off, trying to impress her but all he had succeeded in doing was getting her injured. What had caused the horse to throw her he had no idea; he would think about it later, after he got Maggie some medical help.

He was amazed at how light she was and how good it felt to hold her in his arms. He could smell the perfume she wore more strongly now and, as her head rested against his shoulder, her hair brushed against his cheek. Her eyes were closed and her face was very pale. Wondering if she had fainted again he increased his pace and was startled into almost dropping her when she said in a strained voice, 'It's alright, you can put me down now. I think I can manage to walk through the door myself.' He took no notice and, lifting the latch with his elbow, walked straight through to the living room to lay her gently down on the couch.

'I'm off to fetch the doctor. Don't move from there,' he ordered and strode purposefully out of the room.

As if I could, Maggie thought, wincing and pressing her lips tightly together as she tried to wriggle to a more comfortable position. She couldn't prevent a small moan escaping as her the pain ripped down her arm. Waves of nausea swept over her and, closing her eyes, she sank back against the soft cushions. 'Alright then, I'll just lie here and won't move,' she muttered through clenched teeth.

She thought back to the moment just before Freya had reared. In her mind's eye she could see the mist creeping across the hillside and shuddered as she remembered the way the air around her had turned icy. Maggie felt sure the horse had sensed something strange which had caused it to rear. She, herself, hadn't felt or seen anything apart from the abrupt drop in temperature and the advancing mist.

She recalled reading somewhere that animals are more sensitive to changes in atmosphere than humans; especially the sort of changes which might occur in the presence of the supernatural, Maggie thought. She was convinced Freya had somehow been aware of the spirit of the woman in grey. She shuddered again. The room felt chilly and depressing. Through the window she could see the sky was overcast and the clouds had an ominous tint to them. She began to shiver uncontrollably. Her shoulder pulsed with pain and she felt bruised all over. Tears of self-pity welled up and she wished Angus would hurry up and return. It was his fault this had happened. If he hadn't gone galloping off over the hill....

There was a loud thud as the back door crashed open and bounced off the kitchen wall. Angus burst into the room and in two strides was standing over her.

'Maggie, are you alright? I got back as soon as I could. This is Doctor Carmichael,' and he turned indicating the man who had entered behind him. Looking up, Maggie just nodded unable to speak for her teeth chattering.

'She's in shock,' the stranger said calmly, and turned to Angus. 'Can you find a blanket or rug to put over her? And a cup of hot, sweet tea would be good too,' he called as Angus disappeared through the door and headed up the stairs. He bent down towards Maggie. 'Now, Miss MacQueen, I'm just going to examine you. Is that alright?'

Maggie nodded again, immensely relieved to see him. His voice was soothing and his touch firm but gentle as he carefully tested for broken bones and any other damage she might have sustained in the fall. He was just finishing his examination when a dour-faced Angus re-entered carrying a blanket which he laid carefully over her, deftly tucking it in around her legs

'What's the verdict, Calum?' Angus's voice was grim. Maggie too looked at the doctor, anxious to hear what he had to say.

'Well, thankfully, there's not too much wrong, certainly some heavy bruising in places but it's mainly a badly wrenched shoulder. Fortunately it doesn't appear to be dislocated,' he smiled briefly as he glanced at Maggie. 'Otherwise, I'm afraid I'd have had to put you through a lot more pain to put it back into its socket. Anyway,' he went on briskly, 'I'll make you comfortable and give you some pain-killers and you should be feeling a lot better after a couple of days' rest.' He turned back to Angus. 'Where's that tea?'

'On its way'. Angus hurried into the kitchen.

Maggie heard him filling the kettle and opening and shutting kitchen cabinet doors but resisted the temptation to call out the whereabouts of the tea things. *Let him get on with it,* she thought, and turned her attention back to the doctor who was fastening her arm into a sling. Her teeth had stopped chattering and she was feeling warmer with the blanket tucked around her. Although her shoulder ached and throbbed like a rotten tooth, she was relieved she had not broken anything. Sighing heavily, she closed her eyes and tried to relax. The doctor's hands were warm and gentle and he talked quietly as he finished tying the sling.

'There that should be okay. You'll find it won't hurt as much with your arm and shoulder supported.' She felt a soft touch on her hand. 'Does that feel easier?'

It did and she looked up at him, grateful for his skill. She hadn't really taken much notice of him before, focused as she was in trying to deal with the pain and her fury at Angus's part in her accident. Now she studied the man standing over her. About thirtyish, fairly tall with short light brown hair. He had slate grey eyes and a long rather angular face. Quite nondescript really and then he smiled. The transformation was remarkable. His whole face altered in an instant as his eyes danced with amusement under her scrutiny.

'Do I pass muster, Miss MacQueen?'

Maggie felt her face burn. He had caught her staring at him. At the same time she was utterly disarmed. How could she possibly have thought him nondescript, she wondered as she took in the friendly, open countenance and teasing expression. She was in the midst of stammering out an apology when Angus came in from the kitchen with her tea.

'Lots of sugar in it, I hope,' Calum Carmichael said and Angus nodded as he passed it to her.

Maggie opened her mouth to protest she didn't take sugar but then thought better of it and meekly took the proffered cup, mumbling her thanks. She swallowed down the painkillers Calum handed her, gasping as the hot liquid almost scalded her mouth and nearly gagging at the sweetness of it. Stoically she said nothing as she felt the warmth of it begin to seep through her.

'It might be a good idea to put a fire on, the room's a little cold don't you think?' Angus nodded and disappeared to fetch some firewood. 'Now Miss MacQueen...'

"Please, could you call me Maggie? Miss MacQueen sounds so formal. It makes me feel like someone's maiden aunt.'

'I can't imagine you could possibly be anyone's

maiden aunt, Maggie,' he replied with a grin. She smiled shyly back. He was quite charming, she decided, or maybe that was part of his cultivated bedside manner. 'I was going to say I'll call in tomorrow when I'm out on my rounds and see how you are. You'll probably sleep tonight as those painkillers are very strong and hopefully you'll find your shoulder will be less sore in the morning. Though it doesn't mean you should start trying to do anything,' he added quickly when he saw the hopeful look in her eyes. 'You need to rest for a day or two. I believe Angus is going to speak to his aunt, Mrs Ferguson.' He raised a quizzical eyebrow and, when she nodded, went on, 'to ask her to look in on you tomorrow and get you anything you need. Is that okay with you?'

'I'm very grateful, Doctor Carmichael. You've been very kind.' Maggie smiled.

'You Maggie, me Calum,' he chuckled, pointing first to her and then to himself. Maggie could not help joining in. 'I'll see you tomorrow then,' he said and took his leave. She was still smiling when Angus came in his arms laden with wood for the fire.

'You're looking a bit better.'

'No thanks to you,' she replied tartly and then immediately felt contrite at the look of regret which shadowed his face for a second. 'My shoulder's feeling a little less painful now.' Her tone softened slightly. 'I expect the painkillers Calum gave me are having an effect.' She watched as Angus set about expertly laying and lighting the fire. 'He seems very nice,' she said finally. 'It was very good of him to come so quickly.'

'Aye, well you find that in rural communities. People tend to look out for each other and the Doctor's no exception...'

Maggie didn't hear Angus's muttered, 'besides I didn't give him any option.'

The flames took hold, the wood started crackling and at once the room seemed brighter and more inviting. Her shoulder still hurt but its previous raw throbbing had dulled to an ache now. She was warm and snug under the blanket as she gazed into the fire. The flickering flames were hypnotic and a welcome drowsiness began to steal over her. Her eyes closed and within seconds she was asleep.

CHAPTER 9

As she slept, Angus watched her and his heart filled with unaccustomed tenderness. She looked so defenceless, lashes as dark as midnight lying softly against her cheeks, lips half-parted, and her breath coming softly and evenly as she drifted into a healing sleep. Despite the blush of pink on her cheeks, her face had an underlying, deathly pallor and every now and then her brow creased as if in pain; for which he was responsible he thought. Then he remembered the blistering look she had given him and her voice shaking with temper when she had chastised him for letting Merlin have his head. She had not seemed so helpless then, and he didn't imagine the accident would keep her confined for very long.

He stared into the fire. He liked that about her; she had spirit. But he also felt drawn to her because beneath all the surface toughness he sensed a gentler, more sensitive nature; it was a potent combination. Angus was confused and uncertain for perhaps the first time in his life and he did not relish the feeling. He swore lightly under his breath, leapt up and in two strides was out of the door. He would go and ask his aunt to keep an eye on Maggie, then he had work to do, a hotel to run, things to organise.

He had no time to moon around like a lovesick schoolboy. He gave a grim smile at the analogy; when he'd been at school all he was interested in was fishing and horses with perhaps a bit of sailing in the summer, girls had never entered the equation though naturally he'd made up for it since. He narrowed his eyes. He'd managed to avoid any meaningful relationships until now and he planned to continue doing so. The hotel took all his time and attention and he had no wish to be saddled with any other responsibilities. He had no intention of being seduced by a pair of blue eyes which made him think of frozen winter days and torrid, summer skies at one and the same time;

eyes which could chill with an icy aloofness one minute, and flash with scorching anger or swim with unshed tears the next. He would stay away and in a few days Maggie would be gone, back to her cosmopolitan life in London. He ignored the sudden tightness in his chest at the thought as he strode along the road to recover the two horses. Then, swinging himself up onto Merlin's back and leading Freya, he rode off to tell his aunt what had happened.

Maggie remembered little of the next several hours. She woke once to see Jessie Ferguson stoking the fire, and recollected swallowing more painkillers on another occasion. Other than that she drifted in and out of dreams, none of which she could recall when she finally woke up the following morning. The fire was alight in the hearth, dispelling the night-time coolness. She heard someone in the kitchen. Cups rattled on saucers, water in the kettle started to boil and a woman's voice hummed softly.

She tried to stretch and felt a sharp stab in her shoulder. She was still lying on the sofa, still in the clothes she had worn yesterday. *I must stink to high heaven*, she thought. As she contemplated moving to get washed and changed, Jessie Ferguson bustled in bearing a steaming cup of tea and a plate piled high with hot, buttered toast. Maggie's mouth watered. She tucked into the simple breakfast with enthusiasm, pausing long enough to thank Jessie for looking after her.

'Och, it's no trouble, lass.' The other woman shook her head, settling herself into one of the fireside chairs. 'Angus told me what happened and it's the least I could do.' Maggie wondered whether Angus had described his own role in her accident but then Jessie continued, 'He said the horse reared and you were thrown. A nasty fall he said it was and he had to carry you back here.'

So, Maggie thought, he hadn't mentioned it was his own reckless behaviour which caused it. She pursed her lips and frowned. A few moments later she realised she had been too quick to judge and was ashamed of herself as Jessie, standing up to take her empty plate, added, 'Mind you he did say he'd acted rather foolishly earlier. Freya can be a little nervy at times and he said she may have got over-excited. He certainly seems to think he's partly to blame. Now, can you manage another cup of tea?'

After Jessie had left, promising to pop in again later, Maggie struggled to get up. Her shoulder ached but the painkillers were doing their job in taking the edge off the soreness. It was awkward trying to wash and dress with one arm in a sling but she managed somehow. Feeling more like her old self, she was wondering whether to set up her laptop and do some more research when there was a gentle knock on the back door.

A cheerful 'Hello there, how are you feeling today?' followed and Calum Carmichael poked his head round the door. Then, pushing it open, he strode into the room, bringing with him the sharp freshness of country air. Not giving Maggie the chance to respond, he continued, 'I've been on a visit along the road and thought I'd drop in and see how you're getting on. Well you're certainly looking a little better than when I saw you yesterday,' he said, looking her over.

Maggie smiled and motioned for him to sit down. 'Hi,' she said shyly. 'I'm feeling much better thanks. Those tablets seem to have done the trick. The pain isn't nearly as bad as it was.' She moved her laptop aside and rose from her seat on the sofa.

'Can I get you a cup of tea or coffee?'

'A coffee would be very welcome.' Calum relaxed back into his chair when she shook her head at his offer of help. 'It's been quite a hectic morning. How are you liking it here in Invershee?' he called as she busied herself in the kitchen.

'I love it. It's quiet and unhurried. People seem to have time for each other here. It's so different in London. I don't even know my next-door neighbours there. In fact, come to think of it, I'm not sure I've ever seen them.' She came back into the room balancing a tray one-handed with two mugs of coffee on it.

Calum moved swiftly to take it from her and place it on the table under the window. He waited until she'd settled herself back on the sofa and then handed her a steaming mug before sitting back down himself. There was a moment's awkwardness as they each sipped their drinks wondering where to take the conversation next.

Maggie broke the silence. 'You haven't been in the village very long yourself have you? Was it Edinburgh you were before?'

'No, actually I was in Perth before I came here.'

For a fleeting moment Maggie thought she detected a shadow of sadness in his eyes but before she could say anything it was gone. She was probably mistaken she thought.

'But my family is originally from this area. They left when I was a young boy. I did my medical training in Edinburgh though. Do you know the city at all?'

'I've never been north of the border before this,' she smiled. 'This is my first trip to Scotland, though I hope to get to see more of it than Invershee sometime.' She told him about her Scottish ancestry but, because her father had died when she was young, she had never learned anything about her forebears.

'Well I might be able to help you there.' Calum leaned forward in his chair. 'That is, only if you want me to,' he added, seeing her look of surprise. When she nodded, he explained he was a keen amateur genealogist and had managed to trace his own family back as far as the Massacre at Glencoe.

'That's fascinating,' Maggie breathed, watching his face becoming more animated as he described the infamous episode in Campbell clan history and how his ancestors had managed to escape the slaughter. It was true she was keen to find out about her own history, but now here was someone who might help her to find out about the 'Maid,' maybe even discover something about the woman in grey too. Her eyes were full of friendly curiosity as she looked at him.

'Have you heard about 'The Unknown Maid?' she asked.

He had, of course he had. He'd been in the village for six months and it would have been well-nigh impossible for him not to know about the local, unsolved mystery, villages being what they are and gossip being what it is. It was a tale which had intrigued him when he'd first heard it, he told her, and he would be more than happy for them to join forces to see if they could put a name to the poor woman. Maggie decided not to tell him about her ghostly visitor; she would leave that to a later date... best perhaps to concentrate on one mystery at a time.

'If I'm feeling alright tomorrow, I plan to go down to the church again and see if the Minister's located the Parish Registers I mentioned. There might be some clue in them which will help us. I'll let you know what, if anything, I find out,' she promised. On that note, he took his leave to continue his rounds, his step a little lighter and perhaps his heart a little less sore.

She liked him, Maggie decided. He had a pleasant, earnest manner and, although he was not what might be considered conventionally good-looking, he had a strong face with well-defined features. His hands were fine-boned and long-fingered and he used them expressively when he talked. Why he had chosen to leave a busy city to come to Invershee, she had no idea. Maybe something in his past, some significant event had prompted such a life-changing decision but that was nothing to do with her. It had no bearing on the fact he'd promised to help her; his expertise in researching the past would be invaluable.

She felt drained after he had gone yet buoyed up at the same time, hopeful that, with any luck, they would soon discover the identity of the woman who had died on the hillside above the cottage all those years ago. She abandoned all thoughts of working on her laptop for the moment and instead took some more painkillers and lay down on the couch to rest. *Just as the doctor ordered*, she grinned to herself.

She passed the rest of the day quietly. Jessie called in to see if she was coping, which Maggie assured her she was. The gnawing pain in her shoulder had eased and she was feeling less bruised, more able to fend for herself. She was sitting down ready to sort through the research notes she had already made when there was a soft rap at the window. She looked up, momentarily startled, and then relaxed as she saw Bridie's anxious face peering at her through the glass. Smiling, Maggie beckoned her in and, putting aside the papers, went to greet her guest.

'It's lovely to see you, Bridie,' she said with genuine warmth. 'I was going to call in on you tomorrow when I was down in the village but this is better. I wanted to ask you a few things and now we'll be able to sit and have a proper chat. I'll explain in a minute,' she continued when she saw Bridie's quizzical expression. 'Let me get you a drink first.'

Accepting a glass of wine, Bridie sat down in one of the fireside chairs. 'First of all how are you feeling? I hope you're taking the tonic I gave you?'

'Yes, of course.' Maggie tried to meet the other woman's eyes, not wanting to hurt her feelings by confessing she had forgotten all about it.

Bridie gazed at her as if sensing the untruth. Maggie's face flushed. 'It will do you some good you know. There's nothing harmful in it, just lots of good things.' Then, reaching into the depths of the voluminous bag she carried, she pulled out a small, prettily wrapped parcel and handed it to Maggie.

'I've also brought you some sweetberry blossom candles. They'll help you to have calm dreams.'

Maggie mumbled her thanks as she placed the candles on the footstool beside the hearth. Still feeling embarrassed at the lie, she promised herself she would follow Bridie's advice and take the tonic every day.

'Though I must say you're looking better than I expected,' Bridie went on. 'To listen to Angus you'd think you were at death's door. By all accounts, he practically dragged Calum out of his surgery yesterday. He's really worried about you and blaming himself for what happened.'

'And so he should,' retorted Maggie, and went on to explain the circumstances leading up to the accident. As she recounted the details, Maggie knew she was being unfair; Angus had not in truth been responsible for her being thrown. Granted the mare had been over-excited after the gallop over the hill but that was not what had caused the horse to rear.

'Actually, on thinking about it, it wasn't really Angus's fault,' she admitted. She took a sip of her tea…she hadn't thought it wise to mix painkillers and wine. 'I think it was the woman in grey who caused Freya to rear like that.' She smiled at the look of bafflement on Bridie's face and plunged into the story of what she had thought was a strange dream but now believed to have been some kind of supernatural experience on the hill.

Bridie listened, her eye focused on Maggie's face. 'It's quite common for there to be a sudden drop in temperature when a spirit appears,' she said matter-of-factly, as if she were discussing an ordinary, everyday occurrence. 'Ghosts can only materialize if they draw heat and energy from their surroundings.'

'So you do believe in the supernatural and all that?' Maggie looked at the other woman with interest.

'Of course. You've only got to look at how many stories there are of people seeing phantoms and experiencing all kinds of psychic phenomena. They can't all be fantasy or the result of some sort of mental aberrations. Our ancestors wouldn't have seen anything unusual in supernatural occurrences. If you believe in an afterlife it's not much of a stretch to believe that disembodied, distressed souls may have issues with the past which keep them earthbound.'

'Jessie Ferguson told me Morag MacIver

encountered the mystery woman too.'

Bridie nodded. 'Yes, I seem to remember hearing something about it at the time. You haven't seen her again?' When Maggie shook her head, she continued, 'Well, I think you probably will. It sounds as though she's a really troubled spirit and is somehow linked to this particular place.'

She paused as Maggie got up to refill her glass and put another log on the fire. When they were both settled again, she went on, 'Maybe there could be something in the shared sorrow idea of yours too. Obviously Morag was unhappy because she'd just lost her husband and you were clearly very upset when you arrived.' She put up her hand as Maggie looked as if she were about to interrupt. 'No, wait. Let me continue for a minute before you say anything; I'm just kind of thinking aloud. So there's some sort of connection here. You said the woman was weeping, as if she'd experienced some great sadness and loss?'

When Maggie nodded, Bridie carried on, her soft voice and composed tone soothing Maggie's fears the other woman would think her delusional. 'Has anything else strange or untoward happened since you came here?'

'Well, there was the old man who appeared and then disappeared. He sat where you're sitting now.'

Maggie described how she had believed her visit from the Bodach was a dream too until the pebble he had shown her turned up on the doorstep and kept moving, seemingly by itself, from where she knew she'd left it. 'In fact, it's in the pocket of my jeans now. I was going to ask you about it when I called in to see you after the horse-riding.' She jumped up and ran upstairs. A moment later she was back. 'Here it is,' and, standing in front of the other woman, she held out her hand.

Slowly, Bridie took the small, round pebble and let it rest in her own upturned hand. 'It's a rune,' she said, gazing at it. 'I wondered if it might be when you described it.' She looked up. 'Do you know anything about runes, Maggie?'

'A little. They're a very old form of divination,

aren't they? Each symbol means something and when they're cast people believe they can tell the future depending on how they fall.' Maggie sat back down, listening with interest as the other woman explained.

'That's right.' Bridie sat back in her chair, her eyes once again focused on the object lying in her palm of her hand. 'They're thought to have originated in about the second or third centuries AD so they've been around for a pretty long time. This one isn't that old of course.' She turned the pebble over in her hand rubbing her fingers gently over its smooth surface. 'People used to make their own sets from pebbles or even pieces of wood. They had to use them in secret though because, at one time, if you were found with them you could be put in prison or even executed.'

She smiled at Maggie's astonished expression. 'It's true. They were thought to be a very powerful means of magic.' She paused, glancing again at Maggie who was leaning forwarding with rapt attention. 'I think there were about thirty something symbols in the original runic alphabet but traditionally only twenty-five were ever used, and are still used nowadays' she added. 'This particular symbol is one I happen to know.'

Maggie leaned even further forward, hardly able to restrain her impatience. 'What does it mean?'

'Well, if my memory serves me correctly,' Bridie said slowly as she traced the outline of the letter on the pebble, 'it's called Beork and it represents life; it's connected to the cycle of birth and death and rebirth. I suppose you'd interpret its meaning as signifying a new start, a recovery, a fresh beginning.'

The two women sat in silence for a few moments, each contemplating the pebble and wondering what its appearance might signify.

'Jessie also told me about The Unknown Maid,' Maggie suddenly said.

Bridie looked at her in surprise.

'I was thinking I might try and find out who she

was.' Maggie paused as an idea struck her. 'Do you think there could be some kind of connection between her and the woman in grey?'

'I don't know. No-one's ever discovered anything about the Maid or where she came from.' Bridie looked thoughtful. 'It'd be interesting if we could find out. Though whether it's possible after all this time....' Her voice trailed away and she frowned.

'My head's aching and my thoughts are all over the place.' Maggie gave a deep sigh. 'I'm so confused.' She looked at the other woman. 'Have you any idea what it all means, Bridie, why this is happening?'

Bridie shook her head. She hesitated. 'I'm not sure.' She sat up abruptly. 'But what I do know is I need another drink.'

'Sorry, that was the last of the wine I'm afraid. I'll have to get some more tomorrow when I go to the village. I'm hoping the Minister will have found the old Parish Registers by now.

'Can't wait that long,' Bridie grinned and delved once more into the depths of her capacious bag. 'So it's fortunate I brought my own supply,' she said, brandishing a bottle of Chablis.

The two women sat beside the fire quietly talking, going over again the strange events of the past few days, trying to discern a pattern in what had been happening and puzzling over the initials scratched on the stone's surface. Maggie was relieved Bridie was taking her seriously. Maybe, with her and Calum's help, she might discover the reason behind the 'sightings' and somehow solve their mystery.

'I've been having some weird dreams lately too,' Maggie confessed and described them in as much detail as she could remember.

'That's interesting, especially the fact horses figure in them. And in two of them the horse was white?' When Maggie nodded, Bridie went on. 'According to folklore, a white animal, particularly a deer, a bird or a horse is a traditional symbol for a quest. And I suppose, in a way, trying to find out the identity of the woman in grey and of the Maid too is a kind of quest.' She broke off for a moment and was silent, deep in thought. Then she continued, 'You know, Maggie, the more I think about it, the more I think you might have hit on something. That all this could be somehow linked together.'

Maggie frowned. 'But what does it have to do with me? Why am I seeing this spirit or whatever she is and how does the old man fit in?'

They spent a little more time tossing ideas and solutions backwards and forwards until Maggie's head was spinning. Finally they agreed there was little they could do until they knew the identity of at least one of the women, one of whose initials could be C.R.

Bridie thought Calum's expertise would be invaluable in this and seemed really pleased Maggie had got him involved. 'He's a fine man,' she said, 'and from all accounts an excellent doctor. He doesn't seem to be at all stuffy or old-fashioned. I may even be able to persuade him alternative methods of healing have something to offer.'

Maggie looked closely at her new friend. She was sure she detected a faint blush spreading over Bridie's cheeks. *So that's the way of it,* she thought, and smiled to herself. Aloud she said, 'Yes, he seems very nice, and I'm sure he'll be a great help. We should get together when I've had a chance to look at the church records.'

With that decided, Bridie gathered her things together ready to leave. 'Before I say goodnight, Maggie, I've another wee gift for you.' She pressed a small, pink-coloured crystal into Maggie's hand. 'It's rose quartz,' she explained as Maggie looked at it and then her friend in surprise. 'It helps to heal heart-ache and sadness.' Maggie felt unbidden tears spring to her eyes and she blinked quickly to hold them back as Bridie patted her arm. 'No need to say anything now but soon we'll have a good long talk. Let's just leave it at that, shall we?' When Maggie nodded, her throat so choked with the unshed tears she couldn't trust herself to speak, Bridie squeezed her arm and left with a final admonishment that Maggie should go straight to bed and get a good night's sleep.

Closing the door behind Bridie, Maggie was glad she'd confided in her. Bridie was taking her seriously and was going to help her discover the reason behind her ghostly encounters. She felt a rush of optimism; together, they would be able to solve the mystery of the woman in grey.

As she put out the lights and climbed the stairs, Maggie realized the aching sense of loss and rejection which had been a constant background to all her waking moments recently had eased a little. This was the first time in weeks she had felt more like her old self and yet, in a strange way, she also felt keyed up as if this were somehow a turning point. She had no idea where this feeling came from, she simply had an intuition her life would never be quite the same again.

CHAPTER 10

Maggie was up early the next morning after a reasonable night's sleep. She had woken just the once, again certain she could hear a baby crying. The bedroom was witch black; not a hint of moonlight relieved the darkness. She had sat up in bed straining her ears, trying to work out where the sound was coming from. She was about to get up and look for the source of the noise when it stopped abruptly. She had listened for a little longer but the sound wasn't repeated. *I really will have to look for that cat,* she thought, before drifting back to sleep. *It can't possibly be a baby, not around here.*

Once dressed and breakfasted, she strolled down to the village. Her shoulder was much less painful but she didn't think jogging would do it any good so she sauntered along the track going over in her mind all she and Bridie had talked about the previous night. The day was dry but overcast, threatening rain later perhaps. Everywhere was still; only the faint thrum of a tractor engine and the occasional harsh, scolding 'karr' of a black-headed gull disturbed the silence.

Excited at the prospect of looking at the Parish Registers and of finding out a little more about the circumstances of the death of the 'Unknown Maid', Maggie began to step along more briskly and soon reached the church. As she lifted the heavy latch on the gate, a little flicker of doubt entered her mind. Maybe after all this time it wouldn't be possible to establish who the woman was or why she had died on the hillside. *No, stay positive,* she told herself. The woman had lived and died and there were records so there must be ways of discovering who she was and where she had come from. Maggie heard her name being called and looked up to see Euan Cameron hurrying towards her along the gravel path.

'I'm glad to see you my dear. I was hoping...' he broke off as he saw the sling on her arm. 'My goodness me, whatever's happened to you?'

'Oh, it's nothing really.' Maggie gave a short laugh. 'I had a fall when I was out riding. The horse was spooked by the lady in grey.'

'Oh dear, oh dear! You've seen her again then?'

'Well, no, not exactly. But I know she was there, and the horse certainly sensed her presence, it's what made her rear.'

The Minister gave her a doubtful glance. 'At least you didn't come to any serious harm, Thank the Lord' and he raised his eyes briefly to the heavens. He began again. 'I was hoping you might call soon. I've been looking out for you. Of course I didn't know about your accident. I expect you've had to take it easy and rest up. ' Maggie smiled, wishing he would stop twittering on and get to the point. 'Anyway,' he said triumphantly, his plump face beaming, 'I've found them, the Parish Records.'

Her heart gave a little lurch and she could hardly keep the excitement out of her voice. 'That's wonderful. Can I look at them now?'

'Of course, of course, though I don't know whether they'll be of any help to you. This way', and he strode off towards the church, Maggie following a few paces behind. Leading her through into the vestry he pointed to a large, leather-bound book lying on a well-worn, oak table beneath the window. 'I found the relevant tome,' he said. 'This one goes from November 1851 to March 1853 so she should be in there somewhere.'

Maggie voiced her thanks and took the wooden stool the Minister passed her, settling herself down ready to begin the search.

'Well, I'll leave you in peace,' he said. 'I've some visits to make so if you leave before I get back just pull the church door to behind you.' She turned to thank him again but he was gone, closing the door softly behind him.

She turned back to the book lying before her. Its

cover was a little scratched in places but otherwise hardly worn. The polished, maroon leather gleamed and the smell of dust and age hung in the air. She wasn't quite sure where to begin but the date on the gravestone had been 1852 so it seemed logical to start with January of that year. Her fingers trembling slightly, she began to turn the pages. It was fascinating reading all the different and diverse events which had been recorded within its bounds; the marriages, the births and the deaths, as well as the various church festivals and services, all inscribed there for posterity. .

As she read, she was increasingly saddened by the number of children who had died during the year, some at birth, and others in only their first or second year. But she knew from the research she had already done that times had been hard. Childbirth had been much riskier then and many young mothers were recorded as having died also and been buried with their infants. The potato famine had also claimed many other lives, both young and old. She was beginning to despair of finding the reference to the Maid when there it was in black and white beneath her tracing finger. Eagerly she scanned the entry.

"October 31st 1852 – A young woman discovered on the hillside above Invershee was interred under direction of the Minister, Malcolm Campbell, in a plot at the west wall of the churchyard. The woman was found to have no means of identification; she wore no ring and was unknown to any local person. Her only possession was a Celtic cross around her neck so she was given a full and Christian burial.
May God have Mercy on her soul."

Maggie slumped back in the chair. Was that all there was? Somehow she had expected more; a detail which might give some clue as to how she should proceed with her search. She read it again more slowly. But there was nothing, nothing at all. Her disappointment was so intense and so bitter she could almost taste it like bile at the back of her throat. She sat motionless staring at the page, reading the entry over and over as if by doing so she could in some way change what it said.

After what seemed an age she carefully closed the book and leaving it on the table made her way out of the church. What should she do now? The one avenue of investigation which she thought held the most promise had yielded nothing, zero, a dead end.

Feeling despondent she decided to visit the Maid's grave. She could at least pay her respects. *I wish I'd brought some flowers,* she mused as she wandered down the path. Just then she caught sight of a black-suited figure up ahead.

'Mr. Cameron,' she called thinking she would thank him for his help. But the person gave no sign he had heard her.

She called his name again more loudly. *Perhaps he's a little deaf,* she thought, and increased her pace. The figure turned down a side path and Maggie hurried to follow. Where had he gone? Then she saw him. He was standing silently looking at a gravestone. He was half turned towards her and she realized immediately it wasn't the Minister…not unless he had suddenly grown a white beard. She stopped in her tracks, her heart fluttering in her chest and her eyes refusing to believe what she saw. It was the old man, her visitor of the other night. It was the Bodach.

There he stood in broad daylight, to all intents and purposes a living, breathing person. But she knew he was not what he seemed. She hesitated then, taking deep breaths to still her jangling nerves, walked very slowly towards him. He turned and watched as she gradually drew nearer, his countenance solemn but kindly and his gaze steadfast. As she paused a little distance from him, uncertain what to say or do, he turned and pointed to the headstone he had been studying. Then as before, that night at the cottage, his figure began to shimmer and dissolve until she was looking at nothing but the empty churchyard.

Again she felt no fear. Her initial shock at seeing him

had quickly given way to a feeling of acceptance and a belief that he was somehow trying to help her in her search for the truth. He meant her no harm, she was sure of it. Intrigued, she approached the grave and read the inscription.

ALEXANDER MACDONALD

1827 – 1898

HE WALKED GOD'S PATH ALWAYS

Quickly she felt in her pockets for a pen and something to write on but finding nothing of use she looked around helplessly. Then she heard the church gate scrape open. She turned and hurried back along the path. It was the Minister returning from his visits.

'Ah, there you are Miss MacQueen. How did you get on?'

'Fine, thank you. I located the entry but it wasn't much help I'm afraid.' She went on to explain she had come across a gravestone which interested her and needed to make a note of the name and dates. He obliged her with a sheet torn from his pocketbook and a pencil. She could see he was curious but fortunately he forbore to ask her any questions. Thanking him once again for his help she hurried down the path and made her way to Bridie's. The shop was closed.

Maggie could have cried in frustration; first of all the disappointment of the entry in the Parish Register and now no Bridie when she had so much to tell her. She glanced at her watch. It was almost lunch time. Maybe she had gone home, but she had no idea where Bridie lived. On the other hand she could have gone to the Inn for something to eat. Maggie hesitated. She did not feel ready to face Angus yet; she was still annoyed with him. Maybe she should go to the surgery and talk to Calum, but he might be out on his rounds. There was nothing for it, she would have to go to the Inn and, if there was no Bridie, she would ask Caitlin for her address.

Maggie saw her friend as soon as she pushed open

103

the door to the bar. She was sitting by the window talking animatedly to Caitlin who stood listening, an intent expression on her face. Bridie glanced over when the door opened and seeing Maggie waved her over. Maggie sneaked a quick look at the bar. There was no sign of Angus and she breathed a sigh of relief.

'Hi there Maggie. You've met Caitlin haven't you?'

'Sort of.' Maggie smiled at Angus's sister. 'Hello again.'

The girl smiled in return and nodded. 'I'll let you know how I get on,' she said to Bridie. 'Enjoy your meal. Can I get you something, Maggie?' Maggie ordered a cheese toastie and a glass of orange juice. She watched Caitlin as she made her way back to the bar. She was very like Angus in looks, the same thick, dark hair and deep brown eyes.

'She's off the Spanish.' Bridie seemed to know what Maggie was thinking.

'What?'

Bridie explained that a Spanish galleon had been wrecked off the coast nearby in the 1700s and the surviving sailors, having been rescued, stayed on and married local girls. Many of their descendants had inherited the dark good looks of their Spanish ancestors.

'She's keen on one of the local forest rangers,' she added, 'and was just asking me for some advice on how to get him to ask her out.'

'What did you say to her?' Maggie eyed the other woman curiously.

'That'd be telling,' Bridie grinned. 'Anyway, more importantly, how did you get on with the Parish Records? You have been to the church, I take it?'

Maggie sighed. 'Not very well, I'm afraid.' She told Bridie of her disappointment at the sparsity of information in the account of the Maid's death and burial.

'What did it actually say?' Bridie asked.

Maggie was able to recite the entry almost word for word she had read it so many times; trying to read between the lines, searching for information which was not there. 'So all we know for sure is she died shortly before the 31st October 1852, she wore a Celtic cross and she wasn't married.'

'That's not necessarily true, that she wasn't married I mean. Not all married women wore a wedding ring in those days, especially if she was from a lowly station in life. She might simply have gone through a Hand-fasting ceremony though that's probably unlikely. The cross suggests she was a churchgoer or at least religious.'

'But there's nothing to tell us who she was or where she came from,' Maggie paused as Caitlin returned with her lunch and, smiling her thanks to the girl, waited until she had left them before continuing. 'Anyway, I haven't told you the most interesting thing which happened yet.' She smiled at Bridie's expression of puzzlement. 'I saw the Bodach again.' She took a sip of juice enjoying the stunned look on the other woman's face.

'What? At the church?'

'Yes. I thought at first it was the Minister,' and Maggie went on to recount in detail her encounter in the churchyard and showed Bridie the paper on which she had recorded the inscription from the gravestone.

'What do you think?' she asked impatiently as the other woman sat silent, a pensive expression on her face.

'I think maybe you're being shown the way.'

'Shown the way? What do you mean?'

'It seems to me,' Bridie said slowly as if she were weighing every word, 'that the Bodach is guiding you. For some reason it seems he wants you to discover the identity of the Maid.'

'I'm not sure I understand what you're getting at. How's he guiding me?' Maggie frowned.

'Well, think about it. The first time you saw him he showed you the rune. Yes, I know you thought that was a dream.' Bridie waved away Maggie's protests. 'But then the very same stone appears on your doorstep and starts to move to different places around the cottage seemingly of its own accord. Come on, Maggie, it's obvious he's the one moving it because he wants you to take notice of it.'

Maggie shivered at the thought of the Bodach wandering about the cottage at night whilst she slept.

'But why?'

'Because it's a message. I told you last night, didn't I, that that particular runic symbol is associated with the cycle of life and death? Maggie nodded, still puzzled.

'And you said you thought you caught a glimpse of him the first time you visited the Maid's grave?'

'Yes but I didn't actually see him, I just got the impression he was there, watching from among the trees.'

'I'm certain he *was* there, and then today you saw him for real on your way to the Maid's grave again. I don't think it's a coincidence, do you?'

'Perhaps not,' Maggie mused, thinking over what Bridie had said. 'So this name on the gravestone,' she glanced again at the piece of paper from the Minister's notebook, 'is a kind of clue?'

'Maybe,' Bridie said. 'At least it's somewhere to start. I think we ought to tell Calum and ask him to research this Alexander MacDonald's family tree. The Maid could be a relative of his.'

'But how will we know which one she is? We don't know her name.'

'Well, maybe that's where the initials C.R. scratched on the rune come in. It's possible her first name begins with a C.'

'Of course, I'd forgotten about that.'

At that moment Angus walked into the bar. He had been to Oban to pick up an order for the Inn from the Cash and Carry. He'd had a puncture on the way back and was tired, dirty and, worst of all, late for his lunch-hour shift. Although Caitlin was perfectly capable of coping in his absence, it was supposed to be her time off.

Maggie looked up and saw him. He did not look to be in the best of moods. She gave him a cool nod and casually turned back to her conversation with Bridie. She heard him approach their table.

'Hello there, Bridie.' Both women looked up, Bridie smiling with her usual warmth and Maggie poker-faced. Angus turned to address Maggie. 'You're looking very much better than when I saw you last. There obviously wasn't any need for me to have been as concerned as I have been.'

'Not concerned enough to visit me, I notice,' retorted Maggie.

Her off-hand manner clearly irritated him. Maggie saw the flash of temper in his eyes but was unable to stop herself. She knew she was not really being fair but continued anyway. 'I'd have thought you'd at least have felt some responsibility for my accident.'

'I was nowhere near when you fell off the horse.' Angus's tone was indignant.

'I didn't fall.' Maggie felt her temper rising to meet his. 'I was thrown, if you remember.'

Angus narrowed his eyes and stared at her. 'If you'd had better control you'd have been able to keep your seat.'

Maggie felt a warm flush rise in her cheeks but she kept her voice flat and emotionless. 'If I remember correctly, you complimented me on my handling of Freya earlier on so I really don't think I was at fault. It was your reckless behaviour racing off like an idiot which made her nervous.' She stared back at him defiantly.

She saw the anger rise in him like a storm. His lips set in a thin line, his eyes were dark pools of fury. When he spoke, however, his voice was cold.

'Well, Miss MacQueen, I'm sorry you think that but as you're recovering well and you'll be leaving us shortly anyway apportioning blame is hardly helpful is it?'

Bridie clearly had decided she had better intervene before things got out of hand. She stood up.

'Come along now children, no arguing,' she said with an amused grin. They both glared at her. Undaunted, she continued, 'Maggie and I have to go and see someone so we'll catch up with you later, Angus.' So saying, she put her hand firmly under Maggie's elbow and steered her towards the door and out of the Inn.

'Whatever was that all about?' she said when they were both outside. 'You know fine well it wasn't Angus's fault that Freya reared.'

'Yes, I know, but he just makes me so mad sometimes. He can be so arrogant and…and…' She paused searching for an appropriate epithet.

'Well, they do say love and hate are two sides of the same coin.' Bridie gave an enigmatic smile.

Maggie decided not to dignify the comment with a reply, contenting herself merely with an exasperated sigh instead and an impatient, 'Come on then, let's go.'

Arms linked they walked towards the surgery in the hope of finding Calum. Maggie put all thoughts of Angus out of her mind and they discussed what to tell Calum, eventually deciding he should be told everything. 'Otherwise how are we going to explain our interest in finding out about Alexander MacDonald?' Bridie reasoned. Fortunately, he had just returned from his morning visits when they arrived. He listened in silence, his eyes never leaving their faces, frowning occasionally as they described Maggie's encounters with the woman in grey and the Bodach and their feeling that somehow these might be connected to the 'Unknown Maid' in the churchyard.

'It's a pretty strange story,' he ventured finally. 'I'm not sure whether I believe in ghosts and all that stuff.' Obviously sensing their disappointment, he hastily went on, 'But I can see both of you are convinced so I'll suspend my disbelief for the moment and go along with it. It'll certainly be interesting to see what I can dig up about this Alexander MacDonald. That's the name, right?' When both women nodded he continued. 'Well, it's a pretty common name hereabouts so it might take a little time to find the right person. At least we've got his date of birth which should help. I don't suppose there was any indication where he was from?'

Maggie explained again that all that was engraved on

the stone were the dates of his birth and death and the phrase, "He walked God's path always." 'I suppose it suggests he was a god-fearing man, but I don't expect that's any of any help.'

'It might be, we'll have to wait and see. Now as he was buried here in Invershee it would suggest he lived here so I'll start by looking at the local birth registers. If I can't find any record of his having been born here, which is quite possible...' Calum paused seeing Maggie's questioning look. 'It could be he was an itinerant worker and moved around from place to place. A lot of men did in those days: labourers, carpenters, stone masons, estate workers, even undertakers.'

He smiled at their bemused expressions when he mentioned the latter, and explained that such folk would travel around the various communities making the coffins as and when their services were required.

'Anyway, as I was saying, if I can't find any record of him locally, I'll widen the search to the surrounding areas.'

'What if he's from outwith this locality altogether?' Bridie asked. 'He could be from anywhere, I suppose.'

'I'll just have to extend the search area until I find him.' He gave her a warm smile and patted her arm.

'Don't forget we think he could have a relation, perhaps a wife or maybe a sister, whose first initial was C.' Maggie said. 'That could help narrow down the possibilities couldn't it?'

'Yes, that should make it easier.' Calum promised he would make a start on the search for Alexander Macdonald that night after evening surgery.

A little later, having parted from Bridie at her shop, Maggie strolled along by the side of the loch, mulling over all they had discussed. Maybe this was the way forward, a means of discovering the Maid's identity. After her disappointment over the Parish Records, she felt a good deal more hopeful. She tried to push her earlier disagreement with Angus to the back of her mind; she wasn't going to waste her time even thinking about it.

He was just a smug, self-satisfied, full of himself know-all who couldn't admit when he was in the wrong, and she hurried back along the track rehearsing what she would say next time they met; she would tell him exactly what she thought of him.

-

CHAPTER 11

Maggie spent the rest of the day quietly pottering around the cottage. She found dusting therapeutic and housework kept her mind from dwelling on her own unhappiness and thoughts of ghostly apparitions. She also managed, even with one hand, an hour or two in the garden pulling up weeds, or what she hoped were weeds. She really was so ignorant about flowers but she felt she owed it to Rachel to at least try and keep the place looking tidy. The evening passed quickly too as she finally got down to reading through the notes she had made earlier in the week. As always she was fascinated to learn about how people had lived in years gone by.

So engrossed was she that when a log from the fire fell onto the hearth in a shower of sparks she jumped as if at the sound of a gunshot. Hastily she gathered it up with the little brass shovel and, making sure the fire was safe, decided enough was enough. She was tired. She would go to bed and hope for a night's sleep free from dreams and the sound of that damned cat meowing. Maybe tomorrow Calum would have some news though she thought it unlikely. It would probably take more than a few hours to research Alexander MacDonald's family tree and, even then, it might prove to be a dead end.

Her optimistic mood of earlier had evaporated and she felt despondent as she went to make sure the back-door was fastened. She knew people in these parts rarely locked their doors but she was not yet quite ready to shake off her city ways. On an impulse she opened the door instead and stepped out into the night.

Light from the kitchen behind her spilled out a little way forming a bright, radiant glow against which her shadow loomed long and large onto the garden path. Beyond that was complete, impenetrable darkness; no ambient glow from a city's sodium lamps softened the inky blackness. She pulled the door closed behind her and moved slowly further into the garden. Everywhere was completely calm and silent and she could smell the peaty, leafy richness of the earth mingled with the scent of wood smoke from the fire.

Gradually, as her eyes attuned to the darkness, she could make out a multitude of stars puncturing the night sky, their light sharp and cold like the tips of tiny, steel needles. How long was it, she wondered, since she had looked up at the stars? Not since she was a girl. She could hear her father's sonorous voice now, saying,

'Look, Maggie, that's Casseopia and, over there's Ursa Major.' And she had looked where he had pointed trying to see what he saw, thrilled at being with him, just the two of them in the garden at night, feeling privileged he was sharing his knowledge with her. She remembered the hairy roughness of his tweed jacket tickling the back of her neck as he laid an arm around her shoulders and held her close. Without thinking, she reached up and rubbed the nape of her neck where his arm had once lain. Lost in her memories, it was a moment before the sound penetrated her consciousness.

The crying of a baby carried faintly on the still night air.

She was aware of her heartbeat, loud and insistent, drumming in her ears, and her mouth felt dry. She stood perfectly still. The sound seemed to twist into her. *That's definitely a baby's cry,* she thought, staring out into the night, striving to see into the shadowed depths stretching before her, straining her ears to listen for the sound again.

There it was, and it sounded quite close. It was the same sound which had woken her for the last two nights, the sound she had dismissed as the mewling of a cat. She stood motionless, every nerve stretched taut, her whole being focused on listening for another cry. *There!* Fainter now but she was sure it was coming from somewhere down towards the bottom of the garden.

She had to find the baby, she had to soothe it and bring it in out of the cold night air. Whirling round and flinging open the door, she dived into the kitchen. She began rummaging through all the drawers, scrabbling among balls of string, odd pieces of cutlery, old biros, discarded shopping lists and all manner of other odds and ends in her haste. A torch, she needed a torch. She was sure she had seen one somewhere earlier this week. Where was it? *Think, Maggie, think.*

She forced herself to stop her frantic fumbling for a moment. It was at the start of the week, she was sure. She had been looking for something else and had come across a torch during her search. It came to her in a flash. It was when she was hunting for the waterproofs. The torch was in the small cupboard in the porch. She ran to get it, praying that it was in working order. Holding her breath, she stood at the back door and pressed the button. 'Thank Goodness,' she breathed as a strong beam of light spread out into the darkness.

She began to make her way carefully and slowly down the path, sweeping the torch from side to side searching for the baby. She was about halfway down the garden when it dawned on her that the crying had stopped the moment she had switched on the torch. But she continued with her search until she was convinced there was no baby hidden anywhere: not under any of the shrubs and bushes, not beside the dry stone walls, not in the deepest, darkest, furthest shadows of the garden. She had definitely heard it, she knew she had but there was nothing to be seen, nothing to suggest from where, or from whom the sound had originated. She stood by the rowan tree at the far end of the garden, confused and puzzled, for several minutes.

She was about to turn and go back to the cottage when intuition made her swing the torch's beam onto the hillside. Its rays illuminated sections of grass and heather and gorse, sending long shadows slithering away into the blackness which hovered at the edge of its radiance. She moved the torch backwards and forwards, to and fro, ranging over the contours of the hill with the searching light.

There! Where the brightness began to fade into darkness, at the very edge of her vision, she sensed someone standing in the watching stillness. Maggie's scalp prickled. Careful not to move the torch's light towards the place, she turned her head slowly and was able to make out, in the invisible darkness, a solitary, stationary shape. Maggie knew without a second's doubt the figure was that of the woman in grey.

A quiver of expectancy shook her but she remained transfixed, her whole body tuned into the image before her; it was as if time had frozen this moment. For what seemed an eternity Maggie stood there, hardly daring to breathe, waiting for something to happen; the woman to move, or to speak, or simply to vanish as she had before. But nothing changed. It was as if they were both locked into some kind of chilling tableau. Finally, Maggie could bear it no longer.

She called out, 'I'll find out who you are. I want to help you to find some peace.' Her voice sounded loud in the silence. Then she sensed, rather than saw, the woman incline her head in silent acknowledgement. The outline of the figure began to soften and diminish until the shape of her was absorbed into the surrounding night and she was gone.

Maggie remained gazing at the spot where, a few seconds before, the woman had stood. Questions buzzed around her head until she felt dizzy. Round and round, over and over again, her mind spun as the thoughts whirled through her brain. She didn't have any answers and she was no longer sure she would find any but she would try.

Knowing she would achieve nothing further by standing there any longer, Maggie hastened back to the cottage. Her feet and hands were icy, her nerves as tense as piano wire. She had just spoken to a ghost, a spirit, an apparition from the past as if it was the most normal thing in the world.

Too tired and overwhelmed by the experience to think

rationally, Maggie dragged herself up the stairs. It was all too much. Her fight with Angus had upset her more than she had realized and this latest disturbing encounter with the woman in grey, not to mention the unresolved question of the crying baby, had left her drained, emotionally and physically. She sought her bed with relief and fell quickly into a troubled sleep.

When she awoke the next morning she felt un-refreshed and uneasy. Trying to shake off her gloomy mood, she had a quick shower. Deciding she could dispense with the sling as her shoulder was much better, she dressed and breakfasted on several cups of strong coffee. Feeling marginally more human, she set off to walk down to the village planning to call in on Bridie and tell her of the night's events. Perhaps, she thought, she would pop into the surgery too and see what, if anything, Calum had managed to find out.

Maggie knew she was foolish to expect he would have been able to achieve very much in such a short time but, if she went on much longer without some kind of explanation for all that had been happening, she thought she might go mad. Her mind occupied with the questions which had tormented her last night, she didn't hear the approaching horse and rider behind until they were almost upon her.

'Are you feeling any friendlier towards the natives this morning?' Angus called down as he slowed Merlin to a walk beside her.

'Not really,' Maggie said shortly and she strode on, keeping her eyes firmly fixed on the road ahead.

He had done it again, making her nearly jump out of her skin, creeping up on her like that, she thought. Then she smiled at herself. She supposed riding up behind her on a huge, bay stallion could hardly be described as creeping. Her mood lifted a little and she glanced up at him. That was a mistake she realised as soon as her eyes met his. He had not expected her to look at him and his expression was unguarded. She was taken aback at the interplay of emotions she saw there; a grim seriousness combined with a naked longing which made the heat rise in her. She looked away quickly, confounded by what she had glimpsed in his face.

Angus had been hoping to see her during his morning ride and was annoyed at the purposeful way she was marching along, stubbornly in his view, refusing to be civil to him. She could at least meet him halfway. After all he was intending to apologise for his boorish behaviour of the previous day. He'd been in the wrong and was willing to admit it…something he didn't do very often… but she was clearly determined not to give an inch. Begrudgingly he acknowledged he admired that about her; she stood up for herself, unwilling to compromise what she believed to be right and proper.

He saw she was wearing her hair loose. It hung in a thick, glossy curtain to her shoulders, swinging as she walked, her back ram-rod straight, eyes focused straight ahead. He imagined running his hands over the polished sheen of it and then tangling his fingers in its silken strands as he turned her face towards his. He could picture moving closer to her so that her body was pressed tightly against his and then lowering his head to taste the sweet softness of her lips.

Suddenly their eyes met and she quickly looked away blushing. Angus realised he had probably revealed something of what he was thinking and quickly reined in the horse, dismounting in one swift, fluid movement. He pulled the reins over Merlin's head and led him along beside Maggie, matching his pace to hers.

'I owe you an apology, Maggie, well two really,' he said quietly and put his hand on her arm to stop her walking on. She turned to face him, her expression less than encouraging but he ploughed on regardless.

'First of all I was a stupid fool the other day. I should never have let Merlin have his head. I ought to have known Freya would chase after him and become too lively for you to handle.' Maggie's features softened a little.

'And I was completely out of order yesterday. I was annoyed because I was late back for Caitlin so I took it out on you. It was unforgivable.' He gave her a searching look, noting the lines of strain and tension were back around her eyes and mouth. He smiled disarmingly. 'But you will forgive me, won't you?'

Maggie gazed back at him in confusion. The arm where his hand held her tingled as if it had received an electric shock. She fought against succumbing to his casual charm but how could she resist him when he looked just like a small boy who had been caught with his fingers in the biscuit tin; that lop-sided smile, those eyes the colour of molasses would be her undoing, she knew it.

Keeping her eyes steady on his and trying to keep the tremor from her voice she said, 'No, Angus, I'm the one who should be saying "Sorry". It wasn't your fault Freya reared. She might have been a bit over-excited after the gallop but something spooked her out on the hill.' She paused, considering whether she should tell him about the woman in grey but decided this was neither the time nor the place; she didn't want him thinking she was some crazy woman.

'And as for yesterday, I was as much to blame as you. I shouldn't have lost my temper.'

His hand tightened on her arm. Her pulse began to quicken and she made as if to step back, but Angus, with practiced ease, slid his hand up to twist his fingers in her hair pulling her towards him in one rapid movement.

'I always seal an apology with a kiss,' he murmured softly, and before she knew what was happening, his mouth crushed down on hers.

Maggie's eyes widened in shock and her hands flew up to push against his chest as she tried to free herself from his determined embrace. She could feel the rapid pounding of his heart under her fingers and was overwhelmed by an awareness of his strength, the powerful maleness of him. Bizarrely, she was also conscious of the hum of insects nearby and a sheep bleating in a far field. He tasted of mint and apples, autumn and apologies, and a quick rush of pleasure surged through her. All thought fled from her mind as she gave herself up to the moment.

Angus felt the resistance leave her. She relaxed and her lips, as sweet and soft as he had imagined, parted as she surrendered herself wholeheartedly to the kiss. Her arms crept up to clasp the back of his neck and draw him more closely to her. Hot waves of desire and exhilaration swept through him and he found himself wanting to touch her, taste her, take her here where they stood.

She trembled and he sensed her need rising to meet his. She nipped his bottom lip lightly with her teeth, teasing, provocative, inviting him to take more. He tightened his grip, feeling his control beginning to slip. His rational mind struggled to assert itself. This was not the way. He needed her, wanted her, longed to feel her body pinned beneath his but in the right place at the right time. That was not now and not here.

Forcing himself to relax his hold on her, he reluctantly dragged his mouth from hers and reached up to loosen her hands from around his neck. He stepped back keeping her hands trapped in his as he gazed at her. Her cheeks were flushed and those ice blue eyes were cloudy with arousal. His lips curved into a wicked smile. 'Well, Maggie MacQueen, you're certainly full of surprises.'

She raised her eyebrows and drew in a deep, tremulous breath before fixing him with a defiant glare.

'You started it, Mr. Cameron,' she retorted.

'Oh, don't get me wrong,' Angus said, 'I'm not complaining. In fact I think I would rather like to do it again' and, before she could step away from him, he tenderly cupped her face in his hands, bringing his mouth down to hers in a kiss so full of gentle promise he felt the heat stir in him again. Before his resolve could desert him, he stepped away from her.

'I think perhaps we should continue this later,' he said, trying to keep his tone light despite the tightness in his chest.

Maggie stared at him. She hated this feeling of not being in control and her unexpected response to him had shaken her to the absolute core. Unsure how to handle the situation, she took a quick step back and saw the passion still lingering in his eyes. What must he think of her, throwing herself at him in such a fashion? She felt the blush rise in her face. She clasped her arms around herself and tried to ignore the throbbing pulse of blood racing through her veins and the fact every nerve in her body seemed to be quivering as if tiny sparks were touching her skin. She needed to make it clear there was no way she wanted a relationship with him; this had been a mistake. She rested her hand lightly on his arm. With her eyes fixed on his she said firmly, 'I really don't think that would be a good idea Angus.'

She saw a flash of incredulity shadow his face. His jaw muscles tightened and his voice was harsh as he looked at her. 'Really? Well, maybe you're right Maggie. It's probably not such a good idea.'

She tried a smile, relieved she did not have to explain herself. Attempting to lighten the tension that hummed in the air between them, she forced herself to adopt a softer tone. 'I really think perhaps you'd better get hold of Merlin before he eats any more of the hedgerow.'

Angus arched a sardonic eyebrow and gave her a

tight-lipped smile. 'Right again, Maggie,' and strode off down the track to recapture the horse. Mounted once more he raised his hand in mock salute and called, 'See you later,' before wheeling Merlin round and trotting off towards the village.

Maggie watched him go. He cut a fine figure on horse-back, she thought, broad- shouldered, capable, commanding. She felt her cheeks warming again as she recalled her wanton actions of only a few minutes ago. It had simply been a kiss after all, though she had to admit she had never before been kissed with such passion, such urgency, such desire. She could still feel the hardness of his mouth on hers, the firmness of his body as he held her close and the raging need which had all but overcome him.....and her, if she were honest. Thank heavens he'd had the sense to pull back because she didn't think she could have. She really didn't need any more complications in her life. In future she would keep her distance; there could be nothing more between them.

Angus was annoyed with himself. He had rushed things and now she probably thought he was some kind of sexual predator. He knew he wasn't mistaken; she had responded to him with an unrestrained passion that had his abdominal muscles tying themselves in knots, but his timing was wrong. He would just have to exercise some patience, not something he was good at he silently acknowledged.

CHAPTER 12

Pondering the encounter, Maggie continued along the track to the village. She felt the hot flush of embarrassment again as she recalled her reaction to Angus's kiss. *For pity's sake,* she'd been kissed by an attractive man that was all. It didn't mean anything, though she couldn't blame Angus if he had got the wrong impression from the way she had moulded her body to his and kissed him back. She was lonely, on the rebound, missing Ben, feeling rejected, she found all sorts of reasons to excuse her behaviour but the truth was something in her had responded to him. From now on, however, she would just make sure she was never alone with him. *Simple.*

Satisfied she had identified the reasons for her brazen behaviour she pushed all thoughts of the encounter to the back of mind and, having reached the surgery, opened the door to find the small waiting-room still occupied by patients. Eager to find out if Calum had discovered anything about the late Alexander MacDonald, she settled down to wait until he was free to see her

She sat idly flicking through magazines about all manner of things: country-life pursuits, cookery, motoring, and home-improvement. The people waiting were soon in and out and just as she was scanning an article about how to make your home resemble a Mayfair penthouse ... *Who on earth would want to?* ... Calum put his head round the door.

'Come on in, Maggie. I hope you're not here to consult me professionally? Your shoulder's not still giving you problems?' he queried, ushering her into his consulting room.

'No, my shoulder's fine, much better, thanks. I was wondering if you've had any luck tracing Alexander MacDonald? I know you've not had long to do much research, but ...' She looked at him expectantly.

'Well, I have found out one thing. He certainly wasn't born in Invershee. His death's recorded here in the Parish Register but there's no record of his birth. There're several people of that name in the records but none for 1827. So I'm going to have to look further afield.'

She screwed up her face in disappointment. Calum smiled. 'Don't worry Maggie, there'll be a record of him somewhere, it just may take a little longer that's all. I've got some free time this afternoon so I'll start another search.'

'I'm really grateful to you Calum. I just hoped...' her voice tailed away and she bit her bottom lip in frustration. Maggie knew she'd been expecting too much. 'You'll let me know as soon as you do find anything?'

'Of course I will,' he promised.

And with that she had to be satisfied. She took her leave and walked over to Bridie's shop. It was closed. She checked her watch. It was too early for Bridie to be at the Inn so maybe she was still at home. Maggie didn't want to go back to the surgery and bother Calum again so she made her way along to the village shop. Someone there would be bound to know Bridie's address.

Sure enough they did and, armed with directions, Maggie walked along the loch-side, passed the Inn... no sign of Angus she noted thankfully her heart giving a little jolt at the memory of their earlier meeting...and towards the start of the road coming in to the village.

There was the post-office Rachel had mentioned Maggie noted as she strode past a long, low, whitewashed stone building on her right, hunkered down by the roadside, a red post-box set into the wall beside the entrance door, and two petrol pumps located in a parking area close by. She resolved to call in on her way back from Bridie's.

She had made up her mind she was going to stay in Invershee a little longer; although she didn't recall when she had actually made such a decision, she knew that was what she wanted. She couldn't leave yet, not while the mystery of the woman in grey was still unsolved. She was also determined to find out the identity of the 'Unknown Maid' and there was the crying baby too....*Lots of questions and not enough answers*, she mused. There was absolutely no way she could return to London yet.

With these thoughts churning around in her head, her pace quickened and she soon reached the sign which announced, in both English and Gaelic, that visitors were now entering the village of Invershee. She spotted the narrow track leading off up to the left she had been told to look out for. She could just make out the top of a grey slate roof peeping over the brow of the hill and, turning onto the dirt track, she began climbing towards it.

What a lovely spot, she thought enviously as she paused to look back at the view which stretched over the loch to the serried ranks of the hills beyond. It was a cool, grey day but the air was so clear that the hills looked closer than she knew they were. Clouds, like trails of white chiffon, floated above them. She resumed her climb and soon stood in front of Bridie's home.

It was an old, single storey croft house crouching in a dip in the hillside, hidden from sight of the road and sheltered from the harsh rigours of the Scottish weather. The stone of its construction had been left a natural, soft grey, its paintwork glistened saffron yellow. A breathless silence hung in the air as if the world stood still, waiting. There was no sign of Bridie.

She knocked on the open door and called, 'Bridie, it's me Maggie.' There was no answer. She must be somewhere nearby Maggie reasoned and began to wander around the outside of the house. She admired the tall, ornamental grasses with their feathery fronds growing along the dry stone wall enclosing the garden, and the beds of roses still vibrant and blooming. Banks of blue willow gentian and low-growing pink fuchsia bordered a flagged area on which an assortment of coloured and terracotta pots were scattered, overflowing with a diverse selection of herbs and heathers, catmint and Scotch marigolds. Over all hung the fragrant scent of lavender.

She was just rounding the corner of the house when

she heard a faint shout. Looking up she saw Bridie making her way down the hillside her arms full of dark green foliage. As the other woman grew nearer Maggie saw the smile on her face, wide and welcoming. Her bright auburn hair was caught back from her face with a black velvet ribbon and she wore a long, sea-green coloured dress of some soft fabric.

'I thought I heard someone calling my name. I've just been collecting bog myrtle' Bridie explained, as she dumped the bundle of greenery beside the front door. 'I use it to scent some of my candles.' She brushed at her skirt where some of the shiny, waxy leaves still clung, and then turned to give the other woman a quick hug.

'How wonderful to see you Maggie. Come in, come in,' and so saying she ushered her unexpected guest into the house.

Maggie looked around with undisguised interest. It was just as she'd pictured Bridie's house would be. The room they entered was painted brilliant white and slatted, dark wood shelving reached to the ceiling on two of the walls, laden with books and crystals, and all manner of other bric-a-brac. From the mantelshelf over a stone fireplace on another wall hung bunches of dried herbs and grasses and below them, on the hearth, were stacked bundles of kindling sticks. The furniture was mismatched but comfortable-looking and candles shed their soft radiance everywhere, perfuming the room with jasmine and vanilla.

'I hope you don't mind my calling on you at home unannounced like this.' Maggie was suddenly mindful of the fact she hadn't actually been invited to visit. 'It's just that I went to the shop but it was closed and I've so much to tell you I couldn't wait.'

Bridie smiled warmly, 'Of course I don't mind. Let's have a coffee and then we can sit and you can tell me your news.' She disappeared into the back and a few minutes later returned with two steaming mugs. She motioned Maggie to sit on a small, soft cushioned settee in crimson cotton positioned in front of one wall of bookshelves and, after handing her one of the mugs, sat down beside her. 'Now, give,' she said and sat back, sipping her coffee.

'Well, first thing is Calum hasn't managed to trace Alexander MacDonald yet. Seemingly he wasn't born in Invershee.'

'That's not too surprising.' Bridie smiled at Maggie's crestfallen expression. 'We always knew it was possible he wasn't from the village. Don't worry. Calum'll trace him eventually. He's very into this family tree stuff.'

'I know I've got to be patient, Bridie. It's just so hard, especially after what happened last night.' She paused, enjoying the drama of the moment as Bridie's eyes widened. 'I heard a baby crying and saw the woman in grey again. I have to find out who she is and help her to find some peace.' As Bridie pressed for more details, Maggie recounted as much as she could remember of the previous night's events. 'Do you think she and the baby could be linked in some way?' she finished.

Bridie looked pensive. 'It's possible. Your experiencing the two things together, seeing the woman and hearing the child, suggests there might be a connection.'

She broke off for a moment and gazed over towards the window as though the answer somehow lay there. 'You know,' she carried on, turning back to look at Maggie, 'it's interesting you said the crying came from the bottom of the garden. If my memory serves me right, there's a rowan tree growing there, isn't there?' She didn't wait for Maggie's response but went on, as if thinking aloud. 'I don't know if you know this, Maggie, but the rowan's figured in mythology and folklore down the ages. It's sometimes called the Witches' Tree because people believe it gives protection against evil and enchantment and, so, against witches.'

'But what's that got to do with anything?'

'I'm not sure but it could be significant. After all, we haven't yet considered that this spirit of yours might not be what she seems. She might mean you harm.' Bridie put out a restraining arm when Maggie shook her head and opened her mouth as if to protest. 'Wait, hear me out. She always appears on the hillside doesn't she? You've never seen her in the garden or in the house?'

Maggie shook her head again, 'No, but.....'

'I'm not saying she *is* an evil spirit but if she is then the rowan tree's a barrier she can't pass.' Bridie paused, looking at the shelves of books on the wall opposite. She got up and moved across to them. 'I've got a book here somewhere which tells you all about the rowan. People have used it for centuries to protect themselves, their homes and even their animals against the evil eye.' She continued scanning the shelves. 'Cutting down a rowan tree is supposed to be unlucky for that very reason.' She laughed. 'Though I've heard it said if you apologise to the tree before you take an axe to it, then you'll be alright.'

She found what she was looking for and handed the book to Maggie. 'It's a fascinating read if nothing else.' As Maggie began to flick through the pages, Bridie went on thoughtfully, 'It might be a good idea to make sure you have some protection anyway, just in case.' She grinned when she saw Maggie's mystified expression. 'I'm not suggesting you should arm yourself with a big stick, or hire a bodyguard; they wouldn't be any use against a malevolent spirit anyway.'

'That's a relief,' Maggie exclaimed wryly.

'No, I was thinking more about using what we've got. In the old days people used to nail a rowan wood cross over their doors to keep out evil spirits. Even today, some of the older folk in the Highlands still do that. Despite the last witch trial in Scotland being over three hundred years ago, people still cling to the old beliefs.'

'There's no way the woman in grey is an evil spirit, I just feel it.'

'You don't know that for sure. And what about the Bodach? He could intend to harm you.'

Maggie was having none of it. 'I've never sensed

anything malevolent or felt at all threatened when either of them has appeared.'

Eventually, in the face of Bridie's continued insistence that at least it wouldn't hurt, Maggie agreed to hang a rowan cross over the doorway at the cottage.

'It has to be tied with red thread according to the rhyme,' Bridie said, and proceeded to recite it for Maggie's benefit:

'Ran-tree and red thread
Gars the witches tak their speed.'

Maggie looked at her as if she'd taken leave of her senses. 'I haven't got any red thread,' she muttered.

'That's okay, I have.' Bridie's eyes sparkled with humour as she searched through a large, black lacquered box which sat beside one of the fireside chairs. 'There you are,' and she triumphantly handed a length of it to Maggie. 'Now you've no excuse not to do it.'

Pushing the thread into her pocket, Maggie wondered at her own sanity; making a talisman to ward off evil spirits had not been on the agenda when she fled here to get over a broken heart. As Bridie collected their empty mugs and took them through to the kitchen to make more coffee, Maggie dithered over whether or not to tell her about the meeting with Angus.

Before she could decide either way, Bridie came back into the room and set the refreshed coffee mugs down on the stone hearth before walking over to sit beside Maggie. She took the other woman's hands in hers. 'And when were you intending to tell me your other news?' There was a teasing note in her voice.

Maggie felt the colour rise in her cheeks. She opened her mouth and then shut it again, not sure what to say. She cleared her throat and tried to keep her voice steady though she couldn't prevent a little stutter as she stared at her friend. 'I.....er...I don't know...I'm not sure what you mean, Bridie.'

'Come on. I know something's happened. I could

see it as soon as you walked in. You've a sort of spark about you. It's something to do with Angus isn't it?'

'Has he been up here telling you....things?' Maggie frowned, her lips pressed together in a tight line. She felt the temper rising in her; couldn't that man keep anything to himself! 'He has hasn't he? How could he? It's private.'

'Maggie, calm down. I haven't seen Angus since yesterday at the Inn. I promise you, I haven't seen him or spoken to him at all,' Bridie repeated as doubt follow anger on Maggie's face. 'Besides, I've told you before, sometimes I just know things. So what is it?'

Maggie looked down at her hands clasped in Bridie's. *Who'd have a psychic for a friend?* She raised her eyes and met the other woman's inquisitive gaze. 'Well, if you really want to know....'

'Yes, yes! Of course I do. Just tell me…Please!'

'I met Angus on my way down to the village and…..'

Bridie squeezed Maggie's hands. 'And?' she prompted.

'He kissed me…twice.' A little tremor snaked around the pit of Maggie's stomach as her words conjured up the sensation of his mouth on hers. She recalled the swell of passion which had rolled through her when he held her in his arms. She dropped her eyes and pulled her hands free, clasping them together in her lap. She tried to make her tone matter-of-fact. 'But it was nothing.' Even as she said it Maggie knew what a lie it was. She looked up at Bridie again. The other woman's brow was creased in concern.

Maggie went on, '…he apologised, I apologised, he kissed me, and that's all…Really, that's all,' she repeated.

'Well, it's good to see you looking a little brighter than of late. He's certainly managed to put a glow in your cheeks.' Bridie patted Maggie's arm. 'But I'm glad you're not taking it seriously. As I said before, I'd hate for you to get hurt again.' She jumped up from the sofa. 'We should get these coffees before they get cold.'

For a few moments they sat side by side sipping

their now lukewarm coffee each lost in her own thoughts.

Maggie pondered on Bridie's easy acceptance that her encounter with Angus had been nothing more than Maggie had said. After all, she knew him much better than Maggie did. Perhaps, after all, she should go back to London and pick up the threads of her life there again. Forget everything that had happened since she had arrived. Whatever did she think she was doing, chasing ghosts and an old man in black, and searching for a non-existent baby. As for Angus, well she didn't want to get involved with him anyway. No, she didn't need it, any of it.

CHAPTER 13

Maggie was so deep in thought it took a moment for her to realise Bridie was speaking to her. 'Sorry. What did you say?'

'I said why not stay for lunch? I can easily rustle something up for us.'

'Thanks, that'd be lovely,' and she got up and followed Bridie into her kitchen.

It may have been tiny but to Maggie it looked to be the most well-equipped she had ever seen. Pots and pans, bowls and jugs, jars and bottles were either squeezed onto shelves which ran along three of the walls, hanging from the ceiling on big, brass hooks, or stacked on a wooden board next to a large stone sink.

Despite this crowding of every available surface, everywhere and everything was spotless. Stainless steel shone, copper gleamed and glass sparkled. Pots of herbs flourished on the sill above the sink and through the window Maggie caught a glimpse of the hillside behind the house, its lower slopes brushed with the rich, purple bloom of heather.

From a small hook above the window hung a multi-faceted quartz crystal which swung gently in the draught from the partly open back door. Maggie watched it, captivated, as it sent splinters of rainbow-coloured light dancing round the room. Bridie seeing the direction of her gaze paused in her task of chopping tomatoes.

'It's beautiful isn't it? But crystals are very powerful tools in healing too. I use them a lot. They're full of energy and do wonders for your physical, emotional and spiritual life. Have you still got that rose quartz I gave you the other night?' When Maggie said she had, Bridie turned back to her chopping and went on, 'Well, keep it with you, and touch it, handle it, just turn it over in your pocket every now and then. It'll give you strength in any romantic ventures you might embark on.' She grinned broadly, 'and we all need that kind of help at times, don't we?'

Maggie sneaked her hand into her jeans' pocket and closed it around the rose-coloured stone. It felt hard and smooth in her fingers yet, at the same time, it seemed to radiate warmth. If Bridie noticed the slight movement she said nothing. Reaching over to the pots on the windowsill, she tore off some leaves of fennel and basil, and had soon prepared a feta cheese salad with home-made bread. They sat in the front room, at a long, pine table groaning under an accumulation of papers and more books which Bridie cleared away by sweeping them off carelessly into a corner. A small, black cauldron, also on the table, she left where it was.

They chatted easily as they ate and Maggie began to sense some of the tension she had felt earlier start to recede. Bridie told her about a few of her herbal remedies and what they were used for.

'It sounds really fascinating. I never realised there was so much to it. What made you take it up?' Maggie took a sip of wine and looked with interest at the other woman.

Bridie explained that her mother and her mother before her, and hers before her had all been healers so she'd grown up with it, and had never wanted to do anything else.

'What about you Maggie? What do you do?'

So Maggie told her about her work at the museum preparing educational packages on the exhibits for visiting schoolchildren, that she enjoyed the research involved and the organizational part of the work. 'I really like order and method,' she confessed. 'I suppose I'm that way in my personal life too. I can't bear uncertainty. I like to have everything planned out and arranged well ahead.' She hesitated and couldn't help the little note of bitterness which crept into her voice as she added, 'I suppose sometimes people might find it off-putting and hard to live with.' She sat chewing her bottom lip.

Bridie took the other woman's hand in hers and squeezed it gently, 'It takes all sorts, Maggie.' Her tone casual, she went on, 'You've never married then? Or got close to it?'

Maggie's defences crumbled and it all came rushing out like a river released from a dam; how she blamed her mother's frivolous behaviour for the fact the father she had adored had left them; how he had been killed before Maggie had a chance to understand why he had left and had not taken her with him.

Then she told Bridie about Ben.

'I just felt abandoned and betrayed all over again. I can't begin to tell you how awful it was, Bridie.' She struggled to hold back the tears as she continued, 'I had my life planned out, everything was organized. It was all so perfect.'

'It must have been heart-breaking. I can understand why you wanted to get away.'

Bridie's face was filled with sympathy for the other woman. 'The trouble is life has a funny way of turning the tables on you sometimes no matter how much you try to plan ahead. Things don't always turn out the way you expect them to. I remember once hearing someone quite famous...I can't remember who ... say life is what happens when you're busy making other plans. I thought then how true that is.'

She gave a deep sigh. 'I've never told anyone this but when I was about nineteen, I was mad about someone.' She saw Maggie's quick look of understanding and shook her head. 'No not Angus. It was a student from Glasgow University who came to work at the Inn one summer.' She gave a wistful smile. 'I was absolutely crazy about him..... you know the head-over-heels in love with him kind of crazy.'

Maggie wasn't sure she did know, but she nodded anyway. 'What happened?'

'He fell for my friend Annie and at the end of his stay here she went back to Glasgow with him. They're married now with two young boys.'

'I'm so sorry, Bridie. That must have been really

hard for you, especially with her being your friend.'

'I was devastated at the time. The hardest thing was staying her friend. We'd always been very close and shared everything and for a while I felt she'd betrayed our friendship but it wasn't anyone's fault they fell in love. Thankfully neither of them ever knew about my feelings and I often stay with them now if ever I go to Glasgow. They're really good together and very happy. It just wasn't meant to be.'

'I wish I could be as philosophical as you. I just feel I daren't love anyone ever again because in the end they'll leave me and I don't think I could bear it.'

'Oh, Maggie, don't say that.'

Maggie felt the tears she had been holding back spring to her eyes. 'I just think I must be unlovable, that's why they don't stay with me.'

Bridie leaned over and, putting her arm round Maggie's shoulders, let her cry out all the hurt and misery she had carried with her for so long.

'I didn't think I had any more tears left.' Maggie mopped her eyes with the last of a packet of tissues Bridie produced. 'Thanks for listening.' She turned a tear-sodden face towards the other woman, a tremulous smile quivering at the corners of her mouth, her eyes red-rimmed and still full of hurt. She felt totally spent 'You must think I'm pathetic,' she managed. 'Other people suffer far worse and they cope somehow. They don't fall to pieces like me.'

'You're far too hard on yourself, Maggie. You've suffered two extremely traumatic events so you're entitled to feel a little bruised and battered. And besides,' Bridie squeezed Maggie's hand, 'everyone's entitled to a good old cry now and then.'

She rose and began to clear away their dirty dishes. 'Come on, you can help me wash these and then we'll have another glass of wine and put the world to rights.' A little while later, the two women wandered out into Bridie's garden.

'It's so beautiful here.' Maggie took a sip of crisp,

cool elderflower wine and felt the wild, dramatic scenery and the tranquil location soothing her jagged nerves and jumbled emotions. 'I do envy you living in such a wonderful place.'

'It's not so wonderful when a gale-force wind's blowing straight off the loch or there's a foot of snow outside your front door.' Bridie grinned happily, 'but you're right, it's a perfect place to live if you want peace and quiet and nature on your doorstep. I wouldn't want to live anywhere else.'

They continued strolling around Bridie's little plot of land as she pointed out various plants to Maggie, naming them and describing how she used them in her remedies and lotions. Maggie was enthralled and full of admiration for Bridie's understanding of and dedication to her craft.

'It must have been truly amazing learning about all the plants and their properties when you were growing up.'

'It was. My childhood was a kind of fantastic, fascinating adventure. My mother taught me everything she knew, so I was learning new skills and gaining knowledge every day. I was very lucky.'

'Where is she now?'

'She drowned in a boating accident on the loch when I was seventeen.'

Maggie was aghast. 'Oh, Bridie, I'm so sorry. I didn't know.'

'How could you? It's okay. It was almost twelve years ago, I'm over it now. But it's as I was trying to say to you earlier, there's no point in trying to plan things too much. Life has a nasty habit of throwing up the unexpected….as we both know.'

She turned and gave Maggie a hug then stood back, looking at her directly.

'Some things are just meant to be, Maggie. I really believe that. Your Ben was a fool for giving you up but perhaps you weren't right for each other. I don't mean to be cruel but can you honestly, hand on heart, tell me you're missing him as a person? Do you feel as if you've lost part of yourself or do you just regret all your plans for the future were thwarted?'

Maggie gasped. She felt the brutal force of Bridie's words like a body blow. She swallowed hard and stood there silent and stunned. Then the truth of what Bridie had said slowly began to sink in. She hadn't really missed Ben himself had she? She didn't long to hear his voice or ache to feel his presence? Though she'd been shocked by his betrayal, she began to wonder if Bridie was right and her misery was more down to the fact her carefully laid plans for the future hadn't worked out. Her face flushed in shame and Bridie put an arm around her shoulders.

'It's alright, Maggie. Sometimes we can't see the truth of something because we're too close to it. We're all guilty of that at times.' She hugged the other woman to her. 'Come on, enough of the psychoanalysis. Let's go in and I'll show you some of my water-colours.'

Later, feeling much lighter of heart and spirit as she left her friend's home, Maggie strolled down the track and then along the road back towards the village. She had spent a pleasant few minutes admiring the delicacy and detail of Bridie's paintings of local plant life, as well as enjoying another refreshing glass of home-made wine before taking her leave. She was grateful Bridie's honesty and insight had forced her to see the truth of her situation. There would be no more of the self-pity and despair she had indulged in since Ben's rejection. She had loved the idea of their planned life together but now she was no longer sure she had ever really loved him.

With this thought in mind she entered the post-office, ducking her head to get through the low doorway. As with the village shop it was a delight; a hotch-potch of magazines and muesli, fresh and canned foods, cake and chocolate all arranged on various shelves and counters in what was simply one, long, low-ceilinged room. The post-office part of it was tucked away in a corner and as Maggie approached the glass partition separating the customers from the Post-master, she saw he was watching her with interest.

'You'll be Miss MacQueen I'm thinking,' he said in soft, Highland tones.

Maggie was not at all surprised he knew who she was; she had come to realise it was the nature of small village life. He was a tall, lean man with bony arms and narrow, stooped shoulders; no wonder, Maggie thought, working in such cramped conditions day after day couldn't be conducive to good posture.

'Yes, that's right. I'm pleased to meet you Mr. ……?'

'Murdo Ferguson. Glad to know you Miss MacQueen.' He smiled a toothy grin of welcome.

'Please call me Maggie,' she smiled in return. 'Are you by any chance related to Jessie Ferguson?' she asked, curiosity getting the better of her good manners.

'Yes, she's my sister-in-law. She's married to my brother John,' he added unnecessarily.

Maggie nodded, smiling, and purchased a first-class stamp; she needed to get off her letter asking for a leave of absence from her job. She was about to wish Mr. Ferguson a good day, when he said, 'I hear you're interested in finding out about our Maighdeann.'

Did everyone in this village know her business as well as her name, she wondered and then realised Jessie had probably mentioned it to him. When she nodded, he went on. 'You ought to have a look at the village archive then. There're all sorts of papers and records in there. Could be something in them would help.'

He explained he was the custodian of this collection of past history and would be happy to let her have a root through it any time. Thanking him warmly, Maggie left, pleased to have found another avenue to explore. She was determined to find some way to identify both The Unknown Maid and the woman in grey before she returned to London.

The sky was beginning to cloud over and she scurried along through the village, anxious to get back to the cottage before the rain she sensed in the air. She noticed the lights were going on in the Inn as she passed. *No sign of Angus.* She wondered if he might call on her that night. He had said he would see her later but that was something people said, it didn't really mean anything. She had made herself perfectly plain she thought, though she wasn't at all sure he was the sort of man who would take no for an answer. Well, she would simply have to make him understand she was not interested, if by any chance he did turn up.

She didn't quite make it home…funny how she was beginning to think of the cottage as home, she mused… before the heavens opened. The rain was unrelenting and vigorous, raindrops bouncing on the track before her and forming rushing rivulets so that it seemed as if she were wading through a stream.

A little later, showered and her hair washed, she went downstairs to set a light to the fire and make herself a hot drink. She drew the curtains against the chill greyness outside although it was still only early evening and curled up in her favourite, old leather arm chair. She wrapped the comforting softness of her bath robe around her and sipped her tea watching the flames curling and twisting up the chimney. She mulled over her afternoon with Bridie.

What a good friend she was turning out to be. Not many people were as direct and straight-talking as Bridie; Maggie always preferred people who spoke their minds to those who prevaricated because they didn't want to hurt your feelings. She had felt hurt this afternoon there was no getting away from it but it had made her look at her love-affair with Ben…if it was even that… more honestly. She hadn't liked what she had discovered, but it was something she had needed to do. And Bridie had led her there, very gently, and had then been on hand to pick up the pieces of Maggie's shattered self-delusion with sympathy and understanding. Yes, she valued the other woman's friendship and she would make sure she kept in touch when she returned to her other life in London.

The sound of a car door slamming interrupted her

thoughts. Surely it couldn't be Angus? She wasn't dressed nor was she in the right frame of mind to see him. Starting up out of the chair, she was ready to race up the stairs when the back door flew open and an extremely wet and bedraggled looking Rachel poured herself and a very large suitcase into the kitchen.

'Rachel, how wonderful!' She rushed over to greet her friend. 'Whatever are you doing here?'

'You didn't think I'd let you celebrate your birthday all alone in this God-forsaken place did you?'

Maggie took a step back. She had completely forgotten that tomorrow she'd be twenty-seven years old.

'Have you come all the way up here to help me to blow out a few candles?' she said, laughing.

'Well, and to make sure you're okay too,' Rachel admitted, pools of water puddling at her feet 'Now, for Heaven's sake let me get out of these wet things. I'm drenched and that's just coming from the car to the back door.'

CHAPTER 14

Once Rachel was dried off and sitting beside the fire with a large glass of wine in her hand, Maggie studied her friend.

She grinned. 'You know, there was no need for you to come all this way to check on me. I'm perfectly fine.' She reached out a hand and squeezed Rachel's arm. 'Though of course it's lovely to see you and I'm glad you're here.

Rachel kicked of her shoes and settled herself back in her chair. 'So am I, and I must say, Maggie, you're looking a bit more like your old self. This was obviously a good idea of mine. Now tell me what's been happening. What have you been up to?'

So Maggie told her. She left nothing out and Rachel listened, her eyes widening and her jaw dropping further at each new revelation.

'You mean to say you haven't been moping around, crying non-stop and generally feeling sorry for yourself?' She paused and took a sip of wine. 'It's incredible,' she murmured. 'I spend a couple of weeks up here and nothing more exciting happens than a deer appearing in the garden. You're here for a few days and you end up trying to solve an age-old mystery, having dealings with the supernatural and, if that wasn't enough on its own, you're flirting with the only fanciable man in the place.' She gazed over at her friend. 'That about sums it up doesn't it?'

'Well, except for the flirting bit. Angus just grabbed me and kissed me. I didn't do anything to encourage him.' Maggie felt her face redden; the abandoned way she had kissed him back had probably been encouragement enough, she thought. Rachel raised her eyebrows but did not pursue it.

'Tell me again about your encounters with the supernatural,' she insisted, clearly intrigued. So Maggie did, filling in details she had forgotten in her previous account. She made them a quick supper in the middle of the evening and then they continued discussing the mystery until late.

'I'm shattered,' Rachel finally said and yawned.

Maggie too felt worn out. It had been an emotional day, one way and another. She was relieved Angus had not appeared. Obviously he had taken her at her word. She made up a bed in the spare room for Rachel and, having seen her friend settled, retired to her own room.

Sitting in front of the tiny dressing-table mirror, she began brushing her hair with long, deft strokes. What did Angus see in her, she wondered. She wasn't pretty by traditional standards. The face gazing back at her was unexceptional; heart-shaped but with an over-firm chin … stubborn her mother called it… and her skin was too pale despite the rosy glow in her cheeks from sitting by the fire. Her eyes were her best feature, she decided. She paused in her brushing and leaned forward to examine her reflection more closely. Yes, her eyes were definitely the best thing about her; large and cool blue with long, dark lashes, they looked back at her from the mirror.

The next second the image before her began to shiver and blur. She blinked hard and then froze, her hand poised halfway towards recommencing brushing her hair. The face staring back at her was no longer her own. She felt the hairs on her arms and at the nape of her neck stand erect. Her body tensed until she thought her nerves might snap and the scream which rose in her throat remained still-born. The room took on a deep, gathering gloom and she felt fingers of bone-chilling cold sliding over her skin. Darkness slithered over her and the next thing she knew Rachel was shaking her, calling her name.

'Maggie! For God's sake Maggie, wake up.'

Maggie could feel the roughness of the wooden floor boards through her nightgown as she lay there. She looked up into her friend's face, eyes wide and anxiety stamped in every line.

'Oh Maggie, thank God! You're alright,' Rachel

breathed. She put her arm round her friend and helped her to sit up against the bed. 'What do you think you're doing scaring the hell out of me like that?' her voice rising with every word.

Maggie shook her head, trying to clear her mind. She took a couple of deep breaths but her voice was far from steady when she said, 'I must have fainted.' She looked up at her friend. 'Did I?'

'I don't know what happened.' Rachel's tone was somewhere between annoyance and relief. 'I was just drifting off when I heard this loud thump from your room. I called out to you and, when you didn't answer, I got up and came in here. You were lying flat out on the floor, completely out of it.' Relief won. 'Oh, Maggie, I was so worried. Whatever happened?'

Maggie shuddered. She pointed a shaking finger. 'She was there in the mirror, the woman in the grey dress, the figure from the hillside. She was there looking at me Rachel. It was so creepy...one minute I was looking at myself, the next minute there she was. It was her face, not mine.' Maggie looked up at her friend in horror. 'She came into the house, Rachel. She was here, in this room.' Her voice shook and she began to tremble.

'Well, you're not sleeping in here on your own tonight' Rachel said, taking charge. 'We can double up in my room tonight and talk about it in the morning. You're in no state to do anything else tonight.'

Both women passed a restless night, Maggie waking at every little noise and Rachel wondering what on earth was going on; she had never expected anything like this when she had offered Maggie the cottage.

'Wake up, Maggie.' Rachel's voice was loud in her ear. Maggie winced as her friend launched into 'Happy Birthday to you'; Rachel didn't have the best singing voice in the world. She carefully unwrapped Rachel's gift and was delighted with a biography of Mary, Queen of Scots. By tacit agreement neither of them mentioned the face in the mirror until both were dressed and having breakfast.

'It seems to me,' Rachel said as she took up a spoonful of porridge, 'that your ghost, whoever she might be, is getting a tad impatient with you. That's the first time you've seen her in the house I take it?'

'Mmm' Maggie managed, her mouth full. Bridie's warning that the woman in grey could be an evil spirit came back to her and, although she did not quite believe it, she resolved to make a cross of rowan wood before the day was out – *just in case!* When she could speak she said, 'I think we'll go down to the village and see if Calum's had any luck with finding Alistair MacDonald. When Rachel frowned, she went on, 'You know, the name on the gravestone. The one I told you about. I really think he's the key to all this.'

'That'd be good and I can meet Bridie too. She sounds just the kind of person I'll like.'

Maggie nodded. She stood up and gathered up the cereal bowls, popping them into the sink to be washed later.

'Then, as we'll be down there anyway, I can give this Angus of yours the once over.' Rachel smiled back innocently when Maggie turned and glared at her.

'For one thing, he's not *my* Angus, and for another...' She paused trying to think of a good enough reason... for another, he'll probably be busy with things at the Inn,' she finished firmly.

Rachel gave her a knowing look but just said, 'Right.'

They both enjoyed the stroll down to the village. The rain of last night was evident only in the gurgling and tumbling sound of water rushing along the roadside ditches, and the sun was spilling occasional shafts of light below when the clouds above parted. Maggie was able to catch up with Rachel's news. Apparently the new resident in the flat opposite, on whom Rachel had had designs, turned out to have a male partner, but she had met someone on the plane to Glasgow and they had exchanged phone numbers.

'He lives in London and was just coming to Scotland

on business.'

She chattered on giving Maggie a detailed description of his looks, his single status, his job, his favourite film and whatever else she had discovered about him on their two hour flight until Maggie felt she knew him personally, but she relished this chance to indulge in a little womanly chit-chat. If it did nothing else, it reminded her there was a world out there which didn't involve ghosts, unknown maids or old men in ancient, black suits who appeared and disappeared seemingly at will; it was a world she'd eventually have to return to. *But not just yet*, she thought. She told Rachel of her plans to remain in Invershee a little longer, and, as she had known she would be, her friend was happy for her to stay on at the cottage for as long as she wanted.

'Mind you,' Rachel said, 'I want you to promise me you'll be careful. You don't really know what you're dealing with and I'm sure ghosts can be tricky things if they've a mind to – if they have minds that is?' She looked at Maggie and raised her eyebrows. Maggie shrugged and pulled a face. Both women had a fit of giggles. When they had calmed down, the serious note was back in Rachel's voice. 'I mean it Maggie, you have to promise.' Maggie nodded and Rachel went on, 'and you have to promise too that you'll keep me up to date with all developments. That's *all* developments,' she repeated, giving Maggie a suggestive wink. They were still laughing and chatting as they walked arm-in-arm into the village.

Maggie saw Bridie about to unlock the door to her little emporium and waved. She took Rachel over to meet her. Introductions complete, Rachel turned to Maggie and said, 'I think you should tell Bridie about last night, don't you?'

'What's this?' Bridie looked at Maggie, her face anxious.

'I had a visit from the woman in grey.'

'A visit? You mean she came into the house? Oh, Maggie, I warned you.' Bridie looked as if she wanted to shake her. 'You must be on your guard. We've no idea what's behind all this and until we do you've *got* to be careful.'

'That's exactly what I said,' Rachel nodded. 'You don't know where messing with the supernatural might lead.'

'I'm not, *it's* messing with me,' Maggie objected, but she saw the concern on the other women's faces and conceded that maybe they had a point. 'Okay, okay.' She lifted her hands in mock surrender. 'I'll be careful, I promise.'

'Good,' Bridie said. 'Now come on in both of you and you can tell me about it over coffee,' and she ushered them through into her tiny back office.

Once seated, Maggie and Rachel on chairs and Bridie perched on the corner of her work table, Maggie described what had happened.

'So you see, she didn't actually materialize in the cottage, it was just her face I saw in the mirror.' She gave a little shudder as she remembered the awfulness of that moment. 'But I'm absolutely certain she didn't mean me any harm,' she said in a firm voice.

'I suppose you think making you faint and collapse on the floor wasn't doing you any harm.' Rachel turned to Bridie. 'You should have seen how pale she was when I found her. For a moment I thought she was dead.' Her voice shook a little at the memory of finding her friend crumpled on the floor, barely breathing and her face as ashen as if all the blood had been drained out of her.

'It was just the shock.' Maggie insisted. 'That's all.'

'Well, be that as it may, it suggests she's getting more active. Probably because she thinks you're not doing anything to help her as you promised,' Bridie held up her hand as Maggie started to protest, 'Yes, I know you're doing all you can, and let's hope Calum has had some luck in tracing Alexander MacDonald. In the meantime, make sure you put that rowan cross over your door,' she said, wagging a finger at Maggie, 'just to be on the safe side.'

Maggie looked contrite. 'I was going to do it then Rachel arrived and it just went out of my head. But I will, I promise, as soon as I get home.' She suddenly remembered her chat with Murdo Ferguson, the postmaster, and told her friends of his suggestion that the village archive might provide some answers.

'That's a really good idea,' Rachel said. 'There're often all kinds of things to be found in a collection like that, you know letters and photographs, personal diaries and so on.'

Bridie offered to arrange with Murdo for them to visit the archive as soon as possible. 'I think he keeps it all in a big shed in his garden,' she told them. For some reason this caused great hilarity and it was a few moments before the three of them regained their composure.

Eventually, Rachel said, 'By the way Bridie, it's Maggie's birthday today.' She registered Bridie's look of surprise and went on, 'in case she's forgotten to mention it,' glancing at her friend as she spoke. 'Anyway,' Rachel ignored Maggie's grimace, 'we're planning to go to the Inn tonight to celebrate and it would be lovely if you could come too.'

Maggie raised her eyebrows. She had imagined something more along the lines of a couple of glasses of wine at home with Rachel. On reflection, however, she decided she liked the thought of an evening at the Inn.

'That's a great idea,' Bridie said, 'and you can let me know then if Calum's made any progress.'

Maggie once again noticed the little sparkle in Bridie's eyes when she said Calum's name and smiled to herself. There was definitely something going on between those two she thought, and wondered if either of them realised it. When she and Rachel left Bridie, having arranged to meet later, Maggie felt quite light-hearted.

'Right, let's go and see Calum now,' she said, leading her friend towards the surgery.

Patients had been few and far between that morning

and consultations were finished. As Calum had no visits to make either he was free to see them. Having made the necessary introductions, Maggie didn't waste any time. 'Any news?' Calum looked at her anxious face and he grinned.

'Well, I think I may have found him.' He explained that having widened his search outwith Invershee, he had found several possibilities. 'It's not an uncommon name as I think I told you and birth dates weren't always recorded accurately in those days but I managed to narrow it down and I'm pretty sure this is our man.' Maggie drew in a sharp breath.

'That's marvellous.' Her voice squeaked with excitement.

Calum laid out the family tree he had compiled on his desk and went through it with them.

'His place of birth is given as the Isle of Mull which is why I couldn't find him in the local records and, as you can see, both the dates of birth and death match.' He paused and then went on with the air of Sherlock Holmes about to reveal the name of the murderer. 'He also had a sister called Catherine which ties in with your initial C.'

Maggie beamed at this news and she and Rachel studied the details spread out before them.

'So this Alexander MacDonald had four brothers and two sisters, one of whom was Catherine born in 1833. That would make her about nineteen if she died in 1852,' Maggie's brow furrowed in concentration, 'which would fit in with The Unknown Maid, wouldn't it? She's described as a young woman in the Parish Records I read.'

'Look at this.' Rachel pointed to the different people named on the document. 'It's so sad. The first sister, Elizabeth, died only two years old, one brother, Hamish, died before he was one, and two other brothers, Duncan and Robert, died in their teens, In fact they both died in the same year as the mother. How odd.'

'Not really.' Maggie traced the names and dates with her finger. 'I'm sure, from the research I've done so far, that year, 1847 or thereabouts, was the time of The Potato Famine. Thousands of people died of starvation or famine fever all over Scotland and this area was no exception.'

The two friends continued to scrutinize the information Calum had compiled. 'Duncan seems to have fared a little better,' Rachel observed. 'He was forty-five when he died, though of course that's still fairly young. Alexander out-lived them all. He managed to reach the grand old age of seventy-one.'

Maggie turned to Calum. 'You've got all the dates of death down here, except Catherine's. Why's that?'

'Because I couldn't find one in any of the records.'

'That could be because no-one knows when she died, couldn't it?' Maggie felt her heartbeat begin to quicken. 'And, if she's The Unknown Maid that would make sense because no-one would know it was her who was dead and so it wouldn't be recorded.' Any notion of proper grammar and syntax flew out of the window as she struggled to put her thoughts into words. 'It's got to be her.' She clapped her hands together and grinned. 'It's just got to be.'

'Possibly.'

'What do you mean, possibly?' Maggie ceased her celebration and frowned at him.

'Well, remember the initials on the rune were C.R. So if the C. is for this Catherine here,' he said indicating the family tree, 'she must have married.' He paused to make sure Maggie understood the import of what he was saying. 'So her death would have been recorded under her married name.'

Maggie felt like a child for whom Christmas has been cancelled. She had been so certain she was on the way to solving the mystery of the Maid's identity.

She sank onto a chair. 'So what happens now?' she asked in a small voice as she gazed at Calum, disappointment reflected in her whole demeanour. Rachel too looked down-hearted and moved over to put an arm comfortingly round Maggie's shoulders.

Calum smiled at them both. 'Don't give up yet. I just

have to do a search through the marriage records to see if I can find her and then, once I have her married name, I'll go through the recorded deaths again to see if she's there. If not....' He left the sentence unfinished.

'So if her married name began with R and there's no record of her death...' Rachel pondered the implications of what Calum was saying, 'it's probably her, The Unknown Maid?'

'I should say it's almost definitely her,' Calum replied firmly.

Maggie's head was spinning. She needed to get some fresh air and think this latest development through. She rose from her chair and her thanks to Calum for all his efforts were heart-felt. She was somewhat cheered when he promised to do the searches he had outlined that afternoon. Rachel invited him to join them for Maggie's birthday celebrations and give them any further news.

'I'll look forward to it.' He grinned. 'See you both later.'

Maggie didn't mention that Bridie would be there too. It would give her the chance to see how they were in each other's company, she thought. She definitely had her suspicions there was romance in the air.

'Why are you looking so pleased with yourself?' Rachel asked. 'A moment ago you looked as though someone had stolen your sweeties.'

'I've just decided to be optimistic that's all. If anyone can find the truth I'm sure Calum can. Come on, let's go home and get ready for tonight. I've a feeling I'm really going to enjoy this birthday.'

CHAPTER 15

The Inn was beginning to fill up by the time they arrived that evening, having driven down from the cottage in Rachel's hire car.

'You can't not have a drink, or several if you want to, tonight of all nights' Rachel had insisted earlier as they were getting ready. 'I don't mind sticking to just one glass of wine so I can drive back. Besides, I want to keep my wits about me so I can properly assess whether this Angus of yours is worthy of you.' She ducked, laughing as Maggie threw a cushion at her.

Now, as they walked in, they saw Bridie sitting at the bar chatting to Caitlin. She waved on seeing them and called, 'Be over in a minute.' There was a crackling wood fire burning in the hearth and Maggie thought again what a warm, friendly atmosphere the place had; she didn't think it was entirely down to the décor either. Several of the small tables were already occupied, and she and Rachel headed for one by the fireplace. After a few moments Bridie came over, bringing with her three glasses of wine.

'Happy Birthday, Maggie,' she said raising her glass, Rachel joining her in the toast.

Bridie handed Maggie a packet prettily tied up with ribbons and bows with instructions not to open it until she got home. Maggie was touched; she knew the gift, whatever it was, would have been chosen with care. She and Rachel had just finished telling her what Calum had discovered about Alexander MacDonald when the door opened and Angus walked in.

He was not alone, however. By his side was a small, slender woman with bright blonde hair cut and shaped so it looked as though she was wearing a golden cap. She was clinging to his arm with a proprietary air. Maggie glanced up when she heard the door go thinking it might be Calum. Her heart gave an unfamiliar leap when she caught sight of Angus but then felt as if it had gone into free-fall down to the pit of her stomach when she saw he was with someone. She couldn't help a little 'Oh!' of surprise escaping her. Rachel and Bridie turned together to see what had caused it.

'Ah the charming and... apparently two-timing Angus I believe.' Rachel scowled in his direction.

Bridie shook her head. 'That's Isobel Duncan. She's always latching on to him at every opportunity.' She turned to Maggie. 'You remember I told you the school teacher was sweet on him, well that's her. Angus isn't interested but she won't accept it. I know he's trying to be kind and not hurt her feelings but I really think he's going to have to spell it out for her. 'Hi, there, Angus,' she called loudly raising her arm and motioning him over.

He turned and said something to the woman at his side and then gently disengaged her arm. Pursing her lips and, sending a frosty glance in their direction, she spun on her heels and sashayed her way towards the bar swinging her hips; just like a film starlet trying to attract the eye of a casting director, Maggie thought, and then mentally chastised herself for making such a snap judgement... after all she didn't know the woman.

She turned her attention back to Angus and watched as he approached their table, her nerve ends dancing and her heart beating a little faster than normal. His craggy features and disarming, slightly crooked smile made him appear every inch the vigorous, uncompromising man she sensed him to be as he strode towards them. His welcoming glance swept over the three women and then his eyes locked on Maggie's. She saw the warmth of feeling deepen as they held her gaze and felt a tell-tale rosy hue beginning to stain her cheeks. Unless she was very careful, she reflected, those eyes of his and the languid charm he exuded were going to undermine her resolve to keep her distance. She clasped her hands together tightly under the table to stop herself from reaching out to touch him.

Striving to keep her voice light and emotionless she said, 'Hello there, Angus. I believe you may already know my friend, Rachel?'

'Hello. It's nice to see you again.' Angus said, nodding in Rachel's direction.

He remembered Rachel from her previous visits to the Inn. Lovely-looking, he thought now, admiring the willowy figure, strawberry-blonde hair and penetrating, steel-grey eyes which were currently examining him with undisguised interest. Obviously hers had been the car parked outside the cottage last night. He had driven over to see if he could change Maggie's mind about not wanting to take things between them any further and had been both annoyed and curious when his plans were frustrated.

His gaze swept back to Maggie. She looked vivacious and happy, he thought. Her eyes were shining, her face flushed and she seemed more at ease than he'd ever seen her. The red top she wore certainly suited her, making her hair seem darker and more lustrous. He remembered the silken feel of it in his fingers and the taste of her mouth on his. Quickly he brought his thoughts back to the present; Bridie had told him the reason they were all here tonight.

'I understand "Happy Birthday" is in order,' he said smiling and, before Maggie knew what was happening, he leaned over and swiftly brushed his lips over hers. 'Happy Birthday, Maggie,' he whispered in her ear.

He stood back, nonchalantly hooking his thumbs in the pockets of his jeans, trying to ignore the hot, fierce jolt which had assaulted his senses when he'd felt her warm, full mouth under his.

Maggie sat open-mouthed, unsure whether she was more

shocked he had kissed her in full view of everyone or at the swift burst of excitement which had raced through her at his touch.

'We've another cause for celebration tonight as well,' Angus announced. 'My sister, Ailsa, arrived this afternoon to tell us she's engaged to be married.'

'That's wonderful news.' Bridie clapped her hands together in delight. 'It's to Archie Ogilvie, I suppose?' She turned to the other women and explained. 'Archie plays the bodhran and the whistle in the same Celtic music group as Ailsa. They've been going together for some time.' She looked back at Angus. 'So we can look forward to a lively evening tonight then Angus,' she said smiling broadly, 'lots of singing and fiddle playing?'

'Aye, that'll be right.' He smiled back. 'We'll make a great night of it. Anyway, I'm working so I have to get behind the bar,' and with a quick, 'See you later ladies,' he turned and sauntered off.

'Wow!' Rachel breathed, glancing at Maggie who was gazing after Angus with a bemused look on her face.

Maggie twisted round to look at her friend. 'What?' she frowned, inwardly struggling to make sense of her confused feelings.

'Nothing,' Rachel said grinning, 'just Wow!'

Maggie was saved from further comment by the appearance of Calum at their table. Bridie's face gave her away, thought Maggie, putting aside consideration of her own tangled emotions as she observed her friend's reaction to his arrival. Bridie's eyes danced and her lips curved into a happy smile as Calum greeted them all warmly. His attention, however, kept wandering to Bridie. So she was right, Maggie mused, pleased at her own perspicacity, there was obviously some attachment between them.

Maggie was about to ask him if he'd found out anything more about Catherine MacDonald, when he answered her unspoken question.

'I'm still searching,' he said when he saw her raised eyebrows. 'It takes time, I'm afraid. Now, who's for another drink?'

It was a wonderful evening. Maggie couldn't remember a time when she'd enjoyed herself more. The newly-engaged couple was regaled by all and sundry with congratulations, several drinks and some dubious advice on marriage which brought a huge roar of raucous laughter from the assembled company. Then, in response to numerous, vociferous requests, they played an assortment of spirited tunes which set feet tapping, heads nodding and fingers drumming in time to the music.

How wonderful to have such talent, Maggie thought, mesmerized as Ailsa's nimble fingers flew up and down the fiddle selecting the notes whilst, with her other hand, she made the bow dance across the strings. Interspersed among the livelier reels and jigs were a few slower and more doleful melodies and Ailsa's voice, so clear and pure in tone, accompanied only by the haunting notes of Archie's whistle which seemed to hang on the air like drops of pure silver, left Maggie dreamy-eyed.

As the notes of the final tune lingered in the air before being swamped by appreciative cheering and clapping accompanied by the wild stamping of feet, Maggie felt a hand at her elbow. She turned to see Angus leaning down towards her. Thinking he intended to kiss her again, she shrank back. She did not want to be further embarrassed in front of her friends, not to mention a bar crowded with people. *How dare he presume he can take such liberties,* she thought and glared at him. She felt him stiffen beside her. His fingers tightened on her arm.

'Don't panic, Maggie, I'm not going to kiss you again.' His voice was clipped and cold as he continued, 'I just thought you might like to meet my sister.' She looked up at him. His eyes were dark with annoyance and his mouth a taut line.

Her momentary irritation melted away and she jumped up. She had hurt his feelings and she had not meant to do that.

'I'm sorry, Angus.' She cast around for an excuse

for her reaction. 'I was still so lost in the amazing music I didn't realise you were there,' and she gave him a dazzling smile. 'I'd love to meet Ailsa and tell her how much I admired her playing and singing this evening.' He eyed her uncertainly for a moment and then grinned back, obviously accepting her explanation.

As soon as she met her, Maggie saw the likeness to Angus and Caitlin, but where they were both dark Ailsa was fair with light blue eyes. Maggie liked her immediately. She was chatty and outgoing, full of plans for her and Archie's future. A skinny, young man with eyes and ears for no-one but his new fiancée, he never moved from her side. *How wonderful*, Maggie thought, *to be so in love*. A fleeting stab of envy struck her as she wondered if she would ever experience such a thing. No, she thought to herself, it was better to avoid love altogether, at least that way she would not get hurt again.

By the time Maggie and Rachel got back to the cottage it was past midnight. 'Well, despite my initial impression, I think I approve of your Angus.' Rachel said, hugging her friend.

'For the umpteenth time he's not *my* Angus.' Maggie pulled away and scowled at her friend.

'Oh, I think you'll find he is.' Rachel laughed, as she eased off her shoes.

Maggie stared at her. 'What do you mean?'

'I mean, you ninny, he's yours for the asking. Every time I glanced at him tonight he was watching you.'

'But…..' Maggie bit her bottom lip, and then raised her chin stubbornly, 'but I'm not sure if I even like him and I'm certainly not looking to fall in love again in a hurry.'

'Love, pooh! Love's over-rated if you ask me. Angus seems nice enough so just enjoy yourself and have a good time. I'm not suggesting you should marry the guy for goodness sake. Look what happened the last time you tried that.' Rachel saw her friend's stricken face and immediately her hand flew to her mouth.

'Oh God, Maggie, I'm sorry. Me and my big mouth!

I didn't mean it the way it sounded.'

She rushed over to grab her friend by the shoulders. 'I didn't mean it, truly.' She looked so mortified Maggie couldn't help but smile.

'It's alright. I know what you're saying. I just don't know whether I'm quite ready yet to give up on love.' Despite her previous vows not to get romantically involved again, she realised that deep down she still hoped for someone to come along who would fit in with her plans for a safe, comfortable future.

'I just think it might be therapeutic for you to have a bit of fun for a change. It might be good for you.'

Maggie laughed out loud. 'A love affair as therapy? Now there's an interesting idea. I'll have to think about that!'

'Well, who knows? It could work. Anyway, I'm off to bed. All this good, clean, Scottish air makes me sleepy. Are you coming too?'

Maggie nodded and the two women made their way up the stairs. Halfway up the stairway, Rachel paused and looked over her shoulder at Maggie. 'Oh by the way, speaking of affairs, I knew I had something else to tell you. Ben is back.'

Maggie stopped in her tracks. She felt, for a moment, as if she couldn't breathe and willed herself to be calm. Finally she found her voice though it shook a little as she said, 'How do you know? Have you seen him?'

'No, Sally Norwood told me. You know, she's going out with Graham from Ben's office, she said he was back at work. Apparently things haven't worked out with what's-her- name.'

'Sarah,' Maggie murmured. 'Her name's Sarah.'

'Are you okay?' Rachel made as if to move down to where Maggie stood, but Maggie motioned for her to go on.

'I'm fine, really. I'm just surprised. The … er … the Honeymoon was booked for three weeks that's all. I thought he would still be away…' her voice trailed away. All at once she felt bone weary. 'Go on, let's get to bed and get some sleep.'

But sleep was the last thing that came. Maggie tossed and turned as wild and whirling thoughts ambushed her mind. Eventually she abandoned the idea of sleep altogether and crept downstairs thinking a hot drink might help soothe her. She put on the kettle and busied herself getting a cup and the milk. She paced up and down the kitchen while the kettle boiled and then decided she would have wine instead. She poured herself a glass, and thought better of it. She'd had enough to drink at the Inn so she tipped it down the sink. Then she paced up and down the living room. Why was she so disturbed at the idea of Ben being back in London? What had happened between him and Sarah? Should she go back to London and see him? What about Angus and what Rachel had said? Over and over again the same questions spun round in her brain until she was exhausted, though sleep eluded her until dawn crept into the sky.

When Rachel came down in the morning she found her friend curled up in the old, leather chair, asleep at last. Eventually Maggie stirred to find Rachel standing over her with a steaming cup of coffee.

'You didn't have a good night, I take it?'

Maggie shook her head and took the proffered cup. 'I just had too much going on in my head.' She took a sip of her drink and gazed at her friend. 'I've been wondering whether I should come back with you to London and see Ben.'

'Whatever for?' Rachel stared at Maggie in disbelief. 'Have you lost your mind? He dumped you, remember? Why would you want to see him?'

'Well…I just thought perhaps we could…maybe we ought to talk about what happened. Perhaps I was too hasty rushing up here. I don't know what to do.' She sat there uncertain and miserable, clutching her cup in both hands staring at its contents.

Rachel leaned forward in her chair. Her tone softened. 'For heaven's sake, Maggie, it's over. Why try and resurrect something that's dead and done with?'

'I just thought......' Maggie paused and sighed deeply. What had she thought? She wasn't even sure. 'I suppose I thought it might settle things between us. You know...' her voice tailed away and she looked up at her friend. 'I expect you're right though. There's no going back is there? It's finished.'

The two friends spent the rest of the morning quietly, pottering around the cottage and chatting. They avoided any further discussion of Ben or Angus, speculating instead about The Unknown Maid.

'I wonder what she was doing out here all alone?' Maggie mused as she fastened the two pieces of rowan wood she had got from the garden into the shape of a cross with Bridie's red thread. 'She was obviously far away from her home since no-one in Invershee recognized her.'

'Maybe she was looking for someone or something.' Rachel watched as her friend tapped a nail into the lintel above the back door and hung up the rowan cross. 'And another thing, don't you think it's strange such a young woman should die like that? Unless she was ill of course, or maybe she died of hyperthermia.'

'I wouldn't have thought hyperthermia was likely.' Maggie smiled as she got down off the stool on which she had been standing. 'I know it gets pretty cold in Scotland at times but she died at the end of October don't forget, not in the middle of winter. No, I think it was more than possible she starved to death, given the times.'

Both women stood silent for a moment pondering on the Maid and her untimely and lonely death on the hillside.

After a quick lunch Rachel prepared to leave. She had a two and a half hour drive ahead of her and then an early evening flight back to London. The two women hugged and Maggie promised to keep her friend up to date with any progress she made. She stood waving Rachel off, feeling a little lost and alone as she watched the back of the hire car disappear from view. She gave a heavy sigh and turned to go back into the cottage. She glanced up at the rowan cross above her head as she went through the doorway. Would it protect her she wondered if the woman in grey did mean her harm as Bridie had suggested?

CHAPTER 16

Maggie found it impossible to settle once Rachel had gone. She wandered aimlessly round the cottage. Strange, she reflected, she had been perfectly content with her own company before Rachel's visit but now she felt restless and ill-at-ease. Several times she found herself glancing through the window at the hillside wondering whether the woman in grey would put in an appearance but there was no sign of her. Finally, she decided that moping around was not doing her any good and a brisk walk would help to clear her mind.

Picking up her jacket from the chair where she had casually discarded it the night before, she saw Bridie's unopened present. Carefully she undid the bows and, smoothing out the creases, she put the folded ribbons to one side. Apart from satisfying her need for neatness and order, it prolonged the anticipation and excitement of opening the package and, to her, delaying that moment of discovery, of wondering what lay hidden beneath the wrapping was part of the joy of receiving a gift. It was a habit which always irritated her mother.

'For Heaven's sake, Maggie, do you always have to be so fussy and meticulous,' she would say. 'Open the damn parcel.'

Now she pulled apart the paper to find one of Bridie's own delicate water-colours. Maggie gazed at it with pleasure. Bridie had inscribed the name of the plant, "Oak-leaved Geranium" in fine, black ink beneath the drawing of dainty, pink flower clusters surrounded by dark green leaves on a single stem. Maggie marvelled at the detail and sensitivity with which the whole had been executed. Then she saw the note pinned to the back of the picture:

"Dearest Maggie," she read, *"In the Language of*

Flowers the oak-leaved Geranium is the symbol for true friendship, and I believe that is what we have. I hope you do too. Happy Birthday, Love Bridie."

Maggie had a lump in her throat as she propped the picture carefully on the mantelshelf and stood back to admire it some more. She knew exactly where she would hang it when she returned to her flat in London.

All at once she felt cold. The temperature in the room had dropped by several degrees as if someone had sucked all the heat from it. She clasped her arms across her chest and stood completely still, holding her breath. *The woman in grey's here in this room.* The words repeated over and over in her head like a mantra. She drew in a deep breath and fought the hot panic balling in her stomach. She stood absolutely still and then, steeling herself, she slowly turned her head and looked around. There was nothing to be seen, no ghostly figure waited in the shadows, everywhere looked the same as usual.

The silence was absolute; Maggie noticed even the clock had stopped ticking. And then she heard it, the soft swish of material as if someone in a long dress was moving about the room. She felt icy shivers running up and down her spine and she began to shake. Her breath came in ragged gasps and her fingers dug deep into her upper arms.

'Who....who's there?' she managed in a strangled whisper.

The swishing sound stopped, and Maggie could hear her own heartbeat drumming loudly in her ears. There was a slight movement of the air in front of her as if someone had walked past. Maggie shrank back. The fear she had so far been able to contain stirred again in her belly. Just as the scream rose in her throat, she sensed the atmosphere change. Slowly, the air in the room began to grow warmer and Maggie knew the woman in grey was gone.

Letting out a long sigh, she sank down onto the floor and clasped her arms around her legs, resting her head on her knees. She forced herself to take slow, calming breaths and gradually her heartbeat returned to normal. After a few moments, she got to her feet and went into the kitchen. A hot drink would help to steady her, she thought. Later, as she sat at the kitchen table with a cup of coffee, she reviewed what had happened. For a moment she considered whether she might have had some sort of hallucination but in her heart of hearts she knew she had just had another supernatural visitation. *What on earth does she want from me?* The question rumbled around and around in her brain, but she had no answer.

Tired of thinking about it and wanting to clear her head, she slung her jacket over her shoulders and left the cottage, which, all at once, felt small and claustrophobic. She would tell Bridie about this latest happening when she next saw her but in the meantime, she would put it to the back of her mind. What she needed now, Maggie thought, was lots of fresh air and a change of scene.

The stroll down to the village refreshed her somewhat and she began to feel calmer. The sky, which had been rather overcast, was now brightening up and she could see patches of blue here and there... *Enough to make a pair of trousers for a sailor* her father used to say to convince her that a dismal day would soon see some sunshine. She smiled at the memory.

The tide was out when she reached the loch-side. She had not realised Loch Shee was a sea loch and so subject to the same laws of gravity as the sea itself. She was amazed at how far the water had receded and at the large expanse of shore-line uncovered; rocky and stony in some places, smooth and sandy in others, with great skeins of seaweed like strings of tangled knitting wool forsaken and exposed until the tide turned. Jumping down from the road onto the shore, she began to pick her way across the tidal detritus towards the distant water. She stopped now and again to examine a shell or turn over a stone, tutting at the odd abandoned bottle or discarded plastic container and giving a wide berth to several stranded jelly-fish.

She stood looking out over the loch, recalling happy times on days out to the seaside with her father; her mother never went with them on these outings - she was always too busy, or rushing to meet a friend for lunch, or maybe just resting…too tired, she'd say… and besides, she hated the way sand got into everything.

The photograph Maggie treasured, the one showing her laughing with her father, had been taken on such a day. She thought she remembered him asking a passer-by to snap them. She had brought it with her from London and it now stood on her bedside table at the cottage. She thought that that was probably the last time she had ever been truly happy; a time and an emotion frozen forever in a silver frame.

Lost in her memories, she didn't hear the approaching footsteps. Suddenly a stone went skimming over the surface of the water in front of her and startled she turned to see Angus bending down searching for another to send after it.

'I used to be really good at this when I was a boy. I think the best I ever did was eight skips in one go.' He smoothed his fingers over the pebble he held and then sent it flying after the first one, counting as it skipped along before sinking. 'Only five that time. I'm a bit out of practice it seems'

Maggie laughed. 'My record is ten and I bet I can manage more than five any day.' She raised her chin and her eyes challenged him to test her claim.

'Right, you're on,' he nodded grinning broadly. 'Loser buys the coffee.'

Sometime later, having declared the contest an honourable draw …Maggie wasn't about to admit that her sixth, equalling Angus's score had been a fluke …they wandered slowly back towards the Inn.

'Who taught you to do that?'

'What?' Maggie turned towards him, a slight frown creasing her brow. 'Oh, my father.'

Angus saw a sudden flicker of pain darken her eyes.

'Tell me about him,' he said simply.

So she did.

She told him how alone and unhappy she had been when her father left her and her mother, how grief-stricken when he was killed. 'And I felt so angry too. It was as if he'd left me twice, and there was no way to put things right because he died. I've never been able to understand why he didn't take me with him. Maybe he didn't want to be saddled with a young child, or maybe.... he just didn't love me enough,' she added in small voice.

As if sensing her distress, Angus reached out and pulled gently towards him. He held her close, saying nothing. They stood like that for several minutes.

Maggie found comfort in the strength and protection of his arms around her until finally, she sighed deeply and murmured, 'Thank-you Angus, I needed that,' and touched her lips softly to his cheek. They broke apart, Maggie feeling slightly embarrassed, thinking he might see her as some kind of needy female. She caught the look of relief on his face that she appeared to have regained her composure.

'I think we could both do with that coffee now. Why don't you come up to the flat and I'll make us one?'

Maggie's eyebrows shot up. 'Flat? I thought we'd be having coffee in the bar.'

'Well, we can if you'd rather but I thought we'd have more privacy upstairs. I've a few rooms of my own on the top floor. It makes sense for me to live over the shop, so to speak, for security and of course it's convenient.' He flashed his lopsided smile. 'We could talk a little more. Get to know each other a little better. What do you say?'

Maggie hesitated. Could she trust him? More to the point, could she trust herself to be alone with him given her reaction to him when they'd kissed the other day? But she had to admit she was curious. Perhaps if she saw where he lived, she reasoned, she'd learn a little more about the kind of man he was, and then she might find it easier to decide whether or not she wanted to get involved with him.

Angus must have seen her uncertainty. Gently he

cupped her face in his hands and looked into her eyes. 'I promise I'll behave, Maggie. No stealing kisses. I'll be a perfect gentleman.'

Curiosity won. Maggie felt reassured by the obvious sincerity in his voice. 'That would be nice,' she agreed.

Angus led her down the side of the Inn and through a door set into the side wall. 'We could have gone through the bar but I thought you'd prefer using my private entrance. This way we won't set any tongues wagging. It doesn't take much in this village to start the gossip-mongers.'

At the top of a set of stairs, Angus flung open a door and said casually, 'Here we are, make yourself at home and I'll get the coffee.' He disappeared through at door at the far end of the room, to the kitchen she presumed.

Maggie did not know what she had been expecting but it was not this. The room was light and airy with a large window at the far end overlooking the loch. She walked over to it and stood for a moment gazing out at the shore and the water. The tide was starting to come in and the gentle breeze of earlier had stiffened so that little white capped waves were now skittering across the previously calm surface. She turned and surveyed the rest of the room.

Yellow paintwork had faded to a soft ochre against dark cream walls, and a well-used, scuffed, brown three-piece leather suite was arranged in front of a marble-clad fireplace.

The few other pieces of furniture in the room were in a dark wood and looked as if they might once have belonged to Angus's parents or grandparents. Splashes of bright colour came from the patterned rugs which lay scattered here and there on the oak floorboards but it was very much a masculine room, she mused. There were no flowers or ornaments and the only picture, which looked to Maggie like one of Bridie's water-colours, hung over a large, heavy desk littered with papers pushed up against one wall.

Maggie wandered over to the open shelves ranged either side of the fireplace. They were crammed with books and she ran her fingers along their spines, scanning the titles. Her eyes widened as she saw the wide selection of literature represented: from Proust to Orwell, Robert Ludlum to Agatha Christie, the poetry of Wordsworth and that of Ted Hughes, biographies and travel books, tomes on hotel management and horse-racing, and one title which made her smile, "Accounting for Beginners," sat next to "The Complete Works of William Shakespeare." *You're certainly a man of many parts, Angus Cameron*, she thought.

She was still browsing when Angus came back with their coffee. 'You've a very eclectic taste in reading matter,' she observed turning to face him and taking the cup he offered.

'After a long day in the bar, I find it relaxing to read for an hour or two before I go to bed.' He motioned for her to sit down and then followed suit. He grinned. 'It's one of the few pleasures I have. We won't go into what the others might be…for the moment,' and he leered at her in such a grotesquely comical way she couldn't help but laugh out loud. She took an appreciative sip of her coffee.

'How come you're here in Invershee, Angus, running a hotel cum local bar?' She knew most of his family history of course from Jessie Ferguson but she listened again as he told her about his parents' deaths and about his three sisters.

'They do say it's a painless way to die,' he said, speaking of his father…who, Angus told her, had frozen to death in a ditch one winter's night after rather more than one too many drinks. 'You just go to sleep and don't wake up again but it's pretty painful for the people left behind let me tell you.' He paused and nodded towards her, 'Sorry! Of course you know what I'm talking about. So Ma was left to run this place on her own as well as bring up four children. When I was old enough I helped her as much as I could until she got ill and then I took over.'

Maggie watched the changing emotions in his expression as he talked; there was sadness yet also some anger when he spoke of his father's unnecessary death, and she reached out a hand to touch his. He held on to it as he talked of his mother's illness and she saw the guilt he still felt as well as the relief when the end to her suffering had come. 'She fought so hard, Maggie,' he said simply and she squeezed his hand in sympathy.

When he spoke about his sisters his face became animated and his eyes softened. They obviously meant a great deal to him and shared a closeness she envied. Would her life have been different if she'd had siblings, she wondered. She focused again on what he was saying as he told her of his plans for the future of the Inn. His enthusiasm was infectious and she found herself nodding and uttering words of encouragement as he outlined his proposals to develop it into a five star hotel whilst retaining its popular appeal.

'That sounds wonderful, Angus, I'm certain it'll be a great success.' She stirred in her chair. 'Anyway, thanks for the coffee but I'd better be going. I've been here ages and I'm sure you must have things to do.' She smiled warmly at him and started to rise.

'But we haven't talked about where you and I go from here yet,' he said firmly.

She sank back as a fleeting moment of panic washed over her; *He wants more than friendship and I'm not ready for that.*

She gazed at him, wide-eyed. 'What do you mean, where we go from here?'

'Come on, Maggie, you know perfectly well what I mean. That kiss we shared wasn't just any old kiss. You know it and I know it. There's something between us and I for one want to find out where it'll take us.'

She looked down at her hands. She was still holding her empty coffee cup and began to turn it round and round as if her actions were keeping pace with the thoughts spinning around in her head. Angus leaned forward and gently took it from her, placing it on the hearth beside his own.

'What is it, Maggie? Are you going to tell me I've got it wrong? That you don't feel something too?'

Maggie looked up and met his steady gaze. His eyes were serious but his mouth was set in a half smile as if he knew she could not deny the chemistry between them. The least he deserved, she thought, was total honesty.

'I'm not going to lie to you Angus. Of course the kiss meant something to me. I think you're perfectly well aware of how much it meant.' She felt the colour rise in her face at the memory of how easily she had surrendered to him and how much more she would have given had he asked. 'I just can't get involved with you that's all.'

She saw the temper flare in his eyes and his hands ball into fists. His voice was ominously quiet.

'Can't or won't, Maggie?'

She bit her lip and then abruptly, in a voice rough with emotion, she told him about Ben leaving her shortly before their wedding and how she had no wish to subject herself to that kind of humiliation and hurt again.

'So I suppose the answer to your question is I *won't* have a relationship with you.' She raised her chin and looked at him defiantly.

Angus could see she was near to tears and a torrent of emotion stormed through him. What was it about her which so exhilarated and captivated him he wondered as he watched her fight for control of the feelings that swamped her. He didn't have an answer. All he knew was no women had ever reached him as Maggie had, no woman had touched him in the way she had and there was no way he was going to let her go. He smiled wryly; this from someone who'd avoided, dodged and positively run away from commitment all his life.

He felt a quick chill of apprehension. If he was not careful he could lose her. He had to handle this the right way. He forced the tension from his body and, moving swiftly before she could get up from her chair, he crouched down before her. He took both of her hands in his and keeping his voice light and soothing he said, 'I'm not Ben, Maggie. I'd never hurt you like that.'

His response took her by surprise. She'd expected he would be irritated, annoyed, maybe even angry, but this tenderness and understanding was totally bewildering and she felt herself weakening. Her heart was beating in her throat and the tears which had been close now threatened to brim over. She took a deep breath and tried to keep her voice steady. 'I know that, Angus and I know you wouldn't mean to hurt me but everyone I've ever loved has left me and I don't think I can face that again.'

Now she was being ridiculous Angus thought. He felt like shaking some sense into her but he kept a tight rein on his feelings and said mildly, 'I can't promise you things will work out between us, Maggie, but at least let's give it a try. We can take things as slowly as you want and if, at any time, you feel it's not working we can say goodbye with no hard feelings. What do you say?'

He looked so like a little boy pleading to be allowed to stay up beyond his normal bed-time that she couldn't help but smile.

She raised her eyebrows. 'What do you suggest?'

'Well, how about if you came down to the Inn of a night-time then we could sit and talk when the bar's not busy. That way we'll get to know each other a lot better and you'll have the chance to make up your mind whether or not to trust me.'

Maggie's eyes searched his face and she saw the frankness there. How could she refuse when he was trying so hard to be reasonable? 'Alright, I'm willing to do that and see what happens.'

He leaned forward and gently brushed a stray hair from her face. 'I'll see you tomorrow night then,' he said softly, kissing her gently on the forehead as he led her towards the door.

As it closed behind her, Angus sat back down and grinned. He was glad he had given in to the impulse to join her on the shore. He had happened to glance out of the front window of the Inn earlier and saw her wandering there, such a forlorn figure that he had abandoned his morning tasks and gone after her. And now he was pleased with the outcome of his strategy; soft words and gentleness had reaped a better reward than anger and shouting would have done... it was a lesson to be learned for the future.

CHAPTER 17

As Maggie walked away from the Inn she wondered how she could have been so easily persuaded to agree to Angus's proposition. Now, despite her determination not to let her attraction to him cloud her judgement, she had promised to see him every night. She sighed. Perhaps she should adopt Bridie's philosophy; what was meant to be would be. Thinking of Bridie, she turned towards her shop and found her rearranging shelves, singing softly as she did so.

'I think that's eminently sensible,' she said when Maggie told her of her arrangement with Angus. 'It'll give you both a chance to spend some time together without the spectre of S-E-X' – she spelt out the word, rolling her eyes as she did so …'and Should I? Shouldn't I? hovering in the background all the time.' She eyed Maggie thoughtfully. 'I'm surprised Angus agreed to it.'

'It was Angus's idea.'

'My word!'

Maggie smiled at the other woman's astonished expression.

Bridie was silent for a moment and then went on, 'Anyway, I've got some news for you too. I've spoken to Murdo Ferguson. The postmaster,' she added, seeing the blank look on Maggie's face.

'Oh, yes?'

'He's offered to let you have a look at the archive this evening if it suits you. I thought I might come too if you don't mind. I'd be really interested to have a rummage through whatever's there.'

Maggie's eyes lit up. 'That'd be great, Bridie. It'll be better two of us looking through it so we don't miss anything……that is, if there's anything to miss.' Her face clouded over as she realised how much she was pinning her hopes on finding something significant in all the historical memorabilia, something which might help her to put a name to the Maid. She frowned. 'What if we don't find anything?'

'Come on Maggie, let's not give up before we've started,' Bridie said.

'I know.' Maggie took a deep breath. 'By the way, I've had another visit from the woman in grey,' and as calmly as she could she told Bridie of her recent experience.

'Oh dear. Are you all right?' Bridie had obviously picked up on the note of distress beneath Maggie's matter-of-fact account as she moved to give her a warm hug. 'She's certainly getting more active. I wonder why.' She rubbed her hands up and down Maggie's arms and then stood back to observe her friend. 'Really, are you okay?'

Maggie nodded. 'I was pretty scared at the time, but she didn't materialize or anything. I just knew she was there. I wish we could find out who she was.'

'There might be something in the archive, you never know. When we're looking through all the stuff there, for any clue about the Unknown Maid, we can keep an eye open for anything which might pertain to her as well.'

They agreed to meet later in the village and, as Maggie walked back to the cottage, she mulled over all that had happened. There was nothing more she could do about the woman in grey. Bridie was right, they might find something about her in the archive which would solve the mystery of both her and the young woman buried in the churchyard.

Her thoughts turned to Angus. She had to admit he had surprised her and she felt both excited and nervous at the prospect of their evening assignations. Was she being wise? She didn't know and, she realised, she didn't care. She was sick of being sensible so why not relax and go with it? She would drift with the current instead of trying to direct the stream. She smiled at herself. *Getting metaphysical now.* She began to jog along the track, eager to be home.

She spent the rest of the day mooching about, unable to concentrate on anything for very long. She tried to make a start on her writing about crofting but after several attempts to get her thoughts down on paper she gave it up. She read a little of the book Bridie had lent her and discovered that rowan wood was often used to make runes as well as coffin handles, and farmers would put rowan twigs over the entrance to a byre to protect the cattle within. But it was no good. She put the book to one side and glanced for the umpteenth time at the clock. Its insistent ticking marked the passing of every second, every minute but the afternoon seemed endless.

She wandered out into the garden. There was a dank gloominess to the day now and she shivered, wrapping her arms round herself to keep out the cold fingers of air which tried to steal under her clothes. She looked up at the hillside. It stretched away above her, wild, open heath-land, completely deserted. She wondered once again whether the whole thing could be a figment of her imagination. But no, Morag MacIver had seen her and there'd been the face in the mirror as well as her presence in the cottage that morning. The woman in grey was real enough alright…well as real as any ghost could be.

Maggie smiled grimly. She was going to get to the bottom of this mystery if it was the last thing she ever did. As she went back into the cottage, she reached up and touched the rowan cross above the door. *Just in case*, she thought.

The hours dragged by but finally it was time to go and meet Bridie. She drove down to the village as she didn't relish the idea of walking home alone in the dark later. Bridie was already waiting when Maggie arrived and together they made their way to Murdo Ferguson's house which was in the village opposite the green.

'You'll like Flora, Murdo's wife,' Bridie said as they approached the door. 'She's a pleasant soul. A bit quiet, but that's to be expected with Murdo around. He could talk for Scotland and then some.'

She knocked and Maggie immediately recognized the woman who let them in as the one who had served her in the village shop. Once more she had a sense of déjà-vu, as if she and Flora had met before Maggie had ever set foot inside the store. But she shrugged it away as her imagination again playing tricks on her. Greetings over, Murdo took them through the house and into the back garden where stood one of the biggest garden sheds Maggie thought she had ever seen. In fact 'garden' was probably a misnomer as the shed occupied almost all of the available space with just a very small patch of green lawn in front. She wondered if Murdo had to use clippers or even scissors to cut the grass as there didn't seem enough room to swing the proverbial cat never mind manoeuvre a lawn mower.

'This is very kind of you Mr. Ferguson,' she managed to say as he paused for breath ...he had not stopped talking since they had set foot in the house.

'It's no trouble lass though I don't know there'll be anything of any help to you. I'm afraid it's all in a bit of a muddle at the moment,' he explained as he unlocked the door.

Maggie gasped. He hadn't exaggerated. There were boxes and crates and folders of paper everywhere; on the floor, on shelves, on chairs and, she was sure, crowded into the several cupboards lined up against the walls.

'I keep thinking I should make some kind of catalogue of all that's here but I haven't been able to find the time yet, what with the post-office to run and then the cattle to see to as well as getting called out on shouts.' Maggie looked to Bridie for enlightenment.

'He has a herd of cows up on the hill,' she whispered in Maggie's ear, 'and he's a member of the local, volunteer fire-brigade.'

'And people keep giving me stuff,' Murdo went on. 'Someone dies and the family finds old photos, letters, all sorts they don't want but don't think should be thrown away so they pass them on to me.'

He flicked through a box of papers on a shelf sending dust particles scattering and then floating in the air. He turned to look at the two women who were still standing in the doorway trying to take in the jumble of accumulated local history which lay before them. 'Not that that's any bad thing you understand. It's good to preserve our history otherwise it would be lost forever.' He gave a heartfelt sigh. 'It's just a big job for one man.'

Maggie cleared her throat. 'I'd be more than willing to do that for you Mr. Ferguson. I've got plenty of free time at the moment and, as I want to look at everything here anyway, it would be easy to organise things as I go through them. I could make a list of what's here at the same time.'

'Hmm, I'm not sure if that would be in order.' He scratched his head looking her up and down as if trying to decide whether she was a fit person to be let loose amongst his treasures.

Bridie butted in. 'Come on now, Murdo. You know you could do with the help. And Maggie's got good credentials. She works in a museum you know,' she added. She put an arm round Maggie's shoulders, hugging the other woman to her as if to show the post-master she at least was confident in her friend's abilities and trustworthiness.

The mention of the word 'museum' did it. It was obvious he was impressed. Maggie was amused…she might be a cleaner there for all he knew, but the connection was enough to convince him she was a fit and responsible person and could be trusted to carry out the task she had volunteered for. So she found herself arranging to go down every day and sift through and sort out the collection of memories and artefacts which had found a home in Murdo's shed.

He left them to poke around the boxes and pry into the cupboards while he went back into the house to organise Mrs. Murdo into make them a cup of tea.

'There's an awful lot of stuff here, Maggie.' Bridie gazed doubtfully around the chaotic interior. 'It's going to take you forever to sort through it all.'

Maggie was thrilled at the prospect and was not going to be put off by anyone. 'It won't take that long,' she said firmly. She pulled a cardboard box out of a cupboard and rifled through its contents.

'Look, Bridie. There are loads of old photographs, here,' and she held up a sheaf of fading, black and white snapshots. She began studying them and then, as she turned them over, she said excitedly, 'most of these have got the names of the people in the picture on the back with a date.' Bridie joined her and the two were engrossed in studying them when Murdo came to tell them the tea was ready.

'There's a fair few of them photos and such like around,' he said, 'but I'm not sure where.' He looked around vaguely at the various boxes and cupboards. 'You'll come across them soon enough no doubt when you start going through everything.'

Maggie felt so keyed up she couldn't drink her tea without slopping most of it into the saucer. She was sure there had to be a clue to the Maid's identity in the shed. If not....no, she was not even going to consider that possibility. Anyway, whatever the outcome was, she was going to be spending time doing something she enjoyed... digging around in the past, reading old documents, handling things which had been used by earlier generations ...and she couldn't wait to get started. So for the next hour or so she and Bridie moved boxes, ferreted around in cupboards, and rooted through files.

'Right, I think I've had enough for tonight,' Bridie sighed, brushing her dusty hands over her skirt. 'At least we've managed to clear a space for you to work in and we've got a better idea of what's here and where it is. I vote we go for a drink and leave this for another day.'

Maggie saw the lines of weariness on Bridie's face and reluctantly agreed. She felt she could have stayed there all night she was so keyed up but it was probably sensible to make a proper start in the morning when she was fresh.

When they went into the Inn, the bar was busy. Angus saw them come in and waved, then carried on serving a customer as Maggie and Bridie found somewhere to sit. They were talking about the archive and how Maggie was going to set about the mammoth task of bringing order to the current chaos when Angus came over.

'Good evening, ladies.' He smiled warmly. 'I'm afraid I won't be able to join you for a drink just yet. We've a party in celebrating a birthday as you can no doubt hear.' He indicated a noisy group in the corner, 'and also several pipers back from a competition in Inverness, so I'm a little busy. However, I'd be delighted to buy you both a drink. What can I get you?'

Maggie watched him as he went back to the bar, having taken their order. 'It must be very difficult being a publican if you're a drinker.'

'That was the problem for Angus's father.' Bridie said. 'It's why Angus doesn't drink.'

'Really?' Maggie turned a surprised face to her friend.

'He's never touched a drop in all the years I've known him. I think he's worried that if he does he might end up like Alisdair.'

'He must be very strong-minded,' Maggie mused, a hint of admiration in her voice.

'Oh he's that alright. Once he's set his mind on something that's it.'

So she had been right about him, Maggie recalled thinking when she was at Jessie's he looked the type of man who did not give up until he got what he wanted. She wondered whether that was what was driving his pursuit of her; he had decided he wanted her and was determined to have her. *Well, we'll see about that*, she thought. If he imagined she was a push-over and would give in easily to sweet words and tender looks he had another think coming.

Angus didn't get the chance to join them as he was kept busy for the rest of the evening, so when she and Bridie left, Maggie just waved and mouthed, 'See you tomorrow night.' He gave a wide grin and nodded. He looks too pleased with himself, she thought, and determined that come the following evening she would be cool and distant and not allow herself to be taken in by his easy charm.

'You're looking very serious,' Bridie remarked as

Maggie drove her home.

'I'm just thinking about tomorrow and making a start on going through the archive,' Maggie fibbed. 'I'm certain there'll be something there that'll give us a clue to who the Maid is.'

If Bridie had any doubts, she kept them to herself. As Maggie watched the other woman stride up the track to her cottage, she thought how fortunate she was to have found such a good friend. She drove home still thinking about Bridie. She wondered if the burgeoning relationship between her and Calum would develop into something more serious. She hoped so.

The next few days passed quickly. Maggie spent each one in Murdo's shed sorting and reading through mountains of paper and diaries, old records and documents. She examined photographs and maps and began to organise everything into some semblance of order. She emerged at the end of each day dusty and dirty but satisfied. She had not yet discovered anything which could be linked to the Maid but she had learned a good deal about the community and its history. She still had a file of photographs and a few boxes of papers to go through by the time she reached the end of the fifth day but decided they could wait until the next morning.

She was locking up the shed when, to her surprise, Calum appeared round the corner of the house smiling broadly. 'Bridie told me I'd find you here.'

Maggie's heart skipped a beat. 'You've found her!'

'Come along with me and I'll show you.' He took hold of her hand and led her round to the surgery, refusing to answer any of her questions until they reached it. She was at such a fever-pitch of excitement she felt she could hardly breathe.

When they finally entered his consulting room, Calum pointed to a sheet of paper on his desk.

'There!' he said, unable to keep the note of triumph out of his voice.

It was a copy of a marriage certificate and Maggie

picked it up with shaking hands. It gave details of the marriage of Catherine MacDonald to one Douglas Ross, fisherman, on the sixteenth of May 1851 at Kilmore Church, Dervaig, on the Isle of Mull. Maggie could hardly believe it. This was C.R. it had to be.

'Catherine Ross.' She breathed the name softly and then, before Calum realised what was happening, she had seized hold of him and was whirling him around the room in a wild dance saying the name aloud over and over again like some kind of tribal chant.

Calum managed eventually to put a stop to her crazy cavorting by shouting in her ear. 'There's more. I've more news.'

Maggie collapsed into his desk chair, her breath coming in short gasps. Calum looked at her as if he couldn't believe this normally calm and sensible woman had just danced around his office with such reckless abandon.

When she could speak, her voice shook. 'Please, please don't tell me it's not her.' She looked up at him wide-eyed.

'No, no, I'm not going to tell you that. I'm absolutely certain it is her. Also I haven't been able to find any record of her death. There's nothing in any of the records I've been able to unearth, and I've been pretty thorough, that gives a date of death.' He paused for a moment as if uncertain how Maggie would react to the next piece of information he had unearthed. 'There is a record of her husband's death, however. He died in December 1851. It seems he was lost at sea.'

Maggie eyes filled with tears. The poor girl, she thought, a few months married, widowed and then dying alone the following year on a lonely hillside. It was too much to bear. She gave an involuntary sob and the tears streamed down her face. Calum was immediately alarmed. He was good at dealing with all sorts of physical ailments but a woman's tears, especially from one who had always appeared so in control …apart from a few moments ago of course when she was prancing around his office like a wild thing…were beyond him. He stood there looking at a loss as if wondering what would be the best thing to do. Maggie, seeing the look of apprehension on his face, managed a watery smile.

'Don't worry Calum, I'm okay. It's just it's all so heart-breaking.' She took a deep breath and tried to pull herself together as he silently handed her a box of tissues. 'Thank-you so much for all you've done. I really appreciate all your hard work. It must have taken hours.'

'It was no trouble. I've really enjoyed it. It's been fascinating and maybe at last we've solved an age-old local mystery.' He hesitated and eyed her as though speculating whether or not to relate his other piece of news.

Maggie saw the look. 'What is it Calum? Is there something else?'

'Well, I'm not sure, but…'

'Come on, what is it?' She had a feeling that what he was about to say was of the utmost importance. 'Come on, tell me,' she demanded, sitting upright, all attention.

'It's just that…' he paused again and Maggie bit her lip in frustration. 'You have to understand I've been through so many records that I could be mistaken, but somewhere at the back of my mind I'm pretty sure I've seen those two names together before. Not on the marriage certificate but somewhere else.'

Maggie stared at him. 'What, Catherine and Douglas Ross?'

Calum nodded. 'I think I might have come across them when I first started searching the birth records. The names in themselves aren't that unusual but….' He stopped and frowned. Then he continued, speaking slowly, as if weighing every word. 'It's something I need to check out, but I think it's possible they may have had a child.'

Maggie's jaw dropped open and she gazed at him speechless. It was the last thing she had expected him say. She put her fingers up to her head and began massaging her temples, feeling the sharp spikes of pain which heralded the onset of a headache. She struggled to make sense of what

Calum had just said. It was no good, she needed to go away and think things through calmly. She left the surgery after thanking him again for all his efforts and having secured his promise he would tell her the minute he found out anything more.

She walked slowly along the loch-side trying to get her spinning thoughts under some sort of control. It now seemed beyond doubt that Catherine Ross was the Unknown Maid. But how it had come about she had ended up on the hillside behind Tigh-na-Bruach was still a mystery. And, if she and Douglas had had a child, what had become of him or her?

CHAPTER 18

Maggie was still puzzling over the questions Calum's research had raised when she realised she had arrived home. She had been so engrossed she hadn't even noticed she had left the village. She glanced up at the hill as she invariably did when she was outside the cottage and was relieved there was no a sign of anyone or anything.

Later, having eaten, changed and determinedly put all thoughts of Catherine Ross out of her mind, Maggie drove back down to the village to see Angus. She had enjoyed their meetings over the past few nights and felt she was beginning to know him better. He was forthright in his opinions but listened to hers with interest. He had a wry sense of humour, did not suffer fools gladly and, though he could be sarcastic, he also had a sympathetic side to his nature. They were very alike in lots of ways she mused, except for his taste in music… *How could any sane person enjoy Rock and Roll?* Nor could she deny there was a strong physical attraction between them but she had kept to the promise she had made herself to remain composed and a little off-hand during their conversations.

Tonight, however, she was going to ease up and perhaps even indulge in a little flirting. Maybe she had been too hasty in holding back and it was time to move their relationship forward. Thinking of him now, her pulse began to accelerate and she had a sudden longing to be held close again, to have him kiss her and touch her and make her lose control as she so nearly had that first time.

So, with a light step and a quickened heartbeat, she pushed open the door and stepped into the Inn. The first person she saw was Isobel Duncan. She was perched on a stool at the bar, her long legs swinging provocatively and her gaze fixed on Angus who was leaning towards her. His back was to Maggie and she could see the other woman's face, mouth half open, tongue flicking in and out moistening her parted lips, her eyes full of undisguised longing. She reminded Maggie of a boa-constrictor she had once seen on a wild life programme on television just before it stretched its huge jaws to swallow down a fully-grown antelope. Neither of them had noticed her.

She went and sat quietly at a table near the fire which had already been lit now the evenings were becoming cooler as the nights drew in. She watched Isobel lean forward and put a possessive hand on Angus's arm. He stood back and said something to her which made Isobel drop her eyes and move her hand. For a moment she sat twisting her fingers and then jumped down from the stool and stormed out of the door, her face a picture of misery.

Maggie almost felt sorry for her. Angus clearly had not made a very good job of letting her down lightly. He stood at the bar for a moment or two, probably thinking he should have handled things better, Maggie guessed. Then he turned and glanced around the room. She saw his expression change the moment he caught sight of her. His face split into a wide grin and he strode over towards her.

He caught hold of her hands. 'It's really good to see you. Maggie,' he said his voice low and throaty.

She returned his gaze steadily as the treacherous colour crept up her cheeks. 'You too, Angus,' she murmured.

How on earth could she have denied it for so long she wondered as she stared into those warm, brown eyes and felt the blood heating up in her veins. She was falling in love with him and, shocked at the realization, she pulled her hands free of his. He mustn't know she thought, as she tried to maintain her composure. This was her problem and she would have to deal with it as best she could. She didn't want to be in love with him; love made you vulnerable and besides, it hurt too much.

She saw Angus look more and more confused as the evening wore on as if he sensed her change of mood. For a while their conversation was desultory and half-hearted.

She knew the fault was hers as she struggled to come to terms with her emotions but there was no way she could tell him her true feelings. Finally, he leaned towards her, his face anxious.

'What is it Maggie? What's wrong?'

She needed to go home and think things through, to work out what she was going to do, if anything, about their future relationship. 'I'm sorry, Angus,' she said, 'I'm going to have to go home. I've got the most dreadful headache.'

He was immediately all concern but Maggie refused his offer of a lift home saying she had her car and would be able to drive herself the short distance to the cottage.

'It's probably pouring over those old documents all day that's brought it on. I'll be okay after a good night's sleep.'

After her first day at the archive she had told him she was helping to sort it out and catalogue everything in it and had also mentioned she hoped to find something which would help to solve the local mystery of the Unknown Maid.

'I shouldn't think that's very likely after all this time,' he'd said dismissively.

'Well, I'm enjoying it and it'll keep me out of mischief,' she had retorted and laughed when he suggested he would be happy for her to be involved in some mischief as long as it was with him.

Now she took her leave, promising to see him the next evening as usual. When she arrived back at the cottage she was not at all surprised to find the headache she had invented had become a reality. Her head throbbed, her thoughts were muddled and her heart was aching. If this was love, she reflected, she could do without it.

She dreamed that night of Ben and Angus.

Ben was walking towards her, his arms laden with lilies

and chocolates and jewellery. Then Angus appeared and swept away the gifts which turned into dusty old pieces of paper as they fell to the ground. A figure she knew to be Angus stood on the shore looking out over the loch but, as she cried out to him and he turned, she saw he was holding a child and his face was that of the woman in grey. The next moment she was at the Inn watching Angus, with Isobel Duncan on his arm, lead a white stag through the bar. She called out his name but he turned away and Isobel laughed, her wide open mouth flashing fangs instead of teeth.

Maggie woke in a panic, for a moment disorientated, unable to distinguish dream from reality. Angus didn't want her. She felt an overwhelming sense loss and it was a while before she could accept she had dreamt it all.

Eventually, she dragged herself out of bed. There were the few remaining boxes of the archive to go through and their contents to list. Bridie had promised to come and help her go through them and, even if there was nothing about the Maid, she reflected, they at least now knew her true identity from Calum's research. They had still, however, found nothing relating to the woman in grey, or the crying child.

All at once, for no reason at all that Maggie could put her finger on, she felt a surge of optimism and hurried to get dressed and away down to the village. She had no idea why but she had a very good feeling about today; she couldn't wait to get started on unlocking the mysteries of the past.

Bridie had not yet arrived when Maggie got to Murdo Ferguson's so she opened the shed door and stepped inside pleased with what she saw. Shelves were lined with boxes and files all neatly labelled, cupboard doors had sheets of paper pinned to them listing what was within, crates containing old tools and other bulky items were lined up against the wall, all likewise ticketed to identify their contents. Maggie smiled with satisfaction. She had done a good job even though she said so herself.

She decided to make a start rather than wait for Bridie so picking up the final, unsorted box of photographs she began to go through them. She had looked through several when she paused, her hand stilled in mid-air holding a photograph she had been about to consign to the pile of those she had already examined. Something about it tugged at her memory. She peered at it again more closely. It showed several men standing together by what looked like a large barn. The images were somewhat faded but, as she studied it, she thought there was something about the man in the middle of the group which struck her as familiar.

And then, all at once, it came to her…she thought of it later as a Road to Damascus moment. It was the long, wooden crook he was holding. It looked exactly like the one the Bodach had had with him the night he had appeared at the cottage. She could see the signs and symbols carved onto it and she felt her scalp tingle. She stared and stared at the man's face. It could be him….a younger version and of course without the white beard and hair. She was still sitting cross-legged on the floor, completely transfixed, when Bridie breezed in.

'I'm sorry I wasn't here….,' Bridie began and then stopped when she saw Maggie sitting motionless, her expression somewhere between shock and wonder. 'Maggie, whatever is it?' Bridie rushed over to her friend.

Maggie held out the photograph. 'It's him.' Her voice shook. 'It's him, it's the Bodach.'

'Are you sure?' Bridie took the picture and stared at it. 'Which one is he?'

Maggie scrambled to her feet; the initial shock of recognition was passing and excitement began to seize her. 'There,' she said pointing with a shaking finger to the figure in the middle of the group. 'That's him. Of course he's a lot younger there but I'm absolutely certain that's the man who was in the cottage and in the graveyard.'

Bridie turned the picture over. 'There are some

names written here and a date.' She began to read them out. 'Thomas MacIver, Jamie Robertson, Robbie Findlay, Sandy MacDonald...'

She paused and then said slowly, 'You know, Maggie, Sandy is a familiar name given to someone called Alexander ....like Bill for someone called William.' The two women stared at each other hardly able to believe what they had found. 'The date would fit too,' Bridie looked again at the back of the photograph. 'Invershee, 1866... That would make him in his late thirties when this was taken.'

'So that means that the old man, the Bodach, I've been seeing, is....or rather was....Catherine Ross's brother?' Maggie shook her head; it seemed incredible.

'Yes. Don't you see? He was the one who left you the rune which, if you remember I told you, was to do with life and death. And all those dreams you've been having that point to some kind of quest?' Bridie was impatient for her friend to understand what was now so obvious to her. 'He's been searching all this time for his sister and, even after his own death he couldn't let it go, so he's been using you to find her.'

Maggie stared at the other woman in astonishment. Bridie actually believed all this. Then it occurred to her there really was no other explanation. Unless of course they had both taken complete leave of their senses...which was quite possible as they were seriously discussing ghosts or spirits as if they were an accepted part of day-day existence and it was their normal practice to enlist a living person's help in finding missing, dead people. Maggie sank to the floor again, putting her head in her hands. 'I can't deal with this,' she muttered.

Bridie smiled. 'I know it's a lot to get your head round.' She took hold of Maggie's arm, pulling her to her feet. 'Come on, let's go and have a coffee and think it through. It must all seem totally weird to you.'

Maggie nodded. A coffee was just what she needed together with a chance to talk everything over with Bridie.

That the Bodach had been a real person had completely thrown her. Up until this moment she had more or less accepted he was some kind of apparition, a figment of her own fevered imagination...despite the concrete existence of the rune ...with no connection to the real world. To find proof he had been a living, breathing person, a man with flesh on his bones whom people had known as a friend, as a workmate, someone they had had a drink with, who knew the sound of his voice and his laughter; a man with a home, a job, possibly even a family, took her breath away. It was all becoming decidedly surreal.

When they were finally seated in the shop's little office, it was Bridie who broke the silence. 'I was right about The Bodach showing you the way. He pointed out his gravestone at the churchyard so you would know to look for him in the records and in that way find the identity of the Maid.'

'I just can't believe it. After all this time we know who she is.' The significance of what she had just said sank in and Maggie looked at her friend with shining eyes. 'Oh Bridie, it means we can put her name on the gravestone, she doesn't have to be the Unknown Maid anymore.'

Bridie nodded. 'We may have to get all kinds of permission and such like, but I think it should be possible.'

The two friends hugged and discussed what they should do next. Maggie said she would approach the Minister as he should probably be the first to know, and Bridie offered to bring Calum up to date. Maggie smiled. 'What's going on between you two anyway?'

Bridie looked at her in mock surprise. 'I don't know what you mean, Maggie. What should be going on?'

Maggie laughed. 'Alright, don't tell me, but I know something is,' and she left it there. She didn't want to embarrass her friend and it really wasn't any of her business. The two women parted agreeing to meet later to compare notes.

As she wandered along to the church thinking about what she was going to say to the Minister, Maggie heard her name being called. She looked round and saw Angus striding towards her. She stopped walking and watched as he approached, feeling the stirrings of excitement flutter in the pit of her stomach but resisting the impulse to run up to him and fling herself into his arms. She had been watching too many movies she thought, cross with herself for even imagining doing such a thing.

'Well, by your face, I guess you're not that pleased to see me,' Angus said as he reached her.

Maggie realised she was frowning and quickly summoned up a smile.'I'm sorry, Angus, I was thinking about something.'

'How are you feeling today?'

Maggie raised her eyebrows.

'The headache,' Angus reminded her.

'Oh, that's gone. I'm fine. A good night's sleep did the trick,' she lied recalling her night of weird and wonderful dreams. 'Actually I've got some good news,' and she proceeded to tell him of Calum's discovery. She didn't say anything about finding the photograph of Alexander MacDonald because she hadn't mentioned the Bodach, nor had she yet told him about the woman in grey. Angus struck her as very much a man of this world and she didn't know how he would react if she started going on about seeing ghosts.

'That's amazing,' he said. 'Well done. So the mystery's solved and the Unknown Maid finally has a name.' He eyed Maggie thoughtfully. 'Does that mean you'll be going back to London shortly?' His tone was casual but Maggie saw the shadow flit across his eyes and his lips tighten as he stared at her.

He minds that I might be leaving she thought and felt a little tug in her belly.

Aloud she said, 'Well, not just yet. I want to arrange for her name to be put on her gravestone and that'll probably take a little time. I'm off to talk to the Minister about it.' She gazed back at him. She didn't know what came over her but for once in her life she threw caution to the winds. 'Why? Would you miss me?' She fluttered her eyelashes at him and smiled coquettishly.

'Yes,' he said simply.

Her smile vanished as she stared at him. His gaze was unswerving and she saw the total honesty in his face. Her pulse quickened and she dropped her eyes, studying her hands as if all the answers to all the questions which troubled her lay there in their lines and creases... 'I..... I....I'm not sure what I'll do after that's been organised.' She still had to find out about the woman in grey although she didn't say that to Angus. Nor did she tell him the thought of leaving Invershee and, more importantly, of leaving him wasn't something she wanted to contemplate.

Maggie stole a quick glance up at him. He looked bemused, as if he had expected more of a reaction when he'd said he would miss her. He reached out and took one of the hands she was examining so intently.

'Come for a ride with me,' he pleaded, his voice gruff as if he was fighting the urge to simply sweep her up into his arms and kiss her into submission. 'I was just about to take Merlin out for a gallop. Why don't you take Freya and come too?' As if he sensed her hesitation, he pressed on. 'The Minister can wait and I could do with the company. Besides, you know you really should get mounted again after your fall the other day.'

Maggie gave in. He was right. She really ought to get back up on a horse after such a bad fall. If she left it too long she might lose her nerve. After all, there wasn't any urgency about seeing the Minister; the Maid had waited all these years to be identified, another hour or so wasn't going to make any difference. A brisk canter in the fresh air would help to blow away the cobwebs and maybe help her to see things more clearly. She seemed to be living in a state of permanent confusion these days; ghostly mysteries and an uncertain love-life were definitely not conducive to calm, level-headed thinking.

As they walked together to the Inn to fetch the horses, Angus reached across and took her hand in his.

Maggie's instinct was to pull away but she told herself not to be foolish, all he was doing was holding her hand, nothing more. His fingers felt warm and strong and she noticed how comfortably her hand fitted into his. She began to relax and Angus, as if sensing the change, turned to her and smiled. He lifted her hand smoothly to his mouth and gently kissed the back of it.

'Right, Miss MacQueen, let's see if you're as good on horseback as you are at skimming stones.'

Maggie looked around, startled. They were at the field where the horses were waiting and she had not even been aware of passing the Inn so wrapped up was she in trying to sort out her confused emotions. She sought to keep her voice steady. 'If that's a challenge, Mr. Cameron, then you're on.' Her eyes dared him and she flashed him a spirited grin. 'What are we waiting for?'

CHAPTER 19

Once they were mounted, Angus led the way towards the top of the hill but this time, instead of taking the trail through the woods, he continued passed it until Maggie saw a stretch of rough, heather-clad moor land spread out before them, reaching towards other hills away in the misty distance.

Angus turned in his saddle towards her and shouted, 'Ready?' but Maggie, anticipating this moment and determined he was not going to get the better of her, had already dug her heels into Freya's sides and was off. The horse sped across the open ground and Maggie clung on to the reins as if her life depended on it, which it probably did she thought grimly as she fought to stay in the saddle. She could hear Merlin's hooves pounding the ground behind her and she urged Freya on to greater effort.

She felt exhilarated and free; no room for thoughts of ghosts or mysteries or even of Angus, just the sheer joy of the gallop, her hair being blown about her head, her cheeks stinging from the wind in her face and the tingling thrill of the chase.

The next moment Merlin was passed her, the big, powerful stallion stretching out to overtake the smaller horse in a blur. Maggie saw Angus punch the air in delight and give a shout of triumph. She drew back on Freya's reins and gradually the horse slowed down to a steady canter. Angus had pulled up Merlin a little way ahead and was already dismounting.

'That was wonderful,' she said, trying to catch her breath as Freya trotted up to him. 'Of course, I had to let you win.' Her eyes were teasing, 'It would've been too damaging to your male pride otherwise.' She grinned down at him and then yelped as he got hold of her leg and tugged.

'Come down here and say that,' Angus challenged.

He pulled harder and suddenly Maggie found herself unsaddled and slipping down the horse's flank. As his arms reached up to steady her and help her to the ground, she felt his hands slide up her body and a tremor ran through her. Then he swung her round to face him, pulling her roughly against his chest. 'I do hate a poor loser,' he murmured and crushed her lips under his.

She could barely breathe he was holding her so tightly. She felt as though she might faint and then her mind emptied of all thought. Sensation took over and she gave herself up to it, relishing the hardness of his mouth, savouring the taste of him as his tongue probed ever deeper, and delighting in the passion she aroused in him. He smelled of pine-scented soap, sharp, spicy after-shave and fresh coffee. She felt herself overwhelmed by the sheer physicality of him. Linking her hands round his neck, she pulled him even closer. Her senses whirled and she kissed him back with an urgency and intensity which surprised them both.

Finally, he drew back a little and gazed at her face. She was flushed and her eyes, heavy-lidded, were clouded with desire. He ran his thumb softly over her cheek and along the strong line of her jaw. She was some woman, he thought, one moment composed and as controlled as if she didn't have an ounce of feeling in her and the next she was all heat and flaring passion.

'Tha gaol agam ort,' he whispered softly. He paused, stunned by what he had just said. Was it true? He wanted her that was true enough. He wanted her as much as…..more than….he'd ever wanted anything or anyone in his life. But did he love her? He gazed at her standing there within the circle of his arms, her eyes now dreamy and her face glowing with the warmth of arousal and he knew, in a sudden moment of clarity, it was true; he was in love with her.

Maggie, still in the grip of feelings so powerful she felt that if Angus let go of her she would crumple into an untidy heap, leant her head against his shoulder. 'What did you say?' she murmured. She lifted a hand to his chest and could feel his heart beating so hard against it she wondered that it didn't leap out into her fingers. 'What did you say, Angus?' she asked again.

'I just said you're beautiful,' he said softly and, cupping her face in his hands, he stared into her eyes.

Maggie shied away from the compliment, shaking her head and taking a step back. 'No, I'm not, and anyway that's not what you said.'

'Yes you are, and it is what I said only I said it in Gaelic.' He pulled her close again and nuzzled her neck, nipping her ear very gently with his teeth. 'And you smell delicious.'

Maggie wanted to be nowhere else but on this hillside, at this moment, with this man. How things were going to work out between them she had no idea and, for once in her life, she had no plans for the future. She knew beyond doubt she wanted him and it was only a matter of time...if the way she was feeling now was anything to go by...before their physical relationship moved on to another level.

'Kiss me again,' she demanded. 'I want to be sure that one wasn't a fluke and you're up to a repeat performance.' She nibbled his bottom lip and, before he could draw breath, her tongue was flicking between his lips and she was kissing him with complete and utter abandonment. Her small, firm breasts pressed against his chest. Angus moved slightly and cupped one in his hand, stroking the hard, erect nipple with his fingers. Maggie felt as if everything inside her body was in melt-down and, moaning softly, she curled her body sinuously around his.

Angus was losing himself in the feel and taste of her and

it was only the snickering of the horses and Merlin's nose nudging him which made him draw back. He realised he had been only moments away from pushing Maggie to the ground and taking her there and then on the hillside, under the shadow of the watching mountains. He had no doubt she would have been a willing partner but it was not what he wanted for her or for himself. She deserved better than to have him fumble over her like some animal on heat. He wanted to make long, slow love to her, to spend time getting to know every curve and hollow of her body, to caress her soft, creamy white skin, to lose himself in her. Maggie gave a little moan of protest as he drew back.

'We have to get the horses home, lass,' Angus released her gently. He stepped away and, holding her hands in his, he looked directly into her eyes. 'I'll come up to the cottage tonight if that's alright with you?'

Maggie nodded dumbly. She could not think, never mind say anything which made sense at that moment. It was as if every part of her body had, until now, been numb and was now tingling all over. She felt the blood racing through her veins as if her heart was beating at double its normal speed. She had never felt so alive. She took a long, shuddering breath and cleared her throat.

'Yes, I'd like that Angus,' she managed.

He leaned forward and, smoothing her tousled hair back from her face, kissed her again, a long, slow, gentle kiss full of promise and intimacy, hinting at the pleasures to come. They remounted and rode slowly back to the village, each lost in their own thoughts, reliving what had happened between them and wondering what lay ahead.

Maggie's head and emotions were all over the place. It was as if she had been on some kind of fairground ride, tossed and tumbled around until she did not know which way was up but, over-riding everything, was the certainty she loved him and that he had feelings for her too. Whether his amounted to love she didn't know but that didn't seem to matter anymore. She would see him tonight at the cottage and whatever happened after that was in the lap of the gods.

She smiled to herself. *Since when did I become so fatalistic?* She, who always liked everything so cut and dried, to know for sure what was coming because she had planned for it, was now leaving everything up to Fate. She had certainly changed since she came to Invershee, she mused. This place had changed her. Whatever the outcome with Angus, she realised now life was about taking chances.

'I'll see you tonight,' Angus promised as they parted at the Inn a little while later. He kissed her gently, his eyes, frank and direct, looking deep into hers. Then he disappeared into the bar to catch up with the jobs he had neglected that morning. A tight knot of excitement was lodged in the pit of Maggie's stomach and she did not know how she was going to get through the rest of the day. The evening ahead seemed far distant. She sighed and decided the time between then and now would go far more quickly if she kept herself occupied. The delayed visit to the Minister first, she thought, and then she would finish sorting through the papers in the archive. Her plan of action decided, Maggie set off for the church.

She was disappointed. The Minister was absent, off on his parish duties she supposed. She was looking forward to being able to tell him the identity of the Maid and so, shoulders hunched and head down, she wandered dejectedly towards the Ferguson's. She would just have to go and finish up at the archive instead.

She was unlocking the door to the shed when a cheery-faced Flora Ferguson appeared at the back door. 'I'm glad I've caught you, Maggie. Murdo's left some more papers for you.' She disappeared into the kitchen and a moment later was back with a large cardboard box. 'Old Dougie MacKinnon died a couple of weeks back and his son's up from Ayr to sort through his belongings. He gave Murdo this box full of stuff thinking there may be some things here, documents, diaries and so on, which could go into the archive.' She handed Maggie the box with a sympathetic look. 'I don't envy you having to sort through all that in there,' she said, indicating the shed, 'but you're doing a grand job so far.' She smiled, 'Murdo's really delighted at the difference you've made.'

Maggie smiled in return. 'I've really enjoyed myself though I did think I was almost finished.' She sighed as she looked at the jumble of papers crammed into the box.

'You haven't found whatever it is you're looking for then I take it?'

'The thing is I'm not exactly sure what it is I am looking for,' Maggie confessed. 'I don't know if Mr. Ferguson told you, but I'm trying to identify the Unknown Maid.'

She didn't tell the other woman she had already discovered her identity as she wanted to speak to the Minister before it became public knowledge. When Flora nodded, she went on, 'I've found a photograph which more or less confirms what I already know but I was hoping there might be some written record or something.' Her voice tailed away as she peered again into the box Flora had handed her. It seemed unlikely now, she thought.

'Don't lose heart, dearie,' Flora said briskly. 'You know how it is when you're searching for something, it's always in the last place you look and you think to yourself, why didn't I look there first and save myself all that time and bother.' She smiled. 'You never know, what you're hoping to find might be right there. Dougie MacKinnon was in his nineties and he'd lived here all his life, his family before him too. So there may be something in there about the Maid. You never know,' she repeated. 'You go and get started and I'll bring you a cup of tea in a wee while.' She nodded encouragingly at Maggie then turned and went back into the house.

Maggie settled herself down on the floor of the shed. She gave another heavy sigh. She didn't hold out much hope of finding anything significant but she would never know unless she made a start. She tipped up the box, and papers scattered everywhere. Slowly she began sifting through them. Much of it was as she expected; old letters and bills, records of cattle and sheep sales, rent books and even and old ration book from the 1940s. There were also a couple of what appeared to be daily journals written in a very crabbed hand containing accounts of harvesting, market visits, records of sheep shearing and such like.

She began to read some of the entries which detailed the numbers of sheep sheared, the yield of marketable fleeces and the names of the shearers. She stopped and looked again at the names she had just read. There he was, Sandy MacDonald. She checked the date of the entry, July 1866. It was the same date as on the back of the photograph. Eagerly she checked the entries for the following years. Yes, he was there too, named as one of the sheep shearers, every year until 1875 when the journal finished. She picked up the other journal but that was for the previous ten years and there was no mention of him in it. The name scrawled on the front covers was Thomas MacKinnon. She supposed he would have been Dougie's father, or maybe his grandfather.

She stood up to stretch her legs and began to pace up and down thinking about Alexander (Sandy) MacDonald. He could have been an itinerant worker, moving from croft to croft and from farm to farm as and when his skills were needed, or maybe he had lived in the village for a time and had done casual work. She wondered why he had come to Invershee in the first place. Maybe there was no work on Mull though she didn't think it was very likely, or maybe he came to the village to search for his sister.

She stopped her pacing and stood pondering the possibility. That could be it. Catherine had disappeared from where she lived and her brother had been looking for her. Then why had he stayed in Invershee all that time? Because he knew where she was! The thought hit her like a thunderbolt. He knew she was in the graveyard. No, that wouldn't work, because if he knew she was the Unknown

Maid why hadn't he done anything about it?

Maggie's head was beginning to ache. She needed to talk to Bridie. She began to gather all the papers and other bits and pieces together to return to the box until she could come back and sort through them properly. As she did so a sheet of paper slipped out from the back of the earlier journal onto the floor and she bent down to pick it up to put it into the box with everything else. All at once something about it made her pause. It looked pretty old. Its edges were curling and beginning to brown and she could see there was writing on it. Her heart began to race as she reached down to retrieve it. It was probably nothing, an old receipt, a bill, something of that sort. But instinct told her otherwise.

She unfolded it, her fingers trembling as she smoothed it out. She moved to the doorway so the light fell onto the paper. The writing was well-formed and looked to be in an educated hand but the ink was beginning to fade in places. She strained her eyes to make out the words; it was still just about legible. As she read, tiny prickles of excitement ran up and down her back. This was it, the answer to everything. She could not believe it. She read it again. She felt like punching the air as Angus had done earlier when he had won their race. Bridie had to see this.

Very carefully she refolded up the paper and put it into her jacket pocket. She locked the door of the shed and told Flora she would not want any tea just now but she might be back later. As she hurried across the green towards Bridie's little shop, her head was buzzing with this new-found knowledge and she couldn't wait to share it with her friend. To her great relief, she found Bridie busy in her backroom office up to her eyes in paper-work.

'Oh, thank goodness, your coming has saved me from these hateful Tax returns,' Bridie cried gaily, flinging down her pen. 'I was just about ready to throw myself into Loch Shee.' She got up from her chair and went to walk over to the kettle to make coffee. She stopped mid-movement and frowned at Maggie. 'Whatever is it? You look as if you're about to burst a blood vessel.'

Maggie put her hand into her pocket and slowly drew out the sheet of paper. 'You'll never guess what I've just found in the archive.' Her voice was tight with suppressed excitement. 'Well, not in the archive yet, because it was in a box that has just been handed in to Mr. Ferguson and I thought I'd look through it first before I tackled the last one that was left to do.'

She was rambling, she knew she was and she could see from Bridie's expression she was confused. 'Just look at this,' Maggie said and held out the paper to Bridie, her hand shaking.

'Read it. It gives us the answer.' She couldn't keep the note of triumph from her voice.

'The answer to what?' Bridie reached out to take the piece of paper from Maggie's trembling fingers.

'Just read it and you'll see.'

Bridie opened up the paper. 'It's a bit hard to make out some of these words,' she said squinting and then, as she read on, Maggie saw her eyes widen and realization begin to dawn on her face. 'My God, I can't believe it.'

'I know,' Maggie breathed, 'Isn't it amazing?'

CHAPTER 20

The two women looked at each other as if they doubted what their own eyes were telling them. Bridie spread the paper on her desk and they both leaned over to study it again:

"I write this at the behest of Robert, also known as Robbie, Findlay who is unable to do so himself by reason of incapacty (sic). He wishes that I should record his death-bed confession so that he may meet his Maker with no sin upon his soul. This is his confession as it was told to me:

'I have suffered under the burden of a wicked act which I did when I was but a young man. I was out to get rabbits for the pot. Times was hard and there was many mouths to feed, my father not working and me with eight brothers and sisters. So I went up the hills at the back of the village. It was getting late in the year, October as I recall, and I come across a young woman in a bad way.

She was lying in the heather moaning and groaning and I could see she wasna long for this world. She was nae woman of quality, just a maid with yellow hair and a long grey dress, it being covered with stains and dirt as if she'd been crawling, and her hands thick with soil like she'd been digging in the earth for roots - poor lass was gae thin as if starving. She didna have a shawl nor nothing and it was fearful cold. When I leaned over her she was muttering some name, James I think it was, and then she stopped and didn'a move nae more. I saw she had a silver ring on her finger and, God forgive me, I took it off her.

Me Ma hit me round the head when I got home with nae rabbit for the pot but when I told of finding the young maid she sent some of the men to look for her. She was dead when they come upon her and was later buried in the churchyard. No-one knew her, she wasna from hereabouts. I gave Ma the ring some days later and she was glad of it. I told her I'd found it on the hillside, in among the heather. I think she sold it to a tinker because we had food in us bellies for the next few days.

In all this time I've never said nothing to anybody. Not even when Sandy MacDonald came looking for his sister and her wee bairn that had gone missing from where they lived downby Corrieglen. Stealing from a dying woman has weighed heavy with me over the years and now I'm feared to meet the Lord with this badness in me so I beg His forgiveness and do truly repent of my sins.'

Alisdair MacLean. Minister of Invershee Presbyterian Church

October 17th 1899.

Postscript: Robert Findlay died this night. He has no family left in these parts so I shall give this confession to Thomas Mackinnon, his *employer, for safe-keeping in the event any family member should come to claim his belongings, meagre though they be.*

God Rest his Soul and have Mercy upon him.

A. MacLean."

The two friends stood in silence for a moment contemplating the document which lay on the desk before them. Then Maggie turned and gazed at Bridie.

'It is her isn't it? The woman in grey is Catherine Ross?' Her voice shook slightly and she gripped her hands tightly together to stop their tremor. She felt as if she could hardly breathe as she waited with trepidation for Bridie to say something. Surely she hadn't misread it; it did suggest the Maid and her phantom visitor were one and the same?

Bridie straightened up and turned towards her. Her eyes shone and she nodded her head rapidly. 'Oh yes, I would say this more or less proves it. Well done, Maggie. Wherever did you find this?'

Maggie explained about the box Murdo Ferguson had left for her with his wife. 'It was hidden between the pages of one of the journals. It was probably put there for safe keeping and then just forgotten about.'

'Well, it certainly explains why your woman in grey wasn't wearing a wedding ring.' Bridie sighed. 'How sad this Robbie Findlay didn't tell Catherine's brother what he knew but I suppose he was too ashamed of what he'd done.'

'Maybe he didn't connect the two, because he says in this,' Maggie tapped the paper 'that Alexander MacDonald was looking for his sister and her bairn. That's a child isn't it?' When Bridie nodded, she went on, 'So Calum was right in thinking he may have come across a birth record naming Catherine and Douglas Ross as parents.' Maggie frowned in concentration. 'But, when she was found, she didn't have a child with her otherwise it would have been mentioned by Robbie Findlay and it'd be in the Parish Records too.'

'She could have left him or her with someone before she left home.'

'Robert Findlay says she was muttering a name when he found her.' What was it? Maggie quickly scanned the document again. 'Yes, here it is, she was saying the name James so I think we can safely assume she had a son.'

'Unless of course she was coming here to meet a lover.'

Maggie looked at her friend askance. 'That's ridiculous. You don't really think that do you?' Her voice rose a couple of notches in disbelief.

'No, I don't, but I think we should consider every possibility, however unlikely.' Bridie was amused at her friend's quick defence of a woman she had never known.

'Well, I certainly don't believe it,' Maggie declared. 'I can't see a woman, recently widowed with a young child, would be off gallivanting to keep some secret tryst miles away from her home. No, I think when Calum finds the birth record it'll show she had a son called James.' She paused and then continued thoughtfully, 'though I can't imagine what on earth would have made her leave a young child behind. Any mother would have to be pretty desperate to do that.' She thought of her own mother; she would not have thought twice about leaving her but somehow Maggie did not think the same applied to Catherine Ross.

'Perhaps she had to leave him on the way,' Bridie mused aloud. 'Maybe she couldn't carry him anymore because she was too weak or ill and she left him in what she thought was a safe place, meaning to go back for him later.'

Maggie's hand flew to her mouth. 'Oh Bridie, that would be terrible. If she left him hidden somewhere and then she died and couldn't go back for him.' Her eyes filled with tears. 'Maybe that's why I keep hearing a baby crying.' She looked so distressed at the thought Bridie put her arms round her and hugged her.

'Don't upset yourself, Maggie. We don't know what happened, we're only surmising. For all we know she gave him to a member of her family to look after before she left.'

Bridie was right, of course she was, Maggie realised. There was no way of knowing what had actually happened and it was silly to get so worked up over something which happened over a hundred and fifty years ago. She gulped back her tears and dashed a hand across her eyes.

'Perhaps we should go and see Calum and let him know what we've discovered. He might have had some luck too and found a record of the child's birth. If not, at least we'll be able to tell him where Catherine was living. That might help.'

When Bridie agreed, Maggie carefully folded up the sheet of paper and tucked it back into her pocket. The two women made their way quickly to Calum's surgery which he was just locking up when they arrived.

'I was on my way to see you two,' he called cheerfully as they approached. The smile died away as he saw their serious expressions. 'What's up? You both look as if someone's told you the world's going to end tomorrow.' They continued to look at him solemnly. 'It isn't is it?' He gave a sigh of mock relief when Bridie's face split into a broad grin and Maggie giggled.

'We've got the most amazing news,' Bridie said, putting her hand on his arm. 'Maggie has found something which proves that the woman in grey and the Unknown Maid is one and the same person.'

She and Maggie enjoyed seeing his look of amazement and both began talking at once until Calum raised a hand in protest.

'Hold on a minute you two. I can't make head or tail of what you're saying. Let's go to the Inn and sit down and discuss this properly.'

When they walked into the bar Maggie gave a sigh of relief. Angus was nowhere to be seen; she wanted to concentrate on Catherine Ross and she didn't need the distraction she knew his presence would be. After Caitlin had served them with coffee, Bridie told Calum clearly and calmly what Maggie had discovered and he read the 'confession' for himself.

He cleared his throat. 'That certainly seems to settle it and it fits in with what I was coming over to tell you. Catherine and Douglas did have a child, a son called James Douglas; named after his maternal grandfather and father it seems.'

Maggie let out a little whoop of delight and clapped her hands.

'That's it then.'

Calum smiled at her exuberance and continued, 'He was born on 7th February 1852 at Corrieglen.'

'That fits in with what Robert Findlay told the Minister,' Bridie interrupted. 'He said that Sandy MacDonald told him his sister had disappeared from Corrieglen.'

'Where is this place? 'Is it far?' Maggie looked from one to the other.

Bridie nodded. 'It's about thirty-four miles away on the coast.'

'So she walked all the way here to Invershee. She must have had a very good reason to do that,' Maggie mused. 'And there's something else. I've just realised her brother said he was looking for her and the child so she couldn't have left him to be cared for by someone else. She had to have had him with her.'

The three of them sat in silence contemplating the desperation which must have driven Catherine Ross to leave her home and embark on what must have been a pretty arduous journey with her young son.

'If you like, now we know where she came from, I can do a further search to see if I can find out anything about the conditions for families living in the area at that time,' Calum offered. 'There might be a clue there as to why she would do such a thing. I'll also see if I can find any further record of the boy, you know, a death certificate perhaps.' He sipped his coffee and looked questioningly at the two women.

'But we know she had him with her.' Maggie's tone was indignant.

'Actually, we don't,' Bridie said, gently. 'We're only supposing that because of what Alexander MacDonald told Robbie Findlay...that he was searching for his sister and her child. She could have left James with someone her brother didn't know about.' She turned to Calum. 'I think it's a good idea if you really don't mind. You've spent an awful lot of time on this already.' She smiled warmly at him, putting her hand on his arm.

'I don't mind at all. I've found the whole thing fascinating. I'm really quite happy to do a little more digging.' He put his hand over hers and squeezed it gently. 'When you think how little we knew when we started this and how much we know now, it would be a shame not to see what more we can find out.'

Maggie leaned forward. 'It would be great if we could find out what made Catherine undertake such a hazardous journey and I want to know what happened to her son.' She sighed and swirled the remaining coffee round and round in her cup, watching the milky brown liquid circle and eddy with the movement. She lifted it to her lips and drank it down in one swallow. 'I'm so glad of your help,' she said as she put the cup down firmly on the table. 'I'm sure that between us we'll get to the truth and then maybe Catherine will be able to rest in peace.' She paused and then went on, 'You know it's odd but I haven't seen her for a while, not since she appeared in the mirror.' She shuddered again at the memory. 'And yesterday I just sensed her presence. She didn't materialize. Perhaps she knows I've found out who she is and isn't going to haunt me anymore.'

'I wouldn't bank on it.' Bridie said. 'Ghosts aren't rational beings like you and I. They're very unpredictable so don't be surprised if she does turn up again.'

'Thanks for that.' Maggie looked alarmed.

Bridie laughed. 'Don't worry, I'm only teasing. She probably won't appear again and, if she does, you can tell her we know who she is and where she's buried and we'll see to it her name is put on the gravestone.'

'I'm not sure that's all she wants though. I've a feeling she's not quite finished with me yet.' Maggie shivered as if someone had walked over her own grave. 'No, I don't think I've seen the last of her.'

Bridie looked immediately contrite. 'Would you like me to come over and stay with you tonight? We can face her together....if she turns up.'

'No, of course not, I'll be fine. Besides Angus is coming by later,' Maggie blurted out without thinking. She wished she could have bitten off her tongue when Bridie's eyebrows shot up and her eyes sparkled with curiosity.

'Oooooh! When did this happen?'

'This morning,' Maggie blushed to the roots of her hair.

Calum looked from one woman to another bemused. 'What's all this?'

'N...nothing,' Maggie stammered. 'It's just Angus said he'd call at the cottage tonight.' She lifted her chin stubbornly. 'Really, it's nothing,' she reiterated more firmly. 'I told him I'd found out the identity of the Maid and he's just interested that's all.' She glared at Bridie as if daring her to suggest otherwise.

'Mmmm.' Bridie said knowingly but didn't press Maggie further.

Calum got up from his chair. 'I'd better get off now anyway. I've a couple of visits to make. Fortunately they're not urgent otherwise I wouldn't be here. And I'll get back onto the Internet later and see what more I can find out.' He lifted Bridie's hand to his mouth and kissed it. 'I'll see you two ladies soon,' he said his eyes never leaving Bridie's. She coloured prettily and gently removed her hand from his, looking at Maggie as she did so.

The moment he'd gone, Maggie turned to her friend with eyebrows raised. 'So?'

'So,' Bridie said, 'I do like him and I think he likes me.' Maggie snorted. 'Okay, I know he likes me but things aren't that straightforward.' Bridie considered for a moment as if collecting her thoughts. 'Calum was married. His wife taught primary school in Perth and he worked at the hospital, in the A and E Department. They'd just had a little girl, Fiona May.' Bridie paused, her eyes bright with tears. She swallowed hard. 'Anyway, Moira suffered from severe post-natal depression and was on medication. One day Calum came home from the hospital and she and the baby were gone. She'd taken the car too.'

Maggie reached out and took hold of her friend's hand in sympathy. 'Go on,' she said gently. 'What happened?'

Bridie's look was anguished. 'Moira and the baby were found dead in the car about three months later. Apparently, she'd driven to some remote part of Perthshire...that was where she was from so she knew the area pretty well. She'd given Fiona May some of her anti-depressant tablets crushed into her milk feed and then taken the rest of the medication herself. Of course Calum had reported her missing straightaway and he and the police searched and searched for them but without any luck. Calum was even taken in for questioning but naturally they couldn't prove he had anything to do with their disappearance.'

Maggie stared at her friend. 'But the police couldn't possibly have thought he was involved in any way.'

Bridie wiped the back of her hand across her eyes. 'Well, seemingly the first person who's suspected when a wife disappears is the husband and the thing was, although he was at the hospital for most of the day, they only had his word for it she and the baby were there when he left in the morning. Apparently no-one else had seen her for a couple of days prior to that.'

Maggie sat in shocked silence. What a terrible thing to have happened and to have had to cope with. Her heart went out to him. 'How did they eventually find them both?'

Bridie, lost in her own thoughts, started. 'What?'

Maggie gently repeated the question.

'Oh, a couple of walkers who were camping in the

area. Seemingly Moira had driven the car into a wood and tried to hide it with branches. They stumbled across it when they strayed off the normal path and notified the police immediately.' Her voice less than steady, Bridie continued. 'Calum told me that at the inquest they said Moira had given the baby the milk and then held her in her arms until she died, before taking her own fatal dose. The verdict was recorded as infanticide and then suicide while the balance of the mind was disturbed.'

'It must be so hard for him to bear,' Maggie's voice was full of sympathy.

Bridie nodded. 'It's why he left Perth. I think he believes in his heart he should have done more to help Moira, that perhaps he could have done something to stop it from happening....' Her voice tailed away. She gazed out through the window. 'He's trying to make a fresh start and sometimes we both forget for a little while but it's always there, lurking in the background.' She gave a deep sigh and looked back at her friend. 'I know he cares for me and I do for him but it's impossible to move on until he can stop blaming himself for what happened.'

'I'm so sorry, Bridie. I shouldn't have teased you about him but I'd no idea.'

'How could you have, Maggie? Anyway now you know the situation,' and she shrugged her shoulders and smiled weakly. 'I just pray that one day he'll accept it wasn't his fault and then he can get on with his life.' She looked so downhearted Maggie reached across and took Bridie's hand in hers.

'He'll work things out, you'll see. Everything will turn out alright I just know it,' and she patted her friend's hand reassuringly.

Bridie nodded and tried to look as if she believed it too. Then she lifted her cup and drank the remaining coffee. 'We'd better get on,' she said, trying to make her tone business-like. 'You've still got the Minister to see... and I've got things to do as well,' she added vaguely.

The two friends returned their cups to the bar,

exchanging a few words with Caitlin as they did so. Maggie was tempted to ask her Angus's whereabouts but decided against it. Bridie seemed to have forgotten Maggie's earlier revelation and she didn't want to remind her of it and have her quizzing her again. As they left the Inn, she turned to her friend. 'By the way, did your advice to Caitlin work?' Bridie frowned and then her brow cleared.

'Oh, about the young man she fancies? Apparently so.' She smiled. 'She's got a date with him tonight.'

They walked along the loch-side in companionable silence. Bridie was lost in her own thoughts and Maggie was day-dreaming about Angus's visit to the cottage that night. She felt a thrill of anticipation, tinged with a little apprehension as she wondered what the evening had in store.

They reached the green and she was just about to take her leave of Bridie when she heard the roar of a powerful engine. The two women turned at the same time to see a smart red sports car draw up in front of the village shop.

Maggie thought for a moment her heart had stopped; it was like everything inside her had shut down. She stood there unable to move a muscle. It felt as though her feet were encased in concrete boots. Bridie must have sensed Maggie stiffen beside her and twisted round to look at her friend. 'Good Heavens, Maggie, whatever's the matter?'

Maggie's eyes were huge in a face completely drained of colour. She made a strangled sound and then with a sharp intake of breath she gasped. 'It's Ben! My God it's Ben.'

-

CHAPTER 21

Bridie turned to watch as the car driver extricated himself from behind the wheel and stretched his legs. Good-looking she thought as she took in the tall, slim build, regular features and light blond hair. He wore a pair of pale grey slacks with a light blue sweater over an open-necked blue and white checked shirt. Probably his idea of casual dress suitable for the Highlands she thought derisively, conscious of her own well-worn colourful skirt and top and Maggie beside her in faded jeans. He reached into the car and pulled out a dark blue jacket, swinging it carelessly over one shoulder as he slammed the car door shut and began to saunter towards them.

'Maggie!' he called

Maggie didn't move. It was as if she were made of glass and the slightest movement would cause her to shatter into tiny pieces. Ben, a big grin on his face, waved and quickened his pace to stride across the green. *As if nothing had happened* Maggie thought resentfully watching him approach.

'I thought it was you,' he said. 'It's hard to mistake that lovely hair of yours,' and he reached out a hand to stroke it. Maggie flinched; she couldn't bear the thought of his touch. After the initial shock of seeing him here in Invershee, she felt an icy calm sweep through her.

'What are you doing here?' Her voice was as cool as if she were addressing a perfect stranger.

'I've come up to see you of course, what else?' His eyes slid away from her direct gaze and over to Bridie. 'Hello, I'm Ben, Maggie's fiancé.' He took no notice of Maggie's muttered 'ex-fiancé' and continued as if she had not spoken. 'And you are...?' He left the question hanging in mid-air and looked enquiringly at her.

'I'm Bridie, Maggie's friend, her very good friend,' Bridie answered emphatically, ignoring the hand he held out to her. 'Are you alright Maggie?' Bridie put her hand on Maggie's shoulder and peered into the other woman's face.

Her first, frozen astonishment at Ben's unexpected appearance had passed and Maggie reached over and patted the other woman's hand. 'I'm fine, Bridie, don't worry.' She turned and gave her friend a quick smile. There was a steely glint in her eyes Bridie had never seen before.

Maggie swung her attention back to her former lover. 'What do you want, Ben? Everything's over between us. You made that perfectly clear.' She could not help a note of bitterness creeping into her voice.

For the first time, Ben looked a little unsure of himself. A flicker of doubt crossed his face and he passed a hand over his carefully barbered hair.

'I need to talk to you Maggie. I know I've got a lot of explaining to do…' His voice trailed away and he looked at her sheepishly.

Maggie couldn't help it. She felt herself soften, just a little but there was a definite weakening in her resolve. His brash demeanour had vanished and he looked lost and, she thought, maybe a little afraid. He had probably come up here ready to confess he had made a mistake and expected her to fall thankfully into his arms; that they would put his betrayal behind them and start again. Well he certainly had made a mistake if he thought she was going to do that.

'How did you know where I was anyway?'

'I went to see Rachel first but she wouldn't tell me a thing. She just said you'd gone away and then more or less slammed the door in my face….which I suppose I should have expected.' Ben smiled self-deprecatingly. 'Then I thought the people at the museum might know where you were so I gave them a sorry tale about how much I regretted what had happened and said I was desperate to see you. Your boss suggested that if you wanted me to know where you were you'd have left an address for me and told me, in no uncertain terms, to clear off.' He smiled at her again and reached out as if to take her hand. Maggie thrust her hands deep into her jeans' pockets and took a pace back.

'Well, fortunately for me,' he went on, looking taken aback as she stepped away from him, 'there was a young woman nearby who'd overheard our conversation.' Maggie raised her eyebrows.

'Fair-haired with glasses, about twenty-two, twenty-three, something like that. I think she may be a secretary?'

Maggie nodded. *Amy! A real romantic. Always reading "Real Love Stories" and "True Romance" type magazines.* Maggie imagined she would have thought she was helping to smooth the path of true love and reunite star-crossed lovers.

'Apparently you'd written to the Museum Director?' Maggie remained silent, staring at him.

'Well, she got me the address from your letter.' He looked pleased with himself as he continued. 'The rest, as they say, is history. I hopped in the car and drove straight here. I was going to ask at the shop the whereabouts of this Tigh-na-Bruach, but then I saw you standing there with your friend.' He nodded at Bridie who thinned her lips in response.

'Look,' he continued as he stared at Maggie's expressionless face, 'isn't there somewhere we can go and talk?' He looked pointedly at Bridie. 'In private,' he added.

'I suppose we could go up to the cottage.'

If nothing else, Maggie was curious to know what had gone wrong between him and Sarah and she also realised the feelings she had once had for him were not completely dead and buried; such emotions were not so easily dismissed. She didn't blame Amy and she supposed now Ben was here it might be good to talk things through, clear the air between them.

'I'll show you the way' she went on, and leaning forward to give Bridie a quick kiss, she whispered, 'I'll see you later.' She saw Bridie's look of concern. 'Don't worry, it'll be fine.' She turned to Ben, 'Come on, though I don't think that car of yours is going to be too happy, the track to the cottage's a little rutted.' *Serve him right*, she thought grimly, *if the suspension takes a hammering.* Maggie climbed into the car and, once out of the village, they bounced and bumped their way along, Ben gritting his teeth every time the car grounded on the track.

He was not in the best of tempers when they arrived. 'Good Heavens, Maggie, did you have to hide yourself away in this god-forsaken place? Why couldn't you just book yourself into a health spa or somewhere for a week or two?' He looked around as she opened the back door. Maggie knew that, like Rachel, Ben was more at home in the city and would not be at all comfortable in the vast emptiness of hills and moor land.

'I just needed to get as far away from London as I could,' she replied tartly, annoyed at having to explain herself to him. 'Do you want a coffee or perhaps some tea?' she offered, trying to quell her irritation.

'Coffee'll be fine.'

There was an awkward silence between them as she filled the kettle and put out the cups. Finally she said, 'Go and sit down, Ben. I'll bring your coffee in as soon as it's ready.'

When she went through to the sitting room he was standing gazing out of the window. 'However do you put up with all this nothingness and quiet? Don't you miss having people around and life going on?' He waved a slim, manicured hand towards the silent hillside.

Maggie gave a brief laugh. 'Oh, life goes on here Ben just as it does in the city and I like the peace and serenity of the place. It seems to suit me.' He took the mug she handed him and moved to stand by the fireplace.

'Now why don't you sit down and tell me what all this is about,' she suggested as she curled up in one of the chairs.

He sipped his coffee but remained standing. 'I made a huge mistake,' he said simply, looking at her expectantly. 'I suppose it was partly pre-wedding nerves and you seemed so wrapped up in all the arrangements, so distant, I felt I couldn't reach you.' He began to pace up and down the small room, his brow creased as he continued. 'Sara seemed so much fun and so uncomplicated.' He gave a deep sigh. 'I got cold feet I suppose.'

He paused as if expecting some response but she said nothing, sitting with her head down hunched over her coffee. He resumed his pacing. 'It was only when we were away that I realised how wearing it is to be with someone who wants to be up and doing all the time. You were always such a restful person to be around but she was never satisfied, never wanted to just sit and talk or soak in the view. She drove me crazy after a few days.'

He moved over and crouched down in front of her. Maggie was immediately reminded of the way Angus had done the same thing when she was in his flat and her heart gave a little flip. She looked into Ben's face and could see the hope in his eyes. 'I've missed you Maggie and I'm so very sorry I hurt you.' He took hold of the hand which lay on her lap. 'Can you forgive me? Will you forgive me? Can we go back to the way we were?'

Maggie slowly withdrew her hand from his and shook her head. 'It's far too late for that, Ben.'

He leapt to his feet and began pacing again, talking to himself as much as to her. 'But it can't be. I made an error of judgement and I'm desperately sorry for it.' Only Ben would describe jilting her as an error of judgement she thought wryly and smiled. Taking this as a positive sign he plunged on.

'You would have been Mrs. Henderson now if I hadn't been such an idiot. I miss you Maggie, I need you. You don't mean it. It can't be too late.'

'For Heaven's sake sit down will you, you're giving me a headache,' Maggie snapped. She shook her head. 'I'm sorry. I didn't mean to bite your head off. It's all been a bit of a shock seeing you again.' She hesitated as he sat down in the chair opposite hers. He looked so downhearted she felt a little wrench of sadness that things could not be different. But there was no going back. She was very fond of him, had even imagined she was in love with him, and she didn't want to hurt his feelings but she had to be honest for her own sake as much as for his.

She took a deep breath. 'The thing is, Ben, I don't think it can work between us anymore.' She put out a hand as he opened his mouth to speak. 'No, let me finish. I'll admit I was heartbroken when you left me and I felt betrayed and unhappy but I've had plenty of time to think things over since I've been here...that's one thing all this quiet allows you to do.' She smiled gently at his downcast face. 'If you're honest with yourself, you'll know what I'm saying is true. We were good together for a time but it wasn't really love. We fell into a pattern of behaviour which suited us both but can you tell me, hand on heart, ours was a passionate relationship?'

He looked at her nonplussed as she went on. 'No, it was comfortable, it was easy and un- demanding. You went with Sarah because you thought she offered you the excitement missing from your relationship with me.' She leaned forward in her chair and said earnestly, 'You know I'm right Ben. When did we ever have a row or disagreement?'

He shook his head. 'Never. I can't remember us ever falling out over anything but that's good surely, Maggie? It means we're on the same wavelength, that we both want the same things.' He leaned forward in his chair, his face eager.

Maggie shook her head. 'It means our relationship wasn't dynamic. It would never have grown and developed. People change, Ben. We'd both have changed and in the end our marriage would have been dead.' She studied him for a moment.

A small frown creased his brow and he gave a doubtful shake of his head as he sat back 'But I thought we were happy.'

'Come on now,' Maggie countered. 'You certainly can't have been happy or you'd never have turned to Sarah. I'm very fond of you Ben and I know you are of me but surely you can see it isn't enough on which to build a lifetime together.' There was a hint of regret in her voice.

It was always sad, she thought, to have to let go of a dream but she recognized now it had been a false dream. Her time here in Invershee and meeting Angus had proved that. She wasn't going to settle for anything less than she deserved and she deserved to be loved with passion and fervour and total commitment. She would settle for nothing less.

Ben interrupted her reverie. 'Isn't there anything I can say to change your mind, Maggie?' When she shook her head, he groaned. 'I just thought…hoped...' His voice tailed away and he sat, head bowed, clasping and unclasping his hands.

How easy it would be she thought, looking over at his bent head, to just give in and go back to London, pick up where they had left off and try to put all that had happened behind them. But she knew in her heart it wouldn't work. In the end they would both be unhappy and miserable.

'I'm really sorry, Ben, but I'm afraid you've had a wasted journey.' Maggie reached over and put her hands soothingly over his.

'It wasn't wasted, Maggie. At least I've seen you and tried to put things right, even if it didn't turn out quite the way I imagined.' He gave a sardonic grin. 'You can't blame a guy for trying.'

Maggie smiled back and, wanting to lighten the mood, she said briskly, 'Now let me fix you something to eat. You must be starving after driving all that way.'

Ben admitted he *was* rather hungry and wouldn't say no to a sandwich. Maggie laughed. He had always had a good appetite despite his slim build and she could not imagine he would be satisfied with a mere sandwich. She disappeared into the kitchen and he wandered in as she was putting together one of her favourite pasta dishes.

'You really don't have to go to all this trouble just for me,' he protested weakly, at the same time sniffing the piquant aroma of tomatoes and herbs simmering away on the stove. Maggie just ignored him and carried on with what she was doing 'The secretary woman said you were planning to stay on here for a while.' Ben watched Maggie cut a French stick into slices and smother them in garlic butter before slipping them under the grill. 'Whatever will you do with yourself all day, won't you get bored?'

So, as she drained the pasta and assembled their meal, Maggie told him about sorting out the archive ....omitting to mention the reasons for her interest in it... and that she planned to do some research into the crofting history of the area. 'So you see I'll have plenty to keep me occupied.'

'Well, I suppose if it makes you happy,' Ben said glumly. 'I'm just sorry I can't.'

Maggie gave a sigh of exasperation as she carried their plates over to the small table in the corner. 'Don't let's go through all that again. You know I'm right and going over and over it won't make me change my mind.' She put the plates down with a clatter and wondered whether she should tell him about Angus. *Perhaps not a good idea*, she thought and flashed him a bright smile instead. 'Come on let's get this before it gets cold.'

After they had eaten and cleared away, she lit the fire and they sat in silence for a while watching the flames, each with their own thoughts.

Finally Ben said, 'I've been going over what you said Maggie, and I think I do understand how you feel.' He gave a wry smile. 'It was easy being with you because you took charge of everything.' She made as if to speak but he carried on, 'And I let you. We just sort of drifted along in a fairly unchallenging way and marriage seemed the next logical step...not very romantic I know.' Maggie nodded. 'So I kind of get what you mean about there being no passion and I suppose that's what I was looking for when I went off with Sarah.' He looked up at her and grinned. 'She's left the office by the way. She's working for some high-flyer in corporate finance now.'

Maggie relaxed. Ben seemed to appreciate what she

had tried to explain to him and accepted that, for them, there was no going back. She felt a rush of affection for him and, reaching out, she touched his cheek. 'I know there's someone out there who'll make you happy, Ben, it's just not me.'

He gave a low chuckle. 'I hope so, otherwise there's every likelihood I shall turn into a crusty old bachelor.'

Maggie laughed, gaily. 'Not a chance, you'll be a good catch for someone one of these days.' She relaxed. It was going to be alright, she thought. They chatted for a little, mostly about people they both knew; he could be very entertaining company and Maggie found herself laughing at his witty observations. He didn't mention Sarah again which Maggie thought tactful.

After a while he stirred and reached for the jacket he had flung carelessly over the back of the chair.

'Well, I suppose I ought to be getting back. It's a long drive.'

Maggie glanced at the clock. It was late and, she saw, already dark. She considered Angus and their planned evening together. She hoped he would understand. If not he would have to lump it, she thought, already regretting the offer she was about to make.

She looked at Ben and said firmly, 'You can't possibly drive all the way to London tonight. You'd better stay over and start out fresh in the morning.' She gave him a mock scowl when he raised his eyebrows and looked sideways at her. 'You can have the spare room,' she said dryly. She quickly made up the bed and wished him good-night. As she was going out of the door he caught hold of her wrist and swung her round to face him. Maggie's heart almost stopped. What was this?

Ben released her as soon as he saw her startled look and took a step back. 'I just wanted to say again Maggie I'm truly sorry for the way I behaved and for hurting you as I did and I hope we can at least be friends?' He gave her a tentative smile.

Maggie breathed a quick sigh of relief and smiled

back at him. 'Of course, Ben, I'd like that too.'

She gave him a quick peck on the cheek and closing the door softly behind her, went to her own room not bothering to switch on the light. She undressed quickly and crawled under the covers, snuggling down until she was warm and cosy. She was glad Ben had come and they had sorted things out between them. She knew there would always be a bond between them, but Bridie had been right, it was not meant to be. Their marriage would have been a disaster... for both of them. She wondered vaguely why Angus had not turned up but then realised Bridie would have told him about Ben's arrival. She would see him tomorrow and explain everything. He would understand. With that thought in mind she quickly fell asleep.

She woke once in the night, uncertain for a moment what had aroused her. Then she became aware of a weight at the end of her bed as if someone was sitting there. *For goodness sake*, she thought. She'd made her feelings plain enough, surely? She reached out and snapped on the bedside lamp. 'Really, Ben....' The words died on her lips. The soft rays of light lent a faint radiance that did little to dispel the almost-dark but Maggie saw she was alone.

A deathly pall hung about the room and inch by inch a piercing coldness crept over her. Her teeth began to chatter. Hauling the covers up tight to her chin, Maggie's eyes flicked around as she strained to see into the deeply shadowed corners, her heart hammering. Her breathing was ragged and she fought to bring it under control. A sense of expectancy hung in the air.

'Is... is that you, Catherine?' she managed to stammer.

There was a slight movement as the weight on the bed shifted. The hairs on Maggie's arms rose like those on the back of a frightened cat; she felt as though she was enveloped in a cloud of utter despair. She shrank back against the pillows as if hoping they would somehow swallow her up.

Then all at once, she felt the weight lift away from

the bed as if someone had stood up. She heard the same soft swish of material she had heard before downstairs and then there was utter silence. The atmosphere of bleak emptiness melted away and the air began to lose its chill. The ghostly presence was gone.

Maggie waited for several moments still hugging the bedclothes around her until she was certain she was alone again. Snuggling back down in the bed, she felt the warmth seep back into her body and her heart gradually resume its regular beat. She lay there, wondering again what it was Catherine Ross wanted of her…it wasn't to harm her, of that she was sure. She closed her eyes and, despite what had just happened, was soon drifting off into a dreamless sleep. Beside her bed, the light cast its faint glow over the room throughout the rest of the night.

Outside, in the dark, Angus sat fuming in his car.

CHAPTER 22

As Maggie had surmised, Bridie had told Angus about Ben's arrival in the village and he was staggered at the powerful jolt of jealousy which shot through him. He had to concentrate so as not to grip the glass he was polishing so hard that it smashed in his hands. He tried to keep his voice casual. 'That's the bloke she was engaged to isn't it? The one who ran out on her before the wedding?'

Bridie must have heard the tension in his voice, seen the way his eyes narrowed, and she reached out to stay his hands of their frenzied polishing. 'Don't worry Angus. Maggie's over him. She simply thought it only fair to hear what he had to say after he'd driven all the way up from London.'

'She must have been in touch with him if he knew where to come,' Angus said curtly.

He felt a rising tide of anger sweep through him. She had played him for an idiot and he had been taken in by her. God Dammit he had even fallen in love with her. What a fool he was. All this time he had steered clear of commitment only to be seduced by a pair of ice-blue eyes. So caught up was he in this self-condemnation he hardly heard what Bridie was saying.

'What was that?' he said.

'I said,' Bridie repeated, 'Maggie didn't tell him where she was. He managed to wheedle her whereabouts from some ditzy employee at the museum where she works.'

'Oh.' Angus scowled and leaned heavily on the bar.

'They've gone back to the cottage to talk things over. Seemingly his relationship with the woman he went off with might be over.'

'So he's come to sweet-talk Maggie into giving him

another chance has he?' Angus could not keep the bitterness out of his voice. 'Well, she's stupid if she does go back to him. He's obviously not heavily into commitment, he's proved that.'

'That's a bit rich coming from you, Angus,' Bridie retorted but smiled to take the sting out of her words as she went on. 'One thing Maggie is not is stupid. You'll see, she'll send him packing when she's heard him out.'

Angus merely grunted and turned away. How he got through the rest of the afternoon and evening, he hardly knew. He alternated between a firm belief that Maggie had feelings for him and was no longer interested in her former fiancé, and certainty Ben would charm her into his arms again and carry her off back to London.

He had never known time to pass so slowly and the moment the last customer had left the Inn he was in his car and driving off into the night as if he were racing in a Formula One Grand Prix. He had to slow down a little when he reached the track leading up to the cottage and roundly cursed the local council for not taking more care over its upkeep. He was still swearing under his breath when the cottage came into view.

He slowed down the minute he spotted the red sports car in the driveway and stopped at the side of the road wondering whether he should march in, confront his rival and demand an explanation. There was a light still on in the sitting room. As he watched, undecided as to his best course of action, it went out. A moment later a light went on in one of the upstairs bedrooms and he saw Maggie come to the window and draw the curtains. He waited, his belly twisting itself into knots. His sense of disappointment and anger was so strong he felt it gnawing away at him relentlessly like a termite eating its way through a block of wood.

He watched and waited for another upstairs light to come on but none did.

Finally the one light went out and Angus banged his fist so hard on the steering wheel he felt his knuckles bruise. She had called him an idiot once and that's exactly what he was, he thought. He felt sick to his stomach at the idea of her lying up there in the dark in someone else's arms. He vowed there and then he would never, ever put himself in this position again.

Eventually he started up the car and drove slowly back to the Inn. His mind was in turmoil and he decided this was the night he might, for the first time in his life, take a drink.

When Caitlin came into the bar early the next morning she found him passed out on one of the settees, reeking of whisky.

Maggie awoke the next morning to the sound of a cheery 'Good Morning' and a cup of tea thrust under her nose. She struggled to sit up and it took her a moment or two to gather her thoughts. She managed to mutter a return greeting and gratefully took a sip of the scalding tea.

'I thought I'd make an early start,' Ben said. 'Try and get through Glasgow before the morning rush hour.'

Maggie looked at him bleary-eyed. 'What time is it?' She could see it was still dark outside.

'About six-thirty.' Ben smiled. 'I'd forgotten how good you always look in the mornings.' Leaning over he gave her a quick kiss on the forehead. 'Don't bother getting up, I can see myself out.' For a moment he stood irresolutely in the doorway then with a quick grin and a 'Take care, Maggie,' he was gone. She heard the back door close and then the noise of his car starting up. She listened, sipping her tea, as he drove away until she could no longer hear the sound of the engine.

The events of the previous night suddenly came back to her as she saw the bedside light still emitting its feeble glow. For a moment she had been frightened certainly but nothing bad had happened, she had come to no harm and she was determined she was not going to let it trouble her today. Pushing all memory of it to the back of her mind,

Maggie turned her thoughts back to Ben.

She was glad he had come, glad his visit had afforded them the opportunity to talk things over. She was certain in her own mind now he had done them both a favour by walking away from their wedding. She knew with absolute certainty she had never truly been in love with him. Her feelings for Angus were so much more than she had ever felt for Ben and she was grateful that seeing him had dispelled any lingering doubts she might have harboured.

She would see Angus today, explain what had happened and tell him she loved him. If he didn't return her feelings then too bad, she would have to deal with it. *Nothing ventured, nothing gained,* she thought, resurrecting one of her father's favourite axioms. She felt brave and adventurous this morning and resolved not hide behind her normal reticence any more. She leapt out of bed, determined to make the most of the day and full of nervous expectancy at the prospect of seeing the man she loved.

She showered, enjoyed a leisurely breakfast and then wandered out into the garden. It was a pale, powder-grey morning with a faint breeze stirring the branches of the rowan tree. Dew glistened on every blade of grass and she detected a hint of frost in the air. She wondered idly what it would be like here in the winter. She imagined the hillside thick with virgin snow and pictured herself curled up inside the cottage in front of a blazing log fire, a glass of wine in her hand and Angus beside her.

The shrill shriek of gulls wheeling in the sky above broke into her daydream and brought her back to reality. She smiled. There was no reason why her dream should not come true she thought and hurried back into the cottage to get ready for her walk down to the village. She felt keyed up and excited. Who knew what the day would bring but it stretched before her full of hope and possibilities.

Maggie hummed softly to herself as she turned out of the cottage gateway onto the track. She saw a figure striding towards her. Arms swinging and red hair tumbling unbound over her shoulders, Bridie hurried up to her. 'I was just coming to see you. I didn't know if you were planning to come down to the village today or not.'

'Well, I thought I'd go and finish up at the archive.' Maggie looked at her friend curiously. She linked arms with her and the two of them strolled back along the track in the direction of the village. 'Was it something specific you wanted to see me for or is this just a social call?' She smiled inwardly, guessing Bridie was keen to know what had happened with Ben.

Sure enough, Bridie said casually, 'Has he gone then?'

'Who?' Maggie looked at her friend, her face the picture of innocence.

'Your erstwhile fiancé of course, who else?'

'Oh him! I wasn't sure if you meant Angus. You know he was supposed to come up and see me last night but he didn't turn up. I don't know why.' She paused and pulled a wry face. 'It's probably a good thing he didn't with Ben still being at the cottage'

Bridie halted mid-stride and turned to stare at her friend. 'Ben stayed the night?'

Maggie nodded. 'By the time we'd talked and had something to eat it was far too late to let him drive all the way back to London,' She saw the stunned look on Bridie's face. 'He slept in the spare room,' she said laughing. 'I'm well and truly over him and he accepts that. I'm very fond of him but I don't love him and, if I'm being perfectly truthful, I don't think I ever did. We parted as friends and I hope he always will be that. I think even he realises now we've both had a lucky escape.' She sighed. 'I'm glad he came up and we were able to be honest with each other. I feel a huge sense of relief and I've absolutely no regrets. I can just get on with my life now.'

Bridie grinned. 'I'm delighted to hear it. I always thought a tiny part of you was still wondering, "What If?" Now you can put the whole sorry business behind you.' She hugged Maggie and they recommenced their walk to the village.

'I suppose you told Angus Ben had turned up?'

Bridie nodded. 'He didn't take it too well. In fact he seemed rather put out. He thought you must have been in touch with Ben for him to know where to come.' She saw Maggie's horrified expression and hurried on. 'Don't worry. I soon put him right.'

Trying to keep her voice casual, Maggie said 'I don't suppose you've seen him this morning by any chance?'

'No, nor do I want to. I'm very cross with him. I spoke to Caitlin this morning and apparently she found him more or less comatose stretched out in the bar when she went in to work today. He'd been drinking,'

'Angus?' Maggie could not believe her ears. 'Angus was drunk?'

'I know. I could hardly credit it either. In all the years I've known him, and that's a long time, I've never, ever known him to touch a drop of alcohol. Even when his mother died and he was really unhappy, he never took a drink. But Caitlin said he stank of whisky when she found him. Mind you, she did say he seemed to have poured most of it down his shirt.' Bridie smiled grimly, 'I imagine he would only need to down a glass or two for it to affect him.'

'Why ever would he turn to the bottle now when all this time he's been so determined not to drink?'

Bridie shrugged. 'I don't know and I'm certainly not going to ask him, not today at any rate. Caitlin said he nearly took her head off when she woke him, and he's been mooching around ever since as grumpy as a bear woken up in the middle of hibernation.' She nodded at Maggie. 'And if you take my advice, you'll give him a wide berth too, at least until he's over the worst of his hangover.'

Maggie agreed it was probably the wisest course of action and then told her friend about her visit from Catherine Ross during the night. 'I didn't see her, but she was there all right.'

'She's clearly intent on making her presence felt,' Bridie murmured. 'Sorry, no pun intended,' she added laughing when she saw Maggie's pained expression. 'Until she lets you know what it is she wants though, I don't see what else we can do.'

The two women walked on discussing the haunting and soon reached the village. Leaving Bridie at her shop, Maggie went round to the archive and spent the rest of the morning busily sorting out what was left of the papers and other bits of local history in the remaining cardboard boxes. As soon as she had put everything in its appropriate place and labelled it, she stood back looking at the neatly lined up folders and boxes with their contents clearly identified and congratulated herself on a job well-done.

Pleased with her efforts and relieved too the work was finished, she resolved to seek out Angus and find out what was troubling him so much he had broken a life-time of abstinence. She hoped it wasn't anything to do with her and Ben, though she had a niggling feeling it might be.

The moment she walked through the door into the bar she sensed the tension. There was just one other customer, an old man at the bar sitting brooding over his beer whilst Caitlin was wiping down tables with an offended air. Maggie, who had never seen her anything other than cheerful and chatty, was surprised to see her looking so down in the mouth.

'Hi, Caitlin, are you alright? You're looking a bit upset.'

'So would you be if you had a fiend of a brother like mine. Nothing I've done today has been good enough. He's been in a bad mood since early doors and I'm fed-up.'

Maggie tut-tutted in sympathy. 'I hear he's been drinking and he's not used to it. He's probably just suffering from the effects.'

'Oh, he's not got a hangover, more's the pity,' Caitlin grumbled. 'He says his head's fine. He's just in the most foul temper and I've absolutely no idea why.' She stopped what she was doing and went behind the bar. 'I'm sorry, Maggie, I shouldn't be complaining like this. He's usually pretty reasonable. I just don't know what's got him so riled up. Anyway, what can I get you?'

Maggie ordered a ploughman's lunch and went over to her favourite table by the window. She was sitting looking out over the loch, watching the clouds beginning to build into towering, ochre-tinted columns over the far hills, when she sensed someone approaching. She turned her head to see Angus bearing down on her carrying her lunch. His face was as thunderous as the distant clouds. She gave him a bright smile but then frowned when it wasn't returned.

'Caitlin said you were in a temper and I see she wasn't wrong,' Maggie said calmly. She flinched as Angus slapped the plate down on the table in front of her.

'Your lunch, Miss MacQueen.' She recoiled at the abrasive tone of his voice and the way his eyes smouldered with scarcely concealed anger as they swept over her.

She told herself to keep cool and looked up at him. 'You know you'll frighten your customers away if you speak to them in that tone, Angus,' she said mildly. She looked down at her plate and picked up her knife and fork so she missed the spark of fury which flashed in his eyes.

'You're dining alone I see,' he growled. 'Where's your fiancé then? Abandoned you again has he?' It was clear he regretted the words the moment they were out of his mouth. They were unnecessarily cruel and Maggie sat open-mouthed, speechless. All colour drained from her face and her eyes grew wide as they stared up at him.

She finally found her voice. 'Have I done something to offend you Angus?' Her tone was conciliatory and she looked as if she were fighting to hold back tears.

'I don't know. Have you?' His voice oozed sarcasm and he scowled at her.

'Obviously I have.' She tilted her head to one side as she gazed at him in confusion.

'Well why don't you have a think about it Maggie, and let me know.' He gave an abrupt, humourless laugh, turned away and strode back to the bar.

For a moment Maggie couldn't move. What did he mean? The only thing she could imagine had upset him was

Ben's turning up out of the blue and that wasn't of her doing. If he was offended by it then she was sorry. She sat there a moment longer staring down at the food in front of her. She had suddenly lost her appetite and pushed the plate to one side. Perhaps she should talk to him about it. Obviously from his point of view something had gone wrong between them and she needed to put it right.

She stood up quickly before she could change her mind. She had never been comfortable with confrontation, preferring instead to either walk away from it or attempt appeasement. But she recalled that this morning she had resolved to face up to things and not continue hiding behind her normal façade of controlled calm.

Trying to quell the nervous tremors fluttering in her stomach, she approached the bar. Angus watched her, his eyes flinty, his mouth set in a thin straight line. All the time he had been standing over her she had been aware of his temper bubbling away just below the surface and did not relish the prospect of its being unleashed against her now. She took a deep breath.

'What is it that's upset you so, Angus?' She tried to keep her voice steady. 'Is it something to do with Ben coming to see me yesterday? I didn't know he was coming, you know.'

Angus glowered at her. 'I know. Bridie told me,' he said between gritted teeth.

Maggie felt her own temper beginning to rise. 'Oh, for Heaven's sake stop acting like a truculent child and tell me what's wrong. We're grown-ups aren't we? We should be able to talk to each other.'

She saw him bristle at the suggestion he was being childish. Anger sparked in his eyes and he leaned over the bar towards her, pushing his face into hers. 'I don't want to talk anything over with you. Go and talk to Ben if you want to talk.' He said the name as if he was spitting a hot coal out of his mouth.

Maggie's temper flared like a fire racing through a tinder-dry, building. 'I must have been out of my mind to think I could have a relationship with you. Why don't you start acting like a man instead of a sulky school boy?' She pressed her lips together as if to stop further angry words from escaping. Tossing her head she swung round on her heels and made for the door, her back rigid, arms straight at her sides, hands bunched into fists. She could feel his eyes burning into her back but she didn't turn round.

'You clearly didn't think me man enough last night,' Angus flung after her as she barged through the door, letting it slam shut behind her.

She heard his parting shot and now stood on the step outside the Inn chewing her bottom lip, puzzling over what he meant. She had not seen him last night. Unless, he had driven up to the cottage expecting to see her and, finding Ben's car parked outside, had jumped to the wrong conclusion. *I bet that's it,* she thought. She blinked away the angry tears which threatened, thrusting her hands deep into the pockets of her jeans as if trying to contain all the indignation and frustration she felt at Angus's hurtful attack. Why should she bother to try to understand what was going on in his head. There was obviously no reasoning with him in this mood, but if he imagined for one moment she was the sort of woman who would go to one lover having spent the previous night in the arms of another, then he did not know her at all. The day which had begun so auspiciously and which she had embraced with such eager anticipation now looked as black and as stormy as the weather outside.

She stood looking out over the water undecided as to what to do next. Perhaps she should go and talk things over with Bridie or maybe she had better just go back to the cottage and start packing. The anonymity of big city life suddenly appealed... there few people knew her or anything about her, there she could once again be swallowed up in the nameless crowds, there she could lick the wounds of yet another rejection in private.

The grim irony of running back to London to get over yet another failed love affair was not lost on her and all at once the resentment which had buoyed her up and fuelled her temper deserted her. She felt drained and deflated. Angus clearly believed her to be duplicitous and was regretting ever getting involved with her. It just went to show how wrong you could be about someone...just as she'd been about Ben. Would she never learn? She had resisted Angus for a long time but had then opened up to him and had fallen in love. Now, she didn't know if there was a future for them at all. As soon as the arrangements were made to put Catherine Ross's name on her gravestone, maybe she should go back to London and pick up her life there. Perhaps, after all, there was nothing for her here.

CHAPTER 23

As she trudged through the village, Maggie saw one of the Inn's regulars ambling towards her. Obviously making his way there for his daily pint, she thought. She nodded in reply to the old man's greeting.

'Best hurry home lass,' he added cheerfully as he passed her by. 'Them clouds is been ridden by Satan himself. Almighty storm's brewing.' Just then a powerful gust of wind snatched open Maggie's jacket and sent the old man tottering. 'Told you,' he said smugly and chuckling he carried on his way.

Clutching her jacket Maggie eyed the sky. The clouds had thickened and darkened, and now had an ominous purple tinge to them like that of a livid bruise. A dull heaviness hung in the air and then she felt the first drop of rain hit her head. Before she had gone two steps, the heavens opened. It was like being in a car wash without a car, she thought, as the wind buffeted her and flung the stinging rain into her face. She hurried along and was relieved to see the cottage finally loom up before her. She was soaked and shivering. Stripping off in the kitchen, and leaving her clothes to puddle on the floor, she ran upstairs and jumped into the shower.

She closed her eyes and gave herself up to the stream of water as it pounded her skin and its heat penetrated through to her bones. Her thoughts returned to her altercation with Angus. Should she have tried harder to get to the bottom of what was troubling him? But she dismissed the idea as soon as it occurred to her; his attitude had not been exactly conducive to a civilized, reasoned discussion. Clearly he didn't trust her and, without that, what hope was there?

Damn the man. Damn him for the stupid fool he is.

Thank Heavens she hadn't embarrassed herself by telling him her real feelings. At least she still had her self-respect; she ignored the voice inside her head reminding her that self-respect wouldn't keep her warm at night or give her a hug when she needed one.

Then, without warning, she felt a familiar, deep chill sweep over her, as if someone had opened a door and let in a blast of cold air. Her eyes shot open and the next moment her hand flew up to her mouth. The glass wall of the shower had steamed over and there, as plain as day in an old-fashioned, script were the words

James Douglas Ross.

As she stared in disbelief, the writing gradually lost definition and she was left gazing at the spot where it had appeared. There was nothing there, only a section of steamed-over glass. She shook her head and shuddered, rubbing her arms and feeling the goose pimples raised all along them. Maybe she had imagined it but somehow she didn't think so. Quickly she turned off the water and stepped out of the shower, suddenly apprehensive. The wind was screaming even louder outside and the rain, battering against the window panes, sounded as if tiny stones were being hurled against the glass. It promised to be a wild night.

Hugging her dressing gown tightly round her, Maggie ran down the stairs to light the fire. It was already dark outside because of the weather and, as soon as the wood was crackling away in the hearth, she went over to the window to draw the curtains. As she reached up to close them, an explosion of sheet lightning lit up the garden and beyond as if it were day. It was immediately followed by a deafening, ear-numbing roll of thunder which seemed to split the air. The storm was directly overhead. Maggie froze.

Illuminated for an instant by the flash of light, there on the hillside stood the figure of the woman in grey,

Catherine Ross. Maggie's heart beat fiercely and she remained where she was, straining to see through the wall of impenetrable blackness. She held her breath, waiting for the next lightning flash. There it was. For a split second a world of jumbled images was revealed in its silver light; the hillside was empty.

Another crack of thunder growled and echoed across the sky as with trembling fingers Maggie pulled the curtains shut and went to sit by the fire now burning cheerily in the hearth. She held out her hands to the flames to warm her numb fingers. Bridie had been right. It seemed Catherine Ross's spirit was not finished with her yet. She glanced around nervously and then huddled deeper into her chair, staring into the fire. She mulled over all that they had so far found out and wondered what or who it was that kept Catherine tied to this place. Maggie felt she was close to the answer but, every time she thought she had it, it eluded her like a will o' the wisp; in sight but insubstantial, just out of reach.

She closed her eyes and let her mind wander. Then it struck her. The only thing which made any sense was the child. She sat bolt upright as the idea took hold. That had to be it. The name written in the steam had been "James Douglas Ross." He had to be the key to why Catherine's spirit was not at peace. She jumped up and began prowling around the room. She knew, she just knew, that no matter how long Calum searched, however many documents and reports he accessed, he would never find the death of James Douglas Ross recorded anywhere…*because…because he is here!*

Catherine Ross would never have left her son with someone else. She had taken him with her on her journey and something had happened along the way. Maybe, as Bridie suggested, she'd been forced to leave him hidden somewhere, intending to go back for him as soon as she found help. Needing to be reunited with her son had to be the reason she was continuing to haunt the hillside. Maggie collapsed onto her chair. She was right, she knew she was.

Then, without warning, all the lights went out.

The fear was instant; it arrowed straight to her belly. For a few seconds Maggie couldn't think and cowered back in the chair, clasping her arms around her knees, hugging them and trying to make herself as small and insignificant as possible. The storm continued to unleash its fury but after a few moments, when nothing else had happened, reason began to reassert itself and she gave a nervous laugh. *Foolish woman.* The gale must have brought down power cables somewhere. Fortunately the room was not completely dark as the fire was still burning but she needed to find a light. She remembered Bridie's gift of the previous week and scrabbled around at the side of her chair, sighing with relief as her hand closed round the bundle of candles

A little later with several burning, their sweet scent drifting in the air and some extra logs on the fire, she lay back in the chair. The rain was still lashing down, drilling against the walls as if it were trying to find a way through and the wind continued unabated, but the room was warm and cosy and she herself was safe and secure. She supposed power cuts were a fact of life in the Highlands during wild weather and she would need to get used to that if she was going to stay here; though, with all that had happened, it was a big 'if'.

She tucked her feet under her and leaned her head against the soft leather as she mulled over the idea of remaining in Invershee. Now she had calmed down, her earlier thoughts about leaving the village did not seem so attractive. Maybe she and Angus could get over their quarrel. She knew, in her heart of hearts, she wanted to; she had never been a quitter and giving up so easily was not really an option for her. Perhaps they both just needed a little cooling off time. She would go down to the Inn and see him again tomorrow and......

The sudden, splintering sound of breaking glass interrupted her thoughts and she shot upright in the chair. The noise had come from upstairs. She sat motionless, listening, but all she could hear was the wind shrieking and the rain drumming against the thick walls of the cottage. She waited a moment longer but there was nothing further. *Better investigate*, she thought. If her bedroom window had been blown in everything would be getting soaked by the rain.

She lifted one of the candles from the mantelshelf and gingerly made her way up the stairs, pausing every few steps to listen. All she could hear were the violent sounds of the storm. As she reached the tiny landing, draughts of cold air swirled around her and, certain now the wind had somehow smashed her bedroom window, she stepped over to the doorway.

The glow from the candle did not spread very far into the room but she could see shimmers and sparkles on the wooden floor as shards of glass reflected what light there was. The noise of the weather was much louder now and icy fingers of wind clawed at her clothes. The rain was driving in through the broken pane and pooling on the floor. She had to get something to cover the hole in the window before any more damage was done.

She felt her way carefully down the stairs to the kitchen to fetch the hammer and nails she had left in a drawer after fixing the rowan wood cross above the door and then made her way to the spare room and grabbed a rug from the bed

Back in her bedroom, she put the candle just inside the doorway and, careful not to cut herself, picked up those pieces and splinters of glass she could see. She reached for the rug and then paused as she felt the temperature in the room plummet. If it had been chilly before, now it was glacial. Maggie could see her breath hanging in the air like frozen mist

She cried out as a sudden clap of thunder split the air and, with a loud crack, the remaining glass in the window fractured and splintered, falling and shattering on the floor. The curtains billowed and twisted as if being shaken by a giant hand. Then, all at once, the wind died down and there was a tomb-like stillness everywhere. At the same moment the candle in the doorway flared, guttered and went out.

Maggie began to shake. She remained where she was, half-kneeling on the floor, unable to move as if her muscles had turned to water. A sense of dread crept over her and, as if subjected to a charge of static electricity, the hairs all over her body stood on end. There was someone else in the room.

Holding her breath, Maggie concentrated her attention on the far wall where the window was located. She could feel a presence in the room but could see nothing in the inky blackness. As her eyes gradually accustomed to the dark she was able to make out a shape standing motionless about two feet in front of her. Letting out her breath slowly, she whispered, 'Who is it?' and then, when there was just silence, 'Catherine?' Her voice sounded hollow in the empty air. The figure did not move. A sudden flash of lightning lit up the room and in its strange half-light she saw the form of Catherine Ross.

The figure let out a cry of such shattering desolation and despair that Maggie felt her blood freeze and shudders rack her body. She closed her eyes against the sight of such suffering and tried to resist the heart-rending appeal in the woman's tearful lamentation.

'Help me. Please, help me.'

The atmosphere was so heavy with suffering and grief Maggie felt as if an iron band was slowly tightening around her chest. She gripped her upper arms, barely aware of her nails gouging into the soft flesh, as she struggled to control her laboured breathing.

'Find him.'

Again the anguished plea resonated throughout the room. The sound quivered along Maggie's nerves until she thought she would scream.

The air around seemed to be growing thicker and even icier and she felt a shivering breeze waft across her face and ruffle her hair. She forced herself to open her eyes.

At that moment, another explosion of lightning lit up the darkness, and Maggie shrank back as she saw the figure reach out toward her. Hands, as frozen as a winter graveyard, touched her face and she felt clammy fingers crawling over her skin. She shrieked as she tried to scramble away from their unearthly clutch. Shaking and whimpering, she crouched by the door. A mouldering smell of dankness and decay began to seep into the room and Maggie felt her stomach heave. Dry, belly-racking sobs tore through her as she retched until she felt numb and drained of all sensation.

The room was again as black as the darkest midnight and she knew at once that Catherine was gone. But the sound of her terrible cries still rang and echoed in Maggie's ears, and collapsing onto the floor, she began shaking as if she had a fever. She curled up, hugging her knees to her chest. All at once, the words of a prayer her father had taught her flashed into her mind. With her breath coming in shuddering gasps, she began mumbling them over and over again between sobs. 'From ghoulies and.... Ghosties....and long-leggety beasties....'

Outside, the storm continued to rage and howl unabated.

A few hours earlier Angus had watched with mixed feelings as Maggie marched out of the Inn in high dudgeon. A small part of him admired the way she had stood up to him but a far greater part was aggrieved and angry at the way he had been taken in by her. Her air of fragility had deceived him, lured him into falling in love for the very first time in his life, and he spent the remainder of the day bitterly regretting his weakness.

Caitlin gave him a wide berth all day, refusing to speak to him whilst he was in such a foul mood unless she absolutely had to. He stood morosely behind the bar with scarcely a civil word for anyone, let alone his regular customers. He did not want to believe Maggie had misled him, but he knew what he had seen last night.

Today, she had pretended she didn't know what he was so upset about and had then stormed out as if he was in the wrong. He would never have believed her capable of such shameless behaviour. His mind was in turmoil and, during the course of the afternoon and evening, he managed to smash several glasses, knock over a pint of beer he had just pulled for a customer and had offended just about everyone. When he was not serving, he stood drumming his fingers on the bar muttering under his breath.

When Caitlin saw Bridie come into the Inn she breathed a sigh of relief and hurried up to her. 'For Heaven's sake will you see if you can find out what's eating Angus?' she said quietly. 'He's been angry and miserable all day. I've never known him to be like this before and he won't tell me what's wrong.' Bridie looked over at Angus, smiled and gave him a little wave. He glowered back at her.

'Hmmm, I see what you mean.'

'He was bad enough this morning but he's been a whole lot worse since he and Maggie had words this afternoon.'

Bridie's eyes widened. 'They had an argument?'

'I'll say. She stormed off afterwards, didn't even touch her lunch.'

'Alright, leave this to me.' Bridie patted Caitlin's shoulder and then advanced towards the bar.

'Can I have a word, Angus?' she said sweetly but her look was steely with determination.

He eyed her with scarcely concealed annoyance. 'What about?'

She gave him a knowing look. 'Maggie,' she said quietly. Angus didn't answer. His face closed up and his mouth thinned into a grim line. Undeterred Bridie continued. 'What's wrong Angus? It's not like you to be such a grump.'

'It's none of you business,' he warned through gritted teeth.

'Of course it is. I'm your oldest friend'. She smiled at him. 'And I'll be your only friend if you carry on like this,' she added dryly.

Angus gave a firm shake of his head. 'I don't want to talk about it.'

'Oh for goodness sake Angus, stop acting like a spoilt child. Tell me what's happened.'

He scowled. Maggie had flung a similar accusation at him earlier. However, he knew Bridie well enough to see she was determined to get to the bottom of what was wrong.

'Maggie's fiancé stayed the night.'

'And..?' Bridie said with amused impatience.

'What do you mean, "And?" He stayed the night with Maggie.'

'Yes, I know. In the spare room, she told me.'

'Really? You sure about that?' Angus's voice dripped sarcasm.

'Yes, I am. I know Maggie isn't a liar. She told me she realised she'd never truly loved Ben, and I believe her. He tried to persuade her to go back to him but, after they'd talked things over, he accepted they don't have a future together.'

Angus's eyes narrowed. 'Well, why didn't he just leave then? There was no need for him to stay.'

'Come on now, Angus, be fair,' Bridie said, a touch of irritation in her voice. 'The poor man had just driven all the way up from London. You surely wouldn't expect Maggie to turn him out so he could drive all the way back again would you?'

'Only one bedroom light went on,' Angus insisted, although he was beginning to wonder whether he had misjudged the situation. He stared at Bridie. 'I thought…'

'I can guess what you thought.' She put her hand on his arm and gave it a little squeeze. 'But Maggie's not like that.'

Angus shook his head. 'But why didn't she tell me that this afternoon?'

'I don't suppose you gave her much of a chance to,

did you?' He had the grace to look shame-faced and Bridie smiled affectionately at him. 'You do realise she's in love with you don't you?'

At that moment all the lights in the bar dimmed, flickered and went out.

Until then, Angus had only been vaguely aware of the storm raging outside. When the room was once again illuminated by the candles he always kept behind the bar for such an emergency, he took Bridie by the arm and led her to sit by the fire.

'How do you know?' he asked quietly.

She gazed at him, puzzled for a moment and then smiled slowly. 'How do I know Maggie's in love with you?' He nodded. His gaze was searching as he tried to assess the truth of what Bridie had said. 'Oh, Angus, I just know. Anyone who's got eyes in their head can see it. Besides, why do you think she's stayed here so long? She could have gone back to London days ago. I know she got caught up in trying to identify the Unknown Maid, and her ghostly visitor, but you're the main reason Maggie's still here, you numpty.'

Angus had stopped listening, however and was staring at her in alarm. 'Maggie's being haunted by a ghost?'

Bridie saw he knew nothing of Maggie's encounters with the woman in grey and she quickly explained, before adding, 'So you see it's the same mystery figure Morag MacIver saw all those years ago and now we know who she is. The only thing we don't know for sure is why she's still haunting Maggie. It's probably connected to the child, James Ross......' but she was talking to empty air.

Angus was already up out of his chair and reaching for the torch he kept behind the bar.

'Maggie's at the cottage alone in the pitch dark with a ghost hanging around, or whatever it is ghosts do. Anything could happen. She'll be terrified. I'm going up there right now' and with that he was through the door and gone.

He didn't remember much of the drive up to the cottage, aware only of the rain lashing down and branches torn from trees flailing through the air to bounce of the car; his overriding thought was of reaching Maggie and making sure she was safe.

CHAPTER 24

Now here he was, sitting on her bedroom floor, cradling her and trying to calm her convulsive sobs.

'She was here, Angus. She was here in this room, Catherine Ross was standing there.' Maggie's voice shook as she pointed to the spot with trembling fingers. 'Oh, and the sound she made....I'll never forget it as long as I live. It was so full of sorrow and desperation.' Maggie shivered and clung to him. 'I have to find her baby. I have to find James for her sake so she can be at peace.' Angus held her closer, whispering words of comfort, letting her cry out her anguish until at last she lay quiescent in his arms.

He could feel the tremors still shaking her body but she was calmer now. Whispering, 'It's alright my sweet lass, I have you now, you're safe' over and over again, he gently smoothed back her hair from her damp face. Her ivory skin was flushed and tear-stained, her eyes shadowed and red-rimmed, but to him she had never looked more beautiful. Angus was amazed he could ever have doubted the woman he held close; he knew now he loved her beyond all reason.

'She's such a tortured soul, Angus. We have to help her.' Maggie's voice quivered with emotion and she gripped his arm tightly.

'We will. Don't worry, we will,' he soothed.

Maggie leaned into him and rested her throbbing head against his shoulder, comforted by his presence. She never thought to question why he had suddenly appeared or how he seemed to know what she was babbling about, she was just so thankful he was there.

For several moments they sat on the floor in silence. Maggie, reliving her latest encounter with Catherine Ross's spirit, hearing the cries of a tormented soul echo in her head. For Catherine's sake she had to find out what had become of her son.

The glow from the torch Angus had flung down when he had taken her in his arms barely illuminated the room but she could dimly make out the swelling movement of the curtains caught by the wind as it gusted through the shattered window and feel its icy blast on her face and arms. She started to shake as the shock of her recent experience and the cold air drained the warmth from her body.

She murmured in protest as Angus released her and stood up swiftly. Then he reached down to lift her effortlessly into his arms. Feeling his way to the spare room he laid her tenderly on the bed, pulling the covers around her. She felt the bed move as he lay down beside her and drew her to him. 'Go to sleep, Maggie, you need it. I'm here. I won't let anything happen to you,' he said softly.

Emotionally spent, and so tired it felt as though her eyelids had sandpaper inside, she burrowed down in the bed, feeling its warmth gradually spreading throughout her body. She was thankful for the reassurance of Angus alongside her and the comforting strength of his arms holding her. She smiled and closed her eyes.

'Thank you Angus. I'm so glad you're here' and then, on a whispered sigh, she added sleepily, 'I love you.'

Angus's arms tightened round her and in the darkness he grinned. 'I know,' he murmured but she was asleep. The night enfolded them both in its careless embrace as the sounds of the storm gradually rumbled away into the far distance.

Maggie awoke to the sound of bird song. The storm was over and the birds twittered and chirruped as they darted passed the slightly open window, diving down to feast on worms drawn to the surface by the sunshine which now bathed the garden. She lay there for a moment wondering where she was. Then the events of the previous night flooded back and she sat up with a start. She was in the spare bed and, turning her head, she saw Angus, fully-dressed, stretched out next to her. He was leaning on one elbow, his head on his hand watching her with an amused glint in his eyes.

'Good morning, Miss MacQueen,' he said, a smile tugging at the corners of his mouth. 'I trust you slept well?'

She stared at him, unblinking. 'How long have you been lying there watching me sleep?' She was still wearing her night clothes and, feeling slightly embarrassed, she tugged the bedcovers up under her chin.

'Ages,' he grinned. 'Did you know you frown a lot and grunt when you're asleep?' There was a teasing note in his voice as he reached his hand towards her and gently smoothed a strand of hair back from her face. It was such an intimate gesture she felt the heat ball in her stomach.

'I do not,' she retorted and, flinging back the covers, she jumped out of bed. 'I'm going to have a shower,' and she was out of the room in an instant.

She began to relax as the hot water stung her skin. She closed her eyes and held up her face to the stream of warmth cascading over her. She heard the bathroom door open. 'I won't be long,' she called, feeling a sudden tension trembling along her nerves. 'You can have the shower in a minute,' she continued trying to hide the tremor in her voice.

She gasped as the shower door opened and Angus stepped in behind her. 'The thing is, Maggie,' he said softly in her ear, 'I'm a great advocate of doing all I can to save the planet and water conservation is a cause close to my heart. After all, why waste water on two showers when we can share one?'

His arms snaked round her waist then slid down over her hips and across the soft mound below her smooth, flat belly before slowly moving up to cup her breasts gently in his hands. His lips nuzzled her neck. Maggie felt as if her insides were turning liquid and her mind focused purely on the sensation of his fingertips moving across her bare skin. She moaned faintly and then groaned as he rubbed his fingers teasingly over her erect nipples.

Angus had meant to be gentle with her but the blood was pounding through his veins and, as she responded to his touch, so his own arousal began to overwhelm him. He felt her tremble as she pressed back against him and his need for her swirled through him. Seizing her arm, he twisted her around to face him. Her eyes were half-closed, her breathing uneven but she managed to murmur provocatively, 'What now, Mr. Cameron?'

'This!' he said, his own breathing laboured and his voice tight with mounting desire. His hands slid down to her hips and he lifted her in one swift movement as his mouth ravaged hers. He felt a tremor run through her and her legs slipped around him, gripping him tightly.

Maggie poured all her longing for him into the kiss. Her back was pressed against the wall of the shower, her breasts crushed against his chest but all she was aware of was the man; his vigour, his strength and the essential maleness of him. A deep purr escaped her throat and, as she opened up for him, he drove into her with an abandonment she had never experienced. She shuddered as he entered her and felt the assault on her nervous system like a rising tide sweep over her, fill her and leave her gasping.

As Angus felt her vibrate against him, he emptied himself into her, the release bringing with it an overwhelming sense of protectiveness and an intensity of feeling that was beyond anything he had ever felt before. She simply took his breath away and he knew he could never let her go.

'Tha gaol agam ort,' he whispered as she nestled her head against his neck.

Maggie tightened her arms around him. 'That's what you said to me when we were on the hill with the horses,' she murmured, feeling as if she could stay locked in this embrace forever. 'What does it really mean?' She drew back her head and looked at him searchingly, her eyes level with his.

'I love you.'

She could see the truth of what he said reflected in his face and she smiled slowly. 'It's a good job you do. I don't have wild sex in the shower with just anyone you know.'

He grinned. 'I'm relieved to hear it.' He bent his head and kissed her so thoroughly that she felt the hot surges of passion once again stirring in her blood.

She put her hand against his chest. 'I think we'd best find somewhere a little more comfortable this time don't you?'

'This time?' Angus raised his eyebrows in mock surprise, his pulse beginning to race again.

'Yes.' Maggie paused and then added with a sideways glance, 'unless of course you've run out of steam. You are a bit older than me so naturally your stamina....' She didn't get to finish the sentence. Angus gripped her round the waist and lifted her bodily out of the shower. Ignoring her faint-hearted protests, he carried her dripping across the small landing and into the spare room.

He flung her onto the bed and growled, 'Now what was that you were saying?'

She laughed up at him and held out her arms. He slowly lowered himself onto her, gazing into her eyes as she wrapped herself around him. She was glowing. Her skin was flushed and her eyes danced as he teased her mouth with darting kisses, flicking his tongue between her teeth, gently nibbling at her lower lip. Then rolling to lie beside her, he ran his hand slowly over her fine-toned body, admiring and exploring every contour, every crevice, every hollow.

Each touch of his fingers sent spasms of anticipation thrilling through her until she thought she would burn up with wanting him. She urged him on with soft moans and sighs of pleasure but he seemed determined to savour their love-making this time, to enjoy getting to know her body and to take delight in her response to his touch. Again and again he took her to the edge of desire with the soft caress of his hands and the gentle teasing of his tongue before drawing back and leaving her frustrated at the peak of arousal.

She grew more desperate, raking her nails down his back, murmuring his name over and over until he could no longer deny her or himself. She was hot and wet as he slipped into her and with unrestrained passion she urged him on until the pinnacle was reached and she gave herself up to the moment and to him. Hot waves of pleasure surged through her; it was if all the bones in her body were melting.

Then she sensed him let go of the control he had struggled to maintain. He plunged deep inside her and with each thrust of his hips she felt renewed ripples of sweet sensation pulse through her body until she was limp and spent. With a final shudder he spilled himself into her and she held him close, feeling his heart thudding in his chest as his body relaxed against hers.

They lay like that for several moments, their bodies slick and shiny with sweat as their heartbeats and breathing gradually returned to normal. Then gently he moved to lie beside her, and so they remained for some time, sated and exhausted, drowsily aware of each other but neither wanting to move and break the spell.

Finally Maggie stirred. 'I think I need some coffee.' She nuzzled his shoulder. 'How about you?'

Angus smiled lazily. 'That's the best idea you've

had all morning.'

'Really?' She grinned back. 'The *best* idea? Are you sure?'

'Well, second best,' he acknowledged with a chuckle and watched with unconcealed admiration as she rose and walked towards the bathroom to retrieve her robe. 'You have a fine body on you, Miss Macqueen,' he said and she threw him a happy smile over her shoulder as she disappeared through the door.

He heard her run down the stairs and settled back against the pillows, relishing the sense of fulfilment and contentment which spread through him. He wondered what the future held for them but knew in the very depths of his heart that his was with her, wherever that might be. She answered a need in him which, until now, he hadn't even known existed. He closed his eyes and in his mind revisited the feel of her, the taste of her….She really did have the most amazing eyes he thought. Today they were the sharp blue of a frozen glacier, bright and shining in the morning light, unlike last night when they'd been dark and shadowed, drowning in tears.

'Well now,' Maggie's voice from the doorway roused him from his daydreaming, 'you're looking mighty pleased with yourself, some might even say self-satisfied.'

Angus opened one eye and grinned. 'I was just thinking how lucky I am to have found myself the perfect woman, sexy, passionate, warm, loving… and one who gets up to make the coffee. What more could any man ask?'

'You should be thankful this coffee's scalding otherwise I might have been tempted to pour it over your head,' she retorted, handing him a steaming mug, secretly delighted he thought her sexy. She plumped herself down beside him and sipped her drink. He had a good body too, she thought, admiring his hard, muscular frame, his arms and face tanned and his legs strong and powerful from the horse-riding he did. She gave a deep sigh of happiness. Who could have imagined they would be here now like this after their dramatic fall-out of yesterday.

Almost as if he read her thoughts, Angus said, 'About yesterday, Maggie…'

She put out her hand to stop him saying anything more but he ignored her and went on, 'I was totally in the wrong. I assumed the worst … that you and Ben were back together. I never gave you a chance to explain.' He paused, collecting his thoughts. 'I was jealous,' he stated simply. 'It's an emotion I've never experienced before and I didn't know how to deal with it.' He looked at her uncertainly.

She smiled and shook her head. 'It's not important Angus. Really, all that matters is us, here, now. Besides, I rather think I like the thought of your being a little jealous.' She took a sip of coffee, 'But nothing happened between Ben and me, I hope you believe that?'

'Of course I do,' Angus nodded. Then with a chuckle he added, 'Anyway I was as much jealous of his red sports car as I was of his being with you.' He ducked quickly as Maggie aimed what remained of the lukewarm contents of her coffee mug at his head.

'Now I'll have to have another shower,' he said in mock dismay. 'Coming?' and he reached out to grab her hand.

Some time later, after a long shower…which, it has to be said, had very little to do with soap or cleanliness… they sat companionably at the kitchen table over a late breakfast of coffee and toast as Maggie told him about her supernatural experiences with the Bodach and the spirit of Catherine Ross, sharing with him too all she'd subsequently been able to discover. Angus listened intently watching the different emotions play across her face as she described what had happened.

'I wish you'd told me about all this before. I could have helped, given you some support.'

Maggie smiled at the glum expression on his face. 'Would you have believed me? I found it hard enough to believe it myself never mind being able to make sense of it. I didn't want you to think I was some hysterical female up from the big city and afraid of every little sound, every strange shadow.'

He nodded, understanding her reluctance, and put out his hand to cover hers. 'So what now?'

'Now,' she replied confidently, 'now we find the baby.'

Angus frowned. 'But where on earth do we start? The body...' She flinched at the word and he squeezed her hand. 'That *is* what we're looking for, Maggie,' he said quietly. When she nodded reluctantly, he went on. 'The baby's body could be buried anywhere. We can't just go around digging up large parts of the Highlands. We have to be realistic about this.'

'But don't you see, Angus,' she put in eagerly, 'that's the whole point. The baby has to be somewhere close by that's why Catherine's still here, why she's still haunting me. She came into the house last night to make sure I understood that identifying her was only a means of leading us to her child. She wants us to find James so he can be buried with her. All we have to do is work out where's the most likely place for her to have hidden him.'

She looked so thoroughly convinced she was right Angus hadn't the heart to go on trying to discourage her. He just hoped she wasn't heading for a huge disappointment. He didn't think for one minute the task ahead of them was going to be easy, despite what Maggie believed. 'Well then, that's what we'll do,' and he stood up to put their breakfast dishes in the sink. As he did so there was a loud knocking at the back door.

'I'll get it,' he said as Maggie started to rise from her chair. Depositing the dishes in a waiting bowl of soapy water he ambled over and lifted the latch but not before the knocking came again.

A voice called out, 'Maggie! Are you alright?'

Angus and Maggie exchanged grins. *Bridie!* Angus opened the door and, leaning casually against the door frame effectively blocking her view of the kitchen, he enquired amiably, 'Hi there Bridie, where's the fire?'

Bridie pushed passed him with a grunt and marched into the room, pulling up short when she saw Maggie sitting at the table licking her buttery fingers with sensuous enjoyment.

'I was worried about you.' Her tone was accusing. 'The phones are out because of the storm and my damn car wouldn't start this morning.' She dropped down on the chair Angus had recently vacated and glared at her friend. Maggie raised her eyebrows and took a sip of coffee. 'I was just worried,' Bridie repeated more mildly, 'that's all.'

'I'm fine, Bridie. As you can see Angus was here to take care of me.'

'Hrmph!' Bridie turned her attention to Angus who had closed the door and was now standing leaning against the sink. 'As for you, Caitlin is as mad as a bear with a honey pot full of bees. You were supposed to be doing the morning shift, remember? I won't repeat what she told me to do to you if I found you.' She laughed. 'I can see I needn't have worried,' she said, her voice heavy with irony.

'No,' Maggie smiled over at Angus, 'you needn't have.'

'I must say I'm glad you two have sorted out things between you....at last.' Bridie gave a nod of satisfaction. 'Now I'd better get back and help out. The storm did a fair bit of damage in the village.'

Angus looked at her with concern. 'Is everything okay at the Inn?'

'Apart from Caitlin wanting your liver for breakfast you mean? Yes, the Inn got off very lightly, just a few pots blown about and a couple of slates off.'

Angus straightened up. 'I'll come back with you and lend a hand. I have to make my peace with Caitlin anyway. She'll be alright once I've apologised and done a bit of grovelling.'

Maggie stood up. 'Why don't I make us all some fresh coffee and then we can go down to the village together. I'd like to help too.'

Whilst the coffee percolated, she told Bridie about Catherine Ross materializing in the bedroom at the height of the storm.

'My God, that's pretty serious. She must be getting really desperate.'

'That's what I thought too.' Maggie shuddered as she recalled the ghastly wailing and desolate, almost animal-like howls which had so unnerved her last night. 'It was really terrifying,' she confessed. 'I was never so pleased to see anyone as I was to see Angus,' and she flashed him a grateful smile.

Angus smiled in return. 'It was my pleasure,' he said giving her an exaggerated wink. 'Really, it was entirely my pleasure.' His smile deepened into a grin as he saw a deep blush suffuse Maggie's face. She glanced quickly at Bridie as she went to pour the coffee but the other woman didn't seem to have noticed the little exchange; if she had, she gave no sign of it.

'There must be a reason she's becoming more active,' Bridie mused.

'I think it's because her son's somewhere around here, somewhere close by,' Maggie said, 'and now we know who she is, she wants us to find him.'

'You know, Maggie, you could be right. It'd certainly fit with what we've found out so far.'

'Angus is convinced I'm crazy thinking I'm going to be able to find the baby.'

'I never said that,' Angus protested. 'I just can't see it being as easy as you seem to expect. Anyway, I'd better off,' he announced as he finished his coffee. 'I'll see you both later.' He bent down and gave Maggie a resounding kiss. 'You and I'll pick up where we left off tonight,' he said with a grin. They could hear him whistling as he walked to his car.

Bridie laughed and hugged her friend. 'I'm so glad things have worked out for you Maggie. Angus is a good man…and a sexy one at that,' she added smiling. 'You're a lucky woman.'

'Aren't I just?' Maggie replied smugly.

CHAPTER 25

Maggie was just closing the back door behind them as they left to drive down into the village, when she heard Bridie exclaim, 'Oh my, that's a shame.'

'What is?' She turned and then looked where Bridie was pointing.

'Your rowan tree's down. I didn't notice when I arrived, I was too concerned with checking you were okay. The storm must have brought it down last night.'

'Oh no!'

Maggie ran down the path to look at the damage. Bridie followed more slowly and when she reached the bottom of the garden, Maggie was crouched down inspecting the tree which was on its side, its slender branches spread out across the ground. Clumps of dark, peaty soil clung to half of its roots now exposed to the late morning air.

Maggie felt unaccountably sad. She had enjoyed seeing the tree, with its scarlet berries and its deep, grey-green foliage, standing like a slim guardian at the end of the garden.

'The Witches' Tree,' she murmured softly, gazing at the gaping, dark hole which now lay revealed beside the dry stone wall. She straightened up slowly as Bridie came up to her and the two women stood together quietly surveying the destruction. 'Maybe, it can be replanted,' Maggie said.

'Maybe.'

As they turned away to walk back down the path something glinting in the black earth at the bottom of the hole caught Maggie's eye. She paused and then went over to the gash in the ground.

'What's that?' She bent down and began scrabbling in the soft soil. Bridie came to stand beside her.

'What is it?'

'I don't know. I thought I saw something shiny. The sunlight just caught it. It looks like a piece of metal.'

'Maybe it's buried treasure!'

'Got it,' Maggie held open her hand in triumph to reveal something the size of a small pebble. It was dirt-encrusted but in places there glinted a touch of silver.

'It *is* buried treasure,' Bridie exclaimed as she took it from Maggie and began to exam it. She brushed off some of the soil and then, picking up a handful of material from her skirt, she began to carefully polish the metal object.

'I think…,' she began rubbing a little harder, 'I think it's a brooch. Yes look, there's a pin at the back here,' and she held it out to Maggie. 'Do you know,' she went on slowly, 'I believe I know what this is. It's a Luckenbooth brooch.'

Maggie turned the object over in her hands. 'What's one of those?' She looked at Bridie who stretched out her hand and took it back.

'It's a traditional Scottish wedding brooch, a love token given by a groom to his bride on their wedding day. Usually it was handed down through different generations.' Bridie cleaned off a little more of the soil. 'Yes, see, it's in the shape of double hearts surmounted by a crown … that's the crown of Mary, Queen of Scots …and I'm sure it is silver.'

Maggie studied the small item of jewellery resting in Bridie's palm. 'Whatever is it doing buried under a tree?' Bridie didn't answer and, when Maggie looked up at her, she saw her friend was staring at the brooch with an excited gleam in her eyes. 'Bridie? What is it?'

Bridie cleared her throat. 'The thing is, Maggie…and I don't want you to get your hopes up…but the thing is, traditionally, a brooch like this would be pinned to the shawl of the first born child of a marriage.' She heard Maggie's sharp intake of breath and knew her friend had immediately grasped the possible significance of their find.

'You mean,' Maggie breathed, her eyes shining as

she gazed at the tiny bauble lying in Bridie's hand, 'this could be where the baby is ?'

'Yes, that's exactly what I mean,' Bridie replied, nodding her head to affirm her certainty.

Maggie stared at her friend. Excitement bubbled up inside her. Was their search at an end? She turned to gaze at the cavity by her feet. Could it possibly be true? Was Catherine Ross's baby son somewhere in that dark, moist earth? 'We'll have to get a trowel or something so we can have a dig about. We don't want to destroy any evidence or anything.'

'You've been watching too many detective films,' Bridie teased but then her expression grew serious. 'Actually you're probably right. Have you got one anywhere?'

'I think there are a couple of small gardening tools in one of the kitchen cupboards,' Maggie called over her shoulder as she hurried back to the cottage.

She emerged a few moments later waving a trowel in triumph. The two women knelt by the void and Maggie began scraping away at the earth with great care. Some of the rowan's roots had torn when the tree had fallen and remained tangled and twisted in the ground. Maggie was gently removing the soil from around them when she felt a faint resistance to her probing as if there were something just below the surface.

'There's something here,' she said, trying to stay calm. It could be anything, she realised: an old pot, a bit of broken china, any old piece of household rubbish. Her instincts told her otherwise, however, and she carried on painstakingly scratching away at the soil, not wanting to break or damage whatever it was she was gradually uncovering. Finally, she sat back on her heels and surveyed what she had revealed.

'What does this look like to you, Bridie?'

Bridie knelt beside her friend and scrutinized the scrap of torn and decaying cloth which lay exposed.

'Well, it could be part of a shawl, I'm not sure, but if

you look here,' she pointed to part of the uncovered material, 'you can see a kind of fringing which suggests that's what it might be. Can you clear any more of it and then we can have a proper look?'

Maggie leaned forward and renewed her efforts, clearing more of the soil from around the object. 'I think you're right Bridie, it is a piece of a shawl of some kind.' She tugged it gently afraid of tearing it. 'I'm not sure but it seems to be wrapped around something,' she said, biting her bottom lip as she studied the way the fabric lay folded over on itself. She began cautiously scraping a little more of the earth away and then stopped and stared down at the dirt. She reached forward and carefully lifted a small piece of what looked to be a slightly curved, very discoloured piece of bone. She turned and silently held it out to show Bridie. She felt almost sick with excitement.

The two of them gazed at the object lying in Maggie's flattened palm. After a breathless moment they looked at each other.

'Does this looks like a bone to you?' Maggie was unable to hide the exhilaration in her voice. Bridie nodded soundlessly looking steadily at her friend. She could sense the tension in the other woman; it was emanating from her in waves. She had to rein in Maggie's enthusiasm. If this turned out to be a false trail she didn't know how Maggie would cope with having her hopes and expectations so cruelly dashed.

'It could be a bone from a small animal. I don't think we should jump to any conclusions.' Bridie saw Maggie's eyes darken with frustration.

'Oh come on, Bridie. What about the shawl? It's got to be the baby's body.' She gave an impatient sigh.

Bridie shrugged. 'I don't know. It could be but it could also be someone's dead pet. People often bury their cats or dogs in the garden when they die and it's quite possible they'd wrap the animal in something before they put it in the ground.' She put a consoling arm round her friend when she saw the despondency etched on Maggie's face. 'I don't think we should do anything more until we get Calum up here.

'Whatever for?'

'Well, Calum will be able to tell if it's animal or human. If it turns out to be human then we really ought to leave it in situ because it's a burial site, or it may even be a crime scene,' she added thoughtfully.

'How do you mean a crime scene?' Maggie was aghast as she stared at her friend.

'It could be Catherine's baby or it could be someone else's, we don't know and if it is we can't tell how it died so we need to leave it here for the experts to look at. But first, before we get into all of that, we need to find out whether or not the bone is human.'

Maggie hesitated, thinking over what Bridie had said. This had to be where James Douglas Ross was buried but the other woman was right, they should go about this properly. Maggie was loath to leave their excavations but they needed Calum's expertise before they went any further. She got to her feet and brushed the soil from her jeans and her hands. The action reminded her of something and she turned eagerly to Bridie.

'Do you remember in Robert Findlay's confession when he described finding Catherine Ross how he said he noticed her hands were dirty, as if she'd been digging in the soil?'

Bridie's eyes widened in understanding. 'You think she could've been digging in the soil to bury the baby.'

Maggie nodded. 'That's it. I'm certain that's it. She swung round and gazed at the dark earth of the hole in the ground. 'James is there, I *know* he is.'

'We still have to identify the bone we found,' Bridie cautioned.

'I know, I know. So let's get down to the village and see Calum.' Maggie hurried down the path without waiting for her friend. She was torn between feelings of elation and doubt. One moment she was sure Catherine's baby son lay buried beneath the rowan tree, the next she wondered if Bridie could be right and what they had unearthed were the remains of a pet cat.

Impatient to get down to the village, she sat drumming her fingers on the driving wheel as she waited in the car for Bridie to join her. When the other woman finally slid into the passenger seat beside her, Maggie quickly started the engine. 'I hope Calum's there,' she said shortly as she crunched the gears before finally driving off.

'Well, if he isn't, we'll wait. After all, if it is James Ross's body buried in your garden, it's not as if it's going anywhere. He's been there for over a hundred and fifty years, a few more hours isn't going to make any difference, is it?' Bridie glanced at her friend and saw some of the tension leave her face.

'I'm sorry. I'm just so keyed up. I feel as if I can't wait another minute to find out the truth, but I shouldn't take my frustration out on you.' Maggie flashed an apologetic smile in Bridie's direction.

'And don't forget,' Bridie reminded her, 'even if the bone is human, it's still going to take time to find out if it is Catherine's son. Then there'll have to be all kinds of tests to establish how he died and when.'

Maggie gave a heartfelt sigh. 'Of course, you're right. I suppose I got carried away with finding the brooch and then the piece of shawl and the bone. I guess I'm just going to have to be patient.' They rounded the corner of the track and she let out a gasp. 'Good Heavens, what a mess!'

She thought back to her first sight of the village from this vantage point; how peaceful and serene it had looked. Now it appeared as if some giant hand had come along and turned everything upside down. She stopped the car and she and Bridie contemplated the scene before them. Part of the school roof had been ripped away and was sitting at a crazy angle in the middle of the green, tiles, bricks, branches and other debris was scattered over the roads and pathways. Several trees had been uprooted and were lying wherever the wind had dropped them, and they could see the sheen of water on the road in front of the post-office.

'It's amazing no-one was hurt,' Maggie said, turning to her friend.

Bridie, who had already seen the damage, nodded. 'It looks as though they're already making a start on clearing up,' she said, pointing to a group of men with chainsaws who were tackling a couple of the larger trees whilst others were loading wheelbarrows with further wreckage. 'We'd best get down there and see what we can do to help.'

The next few hours passed quickly. Maggie left Bridie in the village and then went on to the Inn. Angus was out helping with the clearing up so she made sandwiches, served in the bar and generally gave Caitlin a hand wherever she was needed. All thoughts of Catherine Ross and her baby were pushed to the back of her mind and she threw herself wholeheartedly into the business of catering to the needs of those who came in seeking sustenance. She exchanged pleasantries with all and sundry, pulled numerous pints and dished up soup and if, by the time the evening came, her legs were aching and her feet felt as if they were on fire she didn't care.

When Angus came in, he found her flushed and bright-eyed leaning on the bar chatting to Murdo Ferguson. He stood watching her for a moment, his pulse quickening and his abdominal muscles tensing. She was his; he knew it and she knew it. He saw that knowledge in her face when she became aware he was there and turned towards him, her eyes softening and her mouth curving into a welcoming smile.

'Hello there,' she said, her voice slightly husky as her smile deepened into a grin. 'Can I get you anything?'

He walked over towards her and cupped her face in his hands. 'Just this,' he said and kissed her with such fervour she felt the heat surge up from the tips of her toes through her body until it erupted in her head. When she finally got her breath back, Angus was propped up against the bar, his eyes sweeping over her with undisguised longing.

She shot him a mischievous glance, and said mildly, 'And would you like a beer with that, Sir?'

Angus chuckled. She would do for him he thought and then wondered if he would do for her. What had he to offer her: a life running a hotel when she had her own career; a life in a small rural community when she was used to the big city and all it had to recommend it, a life as a wife and mother when he had no idea whether that was what she wanted for herself?

A cold shiver of apprehension snatched at him and a flicker of doubt must have crossed his face because she reached out and took one of his hands in her two small ones and brought it up to her lips. She kissed it and smiled gaily at him.

'I've had a wonderful day today, Angus. I never knew working in a hotel and behind the bar could be so much fun.' She gazed at him. Her eyes, never leaving his, were full of reassurance and promise. 'I hope you'll let me do it again….often.'

Such a depth of emotion welled up inside him, threatening to swamp him with an intensity of feeling he was unaccustomed to that, before Maggie could protest, he leaned over and seized her by the waist. Lifting her bodily up over the bar, he swung her to stand breathless beside him, his arms holding her so close she could feel every beat of his heart as if it were her own. He laid his face against her hair and, breathing in the intoxicating scent of her, whispered, 'Marry me, Maggie, marry me.' His voice was hoarse with emotion and he held his breath as he felt her tremble against him.

For one fleeting moment Maggie wondered if she had heard him correctly but she knew she had. Her thoughts were chaotic, whirling around her brain like caged wild birds. It was the last thing she had expected him to say. She needed time to think; this was not part of the long term plan for her life.

Angus felt her stiffen against him and relaxed his grip slightly. Surely he hadn't got it wrong; he loved her, she loved him. He had taken her by surprise, that was it…God damn it, he'd taken himself by surprise…but he knew it was what he wanted more than anything.

Maggie put a hand against his chest and tried to push him away. Angus, feeling the movement, released her and stood back staring at her intently. Her eyes were wide with astonishment and she was chewing at her bottom lip. Her hands fluttered up to her face and she pushed her hair back from her forehead.

'I……that is….I don't……we don't know each other well enough to be thinking of ….' Her voice tailed away as if she couldn't bring herself to say the word.

'Marriage?' Angus supplied dryly. 'What is there to know?' He smiled lazily, although beneath the casual demeanour his stomach was performing cartwheels, summersaults and various other acrobatics.

He leaned against the bar. 'I'm nearly thirty-one years old, born under the sign of Scorpio, own and run a hotel, enjoy horse-riding, reading and listening to music. I don't drink,'…he smiled sardonically as she raised her eyebrows and made a little moue of disagreement….. 'apart from one, single, solitary lapse recently for a very understandable reason. I have all my own teeth,' and he grinned broadly as if to demonstrate the truth of what he said, 'and I play a mean game of poker.' He held his hands out to her, palms up, and shrugged his shoulders as if to say 'That's me!'

But that wasn't all there was to him Maggie thought to herself. *He's pig-headed, obstinate and full of himself, with a quick temper.* However, he was also thoughtful, caring, gentle and open-hearted; in other words a complex human–being and one with whom she was in love. She sighed and looked at him uncertainly. Did she love him enough to take a chance, to risk her future, to put her happiness in his strong, capable hands?

Angus stood watching her, waiting for a response. She bit her bottom lip as she gazed back at him, varying emotions chasing through her

'Come on Maggie, you know I love you and you said you love me' he said with a touch of impatience, 'so where's the problem?'

She took a pace back and stamped her foot. 'I won't be bullied Angus. It's a huge step and we both need to think it through. After all you hardly know me.'

'I know all I need to know. You're stubborn, inflexible, always think you're right.' He was ticking each characteristic off on his fingers as he named them. Then he put both hands on her shoulders and stared into her face. His tone softened. 'But you're also loyal, loving, sensitive, feisty and very sexy. You're the one for me Maggie and you know, deep down, that I'm for you.'

'But....' She got no further. Angus gripped her arms and pulled her towards him.

'I forgot argumentative,' he said, grinning. 'You also think too much' and he crushed her mouth under his until all the fight went out of her.

How could she resist him when he sent the blood

singing in her veins and the heat rising in her body; when every nerve and fibre of her being throbbed and ached for him; when he reached so deep inside her that it seemed as if he touched her soul. Perhaps she should stop thinking so much and just trust her feelings, her instincts; maybe it was time to stop trying to channel her life the way she thought it ought to go and let it flow. Finally they both drew back, breathless and besieged by the strength of the emotion hovering in the air between them like a thick mist.

Angus took a shuddering breath and fixed his eyes steadily on hers. 'Well, Maggie, is it to be yeah or nay? Will you marry me?'

CHAPTER 26

Maggie stared into those deep, whisky-coloured eyes, usually so open and so honest, now smouldering with such passionate intensity, and felt as if they burned into the very essence of her. She had known from the start those eyes would seduce her, would cast a spell impossible to resist and ultimately undermine her intentions to remain in control of her own destiny. Her heart took a trembling leap into her throat and she swallowed hard. She held out her hands to him, and taking them, felt a shiver of expectancy race through him.

'I'm afraid...' she hesitated, her voice not quite steady. She cleared her throat and said more strongly, 'I'm afraid that if you insist on an answer now'...she paused again, teasing him.... 'then that answer has to be yes, Angus,' and her mouth curved into a smile of pure happiness. Her eyes danced and she laughed out loud as Angus picked her up and swung her round to the sound of thunderous clapping, cheering and foot-stamping from all those present.

Neither he nor Maggie had been aware of the gradual silence which had fallen over the crowd in the bar during their exchanges as customers and staff alike had listened to, and enjoyed the little scenario being played out before them.

Now with tension abated and relief all round, someone called out. 'Thank goodness for that! Perhaps now we can get on with the serious business of drinking.' A general ripple of amusement swept the room and conversations were gradually taken up again where they had been abandoned.

Maggie felt a tap on her shoulder and turned to see Caitlin's beaming face at her shoulder. The young woman gave her a warm hug. 'Welcome to the family, Maggie. Thank heavens you're going to take this brother of mine in hand, he certainly needs it. He's a terrible flirt, you know,' she said pulling a face at Angus over Maggie's shoulder. 'I couldn't be more thrilled for you both. Can I be a bridesmaid?'

Maggie stepped back from the embrace and laughed. 'I'm sure you can, though it's a bit early to be talking about that yet don't you think?' She turned to look at Angus who was grinning from ear to ear. 'Though we ought to go and tell Bridie the good news.' No sooner were the words out of her mouth, and as if her friend had somehow heard her name being taken in vain, than the door to the bar swung open and Bridie came in.

'What good news is this then? I could certainly use some.' In an instant she took in Maggie's flushed and smiling face and Angus standing beside her looking not so much as if he'd swallowed the canary but had put away the whole aviary.

Before either could speak, Caitlin called out, 'Angus asked Maggie to marry him and the foolish woman said yes.'

Bridie dropped her bag on the floor and clapped her hands together in delight much like a child who's just been given the very gift she wanted for her birthday. 'That's wonderful. I'm so thrilled for you both. It's about time you settled down,' she said going up to Angus and kissing him on the cheek, 'and you couldn't have chosen better,' she added looking towards Maggie. She put her arms around her friend hugging her tightly. 'As for you,' she murmured, 'I'm glad you've let your heart rule your head for a change '

Later, all thoughts of the discovery under the rowan tree had vanished from Maggie's thoughts until, enjoying her second glass of celebratory champagne, she was sitting with Bridie at the bar.

'I told Calum about the bone we found,' Bridie said, 'and he's going to come up to the cottage first thing in the morning and check it out.'

Maggie's hand flew to her mouth. 'Oh Bridie, I'd completely forgotten about it.'

Bridie smiled broadly. 'That's hardly surprising. It's not every day you get a proposal of marriage.' She chuckled as Maggie sighed with pleasure and hugged herself.

'I know. Isn't it amazing?'

'Anyway,' Bridie continued more seriously, 'Calum says if the bone is human he knows someone at the University in Edinburgh who'll be able to give us an opinion on the age of the body and how long it's been buried for. They might even be able to give a cause of death.'

'That's great news.'

'He also told me he hasn't been able to trace any record of James Ross's death so it's looking more and more likely it *is* him in the garden.'

'I'm sure of it,' Maggie declared. 'It has to be.' She smiled happily at her friend. 'So with any luck we'll soon be able to reunite Catherine with her son and she'll be at peace at last.'

The two women sat for a moment or two thinking of the young mother who had met a lonely death on the hillside having first lost her husband and then her baby all those years ago.

Maggie finally broke the silence. 'I really feel we'll have achieved something if we can finally lay Catherine to rest with her name and her baby.' She reached out and squeezed Bridie's hand. 'You and Calum have been marvellous in all this and I hope you know how much I appreciate the support you've both given me.' She grinned, 'As well as being there as a shoulder to cry on when I've needed it.'

Bridie merely squeezed Maggie's hand in return as if too moved by Maggie's words to do more. She sipped her champagne and finally, smiling at her friend, said mildly, 'I think you'd better go and join your fiancé. He looks as though he's going to need rescuing.'

Maggie turned her head and watched Isobel

Duncan saunter through the door and then, catching sight of Angus who was at the bar chatting to a couple of the regulars, head straight for him. Maggie slipped off her stool. 'I think perhaps you're right,' she grinned. 'Besides, I haven't told him yet what we found under the rowan so I'd better bring him up to date with that. I'm sure he'll want to know.'

Bridie looked on with amusement as Maggie wandered over to Angus and put an arm firmly through his. She looked at Isobel and said dismissively, 'Do excuse us.' Then, turning to give Angus a dazzling smile, she murmured sweetly, 'Come along Darling, I've some news to share with you.'

With that she propelled him over towards the door which led to his private quarters. Angus went without protest while Isobel Duncan stood looking as if she'd just been slapped hard across the face, which metaphorically she had, thought Bridie, smiling in quiet satisfaction.

The next week passed in a whirl of activity. Calum identified the bone as that of a young child which caused Maggie some upset; it was what she had been expecting, hoping for, but the confirmation still hit a nerve and she had to disappear into the kitchen for a few moments to recover her composure. Later the police came along and removed a large section of earth along with its contents to the pathologist's office. There the bones uncovered, together with the remnants of what had once been a plaid shawl, were deemed to be more than one hundred years old and so passed on to Calum's friend at the University. Maggie knew she could do no more. She had to wait for the definitive test results but in her heart she was satisfied they had found the last resting place of Catherine's baby son, James Douglas Ross.

Calum's research revealed Murdo Ferguson's wife, Flora as Catherine Ross's nearest living relative. *That's why*

I felt she looked vaguely familiar when I first saw her in the shop, Maggie thought, recalling the sadness in Flora's voice as she had given permission for the grave of The Unknown Maid to be opened.

'To think,' she had murmured 'that that poor soul, my great-great.....however many greats it is...aunt has been lying there in the churchyard all these years and I'd no idea about it. And that poor wee bairn too, all alone under the rowan tree..... It's only right they should be together.'

Several days later, as Maggie sat by the fire in the living room of the cottage waiting for Bridie, she thought back over all that happened since she had arrived at Invershee. There had been no more ghostly visitations since the night of the storm and she hoped Catherine's spirit would soon be at rest when her baby's remains were finally interred with those of his mother.

Apart from all the activity connected to the discovery of James Ross's body, there was also the excitement of her engagement. She gazed down at the solitaire, once Angus's grandmother's, which sparkled and glittered on her finger. They had decided there was no need to wait; as soon as arrangements could be made they would be married in the village church. She remembered how happy and excited she had been. Now she was plagued with doubts.

She twisted the ring round and round her finger, wishing Bridie would hurry up so she could talk things over with her. As if in answer to a prayer, there was a loud knock on the door and a moment later Bridie was settled in the seat opposite. Maggie got up and poured them both a glass of wine; she made her own a large one, feeling she might need it.

Bridie could hardly contain her delight at the prospect of the forthcoming nuptials. 'I'm so very happy for you both,' she enthused as she sipped her wine. 'You're just what Angus needs and I know he's right for you.' Maggie didn't answer. She sat staring into her glass not wanting to meet her friend's eyes.

Bridie gazed at her. Maggie was very pale and seemed withdrawn, nothing like the excited, animated bride-to-be she had expected to find when she arrived. She leaned forward and touched Maggie's hand. 'You're a little quiet tonight. Is everything okay?'

Maggie hesitated, seeking the right words. 'You do think I'm doing the right thing then?' She looked up at her friend, uncertainty reflected in her face.

'You mean in marrying Angus?' Bridie looked at her in disbelief.

'It just seems to have happened so quickly. I'm worried I've simply been swept along by it all. I could be on the rebound from Ben, don't you think? I'm just not sure anymore.' Maggie got up and began pacing up and down the room. 'I mean I don't really know Angus, and what if it all goes wrong? She stopped pacing and faced her friend. 'I could be making a huge mistake.'

'Do you love him?' Bridie's tone was brusque.

'Yes, of course I do but......'

'There aren't any buts Maggie. If you love him that's all you need.' Bridie's tone softened. 'It's quite natural to have misgivings at this stage,' she said and, putting down her glass, got up and hugged the other woman. 'But I've never seen two people more suited to one another than you and Angus and, yes, it may seem as if you're both rushing into this marriage but, if it's right, what difference would another few weeks or months of waiting achieve?'

She stood back, looking earnestly into her friend's face. 'I've said this to you before Maggie, the trouble with you is you think too much. Life's full of surprises and unexpected twists and turns. It's no good planning and having cosy fantasies about the future. Sometimes you've just got to take a chance. You can't let old hurts ruin your life.'

Maggie sighed and smiled. 'I knew I could rely on you, Bridie. I do love Angus and I can't imagine my life now without him. I suppose I've just got a bad case of pre-wedding jitters.'

Angus made her happy, she reflected. He made her feel desirable and needed and in a little under three weeks she'd be his wife. After all that had happened in the past weeks and the emotionally-charged events surrounding the recovery of James Ross's remains, it wasn't surprising she should have a little wobble, a few qualms and uncertainties. After all, marriage was an enormous commitment but she realised now she was ready for it. As Bridie had pointed out to her before, sometimes you had to take a risk because life couldn't always be planned for, mostly it just happened. If a chance of happiness came along perhaps you should just grab hold of it. She felt the first quivers of excitement at the thought of what was to come. She smiled at Bridie, grateful for her friendship and her common sense.

The rest of the evening passed quickly in making wedding plans as well as drinking a few glasses of wine. As Bridie prepared to take her leave, Maggie kissed her warmly. 'Thanks for everything.' Then she remembered she had a confession to make. 'By the way Bridie, I'm sorry but I seem to have lost that lovely rose quartz stone you gave me. I've searched everywhere and I can't find it.'

Bridie looked amused. 'Do you still need it, Maggie?'

'How do you mean?' Maggie frowned.

'If you remember, when I gave it to you I told you it would help ease heart-ache and sadness?'

Maggie nodded, looking puzzled.

'Well, do you still have heart-ache? Are you still sad?' When Maggie emphatically shook her head, Bridie went on. 'The thing is you don't need it anymore, so you won't ever find it. That's the way these things work. Someone who does need it will find it.'

Maggie's eyes opened wide, but she didn't question Bridie's understanding of these mysteries, merely accepted that what she told her was the way things were.

That had been two nights ago and now Maggie sat in the kitchen of the cottage and gazed at the diamond flashing fire on her finger under the lights. She still had things to do. For a start there was the letter to the museum to tell them that she wouldn't be returning to her job. She smiled as she remembered Angus's concern that she was giving up so much.

'But won't you miss it and your life in London?'

'Not at all,' she had reassured him. 'I'll have plenty to keep me occupied here helping you to run this place,' and she had run an affectionate eye around the bar, thinking of the work ahead to bring Angus's plans for the future of the Inn to fruition; it was something they would do together now. 'Besides, there'll be you to keep an eye on and make sure you stay away from designing females. That's more than enough work for one woman.' She had laughed and dodged as he had come chasing after her.

She also planned to do some writing when she had time she told him. Indeed it was the reason she was up at the cottage tonight. She had promised herself that before she got too immersed in the run up to the wedding she would try and write Catherine Ross's story. The young woman had suffered so much and Maggie felt she needed to somehow piece together what had happened to her and record it; if for no-one else at least for herself. She had done quite a lot of research on the times and the area, spoken at length with Calum about conditions in the mid-Victorian years and felt she had come to some understanding of what might have caused the young mother to embark on such a desperate journey with her baby son.

Writing at the Inn was not an option; there was too much to distract her there, not least of these being Angus. Besides she felt close to Catherine's spirit at the cottage and, although she had not seen her since the night of the storm, Maggie was aware of her presence all around her. She took a deep breath and looked at the blank screen of the lap-top sitting on the kitchen table in front of her. *Better make a start. It isn't going to write itself.*

A sudden shiver of unease made her look round; it was as if Catherine Ross was standing beside her. Maggie sensed her spirit as she might the fluttering presence of a moth in the darkness. She began to type and words appeared on the screen she had no recollection of thinking. Her fingers flew over the keyboard and before she knew it the story was written, there in black and white before her eyes. She took a shuddering breath and began to read.

CHAPTER 27

Catherine stared at the man darkening the doorway to the tiny cottage; darkening it in more than just the physical sense for he had brought her the blackest news. Douglas, her handsome, laughing, loving Douglas, was gone, taken from her by a relentless, unforgiving sea to a salty, sea-green death along with five others. 'I'm sorry lass,' the man, a neighbour and also a fisherman, said but she did not hear him. Her tears fell silently, uncontrolled, and unstoppable.

She stroked her swollen belly and thought only that the child she now carried would never know his father, never experience the joy of feeling his strong arms around him, protecting, safeguarding, shielding him from harm. She too would never again see her husband's eyes dancing with fun or misty with love for her; she would never again find joy in his arms at night nor work beside him tending the croft by day.

That day, and for many days after, she wanted to die too but knew she had to go on living for the sake of her unborn son. The words of the wise, old crone from Invershee kept echoing in her mind.

'You'll be delivered of a fine son.'

In the days which followed the accident, Catherine learned more details of her husband's last voyage from the neighbour who had first brought her the dreadful news for he had witnessed it. Douglas and five other fishermen had set sail when the sea was reasonably calm. Since the failure of the potato crop, they and many others had come to rely upon the bounty of the ocean and, although the sixerns they sailed in were lightweight affairs, the men were skilled and rarely returned without something for the table.

The west coast of Scotland, however, was notorious for the storms which often arose without warning and this was what had happened on that fateful day. Iain Mackellar, for that was the neighbour's name, had had a good day's fishing and turned early for home. He was just beaching his boat when, with little warning, the wind got up and in a few minutes the previously calm sea was crashing against the shore. He could see Douglas and his companions away in the distance begin to turn their boat, ready to make a run for it, but at that moment a huge wave smashed into their frail craft and shattered it to pieces.

During the days that followed, their bodies were washed ashore at various places along the coast. Six men were lost that day but Douglas was the one she mourned. She got through the funeral by thinking of their wedding day. She had been so happy, she remembered, so full of joy that she and Douglas were to be man and wife.

She was seventeen years old and living at Dervaig, on Mull, with her family when she had first met Douglas Ross. Her mother, together with two of her sons, had died during the great potato famine four years previously, having caught famine fever from tending neighbours who were ill. So, at just thirteen, Catherine had been left to care for her father and older brother Robert. Her eldest brother, Alexander was away working on an estate in England.

It happened that Douglas had met and befriended Robert on a previous visit to the island and one day Robert had brought him home to meet his family. The moment she set eyes on him, Catherine knew he was the one for her. He was always cheerful, full of fun and laughter and so good-looking. With his dark hair and twinkling deep blue eyes set in a face tanned from his many hours at sea, he stole her heart. His visits to the island became more frequent until finally he proposed and they set a date for their marriage.

She remembered her excitement as the day dawned.

The whole community took part in the celebrations and, as she set off in procession to meet her groom at the church, she saw the traditional, white flag her father had put up fluttering from the roof of their cottage.

It was a poor community yet everyone had been so kind and generous, bringing gifts of eggs and cheese, poultry and whisky, and the barn where the wedding feast was held had been beautifully decorated. It was a day of feasting and dancing, of fiddle playing and lively tunes performed on the accordion. She recalled her joyous laughter as the wedding bannock was broken over her head and the warmth and tenderness in Douglas' face as he looked at her, his bride. It had been the happiest day of her life.

His funeral, when they laid her beloved husband into the cold, dark earth of Corrieglen was the saddest. She had been married just seven months.

Alone and heavily pregnant, she struggled to keep body and soul together. The township of Corrieglen was small, only eight crofts in all, and her neighbours, though as kind and as helpful as they could be, had families of their own to support. The land was poor and any crop was hard won. The kelp trade which had kept many families, like the Ross's, from the breadline had collapsed following the end of the Napoleonic Wars and the Laird, as did others like him, looked for money from letting good hill land to sheep farmers, displacing many of his tenants to smaller, less-productive plots on the coastal strips or barren uplands. The failure of the potato crop through blight in 1846 had forced many families to emigrate to the New World and those who remained were often compelled to work for the landowners as farm-hands or house servants in order to pay their increasingly high rent. So their own land was often neglected and left to fall into disrepair.

So it was at Corrieglen. The croft which had been Douglas' fathers was small and unproductive. Catherine toiled in the fields day after day striving to cope with the heavy work of harrowing, grubbing, planting and reaping despite her continuing pregnancy. She grew kale and more potatoes but overuse had made the soil increasingly less fertile and the long hours of intensive labour yielded a poor return. Good-hearted neighbours gave her the occasional egg or some fish caught by their own menfolk and she had milk from her one cow but life was a constant battle to pay the rent and survive.

She couldn't go home to Mull because her father had died shortly after her wedding, Robert had since married and Alexander was still away working in England. Besides which she felt she owed it Douglas to make sure his son was born in the home of his father.

Her delivery, when it came, was quick and easy. The baby, a boy, was small but healthy and she named him after his grandfather and father. James Douglas Ross came into the world on a cold February day just three months after his father had drowned and from the start he was a great solace and joy to her.

He had his father's dark hair and blue eyes and she constantly marvelled at the perfection of his tiny fingers and toes. She heated beach stones at the peat fire, wrapping them in cloth, to keep him warm and sang him lullabies to send him to sleep. She held him to her breast and he grew lusty and strong. He was a contented child and rarely cried. She loved him more than she thought it possible to love anyone.

Then one day, he was a little feverish. His head felt hot to her touch and his cheeks were red, his face unnaturally pale. Swallowing seemed difficult for him and he constantly turned away from her breast, crying fractiously. Then he vomitted. Catherine knew there was sickness in the township. Two of the other women were complaining of sore throats and fatigue and several of the children were exhibiting similar symptoms.

Over the past day or two she herself had been feeling unwell; she was tired and listless and felt hot and chilled at the same time. She burned sulphur candles in the hope of keeping any infection at bay and now made an infusion of chamomile florets which she spoon-fed to James in the hopes of bringing down his temperature. Nothing seemed to help. He became more restless and she was sure she could feel the beginnings of a swelling in his neck.

She began to panic. What to do? She couldn't lose her precious bairn; there was no way on God's earth she would let that happen. She had to get help. The few other women in Corrieglen, though well-meaning and kind, had no skills in healing and so she thought of the old woman at Invershee. She was known to be a very skilled healer, familiar with many herbal remedies and was reputed to have cured numerous people of all kinds of ailments and illnesses. Catherine had no way of sending for her to come to Corrieglen and, besides, it would take too long; by the time a message was delivered and the old woman made her way to the township it might be too late for her baby son. She took the only decision she could. She would go to Invershee, taking James with her.

She forced herself to drink a little nettle soup though she found swallowing even that was hard; her throat felt as if it had been scratched by thorns. She wrapped her son up as warmly as she could, filled a bottle with some milk and put two bannocks in a piece of cloth; she would need to keep up her own strength if she was to carry James safely to Invershee.

She told no-one of her plans. She knew they would try to dissuade her from attempting such a long trek; James's recovery should be left in the hands of God, they would say, but she knew better. It was up to her to save him and, although she too was now feeling a little feverish, she had made up her mind. Stealing unseen out of the cottage, she began the long trek across rough mountains, through streams and along lonely glens.

It took her four days and three nights to trudge the difficult miles to Invershee. During that time she grew weaker and sicker but sheer determination to save her baby drove her on. It was as she reached the hillside at the back of Tigh-na-Bruach that she realised something was dreadfully wrong. James had stopped breathing.

He had become increasingly listless and pale as they had journeyed on. The last few times she had stopped to feed him he refused her breast and now he lay inert and cold in her arms. She shook him, hoping against hope that she was mistaken and that he was merely sleeping, but she knew deep down in her mother's heart that it was not so. Her precious bairn, her beautiful, dark-haired baby son was dead. All her effort had been in vain and she had lost him. Just like his father he was gone from her and she had nothing and no-one.

For an hour, then two she sat on the cold hillside and cradled her child. No tears came because she felt empty of tears, no cries or moans over her loss issued from her lips because she felt dead within. Instead she cuddled him close and sang him the lullabies he had once loved as he slept the sleep of death.

Finally, the keening began, quietly at first, as from somewhere deep inside her a thin wail rose and then split the air as it grew with such a sharp-edged intensity the whole hillside seemed to be engulfed by it; until it seemed to wear her grief and sorrow like a cloak. Her heart was broken and she had no will to go on, but she knew she had to; she had to do one last thing for her baby boy. She needed to put him somewhere to sleep away from the prowling night-time predators, safe from their curious noses and sharp teeth for she knew they would follow the scent of death until they found him.

She began to look around for such a place and saw a small, grey stone building she had not noticed before. There was no-one about, just a black cat fast asleep on the doorstep. A dry stone wall surrounded it on three sides and, with the little strength remaining to her, she managed to crawl down towards it and push herself over the wall with James bundled in her arms. She lay him down on the grass and rested for several moments. She sensed that for her also the end was fast approaching but she had to complete this final act for the sake of her child.

Looking around for a suitable tool to dig with she found a large, flattish stone nearby, and began slowly and painstakingly to create a resting place for her baby. The earth was quite soft as it had rained the previous night but still it took her a long time until eventually she had gouged out a hole big enough to hold him.

He looked so pale and so cold she thought. How could she put him in that dark hole without a cover to keep him warm? She took off her plaid shawl and wrapped him in it; she wouldn't need it anymore. She fastened it tightly around him, securing it with the brooch Douglas had given her on their wedding day.

Even though it was chilly and she could feel the hint of frost in the evening air strike through the coarse, woven material of her dress, she scarcely noticed. There, her baby would be warm now and tenderly she lifted him up and gave him one last kiss on his sweet face.

'Goodnight my darling laddie, sleep tight. Mamma will come back for you soon and put you in a proper place.'

Gently, she laid him in the space she had made for him and with her hands began to push the earth over him, singing, as she did so, one last lullaby. When finally he was covered over, she sat looking at the mound of earth, hoping he had known how much she had wanted him, how much she loved him.

From the pocket of her dress she withdrew the sprig of rowan she had carried with her as protection for their journey. She placed it now on the tiny makeshift grave of her infant son; its scarlet berries gleamed like drops of bright red blood against the black earth.

'This will protect you from evil spirits my Precious until Mamma can come and fetch you,' she whispered. Then, tears steaming silently down her face, she began to struggle weakly back up the hill, feeling with every step her strength draining away from her……..

Maggie stared at the screen, transfixed. She had no recollection of thinking these thoughts, no memory of writing these words. All at once she was overcome by a feeling of such unutterable grief it seemed to have settled in her bones, to have invaded her body like some virulent disease, running in her blood stream and attacking her sense of self and well-being. It was as though she were in some kind of hypnotic trance.

Then little by little she became aware of her surroundings: the sound of the tap dripping in the kitchen sink, the insistent tick of the clock on the mantelshelf in the next room, the gentle hum of the laptop on the table in front of her. She shook her head and stood up abruptly, all at once unnerved by what had happened. These words, this knowledge, these feelings were not hers; they were Catherine's.

She began to pace through the cottage: round the kitchen, through the living room, back into the kitchen again. Somehow Catherine's spirit had influenced what she had written; Catherine had told her own story through Maggie. It didn't seem possible but the evidence was there before her.

She stopped pacing. She needed to show this to Bridie. She also needed to be with Angus, to feel the comfort of his arms around her, to return to the world of living, breathing humanity. She had had enough of spooks and spirits, of ghosts and the supernatural. Suddenly decisive, she packed up her laptop, switched off the lights and left the cottage; she had a life to live and she was going to live it.

It was growing dark by the time she reached the Inn. She parked her car and sat for a moment trying to collect her thoughts. A tap on the window roused her and she saw Bridie's smiling face and, behind her, Calum.

'I'm so glad to see you both,' she said, climbing out

of the driver's seat.

'Are you alright?' Bridie sounded concerned. Maggie had an unnatural pallor and her eyes looked enormous in her small face.

'I've just had the weirdest experience, but I need a drink first before I tell you about it.' Maggie looked around for Angus but he was nowhere to be seen. She would talk to him later she thought and followed her friends to a table by the fire. As always the Inn felt warm and welcoming and she began to relax a little. Once they were seated and Maggie had had a few sips of a large glass of red wine, she lifted her lap top onto the table and started it up. 'I want you both to read this and tell me what you think.' She sat back and drank some more wine as Bridie and Calum scanned the story she had written.

'That's very good,' Bridie said her voice full of admiration. 'You've really got a great way with words. It sounds so authentic.'

Calum nodded in agreement, and then eyed Maggie curiously. 'But that's not what you're wanting us to say, is it, Maggie?' She shook her head and Calum leaned towards her. 'Tell us what happened.' So Maggie told them; how she had sensed the presence of Catherine's spirit, how the story seemed to write itself, and how she had then found herself in a kind of dazed, dream-like state when she had finally come to.

'It was like a kind of out-of-body experience and the thing is…' She rubbed her forehead as if trying to clear her thoughts. 'I think this is actually her story,' she said slowly. 'Somehow she got into my mind and guided my fingers on the keyboard. It was really uncanny.'

'Does it really matter, Maggie?' Bridie reached over and squeezed her hand. 'This *could* be her story, that's the point. It answers so many of the questions we had about why she made that journey, and what happened to her and James.'

Maggie chewed on her bottom lip. 'I suppose you're right. If she did somehow get into my mind and what I've written is what really happened then it explains a lot.'

Calum looked thoughtful. 'It would certainly give us the reason she felt she had to bring the child to Invershee. People in those days set great store by natural remedies and this old woman she talks about seems to have had quite a reputation. Maybe she was one of your ancestors,' he said, turning to Bridie.

'It's more than likely. That kind of healing's been handed down in my family for generations.' Bridie took a sip of her wine. 'But wouldn't there be doctors then as well?'

'Oh yes, but they'd be located in the larger settlements or itinerant, and people like Catherine wouldn't necessarily have easy access to them, living where she did.' Calum paused and then went on, 'Besides, the old country remedies were tried and tested and people often preferred to trust those rather than anything they were unfamiliar with. Nothing changes much, does it?' He grinned ruefully. 'I still have patients who ask me when Dr. Gordon is coming back.'

Maggie smiled encouragingly at him. 'I'm sure you'll win them over in time, Calum.'

'I wonder what was wrong with the baby,' Bridie mused.

'Well from the symptoms Catherine describes, and what I know about the health of the population at the time, it sounds like Diphtheria.'

Both women looked at him in surprise.

'I didn't think that was a killer,' Maggie said.

'Oh, it can be,' Calum said. 'Nowadays, it's treated with drugs but if it's not caught early enough people can die. It isn't nearly as prevalent as it once was though, outbreaks are pretty rare. But don't forget that in the times we're talking about the rural population in the Highlands was fairly malnourished so wouldn't have had the physical resilience to fight the disease. Children are always particularly at risk especially if the lymph nodes in the neck start to swell because that then interferes with swallowing and breathing. Anyway,' he added briskly, 'enough of the medical lecture. Suffice it to say that, if I were a betting man, I'd put money on it being what killed James, and probably his mother too.'

The three of them sat in silence for a moment or too. Finally, Maggie murmured, 'It's just so desperately sad.' She sighed deeply.

'Come on now,' Bridie said brightly. 'Let's not get too gloomy. You've done amazingly well Maggie to find out as much as you have. At least now Catherine and her son can rest at peace.' Calum started to speak, but she carried on. 'I know we don't have actual proof yet it was James's body under the rowan tree, but I think we all know it was him.'

'Well, we should be hearing something about that soon from the University,' Calum said.

'Right,' Bridie nodded and then changed the subject. 'How are the wedding plans going Maggie?'

CHAPTER 28

When Angus came in to the bar he found the three of them laughing and joking as they discussed the wedding arrangements. As soon as she saw him, Maggie jumped up and rushed over to him. 'I missed you,' she said flinging her arms round him and laying her face against his.

'What's all this?' he grinned. 'I've only been helping put Mrs. Lomax's new greenhouse up. Is anything wrong?'

'No, no, of course not, I'm just glad to see you that's all,' she fibbed. She would tell him what had happened later when they were alone. She didn't want to think about it anymore at the moment. She took his hand. 'Come on and have a drink. I'm just trying to decide whether we should have a themed wedding.' She saw his look of puzzlement and, trying to keep a straight face, added, 'Bridie and Calum are helping me to decide between Hollywood Glamour and The Wild West.' The look of sheer horror on his face was enough to send her into peals of laughter. 'I'm only teasing, you clown.'

She steered him over to the table. 'Sit down and I'll fetch you an orange juice.... unless you'd prefer something stronger?' and, still giggling, she nimbly skipped out of his way as he made a lunge for her.

The rest of the evening passed quickly and, when Bridie and Calum left, Maggie was able to tell Angus calmly about her experience up at the cottage. He took her in his arms and held her close, stroking her hair and murmuring gentle words of love and reassurance. She felt the heat rise in her as he nuzzled her neck and pressed herself against him. The bar was deserted, the outside door locked and Caitlin out for the night with her forrester. Maggie ran her tongue round his ear and whispered, her voice husky, 'Here. Now.'

Angus pulled away from her and gazed into her face. It was flushed, her eyes heavy-lidded with desire. She moved her hands slowly and sensuously across his shoulders and back, feeling his muscles tense and then relax. She smiled at him provocatively, her eyes now wide and full of invitation.

He was intrigued and aroused; she continued to surprise him. His pulse quickened and jumped as a passionate longing surged through him. He lifted her easily and in a moment had carried her across the room and laid her down gently on the rug in front of the dying flames of the fire.

Maggie stretched and twisted as sinuously as a cat as Angus knelt beside her on the floor. 'I know a rug in front of the fire is a bit of a cliché,' she murmured, 'but I won't tell if you won't,' and she gave him a languorous smile so full of promise it was all he could do not to tear her clothes off. Angus's eyes smiled at her in return. He was determined to stay in control. He would take his time to get to know every inch of her, to explore every intimate part of her and take her to places she had never been to before. He lay down beside her, leaning his head in his hand as he began to slowly run his other hand over her body. Then his fingers got busy: undoing buttons, unclasping hooks and easing down zips.

Later, as the warmth and strength of his body crushed down on hers, Maggie heard him murmur her name over and over again. Slowly, rhythmically at first, he took them both to the height of ecstasy and just when she thought she couldn't bear it any longer she felt herself go over the edge into such a maelstrom of feeling and sensation she thought her body would implode; every nerve was on fire and her insides felt as though they had turned to jelly as he filled her. She let out a shuddering sigh as he collapsed against her and she could feel his heart thumping as if it were trying to escape the confines of his chest. They lay like that for several moments, neither able to move or even think coherently.

Finally, Angus stirred. He moved to lie beside her and she turned to cuddle into him, wrapping her legs around him and lifting her face to his. His eyes were dark and smoky as they looked back at her, and his mouth slowly curved into that lopsided grin of his she loved so much.

'I think I rather enjoyed "Here and now,"' he teased. 'Have you any more ideas like that?'

Maggie grinned back. 'I might have but you'll have to wait and see until after we're married,' and felt her heart give a little lurch at the thought. *Married!* It was a huge step. Was she really ready for it? She pushed the insidious thought away; she loved Angus and that was all that mattered.

She could not believe how quickly the time was passing. There was so much to do, so much to arrange. Although the wedding was intended to be a small affair, numbers gradually mushroomed until it seemed as if the whole village was turning out to witness the event.

Maggie chewed her bottom lip as she read an e-mail from her mother.

'To say I was surprised to get your news, Maggie, would be a gross understatement. After your last disastrous attempt at marriage, I just hope you know what you're doing, though I have to say I seriously doubt it. Giving up a perfectly good job and flat in London to bury yourself in some godforsaken place in Scotland, of all places, doesn't seem to me to be the most sensible thing in the world. But then, you always did go your own way, didn't you, dear? Unfortunately, I won't be able to be there.' *Not that she's actually been invited.* Maggie felt murderous as she read on. 'Antonio is off to the Bahamas to shoot a film and I'm going with him...lots of lovely drinks by the pool and meeting *so* many clever and fascinating people, it should be such fun. I suppose I ought to wish you good luck and of course I do. I really think you might need it.   Mother.'

Maggie deleted the e-mail. Although it was what she had more or less expected, she still felt a little pinch of hurt at the rejection. She put it out of her mind and got on with the arrangements.

She, Bridie and Caitlin met Rachel in Glasgow for a weekend of laughter and girlie chats as they chose their wedding outfits. Maggie found an antique lace dress in a small shop down a back street of the city which she fell in love with the moment she saw it. It was exactly what she wanted and when she tried it on the gasps of approval from the others told her she was right. It was simple and understated but its delicate lace, old and intricately worked, lent a soft glow to her flawless skin and her hair looked darker, glossier against the rich, creamy material.

She asked Murdo Ferguson if he would give her away and he had accepted with a tear in his eye.

'It would be a great honour, lass' he said humbly and Maggie had impulsively hugged him, ignoring his faint protestations as his face slowly turned brick red. She was sad her father could not be there to fulfil this traditional role but that was the way things were and she had to accept it; she knew if he were still alive he would have been. At last she understood that he had left her mother, not her, and if fate hadn't dealt such a cruel blow she would have seen him again and rediscovered her relationship with him.

Finally came the news they were all waiting for. The bones were identified as those of a young child, a boy, between six and twelve months old, and had been in the ground for approximately one hundred and fifty years. A few days later came confirmation of a DNA match with Flora Ferguson's family.

Underlying her delight at having found Catherine Ross's baby son, Maggie felt a deep-seated sorrow at the thought of him lying so long and undetected in the ground. 'He should have had a proper burial and someone to mourn him,' she said sadly to Bridie.

'Yes, I know and I'm sure that Catherine would have come back for him and made that happen if she'd been able. But we'll do it for her,' Bridie put her arm round her friend's shoulders and gave her a comforting squeeze.

So, on a cold, misty, autumn morning, just two days before her wedding, Maggie followed Euan Cameron as he led the way along the gravel path to Catherine Ross's grave side. There had been a short, but simple and moving service in the church and it seemed to Maggie that everyone in the village had turned out for the occasion. Many wept, glad to finally have a name for the Unknown Maid but full of sadness at the circumstances which had surrounded her and her baby's deaths. Maggie swallowed back her own tears; she didn't want to break down, feeling that in some way she owed it to Catherine and her infant son to remain strong.

It was a silent procession which wound its way among the gravestones. The cloud was low, sombre-looking, brushing the tops of the distant mountains, and a heavy stillness hung in the air. It seemed to Maggie that even the birds had stopped singing.

The stone which had lain over Catherine Ross's grave had been lifted in the previous days so the names of her and her child could be engraved into the hard, granite stone. Now it leaned against the old wall of the churchyard waiting to be replaced once James had been laid to rest with his mother. Maggie was aware of Angus beside her, standing straight-backed and silent as he held the tiny, white coffin in his arms. The Minister turned and addressed the crowd, the words of the burial service ringing out in the still air.

Finally Angus stepped forward and placed the diminutive casket into the dark earth of the open grave. Stepping back he gripped Maggie's hand tightly, offering her what comfort he could. Still clutching his hand, Maggie bent down and took up a handful of the rich, peaty soil. She threw it onto the top of the coffin, seeing it fall, and hearing it rattle as it hit the wood.

And then, the evocative notes of 'The Dark Island' shredded the silence as Caitlin's young man began to play the haunting lament on his bagpipes. Maggie felt the tears she had managed until now to contain, well up and roll down silently her cheeks, as the melody, redolent of grief and loss, lifted and swelled through the stillness. Its plaintive echoes searched out the distant hills and glens, and flowed through the blood, touched the hearts and entered the souls of all those gathered there to say a sorrowful farewell to Catherine Ross and her child.

Maggie stifled a sob and turned, burying her head against Angus's broad chest, thankful for his solid, dependable presence. It was done. Mother and son were at last together. She felt as though a part of her heart was bruised by the sadness she felt at what had happened all those years ago; like a thumbprint on the soft flesh of a ripe peach, she bore the mark of it and she always would.

The service over, people began to move away, slowly returning to the village to resume their daily lives. Maggie remained for a while quietly looking down at the open grave. Angus stood with her. He seemed to sense she needed a moment longer to compose herself after the poignant ceremony, to think over all that happened and to say her goodbyes to a mother and child she had never known but had cared enough for to bring this day about. Finally he put his arm around her and pulled her close.

'Come along now, lass, it's finished. You've done a grand thing making this happen but it's over. We have to get on with our own lives'

Maggie nodded slowly and then offered him a tremulous smile. 'I know Angus, I know,' and she turned away with him. He was right. There was the future to think of now, the promise of their life together and whatever that might bring.

She hardly remembered the next two days she was so busy finalizing arrangements, helping Caitlin with the food for the reception, which naturally was to be held at the Inn, and then there was Rachel's arrival. By the time the second afternoon came she felt as though she had run a marathon.

'I never knew organizing a wedding could be so exhausting,' she said to Angus as she sat at the bar with a large glass of wine. But she smiled as she spoke the words and little prickles of excitement chased over her skin as she thought of the commitment she and Angus would make to each other tomorrow.

Angus grinned back at her, his eyes warm with loving promise. 'I can't wait,' he murmured, I've never slept with a married woman before'

Maggie's laughter sailed gaily across the room causing heads to turn and Rachel and Bridie, who were sitting nearby with Calum, to catch each other's eye and smile.

A little later, Maggie leaned towards Angus and whispered, 'I'm just going up to the graveyard for a while. There's something I have to do. I won't be long.'

'Hold on, lass. I'm coming with you,' he said as if he knew what she had in mind.

They slipped quietly out of the bar and Maggie took what she needed from her car. Then she and Angus walked quickly to the church. As she crunched her way slowly along the gravel path towards the back of the churchyard Maggie reflected on the future which lay ahead of her.

Tomorrow she would leave the cottage for the last time. It had proved a god-send, she thought, a place of solace and renewal, a refuge that had enabled her to recover her sense of well-being and her self-confidence. Tomorrow she would be married to a man she loved with all her being and she hugged the thought close. Tomorrow she would follow the dictates of her heart.

She glanced at Angus as he strode silently beside her. Sensing her gaze he turned his face towards her and smiled, squeezing gently the hand which held his so tightly. His love for her was there in his eyes, naked, unquestioning and without reserve.

When, at last, they stood before the re-laid granite gravestone Maggie read out the newly carved inscription.

CATHERINE ELIZABETH ROSS
1833 – 1852
JAMES DOUGLAS ROSS
1852 -1852
May they rest in peace together

Catherine Ross had known back-breaking struggle and hardship and then, finally, overwhelming sorrow but she had also known great happiness and joy with the man and the precious son she had loved. If she had known what the future held would she have chosen any differently? Maggie didn't think so.

Bending down, Maggie laid the wedding bouquet Bridie had made for her on the grave; she would carry just a single lily tomorrow. She stood back and looked at the bronze and golden chrysanthemums intermixed with yellow dill and dark sprigs of aromatic bay as they lay against the dark gray stone. Beside the flowers she had placed the runic stone; like the rose quartz, it was no longer needed.

'Catherine and James are both in their rightful place now,' she murmured.

'As are you my love,' Angus whispered in her ear as his arm tightened around her.

Maggie nodded too full of emotion to speak. Angus was right. She was where she belonged. She and Angus had a lifetime together ahead of them, a lifetime of a thousand ordinary moments, a lifetime which she had not planned for but one she now embraced.

A stray shaft of autumn sunlight broke through the greyness of the late afternoon, bathing the weathered stone before her with a sudden warmth and light.

Along the track, not so far from the village, at the bottom of the cottage garden, a faint breeze rustled the leaves of the rowan tree. Its roots held it firmly once again in the dark, deep, peaty soil and it stood tall and strong, ready to face the onslaught of winter winds, storms and tempests. Beside its silver-grey trunk stood the shadowy figure of an old man with faded blue eyes and a shiny black suit. For several moments the Bodach remained there motionless, and then, with a gentle smile on his ancient, weather-beaten face, his form slowly became insubstantial, wavered and finally faded into a ghostly nothingness.

Beyond, the hillside lay silent and deserted, just a few wisps of grey mist curled lazily along its ancient, sloping contours.

* * * * *

Printed in the United States
212148BV00001B/197/P

9 781849 232685